S0-BFD-480

Confessions
of a
Pregnant Princess

Books by Swan Adamson

MY THREE HUSBANDS

CONFESSIONS OF A PREGNANT PRINCESS

Published by Kensington Publishing Corporation

Confessions of a Pregnant Princess

Swan Adamson

KENSINGTON BOOKS
www.kensingtonbooks.com

KENSINGTON BOOKS are published by

Kensington Publishing Corp.
850 Third Avenue
New York, NY 10022

Copyright © 2005 by Swan Adamson

All rights reserved. No part of this book may be reproduced in any form or by any means without the prior written consent of the Publisher, excepting brief quotes used in reviews.

All Kensington titles, imprints and distributed lines are available at special quantity discounts for bulk purchases for sales promotion, premiums, fund-raising, educational or institutional use.

Special book excerpts or customized printings can also be created to fit specific needs. For details, write or phone the office of Kensington Special Sales Manager: Kensington Publishing Corp., 850 Third Avenue, New York, NY, 10022. Attn. Special Sales Department. Phone: 1-800-221-2647.

Strapless and the Strapless logo are trademarks of Kensington Publishing Corp.
Kensington and the K logo Reg. U.S. Pat. & TM Off.

ISBN 0-7582-0810-3

First Kensington Trade Paperback Printing: August 2005
10 9 8 7 6 5 4 3 2 1

Printed in the United States of America

For Donaldo Olsonnini, scrittore

Chapter

1

I believe in love.

At the end of the day, that's all that matters. Not how much money you made, or how many people you cheated, or if you got your name into the papers.

The question isn't *Were you loved?* The question is *Did you love?*

She loved.

That's one thing they could say about Venus Gilroy.

But they don't. They say a lot of stuff about her, but never that.

I thought I was pregnant when Marcello asked me to marry him. We hadn't had sex yet—except for those times when I was working as a lingerie model, back when I was married to Pete, my second husband. It was never real sex. Marcello would ask me to pose for him and then furiously J.O. into a white linen hanky as I lounged around in my negligee. He had this thing about seeing my naked body through thin, sheer fabric. House rules were that girls could pose, and men could watch, but they *could not touch* you. According to the law, if I allowed Marcello to touch me, I became a prostitute and he became a john. Felons. Both of us. Liable to jail time and a fine.

All he could do was look at me and whack off.

That's how we met, dear reader.

I lived strictly according to the letter of the law back then. When was it? Only last year?

I didn't want Marcello or any of them to touch me. When they offered me an extra fifty for some "one on one" out in their car, or in the stinky motel next door, I was always firm but polite. "No, thank you," I'd say.

Working in the sex industry is enough to put you off sex forever.

I wasn't completely coldhearted, though. I picked up on the vibes.

I knew that Marcello wanted more. He wanted all of me. But back then, last year, before I even knew he was a prince, I just never took him seriously. Why would I? He was older than my dads. He was foreign. Wore tailored suits and shirts with starched cuffs and *pearl-studded cufflinks*. To me he was just another horny guy lusting after my body.

But Marcello was persistent. He kept after me, even when I rebuffed him. First he asked me to go out, "just for a coffee and a little *conversazione*." I said no. I couldn't: I was married. I used Pete as my excuse, even though our marriage was getting as bad as my credit rating. I felt kind of sorry for Marcello because he seemed like a nice man, but I was not interested in a platinum-haired lover twice my age.

Then he asked if I'd consider being his mistress. *Me*, a mistress! It sounded weird and so old-fashioned. Conjured up images of sitting alone in an apartment waiting for some dude to show up with a box of chocolates and a hard-on.

I said no. Thank you, but no, thank you. Firm but polite.

And I thought that was the end of Marcello. I stopped the lingerie modeling, divorced Pete, and met Tremaynne, my third husband, in bankruptcy court. I was on my honeymoon with Tremaynne and the dads when I ran into Marcello again.

We were all at the opening of Pine Mountain Lodge, this glamorous new wilderness resort in Idaho. Daddy had designed it, Whitman was writing about it for *Travel* magazine, and Tremaynne and I got to go along for free because I'd never had a honeymoon and the dads thought it was about time. There was this big party with Hollywood stars, and I was coming down Daddy's signature staircase wearing stiletto heels when I tripped and literally fell into his arms. Marcello's arms, I mean.

I was shocked. So was he.

I look back now and think it must have been fate.

I think about fate a lot these days.

Out there in the middle of Nowheresville Idaho I discovered that the man I only knew as Marcello was, in fact, Prince Marcello Brunelli, one of the richest men in Italy and the major money source behind Pine Mountain Lodge. I wouldn't have known any of this if the dads hadn't told me.

Sometimes life is just too weird to be believed.

Well, I was madly in love and on my honeymoon, so Marcello, no matter who he was, was no more than an inconsequential blip on my radar screen. But he came after me again. Caught me alone. Said he thought of me always. Said he "desired" me more than ever. Offered me a thousand smackaroonies just to look at my tits.

No. I wouldn't. I couldn't. I didn't want to. All I wanted was Tremaynne. But then Tremaynne disappeared and all the rest happened. I went out into the wilderness to find my husband and Marcello chased after me. I headed him off at Dead Horse Canyon and pushed on to Devil's Spring, where I found Tremaynne, but the two of us were almost killed by these paramilitary maniacs who were going to set fire to Pine Mountain Lodge and blame it on the environmentalists. The maniacs tied us up, me and Tremaynne, and threw us in the back of their pickup, and if it hadn't been for the dads, who appeared just in the nick of time and chased after us, I wouldn't be here, in Italy, today.

When I arrived at Pine Mountain Lodge, I was on my honeymoon. Three days later, when I left, I was on a marital death march. My husband Tremaynne had vanished into the wilderness, vanished into the mysterious life of a radical environmentalist. He was a revolutionary, Tremaynne was. I hadn't known that when I married him.

I would have done anything for Tremaynne. I would have run off into the woods and foraged for food. I would have lived in a tree. Even sabotaged lumber trucks.

Because I loved him. I would have done anything he asked. But in the end, I knew that it was futile. My husband was wedded to his cause, not to me.

Before he slipped off into the forest, he told me that the marriage had been a mistake and that I should get a divorce.

Oh God, the misery.

But some part of me knew with a cold, dull finality that it was over. Some part of me accepted it, almost at once, and started thinking about what I had to do next.

Before I left Pine Mountain Lodge, Marcello made one last play for me. I was half-dead with misery and exhaustion, but even in my zoned-out state I knew he was for real. When he wrote a number on the back of his business card and said, "This will reach me anywhere," I knew he wasn't just handing me a line. He *wanted* me to call him. He *hoped* that I would call.

Of course I didn't.

Not for two weeks.

When the dads and I got back to Portland, I quickly and quietly filed for divorce. I don't know how I got through that period. I just kept moving forward. I didn't let myself think about it. I just did it. If I had stopped to think about it, about Tremaynne, about my third divorce, about the huge uncertainty of the future, I would have just collapsed in a flood of tears. So I didn't.

It takes two weeks for an uncontested divorce to go through in Oregon.

Suddenly I was Venus Gilroy again, back in my dinky, messy apartment and working at Phantastic Phantasy for minimum wage, seven bucks an hour.

Things looked pretty bleak.

I shut everyone out. I just did not want to interact. I did not want to talk, or explain, or voice an opinion about what I would do next.

I didn't know.

All I knew was that this *desperate* feeling would come over me at times. It was terrible. Almost like a panic attack. My breath would get all shallow, and my head would feel light, like I was going to pass out, and this hideous anxiety would start gnawing at my chest. Fears would start skittering around like cockroaches in the dark. My heart would race for no apparent reason.

Later on, when I talked to the dads about it, they said it was probably post-traumatic stress syndrome. A reaction to almost being killed in Idaho.

Maybe.

All I know is that the rent was due, they were threatening to disconnect my phone, and I was a three-time divorcée working in a stupid and disgusting dirty-video store, but I didn't know what else I could do because the rent was due and they were threatening to cut off my phone and I was a three-time divorcée and . . .

Circular thinking, it's called.

I sat and stared at his card for a really long time. Marcello Brunelli. President, Lumina International. No address. One office phone number with a Los Angeles area code, another with a 396 prefix. I called and asked the operator. She said 396 was Rome.

On the back of the card, a neatly penned number with a really long prefix. I called and asked the operator about that one, too. It took me about ten minutes and about twenty different operators. Finally, one with a foreign accent told me that it was a special "international prefix code" hooked up to a special satellite telecommunications system.

I sat and looked at the card. I chewed on my lips. I wanted a cigarette *so* bad . . . but I'd quit.

Finally, heart pounding, not knowing what I was going to say, or even why I was calling, I punched in the numbers. Funny sounds, a screech of static, then a distant ring. In outer space somewhere, for all I knew.

I let it ring four times. Then I lost my nerve and hung up. Pushed the phone away from me.

* * *

I tossed and turned and sighed and moaned and I was just finally slipping into a light doze when the phone rang. Four A.M. Nobody calls at that hour unless they're drunk, stoned, or something terrible's happened.

My voice was a croak when I answered.

"Hello?" said a male voice. The voice didn't register. It sounded tiny, distant. "Hello?"

"Who is this?" I asked.

"Marcello," the voice said. And a second later, "Marcello Brunelli." And a second later, "I am returning your call."

I hate technology. Some little thingamajiggy in outer space had registered my telephone number even though I'd hung up.

"I was unable to take your earlier call," Marcello apologized. "This is the first free moment I have had."

I was completely tongue-tied. Had no idea what to say.

"Are you there?" he asked.

"Yeah. Yeah, I'm here. Where are you?"

"I am in Osaka."

"Where's that?"

I had never heard him laugh before. It was a deep, friendly sound. "Japan."

"Oh." My mind went blank again.

"You called me," he prompted.

"Well, sort of. Not really."

"But I have your number here in front of me. You are in Portland, Oregon." He pronounced it *Orry*-gone.

"How did you know it was me?"

"I have given that number only to a handful of people. I know every one of them."

"Oh." Tongue in knots. Heart beating fast.

"You called me," he said again.

"I was going to. But I hung up."

"Why?"

"It was so stupid. I wasn't thinking."

"You were thinking enough to call my number," he said. "What did you wish to say to me?"

"I don't know."

"But—something?"

"I guess so."

"May I hope that you were calling because you wanted to see me?"

"I'm divorced now," I blurted out.

"Are you saying you are free?" He sounded cautious but hopeful.

"I'm saying I'm divorced. That's all I'm saying."

"Are you saying that if I were to fly to Portland, you would see me?"

That's how it started.

Chapter
2

Marcello was headed back to Rome on some "family business" but figured out a way to stop in Portland on the way. He said he would have only one afternoon and evening.

Fine with me. I didn't want him hanging around. To tell you the truth, I didn't know exactly *what* I wanted or *why* I had agreed to see him.

I kept flashing on our last meeting at Pine Mountain Lodge, in the back of the dads' SUV, me so miserable, he so comforting, giving me food, flowers, coffee, and his card.

I tried to dredge up some physical feeling for Marcello, but that was difficult because at the time I was totally tuned in to Tremaynne. I didn't have eyes for anyone else. I'd had an intense sexual relationship with Tremaynne, and I still fantasized about him. Ridiculous fantasies. Like, he'd show up and say he couldn't live without me. That sort of bull.

I'd never gone out with an older man, and just thinking about it made me kind of nervous. There suddenly seemed so much experience attached to Marcello. Worlds of experience and a life that I couldn't even begin to imagine. The idea of seeing him was kind of scary. I felt like I was breaking a taboo.

"Did you ever go out with an older guy?" I asked my mom the night before Marcello was due to arrive.

I was over at her house, slouched miserably on her big, soft sofa, trying not to cry as Judy Garland sang "The Man That Got Away" in *A Star is Born*.

Carolee, her eyes brimming, paused the video, freezing Judy Garland's face, her mouth stretched wide, her lips covered with that bright red early-Technicolor lipstick. "Why do you ask, sweetheart?"

"Just curious."

"Oh." She fidgeted with the remote wand. "Are you asking because an older man has expressed an interest in you?"

"Sort of," I said.

"May I ask how much older?"

"I don't know. Maybe twenty-five years. Maybe more."

She couldn't quite hide her shock, or her curiosity. "To tell you the truth," she confided, "yes, I did go out once with a much much older man."

"How old was he?"

"Eighty."

"Jesus. How old were you?"

"I was twenty." Her eyes slid nervously over to Judy Garland's face, then back to mine. "I'd just left the commune. He was my landlord."

"And you couldn't pay your rent," I guessed, "so you slept with him."

"I want that secret to go to the grave with you," Mom said.

"What was it like?" I wanted to know.

"It was—."

"Icky?"

"No. Not icky." Carolee shook her head. "He was very slow and gentle. Well, he had to be, because he'd just had both hips replaced. I remember he took his teeth out. It was like having a baby at my breast." She gave a mysterious chortle and fluffed up her mound of red hair. "If I'd married that old fart, I'd be a rich slumlord today."

"Did he ask you?"

"Sort of."

"What does that mean?"

She got up from the sofa, unwilling to reveal more. "That's all ancient history, sweetheart. Let's talk about you. Who is this older man who's expressed an interest in you?"

"Just a guy."

"Just a guy," she repeated. "Well, how did you meet this guy?"

Even my mom, who knows almost everything about my life, did not know that I had worked as a lingerie model while I was married to Pete. "I met him up at Pine Mountain Lodge," I said.

"Oh. You met him on your *honeymoon*."

"Is there some law that says you're not supposed to meet anyone on your honeymoon?"

"Well, no, sweetheart, but it's usually your husband you're getting to know."

"That's what I was hoping would happen," I said, suddenly teary again. "But it didn't, did it? And Marcello was just there. He was very nice. He . . ."

"Marcello," Mom said. "He's of Italian extraction?"

"Italian Italian."

"A US citizen? I hope?"

I shrugged.

"Sweetheart, you have to be careful," Carolee said in her most authoritative mother voice. "He may just want a green card."

I had to laugh. "You don't get it, Mom. He's not like that."

"How do you know? How does any woman know what a man is really like until it's too late?"

She meant Daddy, of course. John Gilroy was always her frame of reference when it came to Big Mistake stories. When I was five, and just when Carolee thought her life was hunky-dory, Daddy had told her he was gay. He left her for Whitman that same year, the year I was five. Twenty years before.

"Anyway," I said, "I'm never getting married again, so it doesn't matter if he wants a green card or not."

"Don't think so negatively," Mom warned. "Just because the first three didn't work out doesn't mean you can't still find the right man and have a happy marriage and children."

The mention of *children* was like being punched in the gut. The last place I wanted to be punched just then, because I was afraid that I might be pregnant with Tremaynne's baby. I started to blubber.

Mom scooted over to comfort me. She pulled me down to her giant bosom, stroked my hair, rubbed my back, squeezed me, and made her little clucking and soothing noises. But of course with Mom, crying is contagious. She just looks at someone with moist eyes and starts bawling herself. "Oh, sweetheart," she hiccupped through her mounting sobs, "it's not so bad."

"Yes it is," I bawled.

"No it isn't. You have to look on the bright side. Always look on the bright side. Even when it's raining."

"This is Portland," I reminded her. "It's *always* raining."

"No, no, hush, it's not. There are beautiful days ahead for you. The sun's right behind the clouds."

"Bullshit."

"This older man," she said, wiping her eyes. "Marcello. What's he like?"

"I don't know much. Just that he's a prince or something."

"A prince?" Mom, like, totally froze. I think she stopped breathing. "Did you say 'prince'? As in—*royalty?*"

"I don't know. I guess so. He's one of the owners of Pine Mountain Lodge."

"One of the *owners?*" Mom gasped.

"Marielle said he's one of the richest men in Europe."

"Excuse me," Mom said, "but I think I'm going to have a petit mal seizure."

"He's already married for all I know."

"So you've met this prince, but you haven't actually gone out with him yet," Mom summarized. "You met him at Pine Mountain Lodge, on your honeymoon, and he expressed an interest in seeing you again."

"He's flying over from Osaka to see me."

She leapt up as if I'd applied a stun gun to her tit. "From Osaka? Just to see you? And you don't know if he's married or not, but you do know he's a prince and one of the richest men in Europe?" Mom stared at me, almost accusingly, her eyes a little wild.

"It's no big deal," I insisted.

"Where's my inhaler?" she wheezed. "I can't catch my breath." There was a dramatic moment as Mom scrambled for her inhaler, inserted its big nozzle into her mouth, and gave herself a shot of pentamidine. "Venus," she whispered when she got her lungs back, "tell me his name. His full name."

"Marcello Brunelli."

Mom ran for a pencil and paper. "How do you spell that?"

"I don't know."

"There can't be that many Prince Marcello Brunellis," she said, scribbling something down. "When is he coming from Osaka to see you?"

"Tomorrow. Afternoon."

"That doesn't give us much time," Mom said.

"For what?"

"Assembling a dossier."

"What?"

"You'd be amazed at what you can find on the Internet," Mom said, booting up her computer. "We'll start with Google."

I was too stunned to speak. I just sat there staring at her.

"What are you going to wear?" Mom asked. She took hold of my hands. "Look at your nails—you've been chewing on them. I'm calling Sue-Ellen at New Nails for a manicure appointment right now. Don't worry," she said when I began to protest, "I'll pay for it. It's important. One of the first things a man looks at is a woman's nails."

"No, Mom. The first thing a man looks at is a woman's tits. Then her ass, her legs, her shoulders, her face, and her hair, in that order. Nails are pretty low on the list."

"Don't be so cynical. This man is a prince. He's rich. Don't you want to look nice for him?"

My perfect new fifty-dollar nails, a lustrous purplish green, gleamed like priceless Egyptian scarabs against the beat-up steering wheel of my ancient Toyota. The car had been old when I bought her; now she was begging to be released from her misery. I felt sorry for the old gal, with her taped-up windows and battered fenders.

She deserved a nice rust home, some place where she could quietly disintegrate amid other discarded junk heaps. But I couldn't afford to replace her, so even though she did nothing but complain and make rude sounds and threaten to die on me, she continued to haul me around town.

I was afraid to let her idle, though, and that's what I had to do when I got to the Broadway Bridge. The red lights flashed and the barriers swung down and the giant spans began to rise in the air so a huge grain ship could pass underneath. I knew if I turned the car off, she might not start again. If I kept her on, she might run out of gas. My life of late was always full of ridiculous dilemmas like that.

Sudden depression. My beautiful scarab nails turned into giant cockroaches.

Everything, in the end, came down to money. Or rather, the lack of it.

As I sat there, waiting for the bridge to close, my clunky prehistoric cell phone rang.

"Venus," my dad said, "can you come over?"

"Venus? Hello, sweetheart, it's Whitman." He'd obviously snatched the phone from Daddy. "How soon can you get your tattooed behind over here?"

"What's going on?" I asked.

"Sweetheart, *we know all about it.*"

"About what?"

"About you and *Il Principe*," Whitman said.

"Ill who?"

"Prince Marcello Brunelli. Darling, you don't have to pretend. It's OK. We already know."

I was suddenly furious with my mom. "Did Carolee tell you?"

"Yes, but she was only one of our informants."

"Who was the other one?" I demanded.

"Why, the prince himself," Whitman said. "He just called us from Osaka."

"OK," I said, "I'll be right over."

As I clicked off, I heard a voice in the car next to me shout, "Oh my God!"

It was one of those humongous Hummers, the size of a tank, bright yellow. Rap music was threatening to blow out the tinted windows. Someone tapped something sharp and hard on the window and shouted, "Venus!"

The window came down.

JD, my one-time love, shrieked and thrust out her arms.

"Venus! Oh my God, I don't believe it! You're back! Why didn't you call me? Where are you going? Where's Tremaynne?"

The bridge spans were nearly back in place. I figured I had to stall for about five seconds before I could escape.

I put my arm out, slowly, so JD could see my fabulous new nails, and we touched fingers. "Whose car?" I asked. Yelled, rather. The rap music was so loud, I could feel the bass vibrating in my rib cage.

"Mistah Sistah!" JD yelled back. She moved so I could see the big black guy sitting in the driver's seat. Portland's favorite rapper was wearing sunglasses, a blonde wig, and a short white dress. He winked at me behind JD's back and nodded his head. A real flirt.

"We're getting married!" JD shouted.

"What?"

"Married! Just like you! Engagement party tonight! Come!" She passed me an invitation.

The barriers went up, the lights turned green, and the cars in front of us gunned their motors and moved forward. JD waved as Mistah Sistah's yellow Hummer sped away. You could hear it a block away.

I never knew if my old Toyota would make it up to the dads' house or not. They lived high in the West Hills, where the streets are steep and curvy and have names like Bella Mirage Lane and Altavista Circus.

The dads were waiting for me as I sputtered into the driveway. "We heard you coming," Whitman said drily as he watered white birch trees in huge terra-cotta tubs.

My dads. Dad One: John Gilroy, biological father, architect. Dad Two: Whitman Whittlesley IV, faux pa, writer. The Inseparables.

Daddy gave me a hug and a kiss, then turned me over to Whitman, who did the same.

"Let's have *una piccola conversazione nella casa*, shall we?" Whitman steered me toward the open front door. I absolutely hated it when he used foreign words and phrases because I didn't know what he was talking about. Daddy knew. Their friends knew. But I didn't have a clue.

When you walked into the dads' house it was like you were outside, because you faced a wall of glass and a view out across the city to Mt. Hood, everyone's favorite Northwest icon. On this dry, hot afternoon, its white icy summit shimmered in the distance above a blur of heat waves. The dads' hillside house, with its stone floors and giant windows open to catch fresh breezes, was about twenty degrees cooler than my mom's hot little crackerbox on "the flats" of the east side, or my own closet-size convection oven.

As usual, not a thing was out of place in their house. All straight angles and perfect lines. It was like being in a museum.

In deference to the hot weather they were both wearing khaki shorts and T-shirts. Daddy's T-shirt read: GILROY ARCHITECTS, WE DESIGN YOUR DREAMS. It was an old PR gift he'd sent out to all the people who'd worked on the construction of Pine Mountain Lodge, his last big project. Daddy wore sandals, but Whitman, to my surprise, was barefoot. I envied his high arches. He'd recently been to a hair salon and had a very demanding cut, longer on one side than the other and combed over from a side part. He kept flicking his head back to keep his sandy-colored hair out of his laser-blue eyes. Daddy's hair was all mussy. He obviously hadn't shaved and kept stroking the blue-black shadow on his chin.

I followed Daddy and Whitman out to one of their suspended terraces. A bottle of wine and three glasses sat on the round glass table. I eyed the snacks: some kind of pâté and crackers. Not quite enough for supper. We sat down. Whitman poured out some pinot something or other.

"Since John is your real father," he said, "I'll let *him* tell you what happened."

Daddy smiled at me. Took my hand. "Well, sweetheart, the phone rang and—"

"Marcello Brunelli," Whitman interrupted. "Prince Brunelli. He called and asked if he could speak to John Gilroy."

I turned to Daddy, completely puzzled. "Why did he call here?"

"John can tell you the whole story," Whitman said, slicing a small piece of pâté and offering it to me on a cracker.

"Well, the phone rang and I picked it up. This person asked to speak to John Gilroy. I didn't know who it was."

"This was earlier in the afternoon," Whitman explained, offering pâté to Daddy. "About one our time, so late last night in Japan. He was calling us from Osaka. Go ahead with your story, John."

"Well, I said, 'This is John Gilroy speaking.' And he said, 'Oh, John, it's Marcello Brunelli.'"

"OK," I said, "we've established that it was him. Why the fuck was he calling you?"

"Well," Daddy said, "he said he had something he needed to discuss with me. I said, 'What?' He said, 'Your daughter.'"

"Meaning you," Whitman said, eyeing me over his wineglass.

I didn't touch the wine he'd poured for me. No alcohol. No cigarettes. No nothing. Everything I loved had a red circle around it and a big line through the middle.

"'My daughter?' I said. 'Venus? What about her?'"

"We thought you'd gotten into some ghastly new pickle," Whitman said, "only we couldn't figure out why Marcello Brunelli would be the one calling us."

"So you were listening in on the other line?" I guessed.

"Of course," Whitman said. "Your father and I have no secrets from one another."

I turned to Daddy.

"So he said, Marcello said, 'John, I'm going to be completely frank with you. I'm coming to Portland to see your daughter.'"

"Those were his exact words," Whitman confirmed. He shook his head in disbelief.

Daddy took a sip of wine. "He said, 'I don't want to do anything to upset you, John. I know this probably comes as a great surprise to you.'"

"Shock is more like it," Whitman said. "Because we didn't know that you had—"

"Had what?" I asked.

"Stolen his heart," Whitman said. "How? That's what I'd like to know. When?"

"When she tripped coming down the staircase at Pine Mountain Lodge," Daddy said, "and he caught her. These things happen. It's not just in the movies."

My face was burning. It wasn't embarrassment, but it was, sort of. I knew Marcello hadn't told them about our sessions in the House of Peek-a-Boo, where I'd been a lingerie model. He wouldn't do that. So I was left having to play out this weird charade that Marcello and I had met for the first time at Pine Mountain Lodge.

"Such Old World manners," Whitman said with what sounded like admiration. "Not like those other morons you're always getting involved with."

"Thanks, Whitman," I said.

He was oblivious that he'd hurt my feelings. "Of course you can't trust someone just because he has good manners," he said. "Murderers and psychopaths have good manners. Anyway, tell her what he said next, John."

"He said—"

Whitman didn't let him finish. "He said, 'I would like to ask your permission to see Venus.'"

I let out a flabbergasted splutter, not unlike the sound my old Toyota made when I was going uphill and stepped down too hard on the gas. "He asked your *permission* to see me?"

Daddy nodded. "He said, 'I don't want to do anything to upset you, John. I value our business relationship, and I hope it will continue.'"

Marcello had called to ask my dad's permission to see me. It was a weirdly old-fashioned gesture, polite but also patriarchal, as if I were owned by my dad. "What did you tell him, Daddy?"

"I told him that you'd always gone your own way."

"That you *never* listen to a word of advice from us," Whitman added.

"I didn't say that." Daddy took my hand again. "I said you always did what you wanted to do, even when we tried to dissuade you."

Why did I feel like crying? "Did you give him *permission* to see me, Daddy?"

Daddy nodded. "Yes. I did. I gave him permission."

Chapter
3

By the time I left the dads', the temperature had dropped a few degrees and I was starting to think about supper. I hated eating alone. But I didn't feel like calling anyone because then I'd have to explain that my new marriage was over.

Tremaynne. I couldn't stop thinking about him. I knew that I had to let go. But how? He was like a sickness I had to work out of my system.

So far, it had been fairly easy to hole up alone and avoid people. But party girls can stand isolation tanks for only so long.

At a stoplight, I picked up the invitation to JD's engagement party and scanned the info. It was being held at the Lizard Lounge. The invitation said "food." I wouldn't have to get into any heavy conversations at a club party. I could even lie if I wanted to, and pretend that Tremaynne and I were still together.

Who knows, maybe I'd even meet a new guy. Someone closer to my own age than Prince Marcello Brunelli.

Funny, the things that can affect your mood.

On my way to the Lizard Lounge, I passed a man dressed up like a slice of pizza. He was hollering, "Free pizza! Free pizza!" and trying to get drivers to pull into a new pizza joint called Mr. Pizza.

Under normal circumstances I would have gone in and gotten a free slice. But the sight of him standing there on that busy street dressed like a slice of pizza just depressed the hell out of me. I thought, *That could be me.*

It was my old money worry. The constant money worry. The incessant money worry that triggered a bunch of other worries.

Like, about my entire future.

A month earlier, I'd assumed that the years ahead would be spent with Tremaynne. Now that assumption was gone, a vaporized fantasy.

But Tremaynne would always be with me because I was carrying his child. At least, I thought I was. It was possible. My period was due in a couple of days.

And then what?

The glamorous world of single motherhood?

Supporting a baby by working in what Whitman always referred to as "that dirty-video store."

No way.

I hated my job, but what else could I do? I didn't have a college degree. I had no skills to speak of. The economy sucked major league. Oregon had the highest unemployment in the nation and jobs were scarce. For all I knew, the man dressed up like Mr. Pizza had once headed up a rip-roaring dot-com company.

Welfare had been cut to nothing, so scrounging off the government was not an option.

I didn't want to move in with my mom, and the thought of me and a messy crying baby living with the dads in their meticulously perfect home was ridiculous.

It was the worst time possible to bring a kid into the world. Into my world, anyway.

I could get rid of it. Secretly. No one ever had to know.

But I would know.

From a purely practical point of view, it was the best option.

But I'd never been practical in my life.

If I had Tremaynne's baby, I would think of Tremaynne every time I looked at our child. I wouldn't be free of him, not really, for the rest of my life. I didn't *want* to be free of him, but it was stupid and self-defeating to pretend that we still had any kind of relationship.

It was all so goddamned difficult and overwhelming. I sucked in a ragged breath and brewed up another pot of tears.

And of course that's when my old Toyota finally decided to die on me. I was at the stoplight next to the new pizza joint. When the light turned green and I stepped on the gas, the car jerked forward and stopped dead.

I didn't have the money to pay for expensive repairs, and at this stage in my car's life, everything was an expensive repair.

I put my head down on the steering wheel and began to sob.

I was still blubbering when the man dressed like a slice of Mr. Pizza pizza leaned over to look in my window. "You OK?"

I shook my head. Tears spurted from my eyes. So many tears, I could have used them to wash my dirty windshield, if my windshield wipers had worked.

"Hey, what's the matter?" Mr. Pizza asked. "Can I help you?"

"No one can help me," I moaned as the lineup of cars behind me started to honk.

"Shut up! She's stalled!" Mr. Pizza yelled, gesturing for the cars to go around me. He leaned back down and said, "I'm going to push you over to the side."

I nodded and managed to turn the steering wheel as the man dressed like a slice of pizza pushed me from behind. We got off the busy street and into a corner of the parking lot.

"Now, what seems to be the matter?" Mr. Pizza asked.

I looked at him for the first time. He had a big, plain, honest face. Not cute, but not ugly, either. About thirty. He was a big guy with olive-colored eyes and eyebrows the color of pepperoni.

"My car died," I said, wiping away my tears.

"Get out," he said. "Let me have a look."

He folded his sides together, the way those guys in New York used to do it when they wolfed down a hot, gooey slice, and slid into the driver's seat. The car gave a sluggish stutter when he tried to start it. "Had any trouble with the generator?" he asked.

"You name it," I said, "and I've had trouble with it."

He tried again. "I think you need a jump," he said. "I'll get my truck."

"It's really nice of you to help me."

"A beautiful girl like you?" he said. "No trouble at all."

I watched as he headed over toward a battered pickup. He was a cheese and tomato pizza front and back. He must have been really comfortable being a slice of pizza, because he never removed his Mr. Pizza costume. He pulled open my hood, attached the jumper cables, and signaled for me to step on the accelerator.

Electroshock. My old jolted car shimmied and roared.

"Thanks!" I yelled over the noise of the engine.

Mr. Pizza leaned close. He wasn't done with me. I could see it in his eyes. "Can I help you in any other way?" he asked.

"I don't think so."

"You looked troubled."

"I'm OK now. Thanks."

His eyes narrowed and he stuck his head into my car, full of ardor. "Have you ever tried prayer?"

I smiled and shook my head. I hadn't been raised with any kind of religion. Carolee was always consulting psychics and astrologers and having her tarot cards read, but that's not what Mr. Pizza was talking about. The dads were very down on organized religion because of all the pain and suffering it caused gays. When I was a little girl and the dads had taken me to St. Patrick's Cathedral in New York, it was because the church was a tourist attraction, not because it was holy.

"If you give your heart to Jesus," Mr. Pizza said, coming closer, "he'll wash away your fears and disappointments in the river of eternal life."

It just didn't sound very sexy. And somehow I couldn't imagine praying with a slice of pizza. So I leaned over and gave him a quick peck on the cheek and took off.

JD getting married to a cross-dressing rapper?

I suppose weirder things had happened.

Like Michael Jackson marrying Lisa Marie Presley.

But since JD had always said she was a lesbian, I always assumed she would stick to chicks.

Of all my past lovers, JD was the most socially exciting and sexually boring. She put on a good show. She was a performer on stage and off. It was only in bed that she had stage fright.

When I had fallen in love with JD, she was the lead singer and guitar player with an all-girl band called Black Garters. Last I heard, she'd joined a new group called the Go-Go Girls. I'd never heard the Go-Go Girls, but the name conjured up retro images of bouffant hairdos and bubble gum, not the punky sexuality of Black Garters.

JD had been messing around with a lot of heroin when we were together. That's one of the reasons why I left her. That and the fact that she was the world's most uptight lover. In bed, she was as exciting as a piece of cardboard.

It's only when you break away from a lover that you can actually see that person in the cold hard light of reality. When you're in love, a kind of blindness prevents you from seeing clearly.

I'd had plenty of time to think about my relationship with JD. Her world, the band world, had been totally exciting to me. There was this constant rush of drama. People fought and fucked and dressed up weird and showed off on stage. Adorable JD was right smack-dab in the center of it all, and as her bitch, I got to play along.

But there's one thing to remember about performers: they are only interested in themselves. You exist only as part of their show. It's not what they give to you that matters. It's what you do for them.

In other words, they don't know how to love.

Either they can't or they don't want to.

When you fall in love, you have to let go. You have to drop some of your defenses and let yourself be vulnerable. Cute JD, all five feet of her, with her permanently hoarse voice and utterly cool dyke style, was not capable of letting go. She could not or would not lose herself in another person.

So when had she made the big switch and started dating Mistah Sistah? I just couldn't imagine the two of them together. Because JD, for all her streetwise bad manners, was actually the product of a rich, overprotective, white suburban home. And Mistah Sistah, from the little I knew of him, had grown up below the poverty line.

As I pulled up to the Lizard Lounge I could see that JD's engagement party was a big event. It was still early, but the parking lot was already jammed. The big yellow Hummer was parked right by the front door, in the reserved spot.

I looked around for familiar dykemobiles but didn't see a single one. Had JD gone totally straight or what? When she was with Black Garters, she'd been the most popular lesbian in town.

To get in, I had to present my invitation and get my hand stamped. Instead of a sign-in book, there was a computer. I typed in my name and a short message: CONGRATULATIONS. I HOPE IT WILL BE "HAPPILY EVER AFTER" FOR YOU. LOVE, VENUS.

"Presents over there," the check-in girl said, indicating a long table heaped with gifts.

I didn't have a present. I was really there for the food. And to check out the scene.

Which was crowded and kind of strange.

Mistah Sistah was getting all the attention. I stopped in my tracks when I saw him.

He stood in a white spotlight in the center of the dance floor. He was dressed in a strapless wedding gown, the bodice glittering with thousands of sequins, the white organdy skirt puffed out like a bell and trailing a twenty-foot train held up by two white guys wearing dark glasses. On his trademark blonde pageboy wig, he wore a sparkling white tiara. The sunglasses added a weird effect.

Mistah Sistah stood like a queen in a receiving line, extending his gloved hand with regal limpwristedness to all who passed. JD danced around him in a kind of hysterical attendance. She was wearing a red leather tuxedo and had dyed her hair fluorescent green.

I wanted a huge rum and coke but ordered a Perrier with lime and loaded up a plate with greasy short ribs and lime Jell-O with marshmallows. Then I found a dark corner where I could stuff my face and watch the goings-on and forget my own problems.

I looked around for JD's adoring lesbian entourage but didn't see a single familiar face. This crowd was totally into costume. Except for my long, scarab-colored nails, I felt as dowdy as Jane Eyre.

When JD excused herself and headed off to the ladies' room, I gave her three minutes and then followed.

I didn't see her, but one of the stall doors was closed. I washed the grease off my fingers and then went into the stall beside it. A faint, sickly sweet smell drifted beneath the partition. I couldn't identify the smell, but it was illicit, whatever it was. I hoped for JD's sake that it wasn't crack.

I could hear the scratch of her soles on the cement floor and a quiet rustling. Then a sharp intake of breath and a smothered cough, followed by a scary, low-pitched muttering. She mumbled as she rooted around in her purse, then I heard what sounded like a sudden cry or laugh; I couldn't tell which.

"JD, are you all right?" I asked.

There was a moment of silence. "Who's over there?" she whispered. She sounded like a frightened little girl.

"It's me, Venus."

"Venus? Oh my God!"

I wiped and flushed and went out to wash my hands again, expecting that she'd follow. When she didn't, I knocked on the stall door. "JD? Are you all right?"

"Just a minute, just a minute," she said. After another flurry of rustling and rooting, she unlatched the door and looked up at me through bloodshot eyes.

"Oh my God," she said. "Oh, Venus." She clasped me in her arms and pulled my head down for a big wet kiss that smelled of Tic Tacs.

The intensity of her kiss startled me. She'd never given me a kiss like that when we were lovers. I pulled away and looked at her. She was so goddamned beautiful and looked so hot in her red leather tuxedo that I wished for a second that I was just meeting her.

"Are you really getting married?" was all I could think to say.

"Yeah, I am."

"I guess I'm . . . surprised," I said.

"Everybody is." She threw her purse on the counter by the sink and lit up a stinky Gauloise. But that was *not* the smell I had smelled earlier.

"Where's Vida, and Lynjo, and Sarah?" Her closest friends.

"I don't hang out with them anymore," JD said.

My face must have registered disbelief.

"They're so uptight!" JD snapped, examining her face in the mirror. She pulled out a tube of Chanel lipstick. "They act like I'm a fucking traitor."

I didn't know what to say. I didn't know who she was anymore. She'd obviously shaken off her old identity.

"When did you meet Mistah Sistah?" I asked.

"Isn't he *fucking ultra?*" she gushed. "Isn't he like the coolest dude you've ever seen in your life?"

"Is he straight?" I asked.

She spit out a scornful laugh. "Who cares? He just signed with Virgo Records. He's gonna cut a CD and make a music DVD for them."

"Wow," I said. "That's pretty awesome."

"All the Virgo people flew up from LA for this. Someone from *People* magazine is coming. We're going down to LA next week for a production meeting." She eyed me in the mirror as she swiped on her lipstick.

"Are you giving up the Go-Go Girls?"

"Mistah says they're like the worst. Electro-funk-rap is where it's at, Venus. You wouldn't believe how much he's taught me."

"Is he good in bed?" I asked.

JD flinched. I saw it. And I also saw her eyelids flutter and then droop as some drug raced through her body. She dropped her lipstick into the sink.

"What are you on?" I asked.

"Oh God," she moaned.

"Are you sick?" Suddenly I was terrified that she'd OD'd. "JD, what did you take?"

She groaned and retched a pink soup of vomit into the sink.

I lifted her up and shook her. "Tell me what you took! I'll go find a doctor!"

"No!" she cried, turning on the tap, frantically trying to clean up. "It's a big night. *People* magazine. They might put us on the cover."

"Yeah, they sure will if you die of an overdose at your engagement party."

She lurched away. "I'm OK. Really. It's just a little jagged at first."

"What is?"

"It's brand new. Oh my God!" She threw her head back and laughed like Linda Blair in *The Exorcist*. "It is *so* fucking new, Venus!"

"What is? What is it?"

"HGH," she said, touching her green hair and staring intensely at her reflection. "Cooked. They mix in Viagra." She turned around, her lipstick smeared, the sour smell of vomit on her breath. "You want to try it?"

"No!" I cried. "Human growth hormone and Viagra? It sounds really dangerous, JD."

"Your clit, Venus. It swells up like a cock. It's fantastic."

"Where did you get this shit? Are they selling it on the street?"

"The street? Are you kidding?" She laughed and swung back around, jerky as a puppet. "The people at Virgo. They all take it. It's hot in LA."

I didn't know what to do or what to say. I was frightened for her. It was like she'd gone off reality altogether. It was impossible to penetrate to the JD I'd known. The girl who'd had it all, even a bat mitzvah.

"Remember this song?" JD grabbed me by the wrists. Her voice was raspy as a saw blade. "*'You stole my soul. You drank my blood.'*"

"That was a Black Garters song."

"*'You dried my tears,'*" she sang. "*'You ate my love.'*"

"That was one of your best," I said.

"I wrote that fucking song for *you*, Venus. For you!" She rubbed up close.

"I never knew that," I said. "You never told me—ever—that you loved me." I tried to hug her. It was an impulsive gesture, an attempt to reestablish contact, but she froze, just like in the old days.

"I'd better get back to my old man," she said, turning away. "He's gonna do a new rap for the Virgo people. 'Wedded Bliss Diss.' They're going to tape it and see if it works in the new DVD."

I cleared my throat. "Well, then, I'll just wish you good luck, JD. I hope you'll be happy."

"I do, too," she said. "As happy as you are." She gave my hand a squeeze, took a deep breath, and headed back into the din of her engagement party.

They were setting up for "Wedded Bliss Diss" as I made my way to the door. Mistah Sistah was surrounded by makeup girls and lighting men. The white guys holding up his long train were practicing their dance steps.

Chapter

4

What do you wear to meet a prince?

I couldn't find a single thing that looked right.

My entire wardrobe was ready to be handed over to the Goodwill. But then what would I wear? I couldn't go out, like in the old days, and charge whatever clothes caught my fancy. The terms of my bankruptcy were very strict: I wasn't allowed to have a single credit card. For the next seven years, everything had to be cash on the line.

Or in my case, no cash on the line.

I was flat broke. What I earned at Phantastic Phantasy paid my rent and phone with a little left over for lattes and TV dinners.

It was so bad that some nights, for supper, I'd just go around to certain upscale supermarkets and eat the samples. There were a couple of fancy food stores over near where the dads lived that put out all kinds of delicious stuff from their various food departments. If I timed it right, I could start with tostados and a smoked-salmon dip or maybe a soup appetizer, follow that with some marinated pork or Cajun chicken, and end with cookies, biscotti, or chocolate. Then maybe cleanse my palate with some fresh fruit.

There were lots of advantages to dining this way, the biggest being that it was free. No cleanup afterward, either. Everything was sipped, sucked or licked from little paper cups, or scooped up by hand, or stabbed with tiny toothpicks. Long nails came in handy because I could use them like tongs to pinch up bigger hunks of food.

I was always hungry nowadays. Ravenous. Everything looked good. Everything looked edible. But when it came down to spending five bucks for a meal at Burger King or gas for my car, wheels won out over Whoppers.

I had a feeling that Marcello was going to take me out to dinner at someplace very fancy. He'd asked me if I'd "dine" with him.

Luckily, over the years, the dads had taken me to quite a few fancy-schmancy restaurants in New York and Portland. So I knew what silverware to use and how to drape a heavy linen napkin across my lap. Whitman was horribly finicky about table manners.

"We do not drop our heads to the bowl of soup and slurp," he'd say in that royal tone of his, "we sit erect and lift the spoon to our lips."

Just to needle him, I once asked him the proper way to drink milk out of a carton.

"Beverages are *always* poured into glasses," he said.

Not in my household.

But in public, I could, under the proper circumstances, pass myself off as a reasonably well-etiquetted girl.

So what would I wear for an afternoon and evening that included dinner at a fancy restaurant?

I had absolutely nothing dress-uppy. That still fit, anyway. If I squeezed myself into one of my old size eights, I ran the risk of having my head blow off.

The night before, during my late shift at Phantastic Phantasy, I had been hyperaware of the thick stacks of green every time I opened the till. It was a busy night in Pornsville and guys were coughing up fives, tens, and twenties like there was no tomorrow.

Sex, in case you didn't know, is a growth industry. It's one industry, like funerals and toilet cleaning, that always has a guaranteed clientele.

In their never-ending quest for sexual release, guys will buy just about anything. They came into Phantastic Phantasy and spent thousands on videos and magazines. One guy had come in and dropped a hundred and fifty bucks for a new adjustable latex "Sit 'n' Spin."

It was like all I did was rake in money. Saturday night is, of course, the horniest night of the week. I had stacked the bills neatly in their compartments, and pretty soon I couldn't fit any more twenties under the clip that held them in place.

Bruce, the owner, usually came in at 2 A.M. to "cash out" the till. But he was late, so I had to bundle up excess twenties and stash them in the safety bank under the counter.

All that money.

Cash.

Right there in my hand.

I loved the feel of those stiff new twenties with Andrew Jackson's puckered face on one side and a green White House on the other. The older bills, the twenties that had slid in and out of dozens of wallets and changed hands hundreds of times, were as soft and supple as silk pantyhose.

I don't know if you've ever noticed, but money has quite a distinctive and pleasant aroma. I don't think I'd ever been so aware of just how good it smelled.

Efficient as a bank clerk, I counted out fifty twenties, snapping the bills precisely on top of one another.

A thousand bucks.

I looked around the room. The guys were all preoccupied with their illicit fantasies.

I looked down at the money.

There were plenty of ways to skim off a few.

It would have been so easy.

I flipped through the stack of bills like they were a deck of cards. The thick wad of green brought back memories of flusher times. When I had danced topless I used to leave the club with a wad of bread as large as the one in my hand. Back then I never worried about where my next meal was coming from. If I wanted to buy some new clothes, or a two-hundred-dollar pair of shoes, I didn't think twice. I just did it. Back then, prebankruptcy, I had cash *and* plastic.

The coast was clear. I took the money and crouched down behind the counter.

A voice in my head said, *Look at all those greedy-pig CEOs who ripped off their companies and sucked dry their employees' pension funds. Stealing is part of corporate culture, so why shouldn't you steal, too?*

Suddenly, it was like I was outside my own body. I looked at myself, crouched behind the counter, the wad of bills in my hand. I saw my dilemma. Or, rather, the dilemma of this twenty-five-year-old woman who had no money and was contemplating stealing a few twenties so she could buy a nice new dress to dine with a prince.

I thought, *poor her.*

Then I was sucked back into the moment at hand. I looked at the money and said out loud, "No way."

If I was ever going to have money, it would be because I earned it, fair and square, without ripping anyone else off.

That was the American way.

I stuffed the bills into a nylon cash bag and slipped the bag into the slot on top of the safe. It was like a piggy bank that only Bruce could open.

I felt ridiculously virtuous. Patriotic. And very poor.

Which left me, twelve hours later, at two on a Sunday afternoon, still pawing through my closet and digging through the dirty heaps on the floor as I desperately looked for something decent to wear.

The perfect "look." What would it be?

Marcello was due to arrive at three.

The hangers scraped and squeaked as I plowed yet again through my meager lineup of possibilities. Faint puffs of scent rose up from each jarred garment. Stale cigarette smoke. Perfume. Each smell brought up a memory. Dates, dancing. My three husbands. Dreams sowed that never blossomed.

I was standing there in front of the mirror, holding up a slinky pink thrift-shop dress from the 1940s, when the door buzzer let out its angry metallic squawk.

My heart started to pound.

I looked at my watch. Two-twenty.

He was early.

I wasn't ready.

I wasn't even *close* to ready.

I ran to the window and peeked out. A black Lincoln was parked by the front curb.

OK, the problem was this: although the doorbells in my apartment building worked, tenants were unable to buzz anyone in. It was a safety precaution. The intercom and buzzers had been disconnected because people had been letting in anybody who rang, without checking to see who it was. Junkies had been slipping in and shooting up in the hallways. They would say they were delivery boys, or make up other stories to get buzzed in. So now you had to go down to the front door and personally let in whoever was buzzing.

How was I supposed to do that when I wasn't even dressed or made up yet?

I cast a frantic glance around my tiny apartment. It was too messy to let anyone see. Carolee hadn't come over to clean, which meant that *nothing* was put away. Major debris had accumulated over the weeks since I had come back husbandless from my honeymoon. I'd bushwhacked narrow trails through the piles of litter that allowed me to get to my futon, my chair, the refrigerator, and the bathroom.

The bell squawked again.

Part of me wanted to just throw up my arms and say, "Fuck it!" I didn't care what he thought because I didn't really care if I saw him again or not.

Let him wait, I thought. No man in his right mind comes that early to pick up a date.

My phone rang.

"Venus Gilroy?" said a male voice.

I had a sudden vision of Tremaynne. The FBI. Wanting information. Asking how Tremaynne's signature had gotten onto my divorce documents, when he was known to be hiding in Idaho. Did I know that forging a signature was a felony? Etc. "Who is this?" I asked.

"Bobby Clark Florist. Got a delivery for Venus Gilroy."

Bobby Clark was the most expensive florist in town. But I remembered those heroin addicts who'd gotten into the building by saying they were pizza boys. "You deliver on Sunday?" I said suspiciously.

"I'm here, ain't I?"

"OK. I'll come down."

I slipped on my ratty terry cloth robe, the one the dads had brought me years ago from some resort in Hawaii, and peered down the hallway. The coast was clear. I was on the third floor, and the entrance was down two flights of stairs. I didn't bother with slippers. I threw a dish towel over my washed but unstyled hair and tied it up in front, the way Lucy Ricardo does in *I Love Lucy* when she's cleaning that cardboard apartment in New York.

Waiting for me at the front door was the most enormous bouquet of yellow and white roses I'd ever seen. "Jesus Christ!" I cried, toting up the value.

"Someone must love you real bad," the smart-alecky delivery guy said. He was tall and thin, wore blue jeans and a denim jacket, and was about my age and fairly cute.

My hand was shaking as I signed for the flowers. The delivery guy, eyeballing my cleavage, was hot to carry the bouquet up to my apartment. But I pulled my robe tight and cut him off at the pass. "I can do it."

"They're heavy," he warned.

"I'm strong," I said.

"OK." He just stood there until I realized that he was waiting for me to tip him.

"Listen, I'm sorry, I don't have any cash on me," I said.

He gave me a sour smile, turned, and took the front steps three at a time.

He was right. The flowers were heavy. The arrangement was in a silver bucket with a handle on top. It must have weighed twenty pounds.

I lugged it up the stairs, trying at the same time to keep my bathrobe from pulling loose. I know. I *should* have put on some undies before leaving my apartment. But when you're in a hurry, you can't think of everything.

As I was panting up the last few steps, I heard an apartment door slam shut. The slam was sudden and loud, like the wind had blown it.

When I got to the top of the stairs, I saw that the slammed door was the one to my own apartment.

No, I thought. *No, that is not possible.*

But of course it was possible. Not only was it possible, it had happened.

I was locked out, wearing only a robe and a dish towel on my head.

I turned the doorknob very slowly, just in case the latch hadn't caught. But of course it had. I began to turn and jiggle the knob furiously back and forth. "Goddamnit!" I hissed under my breath.

Now what? I didn't want to panic, but it was two thirty-five and Marcello was due to arrive in twenty-five minutes.

I put the roses down, cinched up my robe, and bravely strode down the hallway to the next apartment. Inside, I could hear a TV blaring. I'd never seen the person who lived there, but I knew all the shows he or she watched.

I knocked again. Louder.

Feet scuffled across the floor. The door opened as far as the chain lock allowed. A bleary eye in a nest of wrinkles peered out at me. A sour smell of booze seeped out the crack.

"Hi," I said, "I'm your neighbor in 3A."

The bloodshot eye looked at me. Was it male or female? I couldn't tell. There was some slight motion, as if he or she were chewing on something. Maybe I'd interrupted their Sunday dinner.

"I got locked out of my apartment," I explained, "and I was wondering if you could call the manager, Mr. Tilly, and ask him to bring over a duplicate key."

"No phone." The voice was cracked and oddly pitched.

No phone? In this day and age? Creepy. "Well, listen," I said, "would you mind if I crawled out your window to the fire escape? I left my window open, so I could get in that way."

The eye blinked once. The chain was removed. The door opened. A gust of stale, stinky air blew in my face from the hot dark box of the apartment.

My neighbor didn't say anything. She just stared at me, chewing on something. Her lips were pursed and working like a baby's on a nipple. I don't think she had a tooth in her head.

"Hi," I said, taking a tentative step into the apartment, "I'm Venus Gilroy."

She looked at me, chewing.

It was very scary. People ended up this way. Young single women turned into this.

My neighbor was wearing a stained nylon slip. Her feet were stuffed into slippers that had once been fluffy and blue but were now like mummified Pekingese dogs attached to her feet. Oh jeez, I didn't want to look at those scabby hairy legs or the lopsided thrust of her breasts or her greasy strands of grey and white hair. And I really did not want to smell the horrible smell of her life in that hot, dark studio apartment.

I pointed to the window and bravely made my way into the room.

The shades were drawn. The only light came from the television, a prehistoric black-and-white console. A shudder ran down my spine. I thought, *This is what could happen to you, Venus Gilroy, if you're not careful.*

An aimless life that just slowly frayed and unraveled over time until it was reduced to the bare essentials: black-and-white network TV and a bottle of gin.

To reach the window, I had to step with my bare feet on ancient shag carpeting that was trodden flat and sticky. "It's nice of you to let me do this," I said, walking on tiptoe across the room. "The wind slammed my door shut."

My neighbor watched me as if I were part of her phantom world of black-and-white reality TV shows.

I didn't dare to snap up the shade for fear it would disintegrate. I don't think the light of day had penetrated into that apartment for years. Everything I touched was greasy, dusty, filthy.

This is how you're going to end up, a horrible little voice warned.

I unlocked the window and tried to open it. Stuck tight. I was getting panicky, so I gave it a mighty Wonder Woman heave. The window opened—about two inches. Grunting and straining, I managed to get it up about a foot, barely enough for me to squeeze through.

There was no way to be graceful or dignified. I stuck my head out, eased out my shoulders, arms, and boobs, then grabbed hold of the rusty fire escape and dragged the rest of my body out.

I leaned back in and said thank you.

"Close it," my neighbor said in a weird, gargly voice.

I closed her window and danced over to mine, the iron hot on my feet. My window was open about four inches. I crouched down and tried to lift it higher.

It refused to budge.

I sucked in a Buddha breath, stood up, and turned around to regain my composure. It was a technique Whitman had taught me. Whenever I felt myself getting sucked into moments of frustration, rage, or panic, I stepped back, took a deep breath, and closed my eyes for a moment.

I was doing this, trying to forget the fact that I was now trapped on a third-floor fire escape, wearing a bathrobe but no underwear, with an Italian prince due to arrive in approximately ten minutes, when a voice called out, "Venus?"

I opened my eyes. Looked down. Saw him.

I must have looked shocked, or perhaps stunned, because he said, "It's Marcello."

"Oh, hi," I stammered, trying to sound casual.

Marcello Brunelli stood on the sidewalk below me, looking up with a puzzled grin. In one hand he held a bouquet of flowers, in the other a cigarette.

"I am early," he said.

"Yeah, you are," I said.

There was no way to escape his gaze. He looked up at me with a kind of dazed smile. I pulled my robe tight and kept my legs together.

"I am very sorry," he said. "I was perhaps too anxious to see you."

"Well, here I am," I said caustically.

"Yes," he said. "Dazzling."

"Yeah. Right."

"May I . . . come up?"

"No," I said. "And I can't come down."

His smile wilted. "Why not?"

"Because I'm locked out of my frigging apartment!"

I explained what had happened.

"Do you think I could get the window open?" Marcello asked.

"You?"

"Si si si," he said energetically. "I am in quite good shape. I am quite strong." He gave his arms a quick flex. "I could try anyway."

The fire escape on my building was a strange contraption. Daddy said he'd never seen anything like it and didn't even think it was up to code. The iron-slatted fire escape dated back to the 1940s, possibly even earlier. It ran the entire length of the building, but for security reasons there were no stairs from one level to the next. Well, there were, but the stair segments were fixed into the third and second levels. You had to undo these big iron hooks to release them.

What the hell, I thought. *Let him play Superman and I'll costar as Wonder Woman.*

The hooks were hard to undo, especially with my new nails, and all flaky with rust. But I finally managed to get them loose. With a terrifying screech, like the sound of some ancient prison door, the rusty stair segment slowly cantilevered itself down from the floor of the fire escape. It stopped about six feet above the second-floor fire escape.

"It's rusty," I said. "I don't think it's ever been used."

"It needs the weight of a body," Marcello said. "That's obviously how it was designed."

"I'm supposed to walk out on it, and my weight will bring it down to the second floor?"

He nodded.

There were handrails but the "steps" were little more than thin metal bars, almost like the rungs of a ladder. I took it one step at a time. When I was halfway down, the staircase screeched again and shuddered down to touch the second-floor fire escape.

"That's kind of cool," I marveled.

"Brava! You were brilliant," Marcello said. "It was like watching Cirque du Soleil. Beauty and grace."

I heard but didn't acknowledge the compliment.

No matter how hard I worked, I could not release the next segment, the stairs that led from the second floor to the sidewalk. I got the hooks undone, but the stairs did not budge. When I took hold of the handrail and stepped out on the stairs, nothing happened. I looked down at Marcello, ten feet below me, and shrugged. "Now what?"

Marcello threw down the bouquet of flowers, tossed his cigarette into the gutter, flung away his jacket and tie, and clambered up on top of some tall garbage bins on the side of the building. He grabbed hold of the lowest but still horizontal stair and began chinning himself up.

He was wearing a beautiful white dress shirt and dove gray slacks made out of some soft-looking fabric. Expensive black loafers and black socks. A Rolex watch on his tanned, hairy wrist. No other jewelry. No wedding ring.

As he strained to pull himself up, his face turned beet red, his nostrils flared, and his lips slid back in a Herculean grimace.

Suddenly the stair segment let out a screech and began to move, with me on it.

I let out a startled cry and turned to climb back up, but the stairs kept screeching and bouncing further down as Marcello frantically tried to lift himself up. If they snapped and came all the way down with him on the end, the weight of them could slice him in two.

"Jesus Christ!" I cried.

"Go up!" Marcello gasped. "Balance it at the top with your weight!"

I wanted to scream or make some kind of appropriately terrified noise, but I just sucked up a huge scared breath and turned to climb back up the hot rusty metal stairs. Near the top, I could feel that my weight was counterbalancing his. The stair ceased its downward descent.

Very carefully and very slowly, I turned around.

Marcello, panting and sweating, looking absolutely terrified, was levered off the end of the stairs. His fingers were gripping the third stair. "How far am I from the pavement?" he gasped.

"About seven feet. If you let go, drop straight down."

"I am not going to let go," he wheezed.

"I'm just saying, if you do fall, try to land on your feet."

"You think I cannot do this?" he gasped, eyes bulging.

As I watched, he suddenly did what looked like a gymnastics routine. Like a hinge, he lifted his legs straight up beneath the stairs, then let go for one terrifying moment and lunged for the next railing. He caught it and pulled himself higher. Finally, his entire body was splayed out on the stairs. He lifted a perspiring face and gave me a kind of goofy grin.

"Now what?" I said.

"Stay where you are. Balance me. I am coming up to you."

Which he did, rung by rung, crawling like a slow but determined lizard, until he was literally at my feet.

"Do not move," he panted. "I am going to stand."

Which he did. He stood up. He was an inch away from me. His shirt was soaking wet and covered with rust and grime. His body was trembling from the exertion. He gave off a deep, dark odor.

His eyes burned into mine. "Venus," he said, his voice low. "Do you make all your lovers work this hard?"

I shook my head. Because the truth was, no, my lovers did not, had not, and would not work that hard for me. He was the first one.

"Venus," he said, still panting for breath, "I would like to claim a reward."

I stared at him. "What?"

"A kiss," he said.

I didn't object. I didn't say no. I closed my eyes and felt the hesitant press of his arms. Then he let out what sounded like a small moan and pulled me tight. His lips were on mine.

I shuddered, boiling with conflicted emotions.

When we moved, the stairway let out a screech and started to fall. I stayed in his arms as it dipped, bounced, and swung up again.

Chapter

5

You can tell a lot about a guy from the way he kisses.

A kiss is like a signature. A personal trademark. You get a big hit of personality from a guy's kiss.

I stood there, in Marcello's arms, listening to what his kiss was telling me.

I remembered the different ways my three husbands had kissed.

Tremaynne, my most recent ex, was the best kisser of them all. He really put his soul into his kisses. He was a great lover because he wasn't interested in power so much as maximum pleasure, however that could be obtained. Sometimes he was forceful, sometimes he was yielding. His tongue held a spark that never failed to ignite me.

Once you experience kisses like that, kisses that instantly flip you into a hot whirlpool of passion, you're damned, in a way, because you feel that no other guy's kisses could possibly compare. You can't imagine even wanting to be kissed by anyone else.

But there I was, on my fire escape, wearing a ratty old terry cloth robe and a dish towel, clasped in the arms of Marcello Brunelli, a stranger who was old enough to be my father.

His kiss was what I would call "romantic." I was supposed to participate in it, but that's hard to do on the first kiss when you're not truly hot for the man. His dark eyes gazed passionately into my own.

His long, dark lids were half-closed and trembling with what must have been a kind of REM bliss. His lips were warm and full, tender but certainly not shy.

Not bad.

Obviously experienced.

When I let him slide his tongue in, he let out a soft moan and clasped me tighter. "Venus," he whispered. It sounded like *Vay-noose*. "I cannot believe you are in my arms at last."

It sounded like dialogue from one of those weird old movies my mom was always watching. Something with Bette Davis or Greta Garbo. I burst out laughing.

"Why do you laugh?" he asked.

I couldn't say "Because of the way you talk," so I just shrugged. "I don't know. It's all so ridiculous."

His eyes flashed a kind of wounded alarm. "What is?"

I just could not stop laughing. It wrenched my gut and brought tears to my eyes.

"I am?" he said, pulling away. "I am ridiculous?"

"No, no. Not you. The situation. Look at me!"

"You are beautiful," he said.

"Yeah. Right."

"You are always beautiful," he insisted.

"OK," I said, still laughing, "but I need to get inside and put on some clothes."

"Must you?" he said, then whispered in my ear, "I want to make love to you."

Which brought on another fit of uncontrollable laughter. I snorted like a horse and looked at him through brimming eyes. Oh dear. He looked puzzled and a little crestfallen, as if I'd somehow made fun of his masculinity.

"Well," I said, "at least I know what you're after."

"Oh Venus," he whispered, "please, I hope I did not offend you."

"You were going to help me get the window up," I reminded him, adroitly changing the subject.

"Ah, yes." He followed me off the stairs and over to my window. "It seems to be stuck," he said, crouching down and pulling up on the sash. He flashed those big dark eyes at me and gave those long black lashes a real workout. "It is *very* stuck," he gasped, standing and straining to pull up the window. The way he stuck out his meaty ass reminded me of those "poses" he had always asked me to do at House of Peek-a-Boo.

Marcello backed away from the window with a look of chagrin. "No," he said. "*Mi dispiace, non posso.*"

"Are you swearing?" I asked him.

He mopped his forehead with a boogerless white hanky. "Swearing? No." He smiled. "Mama never let me swear. If she heard me speak a naughty word, I had to say a hundred Hail Marys."

I found this intriguing but incomprehensible. "What's a Hail Mary?"

Marcello's eyes suddenly dropped into bedroom mode. He came close again and put his arms around me. "Hail Mary," he whispered in my ear. "Full of grace. The Lord is with thee. Blessed art thou amongst women, and blessed is the fruit of thy womb, Jesus. Holy Mary, mother of God, pray for us sinners, now and at the hour of our death. Amen."

"That's what you had to say when you swore?"

"A hundred times." He nuzzled my neck.

That was one of the weirdest things I'd ever heard. That, and hearing a grown man call his mother Mama.

"Isn't there another way we could get inside?" Marcello asked.

I quickly flashed through the possibilities. I could knock on my neighbor's window and see if she'd let me go back through her apartment into the hallway. Then I could knock on another door and see if another tenant would call Mr. Tilly, the manager, for me. The problem with this scenario was that I did not want Marcello to enter the hellhole next door. It was horrible enough that he was going to see my own little pigsty.

"No. I will do it." Marcello bent at the knees like a weightlifter about to press a five-hundred-pound barbell, grabbed the sash, and let out something that sounded like "Aawrghk."

The window, resisting all the way, slid up about a foot. Enough for me to slide back in.

"Shouldn't I go first?" he asked.

"No!" I sat down and slipped my legs through. "Hold on to my arms."

Marcello did as he was told. As I eased myself down, a thread on my robe got snagged in a loose splinter of wood. The robe started to open wider and wider. "Close your eyes, goddamn you," I said, starting to laugh again.

Marcello closed his eyes.

Like a contortionist, I touched the floor with my feet while my torso was curved backward, still outside the window. One breast was now exposed and I was in imminent danger of flashing beaver.

Then I was inside.

My horrible little apartment had never looked so good. Or so terrible.

"May I open my eyes now?" Marcello asked.

I pulled my robe together. "Yeah."

"Shall I come in now?"

"Wait a sec." Like a damsel on Dexedrine, I raced through the apartment snatching up clothes and clutter and flinging it all into my closet. The bathroom was a filthy mess, too. I quickly hung up damp towels and shoved my cosmetics into an orderly line on the sink.

"OK," I yelled. "You can come in now."

It required a bit of agility. Marcello carefully sat down on the fire escape. He poked his legs into the room, one at a time, then took hold of the sash and began lowering himself in.

Suddenly he stopped moving.

"What's wrong?" I asked.

"I've got a sliver or something."

"Where?"

"In my backside."

I went to help. "Lift up your rear end so I can see."

Sure enough, he was snagged on a sharp splinter of wood. The splinter had pierced his trousers, sliding in like a dagger. "You have to pull yourself back out."

Marcello muttered something under his breath and went into reverse. I worked the splinter out of the fabric and then guided him back in.

Finally he was standing in my hot, horrible little apartment.

"Next time I would like to come through the front door," he gasped, mopping his forehead.

Then he started to look around. His eyes darted over everything. "Where do you sleep?" he asked.

"On my futon. It pulls out into a bed."

"Ah." He nodded. "Tell me, didn't you receive some flowers?"

"Holy shit, the flowers!" I'd forgotten all about them. I ran to the door and pulled them in from the hallway. "I was downstairs getting them when the door slammed shut and I got locked out."

He nodded. "Do you like them?"

"They're beautiful!" The truth was, I wanted to cry. I just wanted to bawl. Because no guy had ever thought so much of me that he'd dropped five hundred bucks at least on perfect roses.

"Is there a card?" Marcello prompted.

I looked. There was. It read, "An offering to Venus, my goddess of love. Marcello Brunelli."

"Thanks." I felt suddenly sheepish. And, once again, completely baffled. Why was this guy, this prince, this rich Italian, so hot to trot with me? Nothing in my experience had prepared me for the kind of hyperromantic adulation he was dishing out.

Was it just for a fuck?

That was crazy, because he had his pick of women. Back at Pine Mountain Lodge, Whitman's friend Marielle had told me that Marcello Brunelli had "quite a reputation" in Europe. And before that, when he used to come into House of Peek-a-Boo and have me model lingerie for him, before I knew who he was or anything about him, he had worn a wedding ring.

I looked again. No wedding ring.

We stood there like tongue-tied teenagers on a first date.

"Ah." He turned his full attention to me. "*Allora*—"

"What does that mean?"

"What shall we do now?"

"Well, I'm not ready. As you can see."

"That depends on what we want to do, doesn't it?"

"Aren't we going out to eat somewhere? I thought you wanted to *dine*," I reminded him. I was starving. A bowl of Cocoa Puffs was all I'd eaten since those greasy short ribs at JD's engagement party.

"Oh, yes," he said. "But look at me. I am a mess."

"Do you have other clothes with you?"

"Of course. In my *valigia*. My suitcase."

"Well, go get them. You can change in here."

"Ah. Si. Good idea."

When he was gone, I ransacked my closet one last time. It was all a game of chance. I closed my eyes, reached in, and snatched something off the rack.

The pink 1940s dress I'd found at a thrift shop for $7.50. Whitman had told me it was a "cocktail dress." Which I guess meant that the original owner, now an old lady, had worn it to cocktail parties and stood around with a martini in one hand and a cigarette in the other. "It fits you beautifully, with your Marilyn Monroe figure," Whitman said the one time he'd seen me in it. "Of course, women back then didn't have tattoos on their tits."

I thought it looked hot, the big rose above my left boob right beneath the pink silk spaghetti strap of the dress.

I had never worked so fast in my life. I think I made it into the *Guinness Book of World Records*. I figured I had about ten minutes max before Marcello returned. The wonder is that I did it. I was just putting on the finishing touches when the buzzer squawked.

I'd completely forgotten that he wouldn't be able to get back in the front door.

I ignored the buzzer. Let him cool his heels a little.

Of course it wasn't his heels that needed cooling.

"Venus!"

I was putting on my long, drapey rhinestone earrings as I ran across the room to the window.

"Venus!" he called up when he saw me. "The door is locked."

"Yeah, I forgot. I'll be right down."

I slipped into my pink high heels, scuffed from too many big clumsy feet stepping on the toes while trying to slow dance, and made for the door. Skidded to a halt. Purse! Keys!

I stood there for a moment. Sucked in a big Buddha breath.

Looked at my pink reflection in the cruddy old full-length mirror that hung beside the door. I was completely transformed. You couldn't slouch wearing a dress like this. I pulled back my shoulders, the way they'd taught me in that modeling class years ago. I was proud of my figure. I was tired of grieving for Tremaynne. I was ready for a new life.

He was facing the street, smoking a cigarette and bouncing nervously on the balls of his feet.

When he heard me open the inner door, he flicked his cigarette away, ran a quick hand through his hair, and turned.

His face completely changed when he saw me.

He stared, his mouth slightly open.

"*Dio mio,*" he whispered when I opened the door to the street.

"What's the matter?" I asked. I had a sudden sinking feeling that the pink cocktail dress was a mistake. The whole ensemble was a mistake. *Everything* was a mistake. "Should I change?"

Marcello's face lit up. He laughed. He pulled me into his arms. "No," he said, "please do not change. Do you hear me, Venus? Never change."

"Where's your suitcase?" I asked, slipping out of his grasp.

He pointed to a gleaming black Mercedes sedan. "In there."

"Well, why don't you get it?"

"I cannot get in."

"What?"

"The keys. They are in my jacket pocket."

"Well, where's your jacket?"

He gave a shrug. It was what I now know to be a Roman shrug. His hands came out, palms up, his shoulders rose, his lips pursed, and he said something that sounded like "boo."

"What do you mean, *boo?*"

"The jacket. My jacket. It is gone."

"Gone? You mean someone stole it?"

He shrugged again. "Boo."

His nonchalance was impressive. I would have been in a panic.

We looked for his jacket. He'd laid it down near the trash cans before climbing onto the fire escape. Gonzo. No surprise in my syringe-strewn neighborhood.

"What else was in your pocket?" I asked him. "Not your wallet, I hope." Stuffed with all the cash and credit cards he must be carrying.

"No. Everything is locked in the car."

The gods were having a great time. I could almost hear them laughing.

"OK, then," I said, all practical, "you need to call someone. Is it a rental car?"

"No," he said, then, "Ah! Giovanni. He has a key."

Giovanni was evidently Marcello's assistant. He'd been with Marcello on the trip to Osaka, and now he was holed up in some hotel out near the airport. Very sick. In Osaka, he'd eaten some raw fish or something that gave him food poisoning.

"I hate to disturb him," Marcello said. "Do you have a mobile?" He pronounced it *mo*-bile, not Mo-bel.

I hauled out my huge, heavy old cellular phone and handed it to him.

"My God," he said wonderingly, "how old is this thing?"

"From the Ice Age. It was, like, the first model."

"Why don't you have a newer one? They make them very small now."

"I like this one," I said. "I can use it as a weapon if I have to."

He was punching in numbers. "Have you?"

"Yes, as a matter of fact."

"I will try not to anger you," he said, with a flash of smile. Then it was telephone time. On my nickel. First, directory assistance, which used to be free but now costs a dollar. Then he had them ring the number (another buck). Then a long conversation in Italian with Giovanni at the airport hotel.

I watched him as he talked. He became completely focused on the conversation. The sound of his voice, speaking Italian, was deep and musical—yes, musical, full of ups and downs and exclamations. Western voices sounded flat and twangy in comparison. I had to admit he had a sexy voice. He gestured with his free hand as he spoke and paced back and forth on the sidewalk.

"*Allora*," he said finally, handing the phone back. "May we go there in your car, Venus?"

"Go where?"

"To the hotel. I will pick up the other set of keys from Giovanni."

I looked across the gleaming black roof of the Mercedes to my battered old Toyota parked on the other side of the street. What would he think when he saw what I drove? He would be shocked. One rear window was held up by layers of gray duct tape. There was a huge crack in the windshield. The back was dented in on one side. The vinyl seat covers had split and foam rubber poked out like a hernia. The passenger door wouldn't close properly, so I'd tied a piece of rope between the handle and the neck rest to prevent the door from flying open while I drove. And, like my apartment, my car was littered with an accumulation of trash.

He'd laugh. Roll his eyes. Maybe refuse to enter. Because he drove a carriage, but I drove a rotting pumpkin.

And then I thought, *So what? If he doesn't like it, too bad*. I had nothing at stake here. And I was the one with the vehicle.

"Let's go," I said.

"You have to slide in from the driver's side," I informed him.

Marcello was puzzled. "But why?"

"The passenger door's tied shut."

He peered, a little warily, into the baking-hot Toyota. "How do I get over your stick shift?"

"That's up to you," I said with a laugh.

My laugh was like a goad to him. He slid into the driver's seat, corkscrewed around so he could lift one foot over the center console, then lifted his butt over, sat down, and pulled over his other foot. "I did it, you see?" He gave me a proud look.

Trying to be graceful in a pink satin cocktail dress with high heels is not easy when you're sliding into a beat-up wreck of a car. I buckled up and turned on the ignition. The engine chuffed, shook, whinnied, roared. Music blasted out of the one working speaker. The night before, after my melancholy encounter with JD at her engagement party, I had slipped in her old Black Garters demo tape, just to hear what she used to sound like when I was in love with her. I'd kept playing the song she said she'd written for me, imagined her hoarse voice crooning it to me.

You stole my soul.
You drank my blood.
You dried my tears.
You ate my love.

"That is the kind of music my son listens to," Marcello shouted.

I heard him, but I didn't say anything. A son. How many kids were there?

I lowered the volume and headed for the freeway. His eyes never left me. They were trained on me like magnifying glasses in the sun, burning my clothes away.

You know how, under the right circumstances, you can get kind of hot when a man stares at you? I was starting to feel distinctively warm, and it wasn't just my car's lack of air-conditioning.

Then my oil light blinked on.

"Shit," I muttered, pulling over to the curb.

"What is it?" Marcello asked.

I got out of the car, pulled up the hood, and propped it open. It was a routine I could do in my sleep. My car ate and leaked about a quart of oil a week.

I checked the dipper, then asked Marcello to hand me a can of oil from the backseat. "Shouldn't you have a garage do it?" he asked. He pronounced it *gay*-rahj.

"I can do it myself," I said.

"I will get out and help you," he offered. "May I untie this door?"

"No! Just stay put. It's easier if I do it." I took the oil and poured it down the gullet of my poor old car. Then, without realizing what I was doing, I wiped my oil-grimy fingers across my backside. I didn't realize this until later when I took off my dress and saw the big oily swipes.

"You did that very well," Marcello said as I plopped back into the car.

"I've had a lot of practice."

"Perhaps it is time for a new car," he said.

I laughed. It was like some weird reflex.

"Why do you laugh so?" he asked.

"Let's get something straight, OK?"

"Yes?"

I flashed him a quick I-mean-business glance as we started down the freeway ramp. "I don't have any money, OK? I have, like, zero money. I can't just go out and buy a new car, OK? I can't do that."

"I did not say you should go out and buy a new car," he said. "I said only that perhaps it was *time* for a new car."

"Well, that's what you meant," I said, hating the sour tone in my voice.

"I am sorry if I angered you. Please do not hit me with your mobile."

"Goddamnit," I said, "sometimes it just really pisses me off, the way you people with money just don't get it that some of us don't have any."

"Are you a Communist?"

"No, I'm not a Communist." Not the way Tremaynne was.

"My son is a Communist," Marcello said, looking out the dirty window as we sped down the freeway toward the airport. His face grew pensive. "I think it's nothing more than an intellectual pose. Quite outdated, one might say."

Again I veered away from the subject of his child. I just really did not want to listen to some guy talk about his kids. I was not interested. When it came to the subject of kids, I was in total denial.

"You will like him," Marcello said, turning back to me. "He's a fine boy, despite his politics. But my daughter—well . . ."

I kept my lips buttoned, but my radar was picking up everything.

Marcello seemed to think I was going to go into the hotel with him.

No way.

I was not going to go in and meet Giovanni, some guy I didn't know, some Italian crony. Whitman's warnings, which I had thought were so stupid at the time, now seemed worth heeding. After all, what did I really know about Marcello Brunelli? He might have set this whole thing up just to get me into this hotel room. He seemed gentlemanly enough, but maniacs were expert at playacting.

"I'll wait here," I said, standing beside the car door as he hauled himself out.

"You do not wish to meet Giovanni?"

"No."

"I will hurry." He gave my chin a dramatic caress. "Every moment I have with you is precious."

I checked my laughter. "Right."

I'd been standing there about five minutes when my phone rang.

"It's your faux pa," Whitman said. "Is he there?"

"Not at the moment."

"But you're with him?"

"Sort of."

"Listen, I know you think my advice is worthless, but I want you to listen to me. Are you listening?"

"Yes, Whitman, I'm listening."

"Do not give him anything he asks for."

"What's that supposed to mean?"

"Sweetheart, don't take umbrage—"

"What does that mean?"

"Don't get pissed off. I'm telling you this for your own good."

"Telling me what?"

"You're all heart, Venus. Like your mother. That makes you gullible."

As usual he was pushing my defense mechanisms. "I'm *not* gul—"

"Just listen to me. Sweetheart, I've observed you for years. You want to be loved. We all want to be loved. It's in our nature. But you always choose the wrong men."

"Thanks for reminding me."

"You choose them without really knowing them. You're too eager, and that's what makes you gullible. Just because someone wants you doesn't mean you have to give in to him."

"The point, please, Whitman?"

"Male Psychology 101. Men want what they can't have. So don't let Prince Charming overwhelm you."

"Whitman, it's a date. That's all it is. OK?" Marcello wanted to get me into bed, of course; that was very clear. But I had no deep desire, and my new rule was that I didn't sleep with anyone unless I truly desired him. The sad truth of it was that the only man I truly desired was Tremaynne, my third and last ex.

"You haven't gone to bed with him, have you?"

I saw Marcello in the lobby, headed for the front door. "Whitman, stop snooping around, OK? I have to go."

Marcello hurried over to the car dangling a set of keys and grinning like a kid. "Giovanni was very sorry not to meet you," he said.

"Maybe some other time."

"He is feeling terrible, and he looks quite awful."

"Maybe you should call a doctor."

"No, he will be fine in a few hours. That's how it is with food poisoning. Damn sushi."

"Uh-oh," I said. "You swore." I stood back and pointed toward the car. "Better hop in and get started on those Hail Marys."

"Yes, but first you must wave. I told Giovanni you would wave to him." Marcello turned and pointed up to a window.

The sun was reflecting off that side of the hotel so I couldn't see very clearly. I waved at what appeared to be a pale figure with a blanket wrapped around him.

"*Va bene*," Marcello smiled and maneuvered himself into the car. "Now we can go. Now our time together can begin."

The world looks very different through the window of a Mercedes. I sank down into my soft leather seat as we pulled away from my cruddy neighborhood. The car was a marvel of engineering. It seemed to purr.

"You can adjust the seat if you like," Marcello said. He pressed a button and my seat started to recline.

I brushed his hand away and pressed myself back up. "I have to sit upright or I'll get carsick."

"Are you comfortable?" he asked. "Is the temperature all right for you?"

"I'd like it about five degrees cooler."

"Yes, Americans like their air-conditioning to be freezing." Marcello fiddled with another control.

"What's that?" I pointed to what looked like a computer screen.

"That is my GPS. Global Positioning System. You see, it tells me where I am at all times."

"Don't you know where you are?"

There was ardor in his glance. He reached over and caressed my hand. "At this moment, with you, I am in a place that exists on no computer."

No one had ever gotten poetic on me before. I felt embarrassed. "So what does this GPS actually do?"

"Ah, well, it is very clever. I can program in where I am, and what my destination is. Then the computer will give me the quickest route and provide verbal directions. Useful if I do not have a driver with me."

"Is that what Giovanni usually does? Drive you around?"

"He enjoys that. I enjoy driving, too, but I am usually working, so someone else must do it for me."

In the backseat, there was a big black briefcase, what I guessed to be a laptop, and a kind of portable desk thing. In the front, there was a telephone with a cord and a wireless computer keyboard that slid into its own special niche.

"Giovanna insisted that we fit out all of our cars, all over the world, with these computer systems," Marcello said. "Just in case we are kidnapped."

"What good would that do?"

"All the computers are networked to each other and to our main office in Roma. The police could track us anywhere."

"But only if you were in one of your own cars," I pointed out.

"Ah!" He flashed me a mysterious smile. "No. You see, we all carry a mobile GPS as well. Giovanna insists on that."

"Who's Giovanna?" I asked. "Head of security?"

Marcello laughed quietly. "Yes, you might say that."

My stomach let out a loud unladylike growl.

"Where would you like to dine?" Marcello asked politely.

"How much time do you have?"

"Ah. Time. The great thief." He glanced at his watch. "I have until midnight. I must be back in Roma tomorrow." He detailed a bunch of complicated plane schedules.

"OK, let's drive out to the beach," I suggested. "We can find a restaurant somewhere on the ocean." I wasn't interested in the crashing surf. I wasn't interested in holding hands and walking on the beach. I was interested in fried oysters and killing time somewhere out of the city, away from the vicinity of my futon. And, in a horribly selfish way, I wanted to enjoy a long drive in a big Mercedes. It might be my only chance. After my Toyota, this was like being in a spa.

My phone rang.

"Hello, sweetheart." It was the cooing voice of my mom. "Am I interrupting anything?"

"No."

"Where are you, sweetheart?"

"We're driving out to the coast."

"Oh?"

"For dinner."

"Oh." There was a pause. "That sounds romantic."

"Not really."

"Oh?" She was obviously waiting for more information, and I was not going to give it to her. "Well, listen, sweetheart, I've assembled a dossier. There was a lot of stuff in Italian, but I couldn't find much in English." She paused again. "I thought you might want me to share some of this *very* interesting information with you."

"Now?"

"He's not married," Mom said. "His wife died. He's a widower."

I looked at Marcello and smiled. "When?"

"Recently. She was sick for years. He was devoted to her."

"How do you know that?"

"I read it in a magazine."

"Then it must be true."

Carolee didn't pick up on my ironic tone. "The wife's name was Fulvia," she continued. "I think she was an heiress or something.

They had two children, but I couldn't find out much about them. The whole family's kind of secretive. Rich but not into publicity."

"Anything else?"

"Holdings all over the world. Believes diversifying assets is the best way to achieve continued growth in a global economy."

"Groovy."

"The important thing to remember," Carolee said, "is that he's a widower, a multimillionaire, and younger than Mick Jagger."

Chapter

6

It takes about an hour and a half to get from Portland to the Pacific Ocean at Cannon Beach. The ride was one I'd made many times with the dads, who liked to drive out there just to walk on the long white-sand beach and eat pan-fried oysters.

As a kid, I had loved going to Cannon Beach. I'd run and run along the windy shore, my special Wonder Woman cape snapping and streaming behind me, almost believing that I was about to lift off and zoom through the salty air. Or I'd help the dads fly big, complicated kites that looked like Japanese dragons. Kids would gather around in awe, and I always felt very special. Sometimes Daddy and I would rent beach buggies, lightweight, low-slung pedal carts, and race along the surf line.

To get there, you had to drive past nut orchards and the rolling vineyard-covered hills of what Whitman the travel writer always called the wine country. Sometimes we'd stop at one of the wineries so the dads could sample and buy a bottle of their favorite pinot. Once you passed the wine country, you climbed gradually into the forested Coast Range, the low mountains that separate the Willamette Valley from the Pacific, and then scooted down again toward the headlands, bays, and wild, windswept beaches of Oregon's Pacific coast.

"You know, I love this part of America," Marcello said. "I find it very grand."

"You have a house up at Pine Mountain Lodge, don't you?" I remembered what Kristin, the young dyke I'd met at Pine Mountain Lodge, had told me about Marcello's enormous "cabin" in the wilderness.

He nodded. "Unfortunately, I do not have much time to enjoy it."

"You must stay pretty busy," I said inanely. "Running companies all over the world and everything."

He glanced at me with those dark, pensive eyes. "I work too much. I never seem to have time to live."

"Just to fuck around, you mean."

His hand crept over to mine. "Yes, just to fuck around."

"I mean, just to be, like, a slacker and do nothing." I slipped my hand out from under his and gave my dress a discreet tug. The satin was slippery and kept riding up on the big, warm, buttery-soft leather seat of the Mercedes.

"I am very bad at doing nothing," Marcello said.

I laughed. "I could teach you a thing or two about slackerdom."

It was meant to be a joke, but he gave my hand an ardent squeeze and lifted it to his lips. "Ah, my darling, would you really do that for me?"

"Teach you to be a slacker?"

"Si." His face lit up. "Teach me to throw off the weight of obligations and responsibilities and worries that burdens me from every morning to every night. If you could teach me how to do that, Venus, you would save my life."

I just sat there like a dummy. I didn't know what to say. I felt like I'd put my foot in it, offering in jest something that he took seriously. He must have sensed my sudden reluctance because he quickly changed the subject and asked me if I'd ever been to Italy.

"Just once. My dads took me to Capri." It had been one of those rush-rush last-minute trips arranged by Whitman to coincide with a travel assignment for some magazine. I was almost thirteen. I'd fallen in love with a boy I met buying a gelato. That's all I remembered of Capri. That and getting horribly sick on the hydrofoil going over there from Naples.

Marcello sucked in a surprised breath. "Capri! But darling, this is too fantastic. Mama lives on Capri. We have a villa there." He pronounced it *Cop*-pree.

"I don't remember much about it."

"Ah, Capri, *la isola bella*. The beautiful island. You do not remember the Blue Grotto?"

I shook my head, suddenly remembering that boy's face, how dark, mysterious, and non-American-looking it was.

"I will take you there. We will go to Capri. You will meet Mama. I will show you the Blue Grotto."

Holy shit, I thought. *Whoa, boy. Slow down.* "You're way over the speed limit," I pointed out, trying to bring him back to earth. "Lots of state troopers hide along this stretch."

"Ah, yes." He slowed the car from ninety to sixty. "But how can one ever get anywhere with these American speed limits? It is like crawling."

"I know. I like driving fast, too." It was just that my old Toyota wouldn't let me.

"Have you ever tried a Lamborghini?" Marcello asked.

"No. What's that, a kind of wine or something?"

He smiled. Quite a beautiful smile, actually. He was handsome and knew it. "No, not wine, a car. My favorite car. On the autostrada? Zip!" He snapped his fingers. "Three seconds and I am up to one hundred."

"Wow. It would take me a whole day to pump my old Toyota up to a hundred."

"You enjoy driving?" he asked.

"I love it. I'm like my dad. I just love to drive." And, if I did say so, I was a fabulous, fearless driver. Driving, Daddy always said, is both a skill and a state of mind. "When you're driving," he'd say as we zipped around town in his BMW on the weekends he had me, "you take control of the road, but you also share it." Daddy was a great driving instructor, and he loved to go fast. A subtle change would come over him when he goosed up the mph and slipped into the danger zone, courting troopers and tickets. That's one thing I did learn from my dad: how to speed. But to speed well you need the right kind of car, one that's responsive as a lover, and my sorry old clunker went into cardiac arrest if I pushed her past fifty.

"Would you care to drive this?" Marcello asked.

I wanted to, immediately, but hesitated. "It's kind of like driving a spaceship, isn't it?"

"It's only a car," he shrugged.

"Yeah, but I know the sticker price." Because I was always longing for a new car. I window-shopped car dealerships the way some girls window-shop Tiffany's.

He cast me a flirty, daring glance. "Are you afraid?"

I looked him square in the eyes. "Pull over."

We were approaching the summit of the Coast Range. Marcello turned into a viewpoint area. We got out and stood for a moment looking out over miles and miles of forest and cliffs with the silver thread of a mountain stream sparkling far below. The sun was still high and cast a dazzling sheet of yellow summer light into the unbroken stand of green fir trees.

For some reason, the scene made me think of Tremaynne. Nature Boy. Now hiding out somewhere in the wilds of Idaho. Maybe in the forest owned by Marcello's lumber company, Lumina International.

I suddenly felt all wobbly inside, like a house of cards about to collapse.

Goddamn you, Tremaynne, I thought, pulling my face taut so it wouldn't explode in a flash flood of tears. *Goddamn you for kissing me like that and making me believe that you loved me.*

But Tremaynne never loved you, a brutally honest voice reminded me. *He never said he loved you. He even tried to warn you off. But you wanted him to be in love with you because he was so cute and the sex was so good. So you pretended that he was. You let your stupid romantic fantasies run away with you—as usual.*

I stood there, lost in my miserable thoughts, and flinched when I felt Marcello's warm arm around my shoulder. He tried to pull me close. I resisted him.

"Tell me what you are thinking," he said.

I shook my head. "Just stuff."

"Just stuff," he repeated, then cleared his throat. "Shall I tell you what I was thinking?"

I nodded.

"I was thinking how beautiful you look standing there in the evening sunlight wearing a pink dress."

I didn't say anything.

"I was thinking what joy you give me every moment I am with you."

I cleared a little frog from my throat.

"I was thinking of asking you to marry me."

I froze.

"I was wondering how I would do it. What I would say. And what you would say."

My voice sounded kind of wavery. "I would say that we hardly know one another."

He nodded.

"I would say that you throw out a really good line."

He shook his head. "I do not understand."

"I would say that you are so full of bullshit that your eyes are brown."

He looked shocked. Speechless.

I pulled free from his embrace. "I would say, all you really want is to go to bed with me."

"I have never denied that," he said.

"I would say, once you get what you want, you'll disappear."

"No. No, that is not true."

"Why should I believe anything you say?" I cried. "You come here all hot and romantic, all the way to Portland, just to see me? You call my dad to ask his permission to go out with me? You send me five hundred bucks' worth of roses? It's nuts. People don't do things like that!"

"Some people do," he said.

"Not for me, they don't!" I let out a choked-sounding cry, as if I were releasing something buried in me long, long ago. "No one in my entire life has ever . . ." I caught myself just in time. "I mean, it's nice and everything, really, but it's just, like, for sex, right?"

"I see I've made a fool of myself." His voice was quietly wounded.

"No, you made a fool of me."

"Of you? But I worship you."

"Oh, yeah, right, you 'worship' me. You call me 'darling.' You think I'm really going to fall for all this?"

"You think I am insincere."

Lying isn't half as much fun as telling the truth. I felt weirdly exhilarated now that I was off and running. I had nothing to lose by telling him exactly what I thought. And somehow I was hoping that maybe if I was forceful enough, it would cause him to back off, go away, leave me alone. "I think you're just a rich playboy who wants to fool around with me for a while," I said. "Well, thank you. It's a compliment. I never thought I was playboy material."

"Venus." He grasped me by the shoulders. "I am in love with you."

"But why?"

He said nothing, just looked at me with those dark, burning eyes.

"Why me?" I asked. "There's no reason!"

"For the first time in my life, I do not care about reasons."

"Are you looking for a trophy wife or something?"

He let out a disgusted snort.

"Because I'm not trophy wife material. OK? For a guy like you, I'm more like the booby prize."

"Is that how you think of yourself?" he asked.

I didn't answer, but my eyes filled up and I didn't know where the hell the tears were coming from. "You could have your pick of anyone," I said, my voice all cry-shaky. I sucked up a noseful of snot. "Rich beautiful women with perfect teeth. Heiresses. You could probably get a movie star."

"But I do not *want* a movie star," he said, exasperated. "I want *you*."

"Yeah, on my back, with my legs open."

"Ah!" He threw up his arms in disgust. "Si si si si si si. Yes! It is all true! I want to make love to you. I want to hold you in my arms. I want to feel your heart beating next to mine. I want to kiss your breasts and feel the warmth of your womanhood. I want all of that, Venus. I want all of you. If we are honest, isn't that where love really begins?"

Yes. He was right. It all started with sexual attraction. And the problem was, he was hot for me, but I didn't really feel any heat for him. I felt kind of guilty, like I *should* feel attracted to him, but every woman knows you can't fake stuff like that. I could accept the fact that he wanted my bod, because I am pretty hot when I want to be. What I could not accept, or understand, anyway, was why he would want anything more than that. What the hell else did I have to offer?

"Is it just because I'm young?" I asked.

"I am not interested in analysis," he said firmly, sounding a little pissed off.

"Well, I don't really know why else you could possibly want me," I said truthfully. "I don't have a penny to my name."

"I have plenty of pennies for both of us," he said, lassoing me with his eyes.

"I never went past junior college," I said.

Then he laughed. It was like a release of tension. He stepped back and opened his mouth and let go. "Oh. Oh." He pulled me into his arms, and this time I didn't resist. But I didn't put my arms around him, either. "You see, Venus, that is why I love you."

"Why?"

"Because you are always you. You do not pretend to be anything other than what you are."

"Yeah," I said, "but the question is, what am I?"

"The most *natural* person I know." He framed my face with his hands and stared tenderly into my eyes. "The most genuine. The most honestly beautiful."

"You don't know anything about me," I said. "Not really."

"I know enough," he said. "I know what my heart tells me."

"Well, my heart's been broken," I said. "A lot."

"So has mine." He kissed me gently on the lips.

I turned away. "Look, I really appreciate everything you've said. Really. I do."

"But you could never love me," he said. "Is that what you're saying? Because I am too old?"

I evaded the question. "I've been married three times already," I said.

"I know."

He must have run a background check. "And that doesn't scare you?"

"I am not easily scared," he said. "Besides, all it means is that you always married the wrong man."

"That's for sure."

Then we stopped talking. We didn't say anything more. We stood there, high up on that breezy mountaintop, with cars speeding past on Highway 6, and we quietly looked into one another's eyes.

What was I hoping to find in his gaze? Something that would attach me. Bind me to him. Something that would give me that crazy high of love, or the reckless desire that I'd always assumed was love.

Maybe it wasn't.

Maybe love was something quieter, softer, more peaceful.

More mature.

But how could I live without sexual passion? I seemed to need that fire. It never got me anywhere; all it did in the end was scorch my heart and singe my self-esteem, but as a directional signal, it was all I had to go on. Once I felt that heat slithering through my veins, I stopped caring about all the little shit that makes most of life so bothersome and boring, and I felt like there was something more, something that made it all grand and mysterious and worthwhile.

A look is as important as a kiss. I tried to fathom Marcello's. A man older than my dad, with a tanned face and silvery hair and the most intense eyes I'd ever encountered. What was he telling me with his look?

He was telling me that he was pretty serious. He definitely wanted me. He wanted to possess me.

And you know what? I wanted to be possessed. Yes, I, a former Wonder Woman trainee, wanted, I *longed*, for some powerful guy who had his shit together to take charge of my life. It was the Carolee in me. Like my mom, I wanted a happily married life with all the traditional trimmings. I wanted the same fantasy most women want: a life of hot sex, plenty of money, and peaceful security. In real life, these were mutually incompatible. Because most guys were dorks, geeks, louses, losers, bores, morons, and heartbreakers. *Clueless.* The only men I knew who had any real class or finesse were gay, usually friends of the dads. And though I was attracted to gay men, I was determined never to fall in love and marry one. I wouldn't make the mistake my mom had made.

So who did that leave?

Marcello, standing there, meeting my gaze.

I looked seriously at that hawklike nose and wondered if I could ever fall in love with him. If I could ever feel hot for him the way I had for Tremaynne. What would it take? More time. Having just lost Tremaynne, the man of my sexual dreams, I wasn't quite ready to open up to someone new.

And yet I was. I was so ready.

"I want to drive the rest of the way," I said.

Never, I repeat, *never,* try to walk on the beach in high heels. My spikes sank down into the sand and had to be pulled up and out with every step. It was like some weird new exercise for the calf muscles. Finally I had enough of trying to look "grown-up."

Marcello stood by, a smile on his face and his hands in his pockets, watching as I sat down on a piece of driftwood, slipped off my shoes, and peeled off my nylons. I could feel the soft damp salt wind all over my body, cooling my breasts and snuffling up my legs.

The second my bare feet hit the sand, a rush of memories flew through me. All those times on the beach with the dads. A long-forgotten sense of freedom, of energy, of sheer, silly joy.

I suddenly wondered what had happened to that old Wonder Woman cape. I'd dragged it around with me the way some kids drag around stuffed animals. The cape gave me special Amazon powers, allowing me to fly, be invisible, jump vast distances, snatch whatever I wanted with my golden lariat.

Marcello held out his hand, but I ran past him toward the surf. "Take off your shoes!" I called.

I ran from the warm, dry sand down to the cold, wet sand. Oh, man, the sudden thrill of the ocean. I'd forgotten. Its titanic breath flowed up sweet and powerful from the vast, churning eternity of waves. I closed my eyes and sucked in a deep breath. I was invisible again, with my Wonder Woman cape billowing out behind me. I walked out further, letting an incoming wave wash over my feet. It was a delicious shock. It made me laugh.

I turned back to see where Marcello was. He was still standing by the driftwood where I'd stashed my shoes. He waved, nodded, and pointed to his feet. No doubt it was hard for him to divest himself of those beautiful Bruno Magli loafers. I watched as he carefully removed them and his socks. He placed his shoes next to mine, then started toward me.

I had to laugh. He just didn't know how to walk without shoes. He lifted his toes and kept them lifted. When he reached the wet sand, he gingerly pulled up his trouser legs the way a woman would pull up a long skirt to keep the hem from getting wet.

OK, I was laughing pretty hard. That's why it happened. I doubled over, my back to the sea, and a big sneaker wave jumped me from behind. I felt the cold jolting force of it slap my backside and drench my pink satin cocktail dress.

I screamed, but I couldn't stop laughing. And while I was laughing, another huge wave crashed in and knocked me down to the sand.

I was shocked. And soaked. Even my hair. But I could not stop laughing. The sand was soft and the August water was cool but not freezing. There was no danger. I was in my swimsuit, digging in the sand with Daddy, helping him build a huge Bauhaus sandcastle. I didn't care about wet, or wind, or cold, or how I looked, because I was happy. And when you are happy, you know you are beautiful, no matter what you look like.

Marcello rushed to help me as yet another giant wave boomed its wet fist on the sand and sloshed me with water. Another one followed.

"Ah!" Marcello's pants were soaked, clinging to his legs.

"Oh my God!" I looked over my shoulder and saw the biggest

wave I'd ever seen at Cannon Beach. "Run!" I grabbed his hand and we flew up the beach, out of its reach, laughing with panic.

For that one instant, we were completely in synch. Something in me registered that.

We looked at one another.

I must have looked like a drowned rat. My dress felt slippery and cold, my skin all sticky with salt. I started to shiver.

"Let me warm you," Marcello said. He pulled me close, pressing me into the warmth of his chest. But he was shivering, too. His clothes were soaked, clinging to his body like a rubber scuba outfit.

"Maybe we should go to the car and turn on the heat," I suggested.

Marcello scanned the beach. "Wouldn't it be better to find a hotel room? Someplace where we could take off our wet clothes and dry off?"

I saw what he was getting at and tried to head him off from the idea of a quickie hotel room. "You need to be back pretty soon," I said. "And we haven't even had dinner yet." All this time I'd been dreaming about a bowl of Oregon clam chowder so thick that your spoon stood upright in it, followed by pan-fried Willapa Bay oysters. The kind of meals I'd always eaten out here with my dads.

"If we're going to eat," Marcello said, "we need some dry clothes."

Shopping in wet clothes is an interesting experience.

It was after seven on a Sunday night and most of the overpriced boutiques along Cannon Beach's cute main street were closed. But it was August, the height of tourist season, so a few stray places stayed open to catch the last dollars of impulse-buying vacationers.

None of the pricey clothing shops that sold long natural-fiber dresses and big-brimmed straw sun hats were open. In our wet clothes we paraded up and down the street, past shops selling expensive kites and handblown glass and handthrown pottery and homemade saltwater taffy, until finally we found a large grocery store with a rack of casual beachwear.

Marcello picked through the possibilities with a look of disappointed chagrin. "This store obviously does not carry Armani," he noted.

I was curious about what he'd buy. He was always impeccably dressed. Even his casual attire must have cost a fortune. The only other men I knew who dressed with such exacting care were the dads and some of their friends. The guys I went out with, the guys I'd married, didn't own or wear suits. Ever. Tremaynne had worn blue jeans and hiking boots when we got married.

We left the store wearing matching "Cannon Beach is for Lovers" sweatshirts. Corny, I pointed out, but comfortable. Marcello did look slightly ridiculous in his baggy hip-hop shorts, the kind that hang so low on the ass that your underwear shows and come down wide just below the knee. The shorts looked weird with his expensive black loafers, but his legs were tanned and in good shape.

Me? I must have looked real cute wearing safari shorts and pink high heels.

The restaurant was crowded and when we were told it would be at least an hour before we could get a table, Marcello became very agitated. "I do not have an hour," he muttered.

I stood back and watched him go into action.

First, with a friendly but intimidating snap of impatience, he found out from the girl doing the seating where the manager was. Then he made his way past the waiting throngs to a young man standing near the bar. Marcello gestured as he spoke to the man, miming some kind of story, and pulled out his wallet as he did so.

I'd paid attention to that wallet, the way I always did now that I was bankrupt, when he'd pulled it out in the grocery store to pay for our clothes. It was filled with fifty- and hundred-dollar bills and an assortment of brightly colored foreign currency that I couldn't identify. There were several credit cards, all platinum. That, of course, told me that he had the highest credit limit of anyone I'd ever met. There was probably $100,000 worth of credit lines on those cards. There were no photos in his wallet—no smiling deceased wife, no kids, no grandkids. Just lots of money and lots of credit.

As he was talking animatedly to the manager, he slipped a bill from his wallet. I saw the manager give it a quick, surreptitious look. Then Marcello casually pressed it into the guy's hand, all the while talking.

The manager pocketed the cash, lifted his hand, and summoned the girl doing the seating. He pointed toward an ocean-view table that was just being cleared. The girl, clasping her menus, nodded grimly. Marcello gestured for me, and I pushed my way through the crush at the bar.

"They have found a table for us after all," he said.

Haystack Rock was right outside the window. It humped up from the edge of the beach like a giant Christmas pudding, the kind Whitman made and served with rum sauce every Christmas Eve. Gulls wheeled around the top of it, small as flies. As a girl, a miniature Wonder Woman running and flying and pedaling on the beach, I'd peopled the rock with a mysterious assortment of fairies, gnomes, and monsters.

I just loved being at the ocean, even if it was only for a couple more hours. Behind all the noise and clatter of the busy restaurant I could hear the endless crashing lullaby of the surf. A fiery orange carpet of light shimmered across the waves as the sun dipped into the sea.

I scraped my bowl of clam chowder clean and sucked the last of it from my spoon. I was absolutely ravenous. "You aren't eating," I said, eyeing Marcello's chowder bowl.

He smiled and shook his head. "It is too thick," he said.

"OK, I'm going to be a pig and eat yours, too." I swapped bowls and started in on his.

"You have a good appetite," Marcello observed.

"Mm." I sprinkled a flotilla of oyster crackers across the chowder.

"I like to see that. So many girls nowadays are too thin."

"I'll never have that problem," I assured him.

He fidgeted, watching me. "Venus, do you have any feeling for me at all?"

I slowly and silently scraped up the last of his chowder.

"Or am I simply a ridiculous old man to you?"

"No," I said. "There's absolutely nothing ridiculous about you."

"Have you thought at all about—"

"Marrying you?" I sighed, quietly burped, and pushed the bowl away. I took his hand. "Look, I think you're wonderful."

"You do?" He squeezed my hand.

"Yes, I do. You're wonderful. But I don't feel any—"

"Attraction."

I nodded. Better to be honest. It had to end eventually. The chowder was divine, and pan-fried oysters were on their way, but soon I'd be back to burnt TV dinners and reruns of *Survivor*.

"Sometimes attraction comes later," he said hopefully.

I laughed and pulled my hand away. "You mean, *after* you've had sex."

He took my hands again, stroking them with his thumbs. He lowered his voice so only I could hear it. "I would be a very good lover with you."

"You're very attractive," I conceded. "You're the most attractive older guy I've ever met."

"When you were modeling for me," he said, bringing up our sordid past at the House of Peek-a-Boo, "I felt there was a spark—"

"I did that for money, OK? That was the only reason. I had a debt-ridden husband to support."

"But he is gone now," Marcello said. "And you still need money, no?"

"I have *never* fucked a guy for money," I said, bristling. I'd thought about it, and I'd had lots of offers, but I had never crossed the line into prostitution.

"I think I understand." Marcello took a sip of wine and kept his eyes on me. "You would make love to a guy who had no money and who turned out to be all wrong for you, but you would not make love to someone who had a lot of money and was all right for you."

"You said it yourself. It all starts with sexual attraction." I took a big swig of my ice water, wishing it were a pina colada.

"I will make you an offer you cannot refuse," Marcello said.

"Don't," I said. "It won't do any good."

"*Senti*. Listen. You said you could teach me to become a slouch. A slacker. Am I correct?"

I nodded.

"I will hire you, then. You will come to Roma and become my slouch instructor. I require a total-immersion class. I will pay you for your time, but you must spend it with me." He smiled, showing those even white teeth. "I will be your student."

My heart was beating faster. "I don't think you could ever become a slacker," I said.

He raised a finger. "A slacker instructor must never say such things to her students," he admonished. "You will undermine my determination. How can I ever become a slacker if I do not believe that I can do it?"

"You've got a point," I conceded.

"If you will teach me that," Marcello said, "I will teach you something in return."

"What?"

He took my hands, leaned forward, lowered his deep voice, and said, "How to fall in love with me."

Chapter

7

I sat on the plane trying to remember the last time I'd flown.
New York? Back when the dads were living there? Daddy saw me
every month. Sometimes he came to Portland; sometimes he flew
me out to stay with him and Whitman in New York. I'd done that
from about the time I was eight until I was sixteen.

Otherwise, I'd never flown anywhere. Carolee was a closet agora-
phobic and terrified of flying. She liked to stay at home, in her darkened rooms, on her big soft couch, close to her TV and VCR.

So planes were always charged with this incredible anxiety and
excitement for me. I had flown by myself, alone, cross-country, even
changing planes in Chicago (with the help of a flight attendant),
when I was eight years old. I don't know how I did it. I was scared to
death. All I had had to go on was my hope that the plane wouldn't
explode in flames and that Daddy would be waiting for me at the
gate when I arrived at La Guardia.

He always was.

By the time we'd flown to Italy as a threesome, Whitman, Daddy,
and I, I had my own passport. I used to show it to my uncompre-
hending friends, pointing out the red stamp issued at passport control in Milan. None of them knew where Italy was, or cared. I hardly
cared myself. Europe doesn't mean much to a thirteen-year-old
American girl.

All I'd taken away from that quickie trip to Capri was a little handmade porcelain box and the memory of an olive-skinned boy with dark soulful eyes and thick black eyebrows eating gelato. The box, which Daddy had bought for me in a little shop in Capri, was delicately woven, like mesh, and had tiny clusters of painted porcelain flower petals on top. I had absolutely no idea what I could use it for, but I loved it anyway. It was like a tiny shrine. I thought of it as my "Italy box from Daddy." And then it got lost in one of my endless moves with Carolee.

Or so I'd thought, until she'd produced it a couple of nights before. She'd come over to my apartment to help me clean and brought the box with her. "I found this in the back of a drawer," she said, handing it over. "It's yours, isn't it?"

I couldn't believe it. I looked again at my beautiful little treasure, now chipped on one side and with a porcelain flower cracked off. A gift from Daddy over twelve years ago. From Capri. From Italy. Where I was going now.

A sudden, comforting gust of warmth shot out of my heart and all through my body.

It was like a good omen.

I actually had my Italy box from Daddy with me on the plane, swaddled in bubble wrap in my purse. As I sat there, in my wide comfy window seat, I took it out and studied it.

I stared at it, trying to calm down.

Being on the plane, going where I was going, filled me with a kind of skin-crawling anxiety. Excited but also totally wigged-out scared. The way I'd been all those years ago when I flew out to New York to see my dad.

When the dads moved back to Portland, all flying stopped. I mean, they still flew, but I didn't. I didn't have anywhere to go.

None of my friends traveled. Travel costs money. So I pretty much stayed in Portland from then on.

But, weirdly enough, I'd gotten my passport renewed just before I married Tremaynne. Not because I was planning any foreign jaunts. Once you declare bankruptcy and all your plastic's taken away, all you're left with is your driver's license. So a passport is useful because it's got a picture ID.

"Would you care for a glass of champagne?" the smiling flight attendant asked. She was old enough to be my mother.

I smiled and nodded. I wasn't going to drink it. I just wanted to watch as she poured out a glass of champagne and handed it to me on a silver tray.

When they finally happen, things happen fast.

But it's like falling in love. You have to open yourself up and let it in, no matter what the consequences.

That's my theory anyway. Once you accept the challenge, whatever it is, you are essentially saying, "I'm willing to change. Change everything."

The gods or fates or whatever it is that controls life and destiny always listen to such things and help you figure out what to do.

It was a challenge that Marcello had given me.

✓ He challenged me to stop thinking about how miserable I was.

✓ He challenged me to stop thinking about how poor I was.

✓ He challenged me to fall in love with him.

I had nothing to lose in this contest. I didn't see how I could go wrong. The whole thing was like an adventure that someone else was paying me to have.

So I took him up on his challenge.

✓ I agreed to fly to Rome—or Roma, as he always called it— on a first-class ticket. That ticket was now in my purse. Portland–Los Angeles–Milan–Rome. It cost over four thousand buckos.

✓ I agreed to stay in his house in Rome. I would have my own "wing," he said, with someone named Teresina to cook and clean for me.

✓ I agreed to be his slacker instructor for a salary of five grand a month. Payable in cash. US dollars. He offered more, but I thought five thousand tax-free dollars a month to teach someone to do nothing was adequate. It was a big improve-

ment over the eight hundred I took home every month from
Phantastic Phantasy.

✓ I agreed that I would allow him to try to make me fall in
love with him. I was under absolutely no obligation to do so.
I did not have to sleep with him. But I had to agree to spend
my free time in his company, no one else's.

Oh my God, the scenes with the Parents.

When I made my announcement, the dads didn't know what to
do or say.

Whitman wanted to disapprove, of course, the way he's always
disapproved of my boyfriends and husbands. "Sweetheart," he said,
"I think it's fantastic. But do you know what you're getting into?"

"What do you mean?"

"Oh, sweetheart." He paced around their impeccable West Hills
home like a teacher lecturing me and Daddy as we sat on the hard
leather couch. "Marcello Brunelli, *Il Principe Brunelli* as he's called,
is from one of the oldest families in Rome."

"So?"

"Sweetheart, I don't want to scare you. Promise you won't be
scared?"

I looked at Daddy and rolled my eyes. Daddy understood. "Yes,
Whitman," I said, raising my hand, "I promise I won't be scared."

"Well, sweetheart, that world—that world of old Roman families—
of old *old* Italian nobility—well, sweetheart, it's just *riddled* with secret scandals and intrigue. No American can ever hope to penetrate
the mysteries of old Roman society. Especially not a young American
girl—"

"Woman," I reminded him.

"—woman who doesn't speak the language. Gore Vidal's the only
American who even came close to getting into that society, and that's
because he went there in the fifties and he speaks fluent Italian."

I shrugged. "Marcello says I can study Italian while he's at work.
He'll hire a tutor if I want."

"You want," Whitman nodded. "Having a private tutor is the *only*
way to learn a language."

That's how he was taught Latin, and Italian, and German, and French, and whatever other languages he speaks.

Now it was Daddy's turn. We were sitting side by side. Daddy had his arm around me. "Honey, we're just a little concerned that you might—get *lost* over there."

"What do you mean? Killed?"

"No, honey, that's not what I'm talking about," Daddy said.

"Venus," Whitman cut in, "there is a way of life that goes along with having a lot of money and a lot of power. For the most part, these people are very well educated."

"I may not have a Ph.D., Whitman, but I did go to junior college."

"It's not the same," Whitman said. "We are talking about the best schools in Europe. *Ecoles* and *scuolas* and *academies*. And there's a kind of intellectual sophistication that goes along with all that, with the education and the money and the power."

"And I'm not sophisticated enough, is that what you're saying?"

"Honey, listen to what Whitman has to say," Daddy said. "He's had experience with this sort of thing."

I wondered what Daddy meant by that.

"Thank you, John." Whitman cleared his throat and relaunched. "Venus, if you go on this trip, you'll be entering a world of people who can have anything they want. People who play with things— with other people—and then throw them away, like last year's toys."

"Is that what happened to you?" I asked sarcastically.

And was taken aback when he said, simply, "Yes."

He didn't say anything more about it, and I didn't press. But my imagination was running wild. The truth is, I really didn't know much about Whitman's life before he met Daddy. Hardly anything. Partially that's because he didn't really talk about it, and partially because I never asked him about it. He'd grown up rich and his family had disowned him, that's about all I knew. And that he'd been in the Peace Corps in Africa and spent a lot of time in Europe because at one time he was studying to be an opera singer.

Well, what this discussion with the dads all boiled down to, I finally figured out, was that they were worried that I'd feel left out, lost, and miserable in Rome. That I wouldn't understand the complexities of life in Marcello's family. That the social interactions I'd encounter in this weird old Roman world would be incomprehensible to me, and perhaps cruel.

"After all," Whitman said, "the Brunellis did intermarry with the Borgias. They were both papal families."

"Who're the Borgias?" I asked a little nervously.

"Cesare Borgia and his sister, Lucrezia. The ultimate Renaissance power brokers. Famed for their poisons."

"I don't think Marcello—"

"Mar-*chel*-lo," Whitman corrected. "We have to start immediately on your pronunciation. *Chel, chel*," he prompted.

"I don't think Mar-*chel*-lo would have me poisoned. There's no point."

"I didn't mean Marcello," Whitman said ominously, "I meant the people around him."

"Do you really want to go?" Daddy, ever reasonable, asked.

"Yeah. I think I do."

"Is it because you're trying to get away from Tremaynne?" he asked. "From thinking about him?"

"That might have something to do with it," I admitted.

"You don't love him, do you?" Whitman wanted to know.

I nodded, then began to cry. Daddy pulled me closer.

"You love him," Whitman said. "You've gone out on *one date* and you *love* him."

I looked up, confused. "I meant Tremaynne," I burbled.

"Oh." He sat down on the other side of me and gave my arm a clumsy stroke. "Sorry. Number Three was diarrhea, but I know you loved him."

"And Marcello," Daddy said. "He's in love with you, you know. If you go over to Rome, you're giving him hope."

"Of course he *is* grotesquely attractive," Whitman said. "I'd sleep with him in a minute."

"You would?" Daddy sounded surprised and faintly hurt.

"He reminds me of Rosanno Brazzi in *South Pacific*," Whitman said.

"I don't find him that attractive," I said.

"You mean because he's *our* age?" Daddy said.

I shrugged.

"For the life of me," Whitman said, "I was certain he was gay."

"He's *not* gay, Whitman. That's one thing I do know."

"Well, honey," Daddy stroked my hair and wiped away my tears. "You know we can't keep you from going."

"You know we'd *never* do anything like that," Whitman agreed. "We *refuse* to be overprotective parents."

He and Daddy exchanged glances. They were up to something.

"We don't want to keep you from going," Daddy said. "But we're concerned. We don't want you to get into something you can't handle. We don't want you to get hurt."

"That's why we're coming to Rome," Whitman said.

Carolee had been stunned when I gave her the news.

She looked at me through her supersize glasses. Her face froze, then fell. She gave her big red rat's nest of hair a futile fluff and let out a funny little sound. Then she broke down and started to sob.

"Mom, what's the matter?" I absolutely hated it when she cried. I couldn't bear to see her miserable. I clumsily tried to comfort her. "Why are you crying?"

"Because I'm so h-h-happy." She gazed tenderly into my eyes and reached out to stroke my hair. "My little girl is going to marry a prince."

"No." Better to get this straight immediately. "I never said I'd marry him."

"But he wants you to," Mom said. "He asked you to."

"And I said no."

Carolee's eyes filled up again. Her face was turning red. "Sweetheart, may I share my own personal feelings on this subject with you?"

I nodded.

"Promise you won't get angry with Mommy?"

"What is it?" I asked impatiently.

"I think you're making a huge mistake!" she blurted out.

"Why?"

"You should have agreed to marry him. Immediately!"

"Why? I'm not in love with him."

"Oh. Love." She sighed and reached for a Kleenex. She always kept a box handy while she watched Oprah and her Bette Davis movies. "Sweetheart, love is important, but it's tricky."

"It's not tricky," I said. "You either feel it or you don't."

She sighed. It was one of those sighs that was meant to convey her deep experience and my youthful naiveté. "It's not quite that simple, sweetheart."

"Yes, it is."

"No," she said, standing firm, "it's not."

"So you think I should have agreed to marry him even though I don't love him."

"Love can *develop*," Carolee said. "It doesn't have to hit you over the head like a sledgehammer."

Which was exactly how it had been with Tremaynne.

"I know you have issues with money," Mom went on.

"The only issue I have with money," I pointed out, "is that I don't have any."

Mom nodded. "Well, that's just it, sweetheart. You don't have any. You have even less than I do."

"Just because you fucked your eighty-year-old landlord to pay the rent doesn't mean I'd ever do anything like that."

"Venus!" Her face twitched as she tried to control her shock.

"Well, isn't that what you're saying? That I should marry him because he's rich. Not because I love him, but because he's rich."

"Sweetheart, he wants to take care of you!" Carolee cried. "Don't you understand how—how—how completely and totally frigging *rare* that is?"

Now it was my turn to sigh.

"Sweetheart, there are men who are like that. I know it's hard to believe, given the boys you've been involved with. But they do exist. Men who want to take care of a woman, protect her. *Cherish* her. And pay for everything."

"He's giving me a pretty good deal," I said. "I get to live for free, in Rome, with a maid, in a wing of his house, and get paid five grand a month."

"Yes, but that could all end tomorrow. He could get tired of you and throw you out—"

"I thought you just said he wanted to protect me."

"Well," she said, "he's rich, isn't he. One of the richest men in Europe. He's used to getting what he wants, sweetheart. If you won't marry him, and won't? . . . sleep? . . . with him?"

"We did not sleep together," I informed her.

She nodded. "If you won't marry him, and won't sleep with him, why should he keep you around?"

"I'm a challenge."

"Yes, sweetheart, you're a challenge. The astrologer told me that the day you were born."

My conversation with Mom had continued a couple of days later when she volunteered to come over and help me clean my filthy apartment. That was when she brought my little porcelain box, the box Daddy had bought for me in Capri all those years ago.

Carolee had been hovering very close ever since I told her I was going to Rome. There's something funny with mothers and daughters. Or at least with us. Every time there was something important going on in my life, we'd end up spending more time together than usual. She drove me crazy, but I still found some kind of comfort beneath the irritation.

I watched her as she set up housekeeping detail. When it came to cleaning, she always followed a certain procedure. Kerchief tied up and around her big red hair. Plastic gloves. Sometimes a face mask so she wouldn't breathe the toxic fumes of cleanliness. She had her favorite cleaning solutions, gleaned from her own mother and various daytime talk shows. Vinegar and hot water to clean windows, which were then wiped with crumpled newspaper. Mr. Clean industrial strength mixed with Palmolive dish detergent for bathroom floors. Under her ministrations, the water in the toilet bowl turned into a fizzing bright blue cocktail and the crusty shelves in the dinky fridge gleamed like new.

My job was always to hang up my clothes.

"I can't stop thinking about you going to Rome," Mom said, looking up from the kitchen floor. She was on her hands and knees. She plunged her sponge into a pail of hot soapy water. "You know, that's the one city I've always wanted to visit."

"Rome? Why?"

"I don't know. It might have been *The Agony and the Ecstasy*."

Which was this totally stark raving boring flick I'd watched with her as a kid. Charlton Heston played Michelangelo. Yeah, right.

"I've always wanted to see the Sistine Chapel," Carolee said, leaning forward and swiping her sponge into the crumb-filled corners of my kitchen floor. "It must be totally bee-you-ti-ful."

I didn't say anything. I'd heard of the Sistine Chapel, but I had no idea what it was. Whitman had given me a travel guide to Rome that he'd written years earlier, but I'd hardly opened it. There was too much history to cope with.

"And the Colosseum," Carolee said. "Wouldn't you love to see where they fed all those Christians to the lions?"

"Who fed them to the lions?"

"The ancient Romans did. Back when they had emperors."

"They fed people to lions?"

"Yes, sweetheart. They tied them to stakes in the middle of the Colosseum so they couldn't run, and then they set hungry lions on them."

"How do you know that?"

"I saw it in a movie," she said. "And the Forum. Gosh, I'd love to see the Forum."

"What's that, a store?"

"No, it's more like where all the ancient temples stood. When Phyllis took me into my past-life regression, she said I talked about living in the Forum. I guess I was one of the Vestal Virgins."

"You?" She was totally serious, but I had to laugh.

"The Vestal Virgins were very powerful women," Mom said, wringing out her pink sponge.

"What did they do?"

"Well, I'm not exactly sure," she admitted. "I guess they just stayed virgins. There was some kind of merit in that. Like nuns. They had their own temple. And if they ever got caught having sex, they were walled up alive."

"What?"

Carolee nodded solemnly. "Right in the temple. Walled up alive." She shuddered. "That's what happened to me. All I could remember was that it was completely dark and I was really hungry."

I watched her scrubbing, dressed in her cleaning drag: tight blue jeans that she should never have worn and an old pink sweatshirt. Her breath came in loud gasps, as if she could never get enough air into her lungs. As she heaved herself forward and swabbed the sponge back and forth, I thought, *I never want to do that.*

"There's just so much to see in Rome," Carolee panted. "I suppose that's why I've always wanted to go there."

"Daddy's been. He and Whitman are coming over."

"Oh?" She stopped in the middle of an extended stroke.

"Whitman got some kind of assignment."

"Oh. Well. Isn't that nice. They'll get to be there with you."

"The dads know Rome like the backs of their hands."

"Well," Carolee said, halfheartedly continuing her cleaning stroke, "that *is* where your father met Gabriella, after all."

"Who?"

"His first wife."

"Oh, her. The bitch who ran off after she became a US citizen?"

"The bitch before me," Mom said grimly. She rose up on her knees, pushing her big glasses up on her nose with the sides of her hands. "Well, sweetheart, I'd come to Rome, too, if I could. But I just don't have the money or the connections that the dads have. So I guess I'll just stay here—by myself—walled up alive."

"Mom, even if I gave you the airfare, you wouldn't come."

"Why wouldn't I?"

"Because you're afraid to fly."

She considered this for a moment. "That's true." She looked me in the eye. "But if you offered me a ticket to Rome, I would conquer my fear of flying. I would get on a plane, and come over."

"Careful what you wish for," I said.

"Why?"

"Because I'm giving you that ticket."

As soon as I got my first pay from Marcello, that is.

It would probably be a huge mistake, but I realized how much my mom had done for me, always giving me whatever she had, and how little I'd ever done for her.

If she wanted to conquer her fear of flying and come to Rome, a city she claimed she'd wanted to see all her life, and I could help her realize that one dream, why not?

I figured she could stay with me in Marcello's house. If that turned out to be too hair-raising, she could move into a hotel.

It wasn't like I was going to meet my new in-laws, or anything. But that was sort of how it felt. Whether I admitted it to myself or not, the thought of meeting Marcello's family scared me. I didn't know much about them because I hadn't quizzed Marcello beforehand. I didn't want to pry, and since I wasn't really interested in him anyway, it didn't matter how many kids he had or how old they were or what they thought of me.

But of course it did.

So there were two kids, at least. A son and a daughter. And there was "Mama." Marcello's mother, who lived on Capri. Marcello seemed to hold the old lady in a kind of respectful awe.

There would be other new people I'd have to meet, too. Teresina, who would be my maid. Giovanni, the driver, Marcello's valet, the guy who'd gotten food poisoning in Osaka and waved at me from the window of the airport hotel. And Giovanna, who was evidently the head of security for Lumina International and someone Marcello listened to.

It was weirdly reassuring to know that my own American family would be there, too. Familiar faces in the strange new Roman world I was entering.

I sat back in my big, comfy first-class seat and tried to quiet my racing heart as the plane taxied out to the runway.

The engines suddenly revved and the plane moved forward, down a runway at LA International, bound for Italy. It picked up speed. The vibrational drone grew louder.

Liftoff was always the scariest moment for me. For some reason, in my imagination, that was always the moment when the quickly accelerating plane would explode in flames and plummet back to earth as a deadly fireball.

Those images from 9/11, burned into my memory from all the TV coverage, didn't help my anxiety.

If flying was this bad for me, a veteran, I wondered what kind of anxiety Carolee would have to go through.

The plane moved smoothly and quickly down the tarmac. That gravitational push, I felt it right in my tummy.

My tummy.

If my period didn't come in three days, I would miss it entirely.

That had happened before, now and then, when I'd been really stressed out. So it could happen again because of the post-traumatic stress syndrome resulting from my honeymoon with Tremaynne.

Or it could mean the other possibility. The one I did not want to think about. The one I was chronically avoiding.

You've got another month before you have to start worrying, I told myself.

Faster and faster, the plane sped down the runway at LAX. I looked down at the little porcelain box Daddy had given me when I was thirteen. I tried to think of Marcello. Of his handsome tanned face. Of his romantic style of kissing.

But I couldn't. All I could think of was Tremaynne.

Liftoff.

Chapter

8

Time.
Now there's a weird concept.

When I finally got off the plane in Milan, it was something like 2:30 in the afternoon, their time. I had no idea what time it was for me. I hadn't been able to sleep on the plane, even though my seat in first class actually became a *bed*, with my own little canopy for privacy. So I was exhausted, but also wired, because that's how you are when you're in a strange, new place on your own.

First I had to go through passport control. There was a special line for first-class customers. A cute Italian guy looked me in the eye, said "Welcome to Italy, signorina," and stamped my passport.

On my way to the luggage carousels, I saw soldiers with machine guns.

After claiming my luggage, I was supposed to go through customs and then recheck my luggage onto the Rome flight. But as my new red-leather roller-wheel suitcase (a gift from the dads) was coming down the belt, a thin, balding man wearing a dark blue suit and narrow wraparound sunglasses stepped out from behind me and grabbed it.

Before I could object, he said, "Signorina Venus Gilroy?"

I nodded. Yes, I guess I was *Vay*-noose *Geel*-roy. My heart started pounding. Had I done something wrong? Was he going to arrest me?

Something to do with Tremaynne, maybe, or forging his signature on the divorce document.

"Please come," the man said.

Then I sort of remembered seeing this guy in the plane, sitting in first class. I'd passed him about twenty times on my way to the bathroom.

"Who are you?" I asked.

"A friend of Prince Brunelli," he said.

I followed him to the customs line. With a nod of his head, he steered me through the right door. All the while, he was carrying my heavy bag instead of rolling it behind.

"They must to see your ticket," he said when we arrived at the baggage recheck.

After my bag was checked through to Rome, the man nodded toward another corridor. "I take to your gate," he said.

"OK. Thanks."

He stayed not quite at my side, more like a couple of steps ahead and to my left. He didn't speak to me, just nodded or indicated with his cell phone when we were to turn a corner or enter another corridor.

Everyone in Milan Airport seemed to be wearing dark glasses and talking into a cell phone. My companion began talking into his. A gush of rapid-fire Italian. Then I began to hear the airport announcements, prefaced by the word "attenzione." Very different sounding voices from those in America.

Who was this guy, and who was he talking to? He knew who I was. Had Marcello asked him to keep an eye on me?

My guide ended his phone conversation. "Your gate," he said. "They hold the plane for you."

He escorted me up to the ticket podium, where a uniformed attendant took my boarding pass, flicked it through a machine and handed me the stub. "Grazie, Signorina Gilroy," she said. "Now, please hurry."

I turned to thank my escort, but he was gone.

Hot.

Molto hot.

I felt the heat the moment I stepped off the plane and into the jetway at Fiumicino Airport.

I was in Rome. *Roma*, as Marcello always called it.

Bleary-eyed, I made my way down the jetway. Marcello was supposed to be waiting for me at the gate. I'd tried to freshen up on the plane but felt all puffy and like my hair wasn't doing what it was supposed to do. I figured I'd be a huge disappointment to Marcello, but I didn't care. Why should I? Just because I'd flown four thousand miles to see the guy didn't mean I was interested in him. I didn't have to "attract" him. If he didn't like what he saw, too bad.

I scanned the area around the gate. Saw a squat, sweating, middle-aged guy holding up a sign with VENUS GILROY printed on it. He smiled nervously when I approached him.

"Signorina Gilroy?"

"Yeah, that's me. But where's Marcello?"

"Ah—oh—ah—Signor Brunelli—he—ah—he no can come."

"Are you Giovanni?" I asked.

"Eh—eh—no Giovanni," he stammered.

"You're not Giovanni?"

"*Io?*" He pointed to his chest, raised his shoulders, and shook his head. "No Giovanni."

I looked at his sign. Definitely my name. "No Giovanni?"

"No, signorina. *Giovanni é malato.*"

"I'm sorry, I don't—"

He mimed an elaborate story that had something to do with stomach pains and retching. Evidently Giovanni was sick (again, or still?).

"Who are you?" I asked.

"*Io sono Fabio,*" he said. "I have car. I drive. You come." He bowed and gestured. "*Prego*, signorina."

So, trusting yet another complete stranger, I went down to claim my luggage. Fabio snatched it from the conveyer belt, hoisted it to his shoulder, and indicated for me to follow.

A blast of the hottest, muggiest air I'd ever felt hit me the moment we stepped outside. Worse than New York in August, if that's possible. There was a din of cars, cabs, buses, all honking and spewing gas fumes.

"You can wheel that!" I shouted at Fabio.

"Eh?"

"My suitcase! It has wheels. You know, *wheels*." I made circular motions. "You don't have to carry it on your shoulder. It weighs a ton."

My new suitcase was loaded down with a whole new wardrobe, half Versace coordinates from the dads, half Victoria's Secret lingerie from Carolee.

Fabio didn't understand. I tapped him on the shoulder and indicated he should put the suitcase down. When he did, I pulled up the handle. "See? You can pull it along. You don't have to carry it."

"Si, signorina." Fabio hoisted it back up on his shoulder.

The car was parked just a few yards away in some kind of privileged zone. It gleamed. A black limo. Fabio opened the back door and I slid into a world of soft white leather. There was a glass vase with three red roses on a wooden table. I spied a small gift-wrapped box on the seat.

Fabio stashed my bag and slid into the driver's seat. "*Aspett'*." He lifted a finger as if to say, "wait a moment" and called up a number on his cell phone. Said something, then handed the phone to me.

"Venus?"

I was relieved to hear Marcello's voice but felt stupidly shy. "Well, I'm here."

"Darling, I can't tell you how sorry I am."

"For what?"

"I was going to be there. To meet you. To welcome you to Roma."

"Where are you?"

"Ah." He sighed. "I am in Torino."

"Is that in Italy?"

He laughed. "Yes, darling, but still too far from you. An emergency at the plant here. They may strike. I had no choice. I had to come."

"OK," I said.

"You are disappointed."

"Sort of."

"Ah. I will make it up to you. Is there a box on the seat?"

I picked it up. "Yeah."

"Open it, darling."

A platinum watch. Glinting with what I assumed to be diamonds and emeralds. I sucked in my breath. "I can't accept this."

"Do you like it?"

"Oh, jeez. It's totally gorgeous. But I can't—"

"Please, do not argue. When a gift is offered, it is rude not to accept it."

"You convinced me," I said. "Thank you."

"You are with Fabio?" Marcello asked.

I couldn't take my eyes off the glittering watch. "Yes."

"He will bring you into Roma. He will get you settled."

"Is Giovanni sick?" I asked.

"Giovanni is—" He was distracted by some kind of commotion in the background. It sounded like people shouting. "Venus, darling, I must go. This important meeting is about to begin."

"The first rule of slackerdom," I said, "is that you skip *all* important meetings."

"Oh, yes, darling. Keep reminding me of that. I want so much to be a slacker with you."

"That's what I'm here to teach you," I reminded him.

His voice dropped to a husky secretive whisper. "I long to see you."

"When will you be back in Rome?"

"Hopefully, tonight. Otherwise, tomorrow afternoon. Teresina will take care of all your needs. Just tell her what you want. Ciao, *carissima*. I send you a thousand kisses."

I handed the phone back to Fabio. "OK," I said. "I guess I'm ready to enter Rome."

It was the ugliest city I had ever seen.

At least the route in from the airport.

My heart sank. This was *Rome*? The city that made Daddy and Whitman cream in their pants every time they talked about it?

"The most *beautiful*, the most *historic*, the most *dramatic* of all European cities," as Whitman the travel writer had said of it.

The traffic was awful. We crawled through what looked like a giant suburb where the buildings all looked like boxes with green shutters. Now and then I'd spot a palm tree.

Then we entered what appeared to be an industrial area with warehouses and giant office parks built in weird shapes. The sun glared down, hot and furious, through a grayish smear of smog.

I looked at my new watch. It sat so lightly on my wrist. Like a jeweled feather. A pleasant distraction from the ugliness of Rome.

I thought of that movie I'd watched once with Carolee. *Cleopatra*, with Elizabeth Taylor. That scene where she enters Rome on a giant sphinx.

Fabio caught my eye in the rearview mirror. "*Ecco*, signorina. *Il Tevere*." He smiled and pointed out the window.

"Il what?"

"Tevere. *Ti*-burr."

"The Tiber River?"

"Si." He mimicked my English. "The Ti-burr *Ree*-ver."

The Tiber River. *So fucking what?* Everything around it was so nondescript, so ordinary. Except for the fact that all the buildings had shutters, lots of them pulled down like half-closed eyelids, and were painted a color like terra-cotta, and had a few dusty-looking palm trees sweeping the dirty gray sky above them, I could have been anywhere. I couldn't believe my eyes. I didn't want to believe my eyes.

"Roma." Daddy would get all rapturous when he talked about it. "The Eternal City."

Get me out of here, I thought. This was a major fantasy turned into curdled milk. I'd come, in part, because I'd been drawn to the mystique of Rome, perpetrated endlessly by the dads. I'd imagined . . . well, I don't know what I'd imagined. Old buildings and giant temples and picturesque ruins and gushing fountains. Some kind of romantic flair. Something like in *Cleopatra*. Not this dump.

Boy, was Carolee ever going to be disappointed.

"Where's the Colosseum?" I asked Fabio.

"Eh?"

"The Colosseum. Where they fed the Christians to the lions."

"Ah, il Colosseo."

"Whatever. Can we go there?"

"Si. But—ah—eh—no can drive to Colosseo. *Strada*—road—no more. *Finito*." He made a gesture of cutting something off.

"Bummer."

He nodded. "Si, signorina. Bum-mer."

We crawled on. We weren't traveling beside the Tiber anymore but on a busy street called Via Ostiense. The cars were so incredibly little. Makes and models I'd never seen before. Tons of Fiats. Lots of cute boys and girls on motorbikes. I saw one guy talking on a cell phone and smoking as he maneuvered his Vespa through the traffic.

It was less suburban now. I could feel that we were moving into a denser part of Rome. But still, like, *big deal*.

Then we entered a busy intersection and something weird caught my eye. "What's that?" I cried, pressing my nose to the window.

"Signorina?"

"That!" I pointed. "That pyramid!"

"Ah, si." Fabio laughed and scratched his head. *"Il piramide di Caio Cestio."*

"Is it real? I mean, like, old?" It was a small pyramid, but a pyramid all the same. Mom had this whole theory about pyramids, about how they attracted a certain kind of energy based on their geometry. She was convinced that UFOs used them for energy refuelings. "When was it built?"

"Eh? *Scusi*, signorina, *ma*—eh—*non capisco*—eh—no speak English good."

"And I don't speak Italian." I shrugged and smiled at him. "OK. I guess we're even."

"OK," he repeated. Then added, a minute later, "Signor Giovanni speak English good. Signor Giovanni tell you story piramide."

"OK," I said.

"OK," he repeated.

We smiled at each other in the rearview mirror.

From the pyramid we sped up a street called Via dei Marmorata and then turned right.

Suddenly we were racing alongside the Tiber again. My jaw dropped as we passed a small, circular temple. You could tell just by looking at it that it was *really* old. I began to see church steeples, and old windy streets, and big old palaces, or what I assumed were those "palazzi" the dads talked about.

"Every piazza has a palazzo," Whitman had informed me in tongue-twisting terms during the dads' crash course on Rome. "*Palazzo* means palace. *Piazza* means square. *Via* means street."

We passed mounds of sand, piles of bricks. They were repairing the road or something, although I didn't see a single workman. Cars were being rerouted. Traffic slowed, then crawled, then stopped entirely. "Ah!" Fabio threw up a hand and muttered something that sounded frustrated and dirty. With a look of grim determination, he turned the limo onto a side street.

And then, suddenly, we were in Rome. Really in Rome. The Rome the dads gushed about. Marcello's Roma. I could tell instantly. I could feel it.

I didn't know what route Fabio was following, and it didn't matter. I was fascinated. We crept down streets so narrow I thought the side mirrors would get scraped off the limo. I pressed my window button and leaned out into the stifling heat. We moved so slowly that I could hear a hum of human noise, voices, laughter, footsteps, echoing through the maze of cobblestone streets.

No trees here, no sidewalks. A scrawny cat eyed me from a doorway strewn with pale worms of spaghetti. Shutters were down, or half-down, lending an air of private mystery to the buildings. People lived in these ancient buildings, entering through doors right on the street.

People walking on the streets squeezed over to the side as we passed. I heard more English than Italian. American tourists.

"Wow," one of them said, "who do you think that chick is?"

Meaning me.

"Hey!" Another one, a doofus about twenty, stuck his head in the window. "How about a ride, babe? It's hot out here. We could use some AC."

He yanked his head out just in time. From the front seat, Fabio had pressed a button to close the window. "Scusi, signorina," he apologized. "No safe."

I tried not to feel guilty sitting in a big, luxurious, air-conditioned car. Flashed on what Tremaynne would have said about it: "Gas-guzzling monster for spoiled, rich capitalists. So they can show everyone else how important they are."

Tremaynne, back in the wilds of Idaho, while here I was, in a gas-guzzling limo, being chauffeured through the streets of Rome wearing a watch encrusted with diamonds and emeralds.

"*Ecco*, signorina." As we entered a giant square, Fabio gestured toward a humongous palace sitting at one end of it. "Palazzo Farnese."

I gave the square a quick scan. On either side stood what looked like huge stone bathtubs that had been made into fountains.

At the corner of Palazzo Farnese, Fabio turned left onto a nondescript street. Stopped in front of a giant steel gate and pressed some numbers on his cell phone.

This is it, I thought, heart racing with fear and excitement. *This is where I'm going to be living in Rome.*

The gate slowly swung open and Fabio guided the car through a dark tunnel into a courtyard.

"*Ecco*, signorina. Palazzo Brunelli."

I heard the echo of the gate as it slammed behind us.

The moment I got out of the car, I was aware of unseen eyes.

A shiver ran down my spine.

Someone was watching me.

Maybe more than one.

Where were they?

I kept my cool and tried to look as if I were giving the shadowy courtyard of Palazzo Brunelli a quick, casual once-over.

I was almost certain that I saw someone quickly move away from an unshuttered window in a dark corner of the third floor.

"Signorina?" Fabio, my suitcase hoisted up on his beefy shoulder, was waiting for me at the bottom of an old stone staircase.

"*Prego.*" He indicated that I was to precede him. *So polite*, I thought, until I turned around and saw his eyes glued to my rear end.

* * *

The front door was up on the third floor.

We didn't have to ring or knock. The door just opened.

"Signorina." A short, buxom woman, about my age, with jet black hair and a dark mustache above her red lips, stood back and indicated that I was to enter the shadowy confines of Palazzo Brunelli.

"Hi," I said, politely holding out my hand. "I'm Venus."

The woman looked down at my hand, clearly flustered and uncertain what to do. She glanced nervously at Fabio.

"Are you Teresina?" I asked.

"Si, signorina." She paused, searching my eyes. "You know my name?"

"Marcello told me."

"Marcello?" She looked questioningly at Fabio, who muttered, "Il Principe" as he put down my suitcase.

"Ah. Il Principe!" Teresina suddenly sounded almost excited. "Si, si. Allora. Prego, signorina." With a grunt, she hoisted up my heavy suitcase and began staggering down a corridor.

"Teresina, wait. *Momento*." My first word of Italian! I had her put the suitcase down, then turned it over and pulled out the handle. "This sucker's way too heavy to carry. It's got wheels. See?" I demonstrated.

"Ah, no, signorina!" Teresina wrested the suitcase away from me. "I carry for you."

"Then use the wheels!"

"No." She shook her head, almost frightened. "*Non posso.*" She bent down and swept her fingers across the marble floor. "*Antica.* Very old."

I refused to let her lift the suitcase by herself. Finally, after much pleading, she allowed me to help her carry it.

We slipped and shuffled down a long dark corridor, along marble floors that were highly waxed and slippery as ice. The corridor was lined with shuttered windows on one side and old portraits on the other. I noticed several dudes wearing weird red hats and crimson robes with fur collars. There was a lady in black velvet with huge, lustrous eyes and a crucifix clutched in her hand.

"Allora," panted Teresina. (I've since come to understand that there are three all-purpose Italian words that mean everything and nothing: *allora*, *dunque*, and *boo*.) We stopped in front of a large wooden door. Teresina pulled a little hanky from her apron pocket and patted her forehead while fishing out an enormous key. "In here," she said. "For you."

The door seemed to weigh a ton. Teresina pushed it open, slid my suitcase across the threshold, and beckoned for me to enter. When I did, she relocked the door behind us. "Allora," she panted. "Dunque." She flipped a light switch.

We stood in a small antechamber, like an air lock on Starship Enterprise, in front of another huge wooden door. This one had no visible lock or handle. Mounted on the door was an electronic keypad.

"Signorina?" Teresina dug a piece of paper from her apron pocket and handed it to me. "Pass-ward," she said, pointing to the keypad. "You—" She made a tapping motion with her finger.

"It's like Fort Knox in here," I laughed, pressing in the password, but Teresina didn't get the joke.

When I'd entered the last numeral, I heard a tiny, precise click. Teresina motioned for me to push.

My heart was racing as I pushed open the heavy wooden door.

I stepped into a vast room. The largest room I'd ever been in.

"*Il salone*," Teresina said, introducing me to the enormous chamber. The "salon." What Americans would call a living room, if Americans had anything to compare with it.

The floors were polished black-and-white marble tiles set in a repeating geometric pattern. We faced a wall of twelve-foot windows hung with gauzy white draperies. The shutters—the push-out kind, not the pull-down kind—were open just wide enough to let in white vertical bars of light. The windows were firmly closed, but the draperies fluttered softly in a steady current of air.

"Air condition," Teresina said. "*Troppo freddo*? Too cold?"

"Feels great," I said. "Nice and cool."

"Si, signorina. Allora." Her eyes bulged and her neck tightened as she heaved up my suitcase and skittered across the treacherous floor to a wing off the salone. In passing, I looked up at the painted ceiling. I don't know what-all was going on up there, but it sure was busy. There were men on horses and in chariots and angels flying around. They all seemed to be looking down at me.

Finally we were in my bedroom.

How could anyone sleep with so much space around them? It was twenty times the size of my entire apartment in Portland.

Weirdly, there were two beds. An ancient-looking thing with carved posts and a dark green canopy hung with tassels and thick velvet curtains was centered on the inner wall of the room, between two wooden doors. What looked like a modern hospital bed, with side bars and wheels, was parked in an alcove, near a small window. It was fitted with tight white sheets but no other coverings. A large crucifix hung above it.

What was it with all these crucifixes everywhere?

I found them intriguing but very puzzling because I hadn't been raised with any kind of religion. I knew only the rudiments of Christianity. Jesus had died on a cross. He'd been nailed to it. Beyond that, I was in limbo. I didn't get it. If he was God, why had he been hung on a cross?

This Portland garage band, Invincible Vampires, always decorated the stage with crucifixes. Vampires supposedly couldn't bear the sight of a crucifix. I guess because the crucifix is a symbol of God, and vampires are damned.

"You wish?" Teresina strained to get my suitcase on a low table, then made motions of opening and unpacking it.

"I can do that," I said. My mom is the only person I've ever felt comfortable with as a maid.

"No, signorina. *Io.* I do all."

"OK." I shrugged, suddenly exhausted, and gingerly sat down on the huge canopied bed. It was about the size of my entire studio apartment. When I sighed and lifted a foot to take off one of my new but painful high heels, Teresina bolted over, grabbed my leg, and quickly removed first one shoe, then the other.

Shoes in hand, she pulled open one of the giant doors next to the bed and disappeared.

Curious, I got up to look. The tile floor was deliciously cool on my hot, throbbing feet. I sort of tiptoed over and peered inside.

A walk-in closet. When I say "closet," I don't mean one of those dinky cramped spaces in most houses and apartments. This was the size of an American bedroom. There were shelves, drawers, cubicles, racks, hooks, softly downlit alcoves with three-paneled mirrors fore and aft.

I saw a glass-fronted inner closet laden with what appeared to be evening gowns. Each one hung from a padded hanger. It looked like each one was wrapped in tissue paper.

Who did they belong to?

It's kind of creepy entering the closet of an unknown woman and claiming space that once belonged to her. Whoever she was.

Teresina set my high heels down on a shelf, then pulled a cloth from a drawer and gave them a vigorous wipe. "Ecco."

"Ecco," I repeated, smiling, trying for some reason to win her over.

"*Scarpe*," she said, pointing to the shoes.

"Shoes."

"Si. Shooes. *Molto caro*, eh?" She rubbed her fingers together in the universal sign for money.

"Yes. Si. My mom bought them for me. She said I needed impractical clothes."

Teresina smiled and stared at me. I couldn't tell if she understood what I was saying or not. I pointed to the evening gowns. "Beautiful."

She looked, then nodded reverently. "Si."

"Who did they belong to?"

"Signorina?"

"Who wore them?"

"*Non capisco*." Which meant, "I don't understand." She pulled together two hidden sliding doors in front of the glass-fronted closet. The dresses disappeared from view.

"OK. How about a bathroom? Where's that?"

She seemed to understand that question perfectly, for she opened a door at the end of the walk-in closet. "Ecco, signorina."

It was very old-fashioned. Huge, of course. A claw-foot tub. A separate shower. A long, low dressing table with a mirror surrounded by lights and a golden stool with a white satin cushion. The floors and walls were white marble grained with gray and slivers of deep crimson.

A scent lingered in the room, faint, mysterious, subtly exotic. *Her* scent. Her signature smell, created from bath oils and face powders and body lotions and obscenely expensive perfumes.

"I'd love to soak in a hot bath," I said. "I've been on planes for about twenty hours."

I made the mistake of turning on one of the spigots. Teresina gasped as if she'd been slapped and darted over. "No, signorina. I do."

Jet lag was starting to kick in. I was too tired to argue.

Well, what it was, was an entire self-contained house within a house. It was a little palace, a *palazetto*, within Palazzo Brunelli.

It was entirely for me, for my use. And Teresina was to be my maid.

It was like one of those fairy tales Carolee used to read to me when I was a bratty kid wishing my dad still lived with us. There was always some girl, usually a princess, who had to go through all these various travails before she could find her prince. The road to getting a prince was not easy. There were always people out to get her, to ruin her quest for blissful love. Evil sisters, witchy grandmothers, poisons, prisons.

I'd had no such problems getting my prince. Marcello had just shown up in my life. How could I ever have known that the guy beating off into a hanky while I sat around "posing" in transparent lingerie at the House of Peek-a-Boo owned all this? To me, when I first "met" him, when he arranged for a "private modeling session," he was just a horny older guy with a million-dollar wardrobe that was *entirely* unlike Portland, a city that had "deified casual," according to Whitman. Blue jeans, sweatshirts, caps, and running shoes, that's

Portland. And there was Marcello, in House of Peek-a-Boo, wearing ten-thousand-dollar Armani suits and shirts with starched collars and cuffs.

He was the best-dressed horny man I'd ever met.

I could never have known that he harbored such genuine, ongoing *passion* for me. So much that he'd actually proposed marriage.

It just didn't seem possible that this sort of thing could happen to a girl like me.

And I could not, for the life of me, get a handle on the thoughts and emotions that were flying through my head as Teresina took me on a tour of my little palazetto.

Her heels clicked and echoed through the vast rooms. I was barefoot. I loved the way the cool tiles felt on my feet.

"The dining hall," Teresina said, leading me into an enormous hall with a massive beamed ceiling. A faded tapestry covered one wall. There were paintings. A massive table with twenty chairs and three crystal chandeliers above it.

I just couldn't picture myself dining there. Especially alone. The room had a heavy, gloomy feel to it.

Then there was the salone, which I'd already seen. Again, huge pieces of furniture, arranged like giant chess pieces on the black-and-white floor. It was hard to imagine anyone having a conversation in there. You'd have to sit side by side, or shout.

The painted ceiling disturbed me. I felt like there was all this silent, incomprehensible activity going on above me. It was hard to ignore.

Teresina wore a black dress, sort of stylish, maybe a little too tight in the rump. Her butt was a "plus," as Carolee would have said, and so was her chest. A spotless white apron was tied around her ample waist. The mustache and her red bow of a mouth gave her an oddly mischievous look. Teresina was a girl who just wanted to bust loose. I could tell. But she was paid to be a professional maid, paid to give up her own personality and assume the needs of another. So she tried to assume a dignified manner at all times.

Her heels clicked as we went from room to room, down the corridor that led to my giant bedroom. There was another, smaller bedroom, another, smaller bathroom, a gloomy library, and an old-fashioned-looking kitchen with a big table in the middle.

I pointed to a door. "What's in there?"

Teresina colored. "Eh—eh—"

I opened the door. Saw a bed covered with stuffed animals. A crucifix on the wall. An old poster of Prince, before he became the Artist Formerly Known As. And another poster, of a mean-looking girl in a leather cap and bikini, pointing a machine gun.

Teresina, flustered, shuffled over with her head lowered, as if she'd done something wrong in school and was about to get a whipping. "Signorina," she whispered. "*My* room."

I immediately closed the door. "I'm sorry."

"*Ha fame*, signorina?" Teresina asked. "Do you hunger?"

I did, actually.

"I cook for you. You like spaghetti?"

I nodded. "Sure."

"You rest, signorina. I make."

It was still afternoon, but my eyes were so heavy I could barely keep them open.

I looked at my new watch. Lifted it up and rocked it back and forth so the jewels would catch and sparkle in the light. Time had never been so beautiful. My wrist, adorned with flashing gems, became an entirely new body part. I could tell from the shape of the dial and the style of the numbers that the watch was an antique. It was so old that it had to be wound.

Was I supposed to be grateful to Marcello? Overwhelmed? Was that what he wanted? I could see how a girl looking for the good life would fall for all these trappings of luxury.

But I wasn't going to.

I mean, all this *stuff* was not going to make me fall in love with Marcello.

You can fake that feeling from the outside, but not from the inside.

Teresina had turned down the bed for me. I ran my fingers across the pillowcases and exposed sheets. Fine, cool, starched cotton.

I shucked off my clothes. Figured, with a crucifix in the room, that I'd better keep on my bra and panties.

But I was restless. The restlessness you feel in a place you've never been to before, no matter how tired you are. I strolled over to one of the windows. Ever since I'd entered Palazzo Brunelli, I'd had no sense of its placement within Rome, with the streets outside. Despite the size of the rooms, I was starting to feel a little claustrophobic.

All the windows were shuttered in precisely the same way. I've since learned that you cannot mess with Italians and their shutters. The women are in charge of all shutters, both the roll-up kind and the push-out kind. The shutters themselves can be adjusted in several ways. The giant shutters outside the windows of Palazzo Brunelli, for instance, could be opened up to admit a bar of light, and locked in that position.

Peering through the open part, I could sort of see what looked like the wing on the opposite side of a courtyard. I figured out the mechanism for opening the window, heaved it up, undid the lock, then flung out the shutters.

Suddenly I was looking out into the courtyard. I heard a twitter of birdsong.

And immediately, again, I had the sense that someone was watching me. It was so strong, so sudden, that I ducked away from the window, and then was afraid to lean out again to pull in the shutters.

But when I quickly tried to analyze the sensation of being watched, I couldn't say if it came from outside the room, across the courtyard, or from inside.

I slipped into my new pink satin robe. Tried to look brave as I padded around in my bare feet, nervously checking the rooms without Teresina at my side.

The windows in the salone were similarly shuttered. One set of windows was actually a set of doors that opened out onto a stone balcony. Peeking through, I could see a street below, a wall on the other side, a line of trees beyond the wall, then another, busier street, and, past the street, an open expanse with buildings on the far side. This side of my palazzetto looked out on the Tiber.

"Signorina!"

It was Teresina. Her voice was unusually sharp. She waved her hand back and forth, indicating for me to come.

I couldn't figure out what she wanted.

"You stay away," she scolded. "Stand no before windows."

I gave her a puzzled look.

"*Io*," she said, patting her chest. "I make windows. Always me. *Capisce?*"

I shook my head.

"Allora." She got down on her hands and knees and motioned for me to do the same. Together, we crawled across the salone to one of the far windows. Teresina, like a fugitive checking out the terrain, slowly raised her head and peered over the stone balustrade. "Ecco, signorina! Look!" she whispered.

I saw two guys down on the street, talking on cell phones. "Who are they?"

"*Animali*," Teresina spat.

"Are they Mafia or something?"

Teresina let out a disgusted snort. "More terrible than that! They are paparazzi!"

Chapter

9

Troubled sleep.

All my systems out of kilter.

Was it morning, noon, or night for that Venus I'd lugged all the way from Portland, Oregon, to Rome?

Was it yesterday, today, or tomorrow?

That's the strange thing about jet lag. It's like you're two entirely different people. One is still back where you came from; the other is where you currently are, in a totally different place and time. And your job is to bring those two people together.

Teresina's spaghetti didn't help matters. I don't know what was in that heavy, funny-tasting sauce, but after I'd wolfed down a plate of her pasta, I felt absolutely exhausted, tired beyond anything I'd ever felt before.

Outside, it was still daylight, and I felt myself crawling toward total unconsciousness and resisting it at the same time. Sleep was like a comfy hole that I couldn't wait to slip into but was afraid to enter.

I pulled back the sheets and crawled in. My body felt heavy as lead. My eyelids drooped. There was something I had to do, and I couldn't remember what it was. I'd brushed my teeth. I'd peed. Oh yes.

Groggily, I sat up and worked to undo the complicated clasp of my jeweled timepiece. I looked around for someplace safe to put it.

There was an ornately carved bedside cabinet covered with a piece of tapestry. I carefully laid my precious present on that.

I'd never owned jewels before. My last wedding ring was a tattoo because Tremaynne hadn't believed in rings—or marriage.

Jewels. I had to smile. I sleepily looked over and could see them glittering like tiny sparkling eyes.

The sheets were cool as a Portland morning.

The mattress felt strange, but I assumed that was because I usually slept on a futon. And the pillows were weirdly shaped. I twisted and turned, trying to find my perfect, comfortable position. I always fell asleep on my stomach, cuddling a soft pillow.

As I lay there, finally finding the right position, I became aware of a faint, elusive odor. It seemed to emanate from the bed itself.

I sniffed.

The smell was delicate but persistent. A long-lasting scent from long ago. One that had worked its way into the mattress, the wood, the curtains, the tasseled canopy.

Was I smelling the soul of the bed?

Maybe all the generations of Brunellis that had slept in this bed had exuded a kind of ancestral aroma.

Then I thought, *her* scent. The invisible woman who had once rustled through her evening gowns in the closet. The invisible woman who'd bathed in the claw-foot tub and sat on the bidet splashing warm water on her privates. *Her* scent.

Was it friendly or mean, that scented presence?

When I fell asleep in that enormous canopied bed, it was the weirdest sleep I'd ever had. I felt immobilized, as if the heavy bed-cover were imprisoning me. I finally crawled into the sleep-hole and was sucked down a black current toward the deepest part, toward that soup of nutty images and impossible situations, where girls fly and dead people come back to life.

An argument. Hushed but intense voices. Voices charged with emotion. The voices were like a strange kind of music, changing pitch, rising high, falling low. One furious, insistent, demanding, the other weak, abject, pleading.

I was somehow a part of this argument. Maybe I was the subject of the argument. I couldn't be sure because I couldn't understand the words.

A pitter-patter of footsteps. A slight scuffle of soles on a bare floor. Someone coming to find me.

It was in my best interest to remain invisible. I crouched in a deep, dark corner of my dream.

Whatever it was, it came closer and closer. I could hear it breathing. Panting. Sniffing. I was terrified that it would find me.

It came right up to me. Sniffed all around my hiding place. I got a sudden, shocking hint of its pitiless determination to destroy me. It loomed over my hiding place and in terror I crouched down into as small a ball as I could make myself.

But it knew exactly where I was.

It spoke my name. Low. Familiar. "Venus."

It reached out a hand. I knew once that hand touched me I'd . . .

It touched me.

With a baffled cry, I lurched out of sleep. Sat up.

Looked at Marcello.

"*Buon giorno,*" he said, apparently amused.

My voice was rough as sandpaper. "Oh. Hi."

It took me a moment to make the transition from dream to consciousness.

I noticed that Marcello was dressed in his business drag: a beautiful suit, a gray shirt, a pale gold tie with a black pattern. Freshly shaven. He wasn't supposed to look tired, but his eyes were bloodshot.

"Am I too early for my lesson?" he asked.

"What lesson?"

"My slacker lesson," he said.

"Oh. That. No, you're too late." I crashed back down onto the bed, longing for still more sleep. "You've already shaved. Slackers don't shave."

"Would it be inappropriate if I crawled into bed with you?"

"Yeah. Inappropriate. I'm your teacher, remember?" I pulled the warm sheets up to my neck and just lay there, looking at him.

He sat on the side of the bed, stroking my arm, then my face. "I am so happy that you are here. I feel like I have been given a wonderful gift."

When he said "gift," I remembered the watch. And casually turned my head to look at it. I knew exactly where I'd placed it.

My heart gave a stutter, then started to beat fast.

The watch was gone.

Maybe Teresina had removed it. Put it someplace safe. Maids did that sort of thing.

"Are you all right, darling?" Marcello asked.

"Yeah. Why?" I turned back to him.

"You slept right through the night."

"What time is it, anyway?"

He glanced at his watch, then back at me. "Nine." His eyes filled with unmistakable desire. "I have one hour and fifteen minutes."

"Before what?"

"My next meeting."

"So I won't see you today, either."

His face brightened. "Will you miss me?"

I evaded the question. The truth was, I wanted some company. I missed talking. I missed English. "I told you, if you're going to be a slacker you have to cancel all meetings."

An eager smile. He leaned closer. "I wish I could cancel all of them. And spend the time with you."

"Can't you?"

"No," he said, pulling back. "I can't." He rose from the bed as Teresina entered the room with a tray.

"*Buon giorno*, signorina." Her voice was stiff, impassive. I watched her as she set the tray on the bedside cabinet, right where my watch had been. "*Un' caffè?*"

Marcello lit a cigarette and gestured with it as he said something in Italian. Teresina nodded, glanced at me, and quickly left the room.

"May a slacker pour coffee?" Marcello asked.

"Usually not. Slackers are heavy into caffeine, but they never make it themselves. Or pour it themselves. But I guess I can make an exception this one time."

"You are very kind." He poured thick black espresso into a tiny cup. "Sugar?"

"Yeah, as much as you can squeeze into that teeny cup."

"You like it sweet, eh?" He smiled the whole time he was fixing my coffee, then sat beside me, closer this time, holding the cup and saucer. "May I help you drink it?"

I thought he meant "may I have a sip?" So I said, "Sure." But he lifted the cup and brought it to my lips. Held it just so, like a nurse administering medicine.

I sipped.

"Is it sweet enough?" he asked.

I nodded.

His desire was palpable. His dark eyes locked into mine. Cigarette smoke poured out of his nostrils, like steam from a comic-book bull.

Something stirred in me.

My God, I thought, *he's really handsome.*

And then my stomach growled and I laughed, breaking the spell.

He stayed one hour and fifteen minutes. *Exactly.*

Said he had to fly back to Torino but would return to Rome that evening. "We will dine, eh?"

"Sure. But what am I supposed to do all day?"

"Didn't you bring any books with you?"

"Books? I didn't come all the way to Rome to read! I want to go out exploring."

"Not by yourself, no," Marcello said firmly, waving a hand.

"I'm not going to sit around *here* all day, waiting for *you*." I didn't mean for it to sound unkind, but I saw his look of hurt and realized he'd misinterpreted. "Sorry. I didn't mean for it to sound like that."

He shrugged. "You are a perennial challenge, Signorina Gilroy."

"When you're here, I'll spend my time with you. Just like we agreed. But when you're not here—"

"Of course." He sounded resigned.

"I want to see Rome. And if you can't go with me, then I'll go on my own."

He pressed his fingertips together, considering. "I will have Giovanni show you Roma."

Oh great, a chauffeur to drive me around. Not exactly what I had in mind. "I'd rather go on my own," I said. "Just snoop around."

"No. Not on your first day." He was very stern about it. "Roma can be a very confusing city, Venus. You may get lost."

"I can buy a map. And I have your secret cell-phone number."

"That is part of the problem, you see. Numbers." He sighed. "We require a great deal of security here. Codes. To enter, and so on."

I went over to the now unshuttered windows and looked out. Palazzo Brunelli was a big, thick square built around an inner court-yard. The exterior windows were high off the ground and covered with thick metal bars and shutters. The only way in and out was through that gated passageway. Inside, with the steel gate closed, the palazzo was as impregnable as a full-security prison.

"Listen," I said, "there's no way I'm going to sit around in here all day long, day after day, while you're in meetings. I have to be able to go out or I'll go nuts."

"You understand our need for security, don't you? Kidnappings. Terrorists. Paparazzi. We must protect ourselves. We cannot be casual about this, Venus."

"Then maybe I'd better go."

"Go? You mean leave me?" A spark of alarm. "Because of our security systems?"

"*You* can be a prisoner in your own house," I said, "but I won't be. I've got to be able to come and go."

Marcello took a deep breath and ran a careful hand along the side of his head. "Then you will have to see Giovanna."

"Oh yeah, your head of security."

"*Prego?*" He looked baffled.

"Giovanna," I said. "You mentioned her before. When we were at Cannon Beach. You said she was head of security for your company."

"Head of security for my company?" Marcello threw his head back and laughed.

"What's so funny?"

"Giovanna, darling, is my daughter."

I felt like I'd been running and someone had suddenly tripped me. "Oh," was all I could think of to say.

"She is in charge of security here at Palazzo Brunelli. Since her mother died. She needed something to do. Something to be in charge of."

"She lives here?" I asked nervously.

"Yes, right over there. Across the courtyard."

I took a deep breath.

"Giovanna will give you the codes. So you can come and go. But you must promise me that when you are outside, when you are out in Rome, you will always remain alert."

"Of course I will."

"Roma is not like some crowded American mall. It's a different kind of world. I don't wish to frighten you, darling, but I must insist that you be careful."

"*OK*." He was beginning to sound like a parent.

"And today, your first day, I insist that Giovanni accompany you."

"OK." How bad could it be?

"Allora." He glanced at his watch. His face fell. "Darling, I must go."

He took a step toward me. I took a step toward him. Sort of automatic.

"May I kiss you good-bye?" he asked.

I nodded.

I had to admit, he was a pretty good kisser.

I didn't exactly stall for time, but I didn't hurry, either.

His daughter.

I didn't know what to expect. How old was she? What did she look like? Was she a teenager or a young woman? Would she hate my guts on sight?

More immediately, there was the matter of the watch. As soon as Marcello left, I asked Teresina if she had taken it.

"*Io*, signorina?" She looked gravely offended, as if she thought I was accusing her of stealing.

"I thought maybe you put it away somewhere."

"No," she said firmly.

But I still wasn't sure that she had understood me. So I searched everywhere. I went into the closet and opened every drawer and door and felt along every shelf. I went into the bathroom. Fear was making me imagine all kinds of crazy things. Like, *maybe you didn't put it on the bedside cabinet. Maybe it slipped off your wrist and fell into the toilet and was flushed away into the sewers of Rome.*

Or maybe someone really *had* stolen it.

Maybe Teresina wasn't quite as nice as she looked.

I flashed on that weird poster in her bedroom, the chick wearing a leather bikini and holding a machine gun. Definitely a bad girl.

I didn't know what else to do or where else to look. I couldn't very well search her room. "If you find it, Teresina, please let me know."

"Si."

I could tell I'd offended her.

Then I had to decide what to wear. It was going to be a burning hot day. I knew that because I'd found an English-language channel on the radio in the kitchen. "Expect a sweltering high of thirty-seven degrees Celsius in Rome today," the announcer announced. I did some quick figuring. Math is the one thing I'm pretty good at. Before I left, Daddy had taught me how to convert Celsius into Fahrenheit. I doubled the Celsius temperature, subtracted ten percent, and added 32.

It was going to be one hundred degrees Fahrenheit in Rome.

Luckily, those stinky New York summers had given me some experience with extreme heat. I'd fly out from Portland where it was a pleasant 65 and hit that sweltering inferno of New York summer where it was like living in the tropics with garbage rotting all around. There had been so many security bars on the windows of Daddy and Whitman's apartment that they couldn't fit in an air conditioner, so we had lived with the unadulterated heat.

It never cooled down. That New York heat was like a hot blanket of madness spread over the whole city. Everyone was cranky, or pissed-off, or crazy. There were more murders, more rapes, more suicides. My ears picked up the banshee wail of sirens day and night.

It did something to me, that New York heat. I hated it, but I loved it in a weird way because it changed the way everyone looked and lived. You couldn't have any illusions in heat that hot. The subway became a fascinating vision of hell, its dirty, blistering winds howling through a hot stinking honeycomb of tunnels. People stripped down to as little as they dared and moved very slowly.

So I had some experience with American heat. I didn't know what the heat in Rome would be like. All I knew was that I had to dress for cool.

OK, a black sleeveless tube top, black stretch jeans, and how about a yellow neck scarf for a bit of color?

As I dressed, Teresina stood there watching me. Maybe she was accustomed to helping women dress, but I wasn't accustomed to having anyone help or scrutinize me. When I got slightly tangled in the tube top, Teresina stepped forward. I felt her hands gently tugging the fabric down over my breasts.

For some reason, I didn't want her to know how upset I was about the watch. So I acted determined and sure of myself. But all the while, this frantic voice was reminding me that the watch must have cost thousands, and I'd have to tell Marcello that it was gone.

I put on a necklace of silver ankhs that JD had given me when we were lovers, and wondered if my ex-girlfriend was now married to Mistah Sistah. I fastened my silver charm bracelet. Slipped into my new platform sandals that were supposed to be like walking on air but, I immediately realized, would pinch my toes all day long.

I looked in the full-length front- and rearview mirrors in the dressing room. It was me, all right. I was dressed appropriately, or so I thought, for a hot day in Rome. But was I dressed right for meeting Marcello's daughter?

The stretch pants were light and comfy but *very* tight. I didn't want Marcello's daughter to think that I was just some cheap tarty streetwalker her dad had picked up.

On the other hand, I wasn't about to change my look for a total stranger who handed out security codes.

I swung the strap of my new red microfiber purse over my shoulder and turned to Teresina. "Do I look OK?"

"*Caldo*," she said, nodding. "Hot."

I didn't know if she meant the temperature outside or me.

We left the palazetto and made our way through the maze of Palazzo Brunelli. Giovanna lived on the opposite side of the courtyard, also on the third floor, so I just assumed it would be fairly easy to reach her.

But nothing was that simple in Palazzo Brunelli.

We had to go down one internal flight of stairs to the second floor, wind through some corridors, and then climb up to the third floor again.

The layout wasn't anything like an American house. It was totally confusing. I felt like I should leave a trail of breadcrumbs because I wasn't sure I could ever find my way back again.

Everywhere I looked I saw portraits. Dark hooded eyes met mine. They sat at tables, on thronelike chairs, on horses. They were all very erect. Sometimes they appeared to be in a darkish room with a window or door open behind them giving onto a view of a distant landscape. Sometimes their hand rested on a book, or a crucifix, or their breast. In their weird hats, heavy capes, and embroidered collars, they all seemed determined to convey the trappings of power, prestige, and money.

I supposed all these portraits were the Brunelli equivalent of having a bunch of framed, blurry family photographs on top of the TV, the way Carolee did.

Finally, we stood in a long, brightly lit corridor before a low wooden door. Teresina pressed a button, then tapped a code into a keypad.

As we waited, I happened to look up. Saw a camera mounted near the ceiling at the end of the corridor moving slowly back and forth.

The door was opened by a tiny nun.

That can't be Giovanna, I thought. The nun was maybe my mom's age. She had one of those disconcertingly sexless nun faces. No attempt to emphasize the cheekbones or accentuate the eyes. Just a naked face, with eyebrows that almost met and eyes magnified be-

hind gold-rimmed glasses. It was the first time I'd seen a nun in gray
rather than black.

She was holding a stainless-steel tray. A thin white cloth was
draped from her wrist. On the tray there was a small dish, about the
size of a Petri dish, and some object I couldn't identify. It looked
like a miniature turkey baster, or a surgical instrument of some kind,
with a small suction bulb at the end and a thin, four-inch-long glass
tube.

Teresina said something. The nun said something back. We entered a vestibule and the nun closed the door behind us. Then she
disappeared through another door, which she left slightly ajar.

"*Uno momento*," Teresina said. "We wait."

She seated herself in a large chair. I seated myself in another one.
From my vantage point I had an oblique view into the next room.

The background was red. There was a bank of TV monitors or
computers in front of thick red curtains or red-colored walls. Someone—I assumed it was Giovanna—was sitting behind a large desk. I
could see only a bit of the back of her head, a mass of stiff black hair.
She was tilted back like someone in a salon chair getting a facial.
The nun hovered over her, doing something, I couldn't tell what. I
heard what sounded like a whimper. A reassuring voice. Then the
nun moved to Giovanna's other side.

I looked over at Teresina. She saw that I'd been peeking. "What's
she doing?" I whispered.

"*Il naso.*" Teresina lifted her head and flared her nostrils.

"What's that?"

"Her nose!" Teresina repeated in a whisper, tapping her own.
"Sister Angelica, she cleans it."

I looked back in. The nun was squirting something into the little
dish. She dabbed at Giovanna's face with the white cloth. Then
Giovanna shifted her modern chair into an upright position and said
something, and the nun handed her the little dish. A moment later,
Giovanna handed it back and said something. The nun gathered up
her tray, the dish, and the instrument, and rustled toward the door.

I quickly looked the other way.

The nun murmured something in a low voice to Teresina. She

sounded like a nurse in a hospital telling us we could go in to see the patient.

We entered.

Giovanna remained in her chair, behind her desk, facing away from me. She appeared to be looking at the security monitors that lined the far wall and showed the outside of Palazzo Brunelli from different angles and viewpoints. Then I saw that I was an image on one of the screens, seen from high up in a corner.

"Signorina Gilroy," Teresina announced, and left the room.

Giovanna slowly turned her chair toward me.

Oh. My. God.

I stared.

"Signorina Gilroy." She stood. Faced me.

"Hi." I was so flustered I didn't know what to do or say.

Giovanna said nothing. She just stared at me.

Where had I ever before encountered a stare like that? Only a woman was capable of such a look. A very jealous woman. A woman who wanted to put me down and get me out of her way. A woman who wanted to convince me that she was so superior that angels wiped her ass and poured her coffee.

And in response to that look—that glower of imperious self-importance—I just wanted to laugh. But I knew I shouldn't do that. I hadn't come here with any desire to antagonize Giovanna. In fact, just the opposite. But those dark, unfathomable eyes scoured the world for enemies, real or imagined, and I was one of them.

And why?

I'll tell you why.

Because Giovanna Brunelli was one of the ugliest women I'd ever seen in my entire life.

And it was all because of her nose. When I say it was big, I don't mean it was large. It was *enormous*. With a hook in it. She looked like a giant bird of prey. You could almost imagine a string of bloody entrails hanging from her giant beak.

Nose jobs were invented for unfortunate girls like her. Certainly she had the money. So you had to ask yourself, was she trying to prove something with her ugliness? Was she trying to prove that a huge nose was a sign of aristocratic beauty or something? If so, the poor dear was sadly mistaken.

The clothes I didn't get at all. She looked like she'd stepped out from one of those portraits. From another century. She wore a long black-velvet robelike gown with puffed-out sleeves and a high neckline embroidered with gold and lace. Cool, but inappropriate for the twenty-first century. A rope of pearls and a large jeweled crucifix hung around her long, thin neck. She had very pale, almost waxy-looking skin.

And the hair. She needed a stylist really bad. Maybe it was some kind of old-fashioned do, but it was a do that was definitely a don't. Black as a raven's wing. A little fringe of bangs, and then this stiff, constructed mass that rose up like a hood.

I don't want to sound unkind, but Marcello's daughter looked like she belonged in the Raptor House of a zoo.

Finally she said, in an accented, adenoidal voice, "You came for something?"

"Marcello told me you'd give me some codes. Security codes for the doors."

"Did not Teresina give you the code for your rooms?"

"Yeah. She did. But I want to go out for a while. Outside."

She pulled her gown together and sat down in a rustle of fabric, turning to a large flat-screen computer. "Yes," she said, "I'm sure you cannot wait to get back down to the street."

Was that supposed to mean what I thought it was supposed to mean? I got warm. Preparation for battle. But I kept my composure. Rudeness does not come naturally to me. "I'm going to do some sightseeing," I said pleasantly. "I've never been to Rome before."

"Yes," she said, tapping something into her keyboard, pursing her lips as if suppressing a smile, "that's quite obvious."

Was that supposed to mean what I thought it was supposed to mean? I got warmer.

I would not lose control. I would not rise to her childish, jealous bait. To regain my composure, I took a deep Buddha breath and looked around the room.

Giovanna was obviously a computer geek. There were screens and monitors everywhere. At the far end of the room there was a glass wall with a door. Beyond it, a densely green rooftop garden.

"You understand security codes, eh?" She flashed me a scornful glance.

"Of course I do."

"Ours are changed every month," she said. "I determine what they will be. My father and Giovanni and Fabio can access the codes on their mobile GPS systems." She sighed, as if I were a trouble-some child. "Do you have *any* understanding of what I am talking about?"

"Global Positioning Systems."

"The current codes I must give to you on hard copy. I hate to do that. Papers can be lost or stolen so easily."

"I'll take care of it."

"I don't know what else I can do," she said. "I told my father that if I gave you these entry codes it would compromise our entire sys-tem." She gave me a pointed look. "But he would not listen to me."

Her printer suddenly hummed and shot out a page. Giovanna scanned it before handing the sheet to me. "I'm sure it's too much for you to memorize them and destroy the paper."

Her condescending tone pissed me off. "I said I'll take care of it." I snatched the paper from her hand.

We stood there looking at each other. A standoff. Finally Giovanna spoke.

"We are always targets, signorina. That's why we must be so care-ful. Everyone hates the Brunellis." She gave me a dead smile. "They want our money. They want our pictures. They want our lives."

I didn't want to be rude. I didn't want to embarrass her. But oh my God.

"What is it?" She sounded alarmed. "Why are you staring at me like that?"

"Your nose," I said.

She stiffened.

"There's a big drop of blood . . ."

She was horrified. But it was true. A big, bright bead of blood was gathering at the tip of her nose.

She tried to keep her face immobile, eyes staring furiously at me, as she groped in a drawer for a tissue. But before she got one out, the blood dropped onto the white blotter on her desk.

"Ah!" she cried, pressing the tissue to her nose.

"Tilt your head back," I said, moving toward her to help.

"Ah!" Her eyes were wild, terrified. She looked like she was starting to panic. She waved me away and hit a button on her desk.

A moment later, tiny Sister Angelica rushed in. The nun gave me a severe look, as if I'd punched Giovanna in the nose. I saw Teresina's frightened face in the doorway. "It's just a nosebleed," I said.

"Ah. Ah."

Sister Angelica made Giovanna recline in her modern chair. She hovered over her, whispering reassurances as she peered into the huge cavities of Giovanna's nostrils.

I felt like it was a good time for me to go.

"Venus?"

I looked over and saw that he'd been waiting for me.

"I'm Johnny."

"Johnny?"

"Giovanni."

"Oh. Yeah. Right. Hi."

Definitely not what I expected a chauffeur to look like.

Giovanni was leaning against a massive marble sarcophagus in the entrance hall. Why an ancient, empty coffin should be used as decoration, I don't know. But there it was. Johnny tossed the newspaper he'd been reading into the sarcophagus and came toward me. We shook hands.

Looked into one another's eyes.

God help me, I thought.

"Signorina?"

I turned to Teresina. She was speaking to me but staring at Giovanni.

Well, what woman in her right mind wouldn't?

"Do you wish me anymore?" Teresina asked.

"No, thanks. I'm going out with Giovanni."

"Si." She looked furious and crestfallen. Turned on her heel and clicked away into the palazzo.

"So you're Venus," he said.

"So you're Giovanni."

"Johnny, OK?"

"OK."

He was like a big breath of fresh air after all the stiff formality that I'd encountered in Palazzo Brunelli. He was as casual as an American and almost sounded like one. He wore blue jeans and a black T-shirt and black boots. Jet black hair, thick black eyebrows, shiny black eyes caressed by the longest black lashes I'd ever seen. A carefully trimmed goatee. No obvious gym-trained muscular development but lean and strong.

"You got all the security codes?" he asked, opening the front door for me.

We stepped into a blast of hot white heat.

"I've got them."

"They're a drag, but I promised I'd show you how they work."

Which he did, as we stood there in a hot blaze of light, looking down into the courtyard from the third floor. The codes weren't all that difficult. There was an activation code for the front inner door, in case no one was around to open it for me, and a code for a small door set within the security gate at the street. Big deal. Security codes were a part of my and everybody else's life nowadays.

"It's hot," I said inanely as we started down the stairway toward the courtyard.

"It's Rome," he said. "Hot and polluted. Just the way we like it."

There was a small fountain on one side of the courtyard. A trickle of water spurted from the open mouth of a startled-looking stone face and into a marble basin. There was a little fringe of garden around the basin and two lemon trees in huge stone tubs.

Giovanni pointed toward the limo. "I suppose you want to ride in that?"

"Do I have options?"

He laughed. "Sure. But you probably don't want to sit on the back of a Vespa."

"Try me."

He asked if I wanted a helmet and I said no. Unlike in America, in Italy you could still ride bareheaded. Which, let's face it, is the whole point of riding on a motorcycle or motorbike. Freedom. You risk getting your skull smashed, but you get to feel the wind in your hair.

I'd been on a motorcycle but never a motorbike. JD had a huge Harley and we'd gone tearing around Portland on it.

Giovanni's Vespa was small, sleek, and powerful. He turned around in surprise when I expertly hopped on behind him.

"Hold tight, Venus."

I clasped his fat-free waist.

He held up a finger. "First—most important. We make certain that the paparazzi are not outside."

Giovanni was obviously accustomed to avoiding contact with the troublesome photographers. The paparazzi were forbidden to stand within 500 meters of the security gate. If they did, they could be arrested for infringing upon the Brunellis' privacy. Large mirrors had been installed on the street so that you could see, from inside, whether there were any loitering paparazzi outside.

The coast was clear. Giovanni got the security gate open and we cautiously pulled out to the street. Stopped to make sure the gate closed again. Then sped off into the heart of Rome.

Chapter

10

"What do you want to see?" Johnny called back as we eased out onto the busy road beside the Tiber.

"Everything!"

"Do you have a few years?"

"No, but I've got all afternoon."

"What's your primary interest?" he asked. "Art, churches, ancient monuments?"

"Can we go to the Colosseum?"

He nodded and veered off in the opposite direction.

"And then that pyramid?" I had to lean forward and shout in his ear.

He gave me a thumbs-up as we raced down a busy street and turned again, this time into a narrow passageway where he beeped his horn and scattered a group of Japanese tourists.

They scrutinized us as we bumped past on the cobblestones. One of them took a photograph. Weird. Someone in Japan would have a photo of us, of Johnny and me, on this Roman street. Did they think we were a cute young Italian couple?

I kept my hands firmly clenched around his waist as we entered an enormous piazza and joined a stream of cars racing around a fountain in the center. Fizzing jets of water tickled the tits and asses of bosomy bronze ladies capering around an old dude with a trident.

"Piazza della Repubblica," Johnny called back to me. He pointed. "Train station's over there."

I nodded.

I smiled.

Something in me just let go. That ball of anxiety I'd been lugging around in the pit of my stomach since getting on the first plane in Portland finally released its grip.

There was nothing to stop me from enjoying myself in Rome except my own anxieties. I couldn't do anything about the missing watch, or the obviously antagonistic Giovanna, or the fact that Marcello was never around. The only thing I could do, my only obligation, was to live in the here and now of this moment, seeing Rome from the back of a motorbike driven by a very cute chauffeur.

It's funny how you get to know a person by his driving.

I was in the hands of an expert, I could tell. It amazed me that anyone could know how to navigate through this confusing warren of ancient streets and busy avenues, of vast piazzas and tiny squares.

Johnny was not a slow, careful driver like Fabio. He definitely pushed it. On traffic-filled streets he liked to swerve in and out, aggressively passing cars. He darted left and right with agility and authority. It was the kind of driving that required hair-trigger precision and an intimate understanding of your fellow drivers. It was not the kind of driving that you could do anywhere in the States.

Which was why it was so exciting.

I knew I could trust him. If he worked for Marcello, and Marcello trusted him, then this guy was OK.

Johnny pointed straight ahead as we raced along a street that was closed to cars.

There it was. The ancient Colosseum. I was finally seeing it.

Johnny roared up to the building, onto the pavement, and made an illegal circuit before stopping and switching off the motor.

My legs felt kind of wavery as I debiked.

"I can't leave the bike," he said. "I've got to walk it."

"OK."

"Listen," he said, "I may as well tell you. He'll have my ass if he finds out we're doing this."

"Who? Marcello?"

"Yeah. He'll shit bricks."

"Why? What are we doing? I thought you were supposed to show me around."

"In his *limo*," Johnny said. "You know, in a closed car. With bullet-proof glass."

"I won't tell him."

Johnny looked at me.

"This is so much more fun," I said. "I don't feel real in that limo."

"Giovanna scares him with the security stuff," he said. "He shouldn't listen to her."

"That girl would scare anyone."

"She's totally paranoid."

"Must be awful," I said. "What good is it to be rich if it makes you so scared of the world?"

He looked at me again, more intently this time. "That's how I feel. But Giovanna, she just doesn't get it."

"It can't be that dangerous for the Brunellis, can it?"

"People create their own prisons," Johnny said. He nodded toward the Colosseum. "This is where people used to have fun."

"Watching people being fed to the lions?"

"Yeah. Or they'd bring animals over from Africa and let them loose and slaughter them, thousands at a time. Or gladiators would do hand-to-hand combat to the death. Or," he smiled, "if you were an enemy of the state, you might be soaked with tar and lit up like a Roman candle. Wouldn't that be fun to watch?"

"Hilarious."

As we walked, he explained everything about the Colosseum. He was almost better than Whitman at explaining touristy things.

Like, the Colosseum was built in 70 A.D. in the middle of a broad valley between three hills. It was the largest amphitheatre ever built in the ancient world. A giant bronze statue of the emperor Nero, ten stories tall, once stood beside it. "All the emperors were deified," Johnny explained. "Murderers who made themselves into gods."

Johnny offered all kinds of fascinating historical tidbits. He told me that by the middle of the first century A.D., Romans had 160 holidays a year. The Colosseum, with room for 50,000 spectators, served as an open-air arena for holiday spectaculars. Admission was free.

"The emperors gave them so many games," Johnny said, "that the Roman citizens forgot they had any political role to play. It was an ancient form of crowd control. Keep people stupid and amused, and they won't revolt against their leaders."

I recognized the sarcastic tone. Tremaynne had used that tone. It meant there was some kind of political passion brewing just below the surface. I wondered if Johnny kept it under wraps when he was with Marcello.

As we slowly circled the giant, three-tiered building, he explained how the Colosseum had worked. Everyone could go, but you were assigned a seat based on your rank in society and you could never change it. Like sports arenas today, the arcades on the ground floor were numbered, and the number corresponded to a number on your admission ticket and told you which of the 76 entrances you had to use to reach the particular level and wedge of seating you'd been assigned to. Spectators sat on three tiers of marble seating raked back from the arena floor. At the very top there was a fourth level, made of wood, that provided standing room for the lowliest of the low.

"That's probably where I would have sat," I laughed. "Or stood."

"Maybe I would have stood beside you."

I heard it, but I let it go. I knew I mustn't hold on to it.

An enormous awning had protected spectators from the heat of the Roman sun. Johnny showed me where, toward the top of the outer wall, some of the supports for the timber poles that had held this awning could still be seen. The giant sun shade had been maneuvered by a special detachment of sailors sent up from a naval base on the Gulf of Naples.

During shows, the lowest level of seats in the arena was surrounded by metal mesh attached to poles and spiked with elephant tusks. Ivory rollers placed at the top of the mesh ensured that animals could not get a foothold and escape into the stands. Archers were stationed in niches at the bottom tier, just in case.

Subterranean rooms were used to store stage equipment. The

scenery created for shows at the Colosseum had been even more elaborate than the sets for those operas at the Met that the dads used to drag me to. When animal hunts were staged, hills, woods, even small lakes were created in the arena. Sometimes they flooded the whole thing and had fake naval battles.

Men and animals were brought up to the arena by elevators operated by counterweights. First, the animals were driven along underground corridors into cages. Each cage was fitted with a mechanism that raised it to a higher level, where the animals stepped out onto an elevated gangway. That led them to a wooden ramp with a trap door at its upper end. When the trap door opened, the animal entered the arena and became part of the show.

"Once," Johnny said, "they brought a hundred lions into the arena at exactly the same moment. Their roars were so loud that the crowd got scared and became totally silent."

I peered inside the giant arches, trying to imagine the scene.

"Want to go in?" Johnny asked. "I can wait out here with the bike."

"No, I'll come back. I have to show this to my mom when she comes."

"Your mother's coming to Rome?"

I nodded.

Johnny smiled. "Does *he* know that?"

His chummy familiarity suddenly seemed kind of impertinent, like he was trying to cross the invisible line drawn between us. Trying to come closer. It made me uncomfortable. But, I had to admit, I liked being with him. He was smart and cute, a fatal combination.

"Sorry." He held up his hands. "I guess I shouldn't pry into whatever's going on."

"Just out of curiosity," I said, "what do you think's going on?"

"Can't tell," he said. "You're not his usual type."

"What type is that?"

"Older. More—"

"More what?"

"Formal."

"Did he go out with a lot of these older, formal types?"

"Quite a few."

"Even when he was married?"

"If you were married to a crazy person," Johnny said, "you might do the same."

"She was crazy? His wife?"

Johnny turned away and started walking his bike again. "Yes, she was crazy. Very crazy. There was something wrong with her brain, and no one could fix it."

"You know that area where I'm staying, that wing? Was that where she lived?"

He nodded. "That's why they had to lock it."

I was just being polite. It was hot and he'd been tour-guiding me for about three hours. I leaned forward and said, "Can I buy you a coffee or something before we head back?"

It was as much for me as for him. I was feeling weirdly groggy. I wanted to sit down beneath an umbrella at one of those cute outdoor cafés I saw everywhere and think about all I'd seen and watch the passing parade through an enlivening jolt of caffeine.

"I'll take you to a café I like in Trastevere!" he shouted back.

We sped across a bridge and into a hodgepodge of narrow streets. Puttering along, we came out into a big piazza with a church at one end and a fountain in the center. The top of the church was decorated with giant human figures and palm trees against a gleaming gold background. Zip, it was gone, like a thousand other mysterious sights I'd passed that day.

Johnny slowed down still more and we bumped along an uneven cobblestone alleyway into another square, this one much smaller. He pulled up in front of a door hung with red and white plastic streamers. Definitely not fancy, and there weren't any umbrellas.

A dark-haired woman jumped up from one of the tables in front of the café and threw open her arms in greeting. "Giovanni! Ciao, *bello!*" She threaded her way through the tables, her face rapturous.

No, she was not cute. Scarily gorgeous was more like it. *Bellissima.*

With a dark, husky, ferociously sexy voice that came from deep within her "plus" chest.

His girlfriend, I thought. *Be prepared for jealousy.*

"Ah, Giovanni, *caro mio*," she cried, grabbing his face and planting a big fat kiss on his lips. With a sidelong flick of her eyes she acknowledged my presence, then turned back to Johnny.

I couldn't understand what they were saying but could tell from her pouts and smiles and adoring looks that she wanted to sleep with him really bad, or maybe recently had.

She could have been his wife, for all I knew.

But I doubted it.

She rattled on and on, pressing herself into him. And he rattled back, on and on, in Italian. Every now and then her eyes would dart my way, give me a quick assessment, and dart back to roost on his gorgeous face.

Finally Johnny broke loose from her and introduced us. "Venus, this is Flavinia. Deputy chairman of the local Communist party."

She stiffly thrust her arm out, all her animated charm suddenly gone. "Ciao. Come stai?"

"I'm sorry, I don't—"

"Speak Italian?" Flavinia laughed and turned back to Johnny. "She must be an American."

"Yes," I said, "I am."

Flavinia turned back to me. "Your country stinks!" she said.

I felt like I'd been slapped.

"Hey," Johnny said reprovingly.

"It's true," Flavinia said. "Americans think they rule the world. They think they own the world. You've said so yourself."

Never in my life had I been insulted because I was American. I literally didn't know what to say or how to respond. I gave Johnny a confused glance and said, "I'm going to walk down that street over there." As I stumbled away, I could hear the two of them, Johnny and Flavinia, getting into an argument behind me.

Some people hated Americans. I couldn't take it personally. But of course I did.

I turned the corner and left the square. Wandered slowly down a dark, narrow, quiet street. The shouts of excited children echoed from a distant piazza. I heard what sounded like a soccer ball whacking a wall. The air was cooler. The blazing afternoon sun skimmed along the top of the narrow street but couldn't penetrate down into it.

The windows were all shuttered. I tried to imagine the dark, cool apartments behind. The lives being lived, lives completely and utterly unlike my own. But also just like my own, with the same basic needs.

I walked slowly and took deep Buddha breaths to calm myself down. Ahead of me, there was a small square with a fountain. It wasn't a piazza with other streets leading into it, but more of a widening in the street with a tunnel-like passageway leading off from one end.

I didn't see them until I entered the square.

There were about eight of them. Boys and girls. The youngest about six, the oldest about eleven. They looked pretty ragged. Some were barefoot.

"Signorina, signorina, signorina." Their voices were a steady drone of hopelessness. "*O fa-may, o fa-may, o fa-may.*"

I backed away, shaking my head. "Sorry, I don't—"

They came closer, hands extended like little claws, a pleading look in every small face. "*Prego,* signorina. *O fa-may.*"

Some were carrying dirty pieces of cardboard. Their clothes were filthy, their hair stiff with dirt. Their faces looked wild, desperate. "Hungry, signorina. Hungry. *O fa-may.*"

The group surged forward. Some of them scattered behind me. When I looked back, I felt a piece of cardboard shoved in my belly. "Signorina, signorina, signorina." The voices so dull, the eyes so intent.

Obviously they wanted money.

Another piece of cardboard was shoved into my bare midriff. Then another. Something was printed on the cardboard. I tried to read it, but the words were in Italian. And it was all too confusing because the pieces of cardboard were being shifted and turned and jabbed and big, dark, desperate eyes were looking up at me.

And then the nightmare really began.

A hand shot out from behind me and swiped at my rear. Another small hand grabbed my wrist.

Trying to get my bracelet.

The second I pulled my arm back, I felt a hand tugging at my purse.

"No!" I yanked my purse close. But then they were poking at me from behind, from the side, poking with the cardboard and pleading with outstretched hands, chanting with those dull, miserable voices, *"O fa-may, o fa-may, o fa-may."*

In just the blink of an eye it turned from sorrowful pleading to gang warfare. Below the cardboard, the little hands were deftly at work. They were in my pockets, scrabbling for my purse, my bracelet. My top was pulled loose. And then one of them jumped up and snatched at my ankh necklace.

I turned in desperate circles, wanting to strike out, but they were children, and you don't hit kids. And with a terrible flash I realized that they knew that and used it to their advantage.

I lurched from one side of the square to the other and they stayed with me, all those dark eyes trained on me like the eyes of a pack of animals working to bring down their prey.

In one of my gasping turns I saw the glint of a knifeblade.

"Johnny!" I screamed. My voice ricocheted down the dark narrow street.

Working together, they pressed me back into a corner of the square. I didn't realize their strategy until it was too late. I was there, backed into the corner, and the only way to escape was to burst through like a tank and outrun them.

Which I could not do in the shoes I was wearing, on that cobblestone street. They would be on me in a flash, and if I lost my balance, that was the end of it. Bang. Slash. There went my new purse with my passport, my wallet, and all those goddamn security codes.

"Johnny!" I cried. "Someone! Help!"

But the shutters remained shut. No one wanted to look out and see a stupid American girl being robbed by a gang of kids.

Like those hideous, heartless stories you used to hear about in

New York. People screaming as they were stabbed or beaten to death and nobody responding.

"Someone!" I screamed, determined not to be their victim. "Help me!"

The kids' faces. God, what a sight. I'd thought they were pleading, desperate. Now I saw that they were as hard as the old stones beneath our feet. Not desperate so much as determined. They were going to get something from me. I was their chosen victim.

I made a futile attempt to run to one side, but they quickly herded me back to my corner. From there, they began angling me toward the dark passageway leading off from the square. If they got me in there, I knew I was a goner.

I hoped that wasn't a glint of pleasure I saw in that little boy's eyes. The pleasure of power. Of the easy kill.

The oldest boy hissed something and they moved into a new formation, closing in. One of them made a sound and they rushed me. I screamed and flailed and kicked and pushed. I heard a moan, a cry, a surprised gasp. A little girl fell down hard, on her back, and I was afraid she'd cracked her head. But she jumped up with a look of fury.

They would not give up. Neither would I. But then I saw that knife again. Saw it poised to strike, or slit, or gouge. Felt the strap of my purse suddenly go limp and fall from my shoulder. I fumbled but managed to grab the purse before it fell.

I was so busy fighting and crying and screaming and turning in circles that I didn't hear the Vespa until it sped into the square, toward me, toward all the kids.

They scattered like birds. Disappeared into the dark passageway.

Johnny jumped off his bike. Ran to me.

My chauffeur took me in his arms and tried to calm me down.

Marcello returned to Palazzo Brunelli about nine that evening. He looked exhausted. His eyes were red and watery. There was a dark shadow on his face. His beautiful suit was wrinkled and reeked of cigarette smoke.

I had hoped that we'd go out to eat. I wanted to experience Rome by night. I wanted to prowl around those mysterious Roman streets, full of people and laughter and the echoing hum of voices. I wanted to sit outside in one of the giant piazzas lined with restaurants. I wanted to see the ancient churches and temples and palaces and fountains picked out with floodlights.

More than anything, I wanted to confront and conquer my fear of the city before it got any worse. I could only do that, coward that I'd become, with a man at my side.

But Marcello wanted to eat at home and had arranged all the details with Teresina. Plates were set at opposite ends of the massive wooden table in the dining hall. Teresina cast frantic glances at her boss, Il Principe, when I moved my table setting so that I could sit next to him instead of twenty feet away.

Obviously I'd broken some unspoken rule.

"Ah, that's nice," Marcello said. "We will sit together." He patted my arm and smiled, his eyelids drooping with fatigue.

But I was wide awake. For hours my veins had been gushing adrenalin. I hadn't been hurt in the attack, just badly frightened. Nothing like that had ever happened to me before, and I took a secret vow that it would never happen again. I'd had my Roman wake-up call.

✓ No stylish heels or high platform shoes in Rome.
✓ No easy-to-snatch-or-slash shoulder bags.
✓ Avoid deserted streets and gangs of kids.

They were gypsies, Johnny had told me later, when he made me sit down in a café and drink a glass of Pellegrino. Maybe Romanian. Rome was flooded with immigrants, he said. They came from the poorest countries, from Russia and all over eastern Europe, from Africa, from southern Italy.

O fa-may, he said, meant "I'm hungry." *Ho fame*, it's spelled.

Despite his real concern for me, I could tell Johnny was molto worried about what would happen if his employer, Prince Marcello Brunelli, found out. "Jesus, if you'd been hurt—"

"I wasn't," I said, "and it won't happen again."

"When you're with me," Johnny said, gripping my shoulders, "you *stay* with me. Understand? Why did you run away like that?"

"I thought maybe you wanted to be alone with your girlfriend."

"My girlfriend?"

"At the café."

"Flavinia's someone I know from the party," he said. "She's a politician."

"Yeah, and she was really trying hard to get your vote." It slipped out. I cursed myself.

"So are you going to tell him about this?" Johnny asked nervously.

I was still quivering. Taking deep Buddha breaths to calm down. I shivered in the sticky Roman heat, dusted off my low-risers, adjusted my top.

"If you tell him," Johnny warned, "I can guarantee that you'll never sit on that Vespa again."

So I didn't tell him. Marcello, I mean. I longed to, more for the sake of the story than to gain any sympathy, but during dinner I kept my mouth shut on the subject of gypsies.

"Did you have a pleasant day?" Marcello politely asked.

"Yeah. It was great."

"You were with Giovanni?"

"He took me to the Colosseum. And some other places."

"What are your impressions of Roma?"

"It's amazing," I said. "You could spend years just walking around and looking at things."

"Ah!" He smiled. "You like it?"

"I love it." Because that was the terrible truth of it all. In one afternoon, even despite the attack of the gypsy kids, I had fallen madly in love with this hot, ancient, mysterious city with four thousand years of history scattered in fragments around its streets. Portland, which had just celebrated its 150th anniversary, seemed like such a baby in comparison.

"It's like every building, every stone, has a story."

"Yes," he said, "that is true."

"Maybe we could go out for a stroll after dinner?" I hinted.

We fell silent as Teresina removed our plates. I'd slurped down every last noodle, but Marcello had hardly touched his pasta.

Teresina was as formal as a waiter around him. She lifted the wine bottle over his glass. "Signore?"

He waved her away but kept his sleepy eyes on me. "One glass only," he sighed. "Doctor's orders." He yawned. "Ah, forgive me. I was in meetings all day. Back to back until seven o'clock. And more tomorrow."

"Tomorrow too?" I knew what that meant.

"Maybe we can avert a strike," he said. Then he shrugged and shook his head. "Maybe not." He lit a cigarette, the fourth he'd had in about an hour. "Whoever heard of a strike in August? August, for God's sake! No Italian in his right mind works during the hottest month. Only me!"

The meetings he attended were all labor negotiations to avert a strike at a giant food-processing plant he owned in Turin, or Torino, as he called it. The plant made and packaged tomato products— tomato paste, tomato sauce, stewed tomatoes, diced tomatoes. They were going to strike unless they got higher wages and more days off.

"I'm all for that," I said.

"You're siding with the workers?" he said with an incredulous laugh. "Like Giovanni?"

"Yes, if what they want is fair."

"What is fair? Fair is that I am paying their wages and giving them holidays and pensions and health care. No," he said, getting excited, "they want to bleed me dry. They have no conception of what it takes to run a business. If they didn't have these damned Communists running their unions, maybe we could all get somewhere!"

His cell phone played a tune. He looked at the display and scowled. "And still they call me! I am to have no life!"

He rose from the table and had a short, angry conversation with his caller. "Allora," he said, sitting again, shaking his head, "no more work tonight. No more politics."

"Turn off your phone," I suggested.

"No," he said, "not until Mama calls." He drank the last of his wine and called Teresina to pour him another glass.

"Did you enjoy being with Giovanni?" he asked, lighting another cigarette.

I couldn't tell if this was jealousy speaking or not. "Yes, why?"

"So it wouldn't upset you if you had to spend more time with him?"

"No, why?"

"I may have to go to Milano. And Stockholm."

I looked down at my plate, like a disappointed little girl figuring out her next move. What was the point, really, of my being here if Marcello was constantly away?

"Please understand," he said, taking my hand and rubbing it against his bristly cheek. "I didn't know any of this would happen. When it's over, we'll go down to the villa in Capri. So you can meet Mama."

"Speaking of mamas," I said, and told him that my own was coming to visit. And the dads. I thought he might be annoyed, but instead he looked delighted.

"Family is everything!" he exclaimed. "Tell me, did you enjoy meeting Giovanna?"

"I don't think Giovanna likes me very much," I said.

"Why do you say that?" he asked.

"She acted . . . very condescending."

He smiled. "Yes, she can be a very haughty girl. She's more like her mother every day."

That, I knew, was the chief occupational hazard of being a girl. Girls turned into their mothers. And that was why I always prayed to whatever deities ruled the universe that I would never turn into a version of *my* mother, Carolee. It was my worst nightmare.

"I'll talk to Giovanna," Marcello said. "There's no reason why the two of you shouldn't be friends."

"To be honest, I think she might be jealous of me."

"Jealous? Why?"

"Because she thinks I'm stealing her father away from her."

Marcello's eyes gleamed in the candlelight. He grasped my hand. "You are," he said softly.

I deflected his little attempt at romance. "She's probably pissed because you're having dinner with me instead of her."

"But I rarely dine with Giovanna. In the evening, she likes to stay with the nuns."

Which was how I learned about the church and convent attached to the Brunelli palace. I'd seen the church earlier in the day. Now Marcello explained to me that the church and its nuns—the Order of Little Doves, they were called—was connected to Palazzo Brunelli by some ancient matrilineal patrimony. A far-distant female ancestor with a guilty conscience had built the church and founded the order in the fifteenth century, to make sure that prayers would constantly be offered up for her soul. Brunelli money kept the Order of Little Doves going. They were still praying for the founder's soul, and for the souls of all the other Brunellis who had endowed the order over the centuries.

Giovanna, Marcello told me, had spent much of her girlhood with the Little Doves. He didn't tell me why, but I wondered if it was because her mother, Marcello's wife, was crazy and couldn't take care of her. There was apparently some kind of access between Giovanna's wing, across the courtyard, and the convent house. Marcello said his daughter had her own room in the convent and often spent her evenings playing Monopoly with the Little Doves.

"Giovanna's a very religious girl," her father sighed. "More so as she grows older. I doubt that she will ever marry."

With a nose like that, I thought, *she's better off as a nun.*

We sat back as Teresina clicked into the dining room with another course. A cut of broiled meat with some crispy fried potatoes. Marcello tsked, annoyed. "Teresina!"

"Signore?"

The food looked fine to me. But Marcello had words about it with Teresina. I felt sorry for her. Her face fell and she assumed the stance of a girl accepting a beating.

"What's the problem?" I asked.

"*Questi patate!* These potatoes are fried!" He continued to speak English as he turned back to Teresina. "Didn't Giovanna give you my new diet restrictions?"

"Signore," Teresina whispered, "*non capisco.*"

"Ah. *Va!*" He waved her away. "I deal with idiots all day long," he grumbled, "and come home to find another one!"

If I told him about the missing watch now, he'd add me to the list of idiots. So mum was the word for the moment.

"All I do is work for others," he complained. "And what do I get back? *Niente.* I get *nothing* for myself."

"Then why do you do it?" I asked.

"Why?" His eyebrows shot up. "Because—" He thought for a moment, then stuck out his lower lip. "I can't tell you. I used to know why."

"Why?"

"For the power," he said. "For the pleasure of the fight. And the rewards of the win."

"And you don't feel that anymore?"

"Si si. Yes, of course, I still feel it. But it takes an enormous toll. To always be in charge, to always make things happen, to always smooth over the problems, to always make the shareholders happy . . ." He gave me a weary smile. "When you're young, you simply do these things. You think you have unlimited time. Unlimited energy."

"Listen," I said, slicing into my meat, "if you really want to be a slacker, you have to start by canceling some of those meetings."

"And if I did," he said, "would you spend all your time with me?"

I chewed and avoided his eyes.

"How is it that you can understand me so well?" he whispered.

I chewed.

"You know what my needs are." He brushed a finger along my masticating jaw. "They haven't changed from the first time I saw you."

I looked down at my plate.

"Are you worried that I will not be able to satisfy you?" he asked.

I looked at him. A giant yawn caught me off guard. He followed with a yawn of his own. We laughed.

"What a romantic pair we are," Marcello said. "We can't wait to get into bed—to go to sleep!"

* * *

After we'd finished our meal, Marcello said something to Teresina and rose from the table. Teresina disappeared like a well-trained ghost.

Marcello pulled back my chair. "Will you take a brandy?"

"No, thanks. I don't drink anymore." And why? Because if something was there, a few cells attached to my uterus and multiplying daily, I didn't want them to be screwed up with booze.

We slowly strolled, arm in arm, from the dining room into the salone. It was after eleven. The vast, silent rooms were feebly lit by strange little table lamps with rosy fabric shades. Shadows lapped at the dim pools of light, gathering in the corners, in doorways.

"Do you like Palazzo Brunelli?" Marcello asked. And went on, before I could answer, "This house has been in my family for nearly five hundred years. I love it and I hate it."

"I can see why you'd love it," I said, "but not why you'd hate it."

"Because of what it requires."

"The maintenance, you mean?"

"No. The *expectations*. In every room. Memories of all that's happened over five centuries, and expectations that this family, this Brunelli line, must always continue to live here."

Maybe he was worried about the future. I thought of Giovanna. Marcello wasn't likely to see any heirs dropping from her womb any time soon.

"Privilege can be a terrible burden," Marcello said.

That made me laugh. "Yeah. Tell it to the judge."

In a room off the salone, he opened a set of doors and stepped out onto a balcony. Palazzo Brunelli had all kinds of secretive little balconies protruding like stone warts from three sides of the building. This balcony had very high walls—so high and thick that I couldn't see out except by peering through the narrow slits punctuating the wall at eye level.

Looking down, I saw that the balcony overlooked a corner of Piazza Farnese. Sounds of nighttime Rome drifted up from the square. And when I heard them, I wanted to be down there, amid the noise and the people.

Marcello's cell phone played its irritating tune. "Ah, excuse me," he said, fishing it out of his pocket. He looked at the display and smiled. "Ciao, Mama!" he answered.

They must have talked for half an hour. Or, rather, she talked. Marcello, the powerful business executive, was reduced to saying "Si, Mama" about every ten seconds. I continued to peer down into Piazza Farnese but turned around when I heard him say my name, "*Vay*-noose *Gill*-roy."

What was he telling her?

What was she thinking?

It sounded like he was explaining something. Me? Then I heard him say Giovanna's name. The mother-son exchange grew more agitated. But then he laughed. Sounded playful, almost like a husband. Finally he said, "*Buona notte*, Mama" and returned the phone to his jacket pocket.

He beamed, like a little kid who's been kissed good night and knows he's loved. "The principessa wants to meet you," he said.

"The what?"

"The *principessa*. My mother."

He didn't want to go out for a stroll. It was getting close to midnight and he wanted to go to bed.

That meant I'd have to go to bed, too.

A good idea, I supposed, but somehow I'd passed through the comatose agony of jet lag and was now wide awake.

We were walking through the salone when Marcello suddenly pulled me into his arms. The intensity of his grasp startled me, but I didn't resist. He took my face in his hands, looked at me like he was about to die, and plunged down to cover me with hot, smoky little kisses.

"Ah, Venus, Venus," he murmured. "My darling."

I tried really hard not to laugh as we fell back onto a sofa.

There is nothing worse than when a guy wants to make out with you and you sort of go along but are not totally into it.

There was absolutely nothing offensive about him. I dutifully ran my fingers through his thick hair. I stroked the back of his warm neck. I felt the hot chafe of his whiskers against my cheek. I sucked his eager, wine-and-cigarette-soaked tongue into my mouth and let him run his hands up my thighs and over my butt and into my blouse.

And all the while, I was thinking of Johnny. Of what fun it would be to ride around the streets of Rome at night on the back of his Vespa.

And of Tremaynne, out in the Idaho wilderness, fighting to save old-growth trees owned by this man I was making out with.

And my thoughts drifted back even further, to my first husband, Sean Kowalski, and my second husband, Peter Pringle, and to JD.

All those crazy hopes, all those inexperienced passions, all those pains and pleasures and couplings that I believed, or wanted to believe, would last forever and end happily ever after.

Marcello was getting hotter and hotter, but I wasn't. His hands were more insistent, stroking my breasts and trying unsuccessfully to get them free of the sexy but complicated bra that Carolee had bought me. He moaned with joy when I let him stroke my inner thighs.

Get with the program! I chided myself.

There was no reason not to.

But I couldn't.

And so that was the end of it.

Marcello looked at me, incredulous. "No?"

"No," I said. "Not tonight."

"Then when?" he asked.

"I don't know. When it feels right. It just doesn't feel right."

He brushed his fingers across my waist. "That does not feel right?" Then across my breasts. "That does not feel right?" Then took my hand and placed it over his raging hard-on. "It feels right to me," he whispered.

I removed my hand. Gently but firmly pushed him away. "I *want* to," I said, "but I just don't feel . . . *into* it yet. Can you understand that?"

"I only want you, darling, when you want me."

I could tell his masculine pride had been bruised. He'd tried, he'd used all his powers of persuasion, and he'd lost. For the simple reason that *I didn't feel like it*.

He straightened his clothing and I straightened mine.

"I will leave you now," he said with a touch of frosty formality.

"Where do you sleep?" I asked.

"I have my own suite of rooms."

I walked him to the door that led into my wing.

"Would you like to let me out?" he said.

A code was needed to get out and to come in. But I couldn't remember the password. It was written down and stashed in my purse. "You know the code, don't you?"

He pulled out his small GPS device and scrolled through some numbers. Punched them into the keypad. The lock responded with its faint, precise click.

Suddenly I felt kind of mean. Ungrateful. But then I thought, you don't fuck someone because you feel *grateful*. That's, like, the worst reason. With this relationship, I told myself, I'd do what I hadn't done with any of the others. I'd actually give it time to develop. I wouldn't force it because I was needy. I'd be more grown-up about it. More clearheaded. And clearhearted.

"*Buona notte,*" I said, trying to accent the words properly.

He gave me a faint but unmistakably tender smile. "*Buona notte,* darling."

Chapter

11

Marcello was gone for a week, and I wasn't about to sit around and wait for his return. And so began my introductory lessons on Rome.

Roma 101.

Johnny was my private tutor. My classroom was the back of his Vespa.

I kept my eyes and ears open. I watched and listened.

But the trouble with a place like Rome is that the more you learn, the more you realize how much you don't know.

And boy, was I ignorant. *Way* ignorant, as they say in Portland, Oregon.

"Can you read what it says up on that portico?" Johnny asked me.

It was broiling hot and we were sitting in a piazza beneath an umbrella at a café. A pretty fountain with an Egyptian obelisk sat in the center of the piazza, and this huge, amazing building called the Pantheon occupied the far end of it.

"What language is it?" I asked, peering up at the letters.

"Latin."

I pieced out the letters and words, reading them like an eye chart: M. AGRIPPA. L. F. COS.TERIUM. FECIT. "What's it mean?"

"Marcus Agrippa, son of Lucius, Consul for the third time, built this."

It amazed me: I was sitting in Rome at a café with a cute guy who knew a dead language! The only Latin I knew was Pig. Whitman had taught me years ago, after I questioned him about an old movie we were watching. In it, Ginger Rogers and Fred Astaire ing-say an ong-say in Ig-pay Atin-lay.

"When did Marcus Agrippa, son of what's-his-name, consul for the third time, build it?" I asked.

So my private tutor told me: Marcus Vipsanius Agrippa, son-in-law and counselor of the Emperor Augustus, had the temple built between 25 and 27 A.D. The temple was supposed to honor all the gods, so it became known as the Pantheon, after a Greek word meaning "of all the Gods."

Those ancient Romans and their weird gods never ceased to amaze me. They had hundreds of gods. There was a god for every occasion. Every household had its own protective spirits. The hot, muggy Roman air must have been saturated with supernatural deities flying around and meddling in everybody's business.

"But the Pantheon we're looking at right now," Johnny said, "isn't Agrippa's original temple."

"It's not?"

"No. That burned down in 80 A.D."

"So what are we looking at?"

"A reconstruction undertaken by the emperor Hadrian. It was dedicated in 125 A.D."

I did some quick figuring. I was always doing this in Rome. My brain was like a calculator. The building was 1,875 years old.

"Jeez," was all I could say.

"It's the most perfectly preserved building from all of antiquity," Johnny said. He hailed the waiter and paid the check. "Want to go in?"

I nodded eagerly. I'd never been inside an ancient temple before. I couldn't wait to see what it looked like.

As we crossed the crowded piazza, heading toward the Pantheon, this weird sensation swept over me. It's hard to describe. It was a realization that people had been walking in this same spot, toward this same temple, for nearly two thousand years. They dressed differently, they talked differently, they smelled different, but they were all human beings, and if I met one that day, I'd somehow be able to communicate with them.

Generation after generation, they had come here. The old ones died and the young ones took their place. They marched forward through time, continuing on through wars, plagues, famines, and one murderous regime after the next. For a thousand years they were part of the most powerful empire in the world, centered right here in Rome. And then Rome's power vanished. In a couple hundred years, it had gone from being the capital of the world to a malaria-infested backwater. But still this building stood, and people came to it, carrying yearning hopes and blasted hearts and ruined fortunes and personal joys and catastrophes of all kinds.

A world where people walked to temples to talk to their *gods*. That's what really fascinated me. They had this belief that invisible spirits ruled their lives and personal destinies. I wondered if they had continued to believe in their gods as Rome fell apart.

Daddy loved the Pantheon. He said it was the noblest building in Rome, and he had an old engraving of it in his office. I'd never paid much attention when he talked about the Pantheon because I never thought that one day I'd be in Rome myself, standing in front of it, feeling its awesome power.

"That part up there," Johnny said, pointing up to a recessed triangular area above the inscription, "is called the tympanum."

"Tympanum," I repeated.

"Yeah. Originally, it was decorated with gilt bronze reliefs. And the roof was all bronze as well."

From the outside, the Pantheon looked like a giant drum made out of bricks with an attached front porch. The porch was held up by sixteen enormous columns of Egyptian granite arranged in two rows of eight columns each. I felt a kind of light-headed thrill as I looked up at them. I went over and ran my fingertips along the ancient, pitted stone, feeling weirdly superstitious.

"Is this temple something Cleopatra would have seen?" I asked.

"Cleopatra?" Now he did some figuring. "No, she wouldn't have seen the Pantheon. She came to Rome about a hundred and fifty years before it was built."

"Julius Caesar brought her here, right?" I wanted to impress him with my own vast knowledge of ancient history.

"Have you studied Cleopatra?" Johnny asked.

"No, but I saw the video." It was really long, in two parts. My mom had pointed out Elizabeth Taylor's tracheotomy scar and filled me in on the ancient gossip surrounding Elizabeth Taylor and Richard Burton.

"Cleopatra was the queen of Egypt," Johnny said. "Caesar brought her here as a kind of trophy. He was much older than she was."

I shifted uneasily under his gaze. "Cleopatra never married Caesar, though, right?"

"Caesar was already married. She was more like a symbolic concubine."

"Symbolic how?"

"She was Egypt. She was a conquered country. Rome needed Egypt for her wheat. And what Rome wanted, it took."

"You mean Cleopatra didn't have a choice."

"She didn't come to Julius Caesar because she *loved* him," Johnny said with a laugh. "She came because Caesar was the most powerful man in the world. If she didn't come, he could have killed her or made her his slave. Caesar and Cleopatra were playing out the power politics of their time."

"So she didn't see the Pantheon."

"No, but she would have seen other temples, over in the Forum." He pointed. "Look. Those are the original doors. They're made of bronze and weigh twenty tons."

I looked up at them, awestruck.

We followed the stream of tourists toward the massive portals and stepped into the cool shadows of the temple.

According to my tutor, the interior of the Pantheon was unique among the monuments of Rome because it survived, perfectly preserved, in its original form. So I was seeing the same building those ancient Romans had seen when they entered wearing robes or togas almost two thousand years before.

"It has perfect proportions," Johnny said.

I felt his eyes on me as I turned to gaze up at the amazing dome.

"The rotunda where we're standing has exactly the same diameter as the cupola above," Johnny explained. "Together, they exactly equal the building's greatest height."

Some ancient geometrical memory, some mitochondria I'd inherited from Daddy's architectural DNA or a remembered fragment from a geometry class, fired a synapse in my brain. "So a perfect sphere would fit inside the interior?"

Johnny looked at me with surprise. "Right."

"What's that called?" I pointed up at the open hole in the center of the roof.

"The oculus. The eye."

The building was open to the sky, where all the gods lived. On sunny days, a disk of sunlight tracked around the sides of the dome. On rainy days, the rain came in and the marble floor got wet. You were always inside and outside at the same time.

In the seventh century, Johnny told me, the pagan temple had been transformed into a Christian church.

But it still felt pagan to me. Where did that feeling come from? I, who'd never been raised with any kind of religion and knew next to niente about history, suddenly found myself wondering about paganism and Christianity. How far back did they go? Where did they come from?

I didn't want to leave. I stood there looking up and around, pleasurably caught in that perfect, harmonious space.

I thought of the spaces that were part of my daily life in Portland. Phantastic Phantasy, with its tinted windows and porno booths. Fast-food counters and giant food stores, their shadows scrubbed away by the blast of fluorescent lights. My cramped studio apartment. My geriatric Toyota.

Rome was altering my whole sense of time and space. Things that were considered "old" in Portland—like a house from the 1890s—were practically brand-new in the time frame of this ancient metropolis.

Even the people in Portland looked new. I could see a similar newness in the faces of the American tourists crowding around us. I probably looked that way myself. Kind of naive. Gullible, even.

It was a different story with the Romans. Their faces were *old*. I don't mean they all looked old, but they had what Carolee might call "old spirits." Like they'd been around for a long, long time. They'd been jumping into the same gene pool for a hundred generations and coming up with the same set of variations.

Even Johnny. He was only a year or two older than me. He was young and wiry and cute and cool. Yet there was this "oldness" in him. I couldn't quite put my finger on it.

All I knew was that I found it horribly sexy.

He seemed to like me, but I couldn't tell if it was personal or professional. Was he responding to something in me or was he putting on a show because his boss, Prince Brunelli, had told him to be nice to me?

Physically, as we sped around Rome on his Vespa, we were incredibly intimate. Sharing that leather saddle seat, turning together into the curves, we quickly got to know the exact fit and contour of each other's body.

Yet there was definitely a barrier between us.

It came from the fact that Johnny was not a free agent. We hadn't met on our own, we'd met because Marcello had arranged it. There was this weird employee–employer thing. There were lines that weren't supposed to be crossed.

For instance, I knew that he must know every last detail about the Brunelli family. Johnny was *molto* observant. He could probably tell me everything I wanted to know about Giovanna, and about Marcello's crazy wife, and even about Marcello himself. But it would put him in a weird position if I asked about the private lives of his employers. And it would make me sound like I was a snooping gold digger.

But how else could I find out about the Brunellis? My chauffeur and guide was potentially my best source of information.

Though I didn't like to admit it to myself, in some ways I already felt closer to Johnny than I did to Marcello. I suppose it was because, socially, I could identify more easily with a chauffeur than with a prince. With Johnny, I didn't have to worry about social blunders and bewildering laws of foreign etiquette. I could be myself. And he was closer to my own age.

But I couldn't really figure him out. He seemed way too smart to be a chauffeur. Chauffeurs didn't know Latin. It was like he knew everything. Even his English was better than mine.

Marcello, no matter how casual he tried to sound, always spoke with a kind of polite formality. Giovanna had obviously gone to school in England, because she spoke with a strange, nasal English accent. Fabio and Teresina struggled with every word, and I didn't know if they understood what I said. But with Johnny there was no language barrier. None.

"Where'd you learn to speak English so well?" I asked him as we walked down a narrow, pedestrian-only street from the Pantheon.

"I went to school in America," he said.

"Where?"

"A couple different places."

"Like what?"

"Just some schools," he said.

"Where?" I asked.

"On the East Coast."

"Were you an exchange student?"

"Not really."

OK, it was turning into Twenty Questions, and obviously he didn't want to answer any of them.

"Do you like being a chauffeur?" I asked. Totally inane, but I wanted to keep the conversation moving.

The question seemed to stun him. He stopped in his tracks. Then he smiled at me and said, "I like being *your* chauffeur."

Words I wanted to hear, words my heart licked up like whipped cream on top of a hot-fudge sundae, but words I could not let myself absorb, even though a warm current of desire was lapping at my extremities.

"Where are we going now?" I asked.

"You'll see."

* * *

What I saw was Piazza Navona.

The most beautiful piazza in the world.

I sucked in a startled breath as we entered the gigantic elliptical space.

"See how it's curved?" Johnny said. "In ancient Rome this was a stadium for horse racing."

I heard the murmur of voices, the splash of water. There were three fountains, two small ones on the ends and a giant one in the center. The interlocking facades of the buildings around the piazza were painted in shades of ochre, terra-cotta, yellow, and red. A big gray stone church rose up on the far side. Restaurants ringed the perimeter. In the center, artists had set up easels and were doing quick sketches of tourists.

Johnny walked me over to the giant fountain in the center. "The Four Rivers Fountain by Bernini," he announced. "One of the most important baroque monuments in Rome."

Four giant dudes in weirdly dramatic poses sat at each of the four corners of the fountain. Their butts rested on a rocky ledge, but their legs were thrust over the side and their huge feet splayed out in midair. They looked like parachutists about to leap from a plane. Above them, giant stone palm trees waved in an invisible wind. The whole concoction was topped by an obelisk.

I turned to Johnny. "Who are they?"

"They're allegories," he said.

I racked my brain. What was an allegory? Hadn't I heard something about allegories in my lit classes? Or was it a musical term?

"They represent the largest and most famous rivers of the time. Look." Johnny led me around the fountain. "He's the Danube, he's the Ganges, he's the Rio de Plata, and he's the Nile."

"Why is the Nile's face covered with a cloth?"

"Because its source was unknown."

Was that the meaning of "allegory"? I nodded knowingly and sat on the edge of the fountain, dabbling my hand in the cool water. The giant men hovered above me, their legs kicked out like they were about to jump off their perches and into the basin below. "What's that church over there?" I asked.

"Sant'Agnese in Agone," Johnny said. "Saint Agnes in Agony."

"What did she do?"

Johnny shrugged. "She was a saint."

"Why was she in agony?" Maybe her shoes were killing her, the way mine were killing me.

"She was martyred."

"You mean someone killed her?"

"The Romans. At the time of Domitian. Early fourth century A.D. When all the Christians were being persecuted."

I didn't want to know but had to ask. "What did they do to her?"

So my private tutor told me the story of Agnes. She was a Christian girl at a time when it was definitely not cool to be a Jesus freak. When Agnes was thirteen, she was ordered to sacrifice to pagan gods and lose her virginity by rape. No way, she said. So the Romans took her to the brothel that had once stood on the site of her church in Piazza Navona. First the assholes threatened her; then, when she refused to renounce God, they stripped her in front of a jeering crowd. Several young guys came up and offered to marry her, but Agnes told them to fuck off because losing her virginity would be an insult to her heavenly husband. And then a miracle occurred. It was like some heavenly overdose of Rogaine kicked in and all this hair grew out of her head and spilled down her body and completely covered her nakedness. That pissed off the Romans even more, so they tortured and killed her. Johnny wasn't sure if they had beheaded and burned her, or stabbed her to death, or slit her throat. Anyway, that's how she had become a saint.

"But what do these saints do?" I asked.

"The Catholics believe they intercede for people."

It sounded very complicated and bureaucratic. You sent a prayer, like a mental e-mail, to the saint, begging for help. The saint forwarded your request to God, and if God decided to help you, the saint was like the intermediary. There were certain saints you prayed to for certain things.

"If you were praying to Agnes," I said, "what would you pray for?"

Johnny thought about it. "I'm not sure. She symbolizes purity, and chastity"—he fixed me with his dark eyes—"and couples who want to make love . . . but don't."

I looked into his eyes and made a note to send up a prayer to Saint Agnes as soon as possible.

Chapter
12

As I pulled the card from its heavy vellum envelope, I saw her name embossed at the top in a kind of old-fashioned script. The handwriting below was very precise, like her father's, each letter carefully formed.

"Dear Miss Gilroy," I read. "I offer you tea in my chambers this afternoon at five o'clock. Giovanna Brunelli."

Tea? In her *chambers?*

I wondered if Marcello was behind this invitation. I couldn't believe that Giovanna would invite me to tea of her own accord.

Something in me rebelled, the way you rebel when you don't want to go somewhere or meet someone but can't get out of it. But then I thought, *be cool. Put yourself in Giovanna's place. How would you feel if you were ugly as sin, your mom was dead, and your dad suddenly showed up with a stud muffin younger than you were?*

The scenario wasn't too different from what I'd gone through myself, as a five-year-old, when Daddy ditched Mom and hitched up with Whitman. Back then, I'd hated Whitman with the kind of impotent fury only a child can know. I had wanted him to vanish, to disappear, so that the fairy-tale life of Daddy, Mommy, and me could continue. It never had, and for years I felt a kind of sullen resentment toward Whitman. So I could just imagine what Giovanna must be going through. I threatened the stability of her entire world.

Maybe if I was nice to her, Giovanna would stop seeing me as a threat. Was it too much for me to make the effort? I was a guest in her family's palace, after all.

Dressing for this occasion required some consideration. What did Romans wear for tea? I didn't have a clue. I remembered Whitman's words of fashion advice: *A simple black dress with appropriate accessories works for every occasion.*

"Ah, signorina, *molta bella*," Teresina said appreciatively when I emerged from the dressing room wearing my strapless black leather mini.

"Now if I just had that watch, it would be perfect." I studied Teresina's face for signs of guilt, but she just nodded and said "si" in a soft voice.

I was going to ask Teresina to lead me back to Giovanna's "chambers," then thought better of it. I didn't want her to think I was like a little girl who couldn't find her way around a big house.

On the other hand, I wasn't exactly sure of the way.

I set off with a confident stride, my black stilettos clicking sharp and precise on the marble floors. To the servants and staff working in other parts of the palace I smiled and said "*Buona sera*" (the official greeting after four o'clock, according to Johnny).

Quite a few people worked in Palazzo Brunelli during the day. The living quarters were on the third floor, but there were offices below. Old women stared at me as they scrubbed marble and polished giant pieces of wooden furniture and dusted objects on shelves, tables, and in glass-fronted display cabinets. Women wearing dark, demure dresses and carrying file folders, stacks of documents, sometimes briefcases, nodded politely as they hurried by. In one room, guys in blue lab coats were doing some sort of restoration work. A long, wide corridor on the second floor was lined with vast, dimly lit offices. I could hear deep male voices talking on telephones. Men sitting at desks looked up, curious, as I passed by.

So far, so good. I made it down the first stairway and through the maze on the floor below. Now I had to find the stairway that led back up to Giovanna's wing.

I clicked briskly down corridors that became darker and darker and had fewer and fewer people. I felt like I was penetrating into an even older part of the Brunelli palace. Was that the right turn? Had I gone down there before, and through that stone archway? That hawk-nosed Brunelli giving me a dark, hooded stare as I passed his portrait, had I seen him before?

Then I saw a portrait that I did remember: a woman clad in black robes, a tight white collar choking her neck, head covered like a nun, clasping a crucifix and staring up to heaven with eyes that looked like slippery black olives. She looked like she was having a crisis and pleading for someone to help her.

I found the staircase I needed and started up the gray stone steps. The stairs, wide and much lower than American stairs, curved up and around to another corridor lined with closed doors.

The camera was still rotating at the end of the empty hallway.

I wondered if Giovanna was watching my approach on one of her monitors.

I pressed what looked like a doorbell. Teresina, I remembered, had used some kind of password first, but I didn't know what it was. I waited about two minutes, then pressed again. Finally the door was opened and the same tiny, gray-robed nun—Sister Angelica, Teresina had called her—peered out at me.

Her gray eyes, magnified behind strong glasses, slowly looked me up and down, studying me as if I were a statue. Her face was completely impassive, neither welcoming nor hostile.

"I'm here to see Giovanna," I said.

The nun cocked her head to the side. Her eyes flicked to the rose tattoo above my left breast. "Eh?"

"Giovanna?" I pointed toward the inner room. "We're supposed to have tea."

"*Cosa?*"

"Tea," I repeated. "In her chambers."

The nun held up a finger, indicating that I should wait, and closed the door in my face. When she returned, she stepped into the corridor and pointed down the hallway. "*La* Signorina Giovanna. *La prossima porta.*"

I shook my head. "I don't understand."

Sister Angelica sighed. "*Venga*." She pulled the door shut and motioned for me to follow her.

I studied her habit as we started down the corridor. She was covered from head to toe with gray woolen robes that looked hot, heavy, and uncomfortable. On her head, held in place by a long gray veil, she wore a starched white hat with stiff side wings that flapped slightly when she walked.

I'd seen other nuns, always wearing black floor-to-ceiling robes, while speeding around Rome with Johnny. They were like a different species of woman, and they fascinated me. I had visions of them being like Mother Teresa, nursing the sick and poor in the teeming slums. But Johnny said half the nuns in Rome were there on vacation, and the other half worked for the Vatican. "Doing what?" I asked. "Making money," he answered.

Sister Angelica's walk was a kind of determined, headlong rush, as if she were pushing her way through a crowd of invisible demons and didn't dare look right or left. How weird, I thought, to always have those sharp white pointed wings at the sides of your head. And never to show off your body. The only skin she showed was her tiny white hands and white moonlike face.

What did she dream about, I wondered. Maybe she didn't dream at all.

And the idea of erasing your emotional life . . . I just didn't see the point.

JD's lesbian harem had once included an ex-nun. She told me that at a certain time every Friday night, in their darkened rooms, the nuns in her order were supposed to remove their robes and whip themselves on the back, chest, and legs with a little leather whip. She said it was supposed to be painful, but it had always made her giggle.

My heels provided a sharp staccato accompaniment to Sister Angelica's rhythmically clacking beads as we hurried down the corridor. I couldn't see or hear Sister Angelica's shoes. Maybe she was jet-propelled. But shoes of the kind I was wearing are not meant for power walks. I felt like I was in training for the Olympic high heel event.

At the end of the cheerless corridor, Sister Angelica tapped in a password and pushed open a massive door. We entered a large foyer. "*Aspetta qui,*" the nun said. "You wait. She come." With that, she disappeared.

I cleared my throat and looked around the dark, windowless room. There was nothing to sit on. The adjoining room, a grand salone, looked more appealing. I took one careful step into it, afraid I might trigger some kind of security alarm.

Rude, really, not to offer me a chair in the salone. But nuns obviously had other things on their minds than comfort. There was no way that tiny, sexless Sister Angelica in her gray robes could know that my new and very hot high heels were killing me.

As I stood there, at the edge of the salone, waiting for my hostess, I studied Giovanna's "chambers." The rooms were smaller than mine, and looked out across a skinny courtyard to the church that was attached to Palazzo Brunelli. The height of the church and shutters on the small windows blocked out the light. A cheerless gray twilight pervaded the heavily beamed rooms. At the end of the salone, however, there was a glass wall with a balcony garden behind it. The small, luxuriant garden was obviously the same one I'd seen from Giovanna's office.

I tried to suppress my irritation as the minutes ticked past, each second measured by a gold clock sitting on a high stone mantlepiece. Was this Giovanna's catty way of showing me who was boss in Palazzo Brunelli?

The clock struck five-thirty. A bell-like ping was followed by five quiet chimes. Something moved in the clock; a little figure came out of a door, did something I couldn't see, and slid back in again.

Finally I decided I'd go wait in the garden, where I spied a stone bench. If Giovanna didn't arrive in another five minutes, I was out of there.

That weird sense of being watched—*monitored*—as I click-clicked through the salone made me walk very erect. Let no one see that Venus Gilroy, alone in Rome, was unsure of herself in any situation.

I opened the glass door to the garden and waded into a pool of sultry Roman air. Took a deep Buddha breath and felt momentarily released from the dark, enigmatic formalities of Palazzo Brunelli.

Plants and flowers covered every square inch of the balcony, spilling out from terra-cotta pots and old stone planters. Leafy tendrils crept along the narrow walkway. The massed foliage throbbed with a dense green glow.

Then I began to notice details. Sharp, pointed leaves with spines at the tips. Immense cacti covered with hypodermically long needles. Strangely colored plants with odd-looking and not very pretty flowers.

A faint, fishy, feminine odor, almost like menstrual blood, hung in the humid air. It was tempered by a sweet, drowsy smell that drifted over from a far corner.

Instinctively, like a bee on the trail of honey, I headed toward the sweet smell. It seemed to be coming from a plant in a giant stone tub. The plant had glittery leaves of red and gray and weird, waxy magenta flowers that hung open like screaming mouths. Sticking out of each mouth was a long yellow tongue, curled up at the end. I'd never seen anything like it, but then I was a total dodo when it came to plants.

The plant gave off a sweetly hypnotic exhalation that drew me to it like perfume. I was reaching out for the nearest branch, to draw it closer and take a really deep sniff, when a voice said, "Do not touch that!"

I froze, midreach, and looked over to see Giovanna, wearing a long red gown, standing in the doorway.

"It is very poisonous," she said.

"Oh." I straightened up and looked at those ominous screaming mouths. "It smells so sweet."

"Yes," Giovanna said. "It's a very clever plant." She took a tentative step toward me, looking concerned and irritated at the same time. "I hope you did not touch it."

I shook my head.

"You must be careful out here," she said. "Especially with so much skin exposed. Some of these barks and leaves are not kind to human flesh."

"Why do you grow them?" I asked.

She flashed me her dead smile. "This garden is one of the oldest secrets in Rome," she said, lifting the hem of her long red dress and carefully stepping outside. "It's a *medica natura*—a kind of ancient botanical drug store." As she walked along the garden path, I saw, for the first time, that she limped. "There are plants here that have died out in their native lands," she said. "Rare species that have been destroyed because people didn't understand them. Or were afraid of them."

"So you collect rare plants."

"I take care of them," Giovanna said. "They are in my charge." Like a wary, watchful bird, she drew herself up and stood very erect as I approached her. Her breathing was shallow, tense, maybe excited. Her chest pumped like a bellows as she sucked in air through her great beak of nose.

"It's like having your own private jungle," I said.

"This garden was started five hundred years ago by my ancestor, Fabiana Gelsomina. She was an herbalist. She studied plants. She knew the special properties of each one." Her eyes darted up and down, taking in my shoes, my black hose, my leather mini, my tattoo, my hair. "Do you have an interest in plants, Miss Gilroy?"

"Not really," I said. "My dads do, but I don't."

"Your dads?"

"My fathers."

"How many fathers do you have?" she asked.

"Just two. They're coming to Rome next week. So's my mother."

She lifted her chin, swallowing this piece of information. "I see."

"I've already talked to Marcello about it. My mom's going to be staying with me in my wing."

"Your wing?"

"Yeah. The one where your mother lived."

Giovanna abruptly turned away. "The air is very polluted today," she said. "It oppresses my sinuses. Shall we take tea inside?"

She led me back to her salone and gestured to an enormous chair. "*Prego.*"

The chair was upholstered with something hairy and uncomfortable, its proportions strangely inhospitable to normal human bodies. The only way I could sit on it with any poise was to perch on the end and remember to keep my knees clamped.

Giovanna stiffly seated herself on the adjacent sofa and watched as Sister Angelica bustled in with a tray. She pointed to the table in front of her. The nun set down the tray and left, her beads clicking.

I didn't get it. Was Sister Angelica her servant?

Silence, except for Giovanna's wheezing breath, as she leaned forward to pour the tea. The short walk had apparently been an exertion for her. I noticed that she kept one leg extended, as if it had a stiff joint. Her shoes were black, low-heeled, old-fashioned lace-ups, maybe orthopedic, definitely ugly, and totally inappropriate for her long red dress—or *gown*, I guess I had to call it. I had the feeling she was trying to look aristocratic, or important, like those Brunelli women in the portraits. Her jet black hair was done up in thick, complicated braids that sat like charred pastries on the top and sides of her head.

The silence and the sound of her breathing were awful. I racked my brain for inconsequential topics of conversation. "I'm looking forward to meeting your grandmother," I said politely.

Giovanna did not look at me or acknowledge my comment. "Do you take lemon or sugar?" she asked.

"Sugar, please."

"*Quanto?* How many?" She held a teacup in one hand and a small silver tongs, poised over a bowl of sugarcubes, in the other.

"What kind of tea is it?" The greenish yellow color didn't bode well for the taste buds.

She pressed her lips together and stared at the teacup in a way that made me think I'd offended her. "It's an herbal infusion," she said.

"Four, then."

"Four." Her eyebrow arched almost imperceptibly as she dropped the cubes into the cup and handed it to me. "There you are. I hope you can taste the tea."

It looked nasty, like something scooped out of a swamp. I waited until Giovanna had poured her own before taking a sip. A tiny sip. If I'd taken a larger one, I would have spit it out, maybe in her face. I'd never tasted anything so vile in my life.

I could tell she was studying my face for a reaction.

"Do you like it?" she asked.

"Delicious," I said, putting my cup down on the table.

"It's a very old recipe."

"Yeah," I said, "it tastes old."

"Restores one's balance," Giovanna said.

"I have pretty good balance already," I said.

"Yes, you must," she smiled, "or you would not be able to walk in shoes like that." As she reached forward to pick up a small plate of cookies, the bony wrist of her left hand, previously hidden from view in the wide red cuff of her long-sleeved gown, was suddenly exposed.

And on it, quietly glittering in the half light of the room, sat my watch.

I didn't know what to do.

What would you have done?

The watch slipped down over her wristbone and hung like a loose bracelet as she offered me the plate of cookies. "Biscotti? The Little Doves make them."

"No, thank you," I managed to say. My heart was hammering. "That's a beautiful watch."

She drew back the plate. Looked down at her wrist. Gave me a wan smile. "It belonged to my mother."

"It looks like one that I used to have," I said.

Her breathing was faster and louder. "It was my mother's," she said again, tucking the watch back inside her cuff. "Are you sure you won't have a biscotto?"

I just looked at her. What was I supposed to do? Did she mean for me to see the watch, or was it her pleasure to wear it secretly, knowing that I must be frantically trying to find it? I was almost positive it was the watch Marcello had given me. If it had belonged to Giovanna's mother, I could understand why she'd want to keep it for herself. But if Marcello gave it to me, it wasn't hers to appropriate. And how, I wondered, had Giovanna found out that I had the watch and how had she managed to steal it away?

Teresina. Who else could it be?

It gave me the creeps to think about it.

I didn't want to think about it.

I was so preoccupied with the watch, wondering what to do about it, that I hadn't heard Giovanna speak. "What?"

"I said, you seem to be spending a great deal of time with Giovanni."

"He's showing me Rome."

"Mm. And of course there's so *much* to see."

This bitch hates me, I thought.

"He's very stupid sometimes," Giovanna said.

"I think he's brilliant."

"Brilliant? Really?"

"He knows Latin," I said, realizing immediately how idiotic that must have sounded.

Giovanna let out a small disdainful laugh. "Does Giovanni speak Latin to you? Or some other Romance language?"

She was bristling with hostility. I could see it in her eyes, in the tense thrust of her chin. Maybe she'd had an affair with Giovanni herself. Or, for all I knew, she was having an affair with him now.

"He thinks he leads a charmed life," Giovanna went on. "Wants no responsibility. Enjoys danger."

"Danger?"

"It is dangerous, Miss Gilroy, to ride around Rome on a motorbike. Giovanni knows that."

"It's fun," I said.

"Your fun opens us up to exposure."

"Exposure?"

Her hand flew up and made a sharp slicing gesture, as if she couldn't bear my stupidity a moment longer. "No one has followed you?" she asked.

"No."

"Are you certain?"

I nodded.

"Ah, well, perhaps it was someone else in the photographs."

"What photographs?"

She rose, limped over to a tall wooden cabinet, and withdrew a manila envelope. She didn't hand it to me. She tossed it on my lap. "*Ecco.*"

I opened the envelope. A hot flush spread through my body. There I was in black and white on the back of Johnny's Vespa. The photographer had captured me leaning forward, with what looked like a sly half smile on my open lips. I appeared to be whispering sweet nothings in Johnny's ear. The other photos were variations of this shot.

"Where did you get these?"

"From the photographer, of course." Giovanna crossed her arms and looked at me, enjoying my discomfort.

"What photographer?"

She exhaled a disgusted sigh. "Does it matter? One of the vermin that lives outside. A paparazzo! I warned you about them."

Her voice was sharp and shaming. Cheeks burning, I glanced again at the photographs, shocked to see my image. A stranger looking at these photographs would think, *She's in love with that guy.*

"This wasn't taken outside the palazzo," I said. "We're on a street somewhere. We're moving."

Giovanna muttered under her breath. I didn't know what she said, but I could tell it was unpleasant. "Miss Gilroy, the paparazzi are like bloodhounds, do you understand? They trail us. They follow us. When they spot us, they call and alert one another."

"But why should they care about me?" I said. "I'm just a visitor."

Her features rose in an expression of astonished disbelief. "Just a visitor?"

I said nothing but held her disdainful gaze.

"A young woman invited to Palazzo Brunelli by Prince Brunelli himself? That is not being 'just a visitor,' Miss Gilroy. At least not in the dirty eyes of the press. And here she is—Prince Brunelli's girlfriend—with Giovanni, on the back of a motorbike." She scooped up the photos from my lap and looked at them with disgust. "Having what appears to be quite a very good time. *Fun*, as you call it."

"Yes," I said, "I was having fun."

"I'm sure that's what my father would think," she said, "if he were to see these."

"I don't care if he sees them." But some guilty part of me, I had to admit, did care.

"You don't care? Miss Gilroy, I won't tell you how much I paid for these photographs. All I will say is that my father would not be very pleased if he saw them. If he knew that Giovanni was taking you around Rome this way—unprotected . . ." She shook her head and sighed.

"I don't want Johnny to get into any trouble," I said.

Giovanna stood there, arms folded, holding the incriminating photographs and drilling me with her black eyes.

"Johnny's been great," I said, flustered by the hostility of her gaze.

"I'm sure. Giovanni does have a way with women."

The insulting tone of her remark infuriated me. "What is that supposed to mean?"

"You're not the first, Miss Gilroy, and you won't be the last."

"I don't know what you're implying—"

"I'm *implying* nothing," she said, looking down at the photographs with an amused smirk.

I'd been sabotaged. Or was about to be blackmailed. I didn't know what she was after or what to expect next. It even occurred to me that maybe, in some weird way, she was trying to protect me.

Everything depended on what she did with the photographs. If she showed them to Marcello, he might fire Johnny. And, of course, he'd see the photo, see that look on my face, see my hands clasped around Johnny's waist, and assume . . .

"Why don't you give me the photographs," I said, "and I'll take care of them."

She laughed. And with that laugh, I finally knew that I was dealing with a real pro. "Yes, I'm sure you would like to have them," she said. "So would every cheap magazine in Italy. That is why I had to pay so much money for them."

If I was going to bargain, I had to know what kind of value she placed on the images. "How much did you pay?"

"You Americans," she said. "Always so direct." She moved slowly around the giant salone, her gown rustling, and came to a halt beside the grand piano. "Five thousand euros," she said. "For the photographs and the negatives."

My calculator brain whirred into action. Five thousand euros was more than five thousand bucks. All for some photos of me on the back of a Vespa with Marcello Brunelli's chauffeur.

"That's a lot of money," I said.

She put her hand on the gleaming top of the piano, like a singer, and regarded me. "How much are you going to offer me, Miss Gilroy?"

And that was the straw that broke the camel's back. "I'm not offering you a penny," I said. "But I think it might be a good idea if you give me the photos anyway."

"Why should I do that?" she asked.

"Because if you don't," I said, "I'll tell your father that you stole my watch."

She drew herself up, eyes burning with indignation. "How dare you suggest—"

"I'm not suggesting anything," I said. "I'm telling you. Hand over the photos . . . and the watch."

"I have no idea what you're talking about."

"Give it back," I said, "and I won't say anything." I tried to keep the anger out of my voice, tried not to sound overtly threatening.

Giovanna stood there, her face the color of Crisco, taking loud breaths and eyeing me like a hawk eyeing a small rodent.

"Otherwise," I said, "I'll have to tell your father."

"Then tell him!" she cried, suddenly moving toward me. "Tell him!"

"I'll have to." I instinctively leapt up and moved behind the fortress of the chair, blocking her advance. "He gave it to me. He'll want to know where it is."

"It wasn't his to give!" Giovanna turned in agitated circles. "It was my mother's. It belonged to her. She's the one who brought the money to this family. The Brunellis, they had nothing."

"That may be true," I said, "but Marcello gave the watch to me."

"To you!" she cried. "Of all the whores he's slept with, why should *you* be the one to get it?"

My body was in a total burn, but I looked her straight in the eye and said what I knew she didn't want to hear. "Because he loves me."

"Loves you?" She let out a peal of laughter. "Don't be ridiculous!"

Oh man, we were locked in a major battle. "Be careful what you say, Giovanna," I warned. "I'm young enough to be your step-mother."

She let out a high-pitched sound that made me think of an overexcited bird. "You will never marry him!"

"Is that a threat?"

"You cannot!" Her face had become an awful mask with gleaming eyes.

I prepared for battle. A woman knows when it's time. I took my heels off and held them in front of me like weapons as I came out from behind the chair. "Don't ever try to tell me what I can and cannot do, Giovanna."

"He won't marry you," she wheezed. "I promise you that."

"Don't make promises you can't keep, Giovanna. It sets you up for failure. Now give me the watch and photographs or your father will find out you're a thief."

"You're having an affair with Giovanni. Don't think I don't know. That's why you want these photographs. So my father won't find out."

"I'm not having an affair with Giovanni," I said. "But I'm beginning to think that maybe you did."

She sucked in a startled breath. "What are you saying?"

"I just said it."

The implication that she'd fucked Johnny seemed to temporarily unhinge her. She looked left, right, up, down, as if desperately searching for a means of escape. Her breathing became a kind of dry, snorting bull-terrier gasping, as if she couldn't suck enough air through those giant nostrils, no matter how hard she tried. I watched as she lurched over to a dark wooden table and stood beside it, panting and staring down at a large crucifix.

Neither one of us said anything. But then Giovanna's face suddenly crumpled, and she began to sob.

Every time my mom or one of my girlfriends starts to cry, it makes me want to cry, too. It's a female form of bonding, I guess. Crying erases differences and makes you realize how much alike you are, even if you hate one another's guts.

"Giovanna," I said softly. I took a couple of tentative steps toward her. "I don't want us to be enemies."

She looked down at my bare feet, tears dripping from her eyes.

I took a couple more steps. "But you're making it so hard for me to like you."

Giovanna hung her head and ran her finger along the crucifix. "No one likes me," she whispered.

It was such a sad admission. I felt awful for her. To know that you are unloved . . .

I reached out, thinking I would just touch her, acknowledge her pain, share it for a moment. But she backed away. Then turned and fiddled with something. The watch, as it turned out. She was holding it out as she turned back to me.

"I'll talk to Marcello about this," I said. "Maybe he didn't know it belonged to your mother."

"He knew," she said quietly. She dropped the watch into my hand, then gestured toward the photographs. "Take them."

As I walked over to fetch the photographs, carefully clenching the watch in my hand, a horrible little voice in my head gloated, *You won, you won, you won.*

"Where are the negatives?" I said.

She pulled another envelope from the cabinet and handed it to me. "I suggest you be very careful, Miss Gilroy. In Rome, you never know who may be watching you."

Chapter
13

My encounter with Giovanna left me dazed and wary. A heaviness pressed in around my heart. I knew that my freewheeling days on the back of Johnny's Vespa were over. He could still be my private tutor and tour guide, but we'd have to "take precautions," as Giovanna put it.

My conscience was clear. I hadn't done anything wrong with Johnny. But those photos of us seemed to tell another story. Looking at our images, I realized for the first time the power of a photograph and the implication of an image.

I couldn't bring myself to tear up the pictures. Instead, I slipped them into the bottom of my suitcase and locked it.

OK, call me naive. When Teresina pointed out the paparazzi to me on my first day in Palazzo Brunelli, I just hadn't taken her seriously. When Giovanna warned me about them, I thought she was being paranoid and self-important. But now I realized that the guys—sometimes a young woman joined them—hanging around on Via Giulia, down below my windows, were hard-core professionals who would stop at nothing to get a salable shot.

And, weirdly enough, I was the object of their image hunt.

It left me in a real quandary.

As Giovanna pointed out, the value of photographs showing me and Johnny together was the implication that I was having an affair with Prince Marcello Brunelli's chauffeur. That I was cheating on Marcello while he was away on business. If the "evidence" was a photograph, there was no way I could defend myself. Once visible, outside, with Johnny, I was fair game for anyone's camera.

This was a problem for major celebrities like J-Lo and Madonna, not something Venus Gilroy had ever had to deal with.

On my own, I was not cameraworthy. I was a bankable image only because of Marcello. The incident with the photographs gave me tangible proof of just how important he was. Maybe no one in America had ever heard of the Brunellis, but in Italy they were apparently as well known as the Kennedys. They excited media interest because of their wealth and standing in Roman society. The Brunellis weren't movie stars, they were rich aristocrats. Marcello was one of the most powerful businessmen in Europe.

And he was in love with me!

Or so he said.

I wondered if what Giovanna had blurted out in a moment of anger was true: that Marcello's wife had brought a much-needed infusion of cash to the bankrupt Brunelli coffers. Had Marcello married her for her money?

There were a lot of questions I wished I could ask Marcello's wife. But the mad Signora Brunelli, who had been kept locked up in a wing of her husband's palazzo, was dead and unavailable for comment.

When Marcello called later that night and asked how my day had gone, I said nothing about the photographs or the watch his daughter had filched. I told him instead about the sights Johnny and I had visited.

"You love Roma, eh? I can hear it in your voice."

"I love it," I said. "I want to see more and learn more."

"I must say that I'm surprised the paparazzi haven't been trailing you and Giovanni," Marcello said.

"Mm." Looking down from a window of the salone to the street below, I saw a mean-looking woman smoking and gesturing angrily as she talked on a cell phone.

"Maybe they've gone away for August," Marcello said. "Even the dirty paparazzi need a holiday."

"When are you coming back?" I asked.

"Do you miss me, darling?"

"Yes." But it was more than just missing him. I was afraid of what might happen if he stayed away too long. "How can I teach you to be a slacker if you're always working?"

Marcello laughed, then sighed. "Ah, Venus. Do you know what I would give to be with you at this very moment?"

"No. What?"

"A year of my life."

"No way!" His romantic intensity thrilled and embarrassed me at the same time.

We chitchatted about practical matters. When would the dads and my mom arrive? Marcello wanted them all to be met at the airport and be his guests in Palazzo Brunelli. And weird as that seemed—having the dads and Carolee and me all staying together in the same wing of Palazzo Brunelli—I took a funny kind of comfort in it. For once in my life, I wanted to see their familiar faces.

"And, you know, my mama is also arriving," Marcello said. "You may see her before you see me."

"Where does she stay?"

"Mama has her own suite of rooms."

"Have you told her about me?" I asked warily.

"But of course."

"Do you think she'll like me?"

"Mama is a very, mm, *commanding* lady. Many are afraid of her. But there is no reason for her not to like you."

Oh, you stupid, stupid male, I thought. *You know nothing about women.*

"We will have a special dinner," Marcello said. "Both families together. A grand celebration."

After talking to Marcello, I went to look for Teresina. I didn't want to confront her, but I knew if I didn't find out what role she'd played in the watch-snatching incident, I'd never be able to trust her. And if I couldn't trust her, I really didn't want her "working" for me.

She was nowhere to be found.

"Teresina?" I called.

No answer.

I went into the kitchen. No Teresina. I knocked on her door.

I heard a sudden agitation within her room. Whispered voices. A creaking of springs. Then Teresina's voice called out, "Si, signorina! *Vengo subito!*" Scuffles and more whispers. "I come, I come!"

When she opened the door, breathless and red-cheeked, I caught a fleeting glimpse of a naked leg as someone scrambled out of sight.

Teresina quickly pulled the door closed and looked at me with an expression of trepidation and irritation. She was mussed and perspiring, her face and neck blushing pink. Someone inside the room let out a muffled cough. Teresina pretended not to hear it.

"Signorina?" she said.

What I wanted to say was, *Who's in your room?* But it wasn't my place to question her. Or was it? She was supposedly working for me. Shouldn't I know who was coming into "my" wing of Palazzo Brunelli?

"Look what I found," I said, holding out my wrist. Even in the drab light of the kitchen, the jewels glittered and darted their colored flames.

Teresina's eyes opened wider. "Ah! *L'orológio!* Your wreestwatch!"

"Yeah," I said. "I got it back."

She looked at me. Brushed some damp strands of hair from her cheek. Said nothing.

"Where do you think I found it?"

"I do not know," she whispered.

"Are you sure?"

She turned away.

"Look, it's all right. I don't care. I've got it back. But I just want to know."

"Know what, signorina?"

"Did Giovanna tell you to take this from me?"

Teresina sucked in a breath. She couldn't look me in the eye.

"Did she?" I demanded.

My maid bit her lip and nodded her head.

"So you took it and gave it to her?"

"No, signorina."

"Then how did she get it?"

"She take it." A pleading look from those big dark eyes. "I wouldn't do this thing. I said no."

"So Giovanna came in here and took the watch herself."

Teresina bit her lips and nodded. "Ah, please do not tell him, signorina!" she blurted out.

"Tell who?"

"Il Principe. He will get rid of me. He hates me. And I have no place to go. No family." Her eyes filled with tears.

I was instantly sympathetic. "I'm sure he doesn't hate you," I said.

"Yes, signorina. He hates me."

"Why?"

"I take the care of his wife."

"Then he should be grateful to you."

Her eyes probed mine. "I know too much, signorina. I am with La Signora Brunelli for two years. From her, I learn quite a great deal. I see many things."

I'll bet you did, I thought.

"Look, Teresina, I have to trust you, OK? If I can't trust you—"

"You can trust me, signorina! I swear by the Madonna and all the saints."

"If I'm going to trust you, you have to be my friend, not my enemy."

"Your friend, signorina?" She looked puzzled.

"Someone I can trust."

"Ah." She nodded and lowered her voice. "You don't tell Il Principe nothing and I won't tell him nothing neither, eh?"

What could she tell him? I didn't understand, and my face must have registered my confusion because Teresina suddenly leaned forward and whispered conspiratorially, "I say nothing about you and Signor Giovanni."

I had to cool it with Johnny. I didn't want to get him into trouble with Marcello. And I was afraid of what might happen between us.

A woman knows when a man wants her. My radar was turned on and picking up a distinct signal.

The next morning, Johnny was waiting for me, as planned, in the courtyard of Palazzo Brunelli. He was standing by the fountain, staring into it, but when I came out he immediately turned and looked up at me. Our eyes met. And I could see a special shine in his, a look of happy excitement.

My body went hot.

"Ciao," he said, just loud enough for me to hear.

"Ciao."

You have to end this, I said to myself, starting down the long stone staircase. *You have to do it now, before it goes any further.*

Johnny was waiting for me at the bottom of the stairs. "You look beautiful," he said.

"So do you."

And he did. Oh so molto sexy in his black jeans and silk T-shirt and gorgeous black leather loafers with no socks. With that head of thick, curly black hair and black eyelashes as long and soft as paintbrushes, and eyes that were polished disks of mahogany.

"I thought we could begin at the Forum," he said.

Say no, hissed a sharp little voice in my head.

"Then go on to Piazza di Spagna and Piazza del Popolo," Johnny continued.

Tell him you're sick, insisted the voice.

"And I have a few other surprises, too."

I couldn't speak. I simply could not utter the words to break the spell.

Because I didn't want the spell to be broken.

"Let's go have an espresso," he suggested. "I'll tell you a bit more about our itinerary." He started for the Vespa.

"Johnny?"

He turned, smiling. "Eh?"

Our eyes met again. I felt my outlines blur. "Johnny, I—"

"What is it?" A look of concern. A sudden interruption of his good mood.

"I can't go with you," I whispered.

"Eh? Why not?"

I shook my head. "I just can't, that's all."

"Are you ill?" he asked.

I shook my head. Stood there like an idiot, not knowing what to say or do.

He came close. "Something is wrong."

I bowed my head, an alcoholic unable to resist the liquor of his eyes.

He brushed my chin with his finger. Softly. The first time he'd touched me. "Tell me."

"I think you know," I said.

"Does this have something to do with Giovanna?" he asked.

"Why do you say that?" I ventured a quick peek at his eyes. Saw him staring belligerently up toward Giovanna's wing on the third floor.

"Did she tell you something?" he wanted to know.

I turned away, wishing I had a cigarette.

"Did she?" He blew out a noisy breath. "She did."

I said nothing.

"What did she say? Something about me?"

"Sort of," I admitted.

"What kind of an answer is that?" he spat. "Venus, look at me!"

So I did. Leaned back against the carved stone staircase for added support.

"Giovanna has nothing good to say about me or anyone. Understand? Look at her and you can see why."

"Why?"

"Because she is so goddamned *ugly!* And crippled, too. And for that, she blames me."

"What did you have to do with it?"

"Ah!" He turned away with a disgusted exclamation. "All that cocaine she used to take. I think it fried her brain."

"Giovanna was addicted to cocaine?" It was hard to picture the begowned Signorina Brunelli, surrounded by nuns, snorting coke. Her nostrils were so huge she'd need a shovel.

"Giovanna used to be a party girl," Johnny said. "She was one of the wildest girls in Rome. She tried everything, but it was coke she got hooked on. She snorted so much that she destroyed the inside of her nose."

Was that why blood dripped from her nostrils and Sister Angelica had to vacuum out Giovanna's nasal passages? "What about her leg?" I asked.

"One night she went to a party and got so stoned that someone called and told me I'd better come to get her. It was three in the morning, but I went. I got her into the car, but then she asked me to run up and fetch her purse. She said she'd forgotten it. I left the keys in the ignition. And while I was gone, she started the car, drove away, and crashed into a third-century aqueduct. Smashed her leg."

"God."

"So you see, I am to blame."

"Right. You forced her to get high and steal the car and lose control."

"Exactly. And now, of course, she's entirely different. Never goes out. Practically lives with those damned nuns."

"The Little Doves."

"They need her money to survive. So they dance around like her servants."

"She seems like a really unhappy person," I ventured.

"Giovanna? She knows it's only her money that people care about. It's made her paranoid. She suspects everyone and everything is out to get her and her precious fortune."

We looked at one another.

"What did the bitch tell you about me?" Johnny asked.

I shook my head. "It doesn't matter."

"Doesn't it?" His voice challenged me. "She poisoned you. I can tell. Turned you against me."

"No," I said miserably. "I haven't turned against you. It's not that."

"Then what?"

He reached out. I saw his hand. I knew he wanted to stroke me, to coax me back to him. And I knew if I let his fingers so much as graze my skin, I'd be lost. So I twisted away and ran up the stairs.

"Venus!" he called.

All I could think to say was, "I can't!" I huffed my way to the top landing and fumbled with the keypad beside the door. I wasn't crying, but my eyes were blurry and wet.

The electronic lock released. I pushed open the heavy door. Before I darted back inside, to the gloomy safety of Palazzo Brunelli, I looked down and saw Johnny standing at the bottom of the stairs. He looked hurt and angry and insulted.

Oh, Johnny, I thought, *if you only knew.*

I stayed inside all that day, a self-imposed prisoner in my wing of Palazzo Brunelli.

I tried to keep myself occupied by reading Whitman's guidebook to Rome. It was fascinating, especially a chapter called "Rome Underground," all about catacombs, and sewers, and ancient pagan temples buried beneath Christian churches. I marked a few places that looked interesting and located them on a map.

There was no reason why I couldn't explore on my own, without Johnny. I'd been so lazy, so passive, expecting that Marcello or Johnny or someone else would always squire me around. But I was perfectly capable of figuring out how to find my way around a foreign city on my own.

All day I kept a close watch on the paparazzi down on Via Giulia. They had a routine. There were periods when they disappeared for half an hour or longer. I noted times and roughed out their schedule. If I timed it right, I could slip out, unnoticed, the next day. If I went alone, without Johnny, there'd be even less chance of drawing anyone's attention.

I have to admit, it gave me a weird little thrill to think of outsmarting the creeps who made their living from spying on innocent people.

As the hours dragged by, it became harder and harder to concentrate. I didn't want to *read* about Rome, I wanted to be out *in* it, zipping around the hot, traffic-clogged streets on the back of Johnny's Vespa. I read what Whitman had to say about the Forum, and Piazza del Popolo, and Piazza di Spagna, and all the places that Johnny would have shown me.

If there was one thing I couldn't stand, it was being cooped up at home. Back in Portland, I had spent as little time as possible in my dinky apartment. I was a car girl at heart, a girl accustomed to unlimited mobility so long as her decrepit Toyota kept sputtering and she could pay for the gas.

When I was fifteen and starting to get into trouble, my mom dragged me to her energy analyst for a "reading." The energy analyst had me stand in my bra and panties under a bright white light. She ran her hands up and down my body, never touching me, staying about an inch away from my skin. She paused near my crotch, nodding meaningfully and saying "Hm," and paused again near my boobs, saying, "Aha." Then she turned to my worried-looking mother and said, "Her energy's all turned outward."

According to the energy analyst, I had overactive chakras. All it meant was that I hated staying home and I liked boys.

The trouble was, I always liked the wrong boys.

And they liked me.

Anyway, beautiful as my wing in Palazzo Brunelli was, by one that afternoon I thought I'd go crazy if I didn't get outside and be around people for a while. I wanted to stroll and window-shop and sit down somewhere for a cappuccino, which I could pay for no matter how expensive it was because I had my first month's salary from Marcello and it was burning a hole in my new and very cool microfiber purse.

Every time a tantalizing image of Johnny popped up in my thoughts, I replaced it with one of Marcello. But Marcello had told me that I probably wouldn't be seeing him for several more days. The strike in Torino was dragging on and he had to be there for the negotiations. He was not good slacker material.

Another hour passed and my desire to escape grew stronger. To keep myself occupied, I did a meticulous snoop through my rooms.

The funny thing about my part of Palazzo Brunelli was that it was weirdly devoid of human touches. There weren't any photographs or cute little knickknacks or anything else to suggest that Marcello's wife, Signora Brunelli, had lived there for many years.

The enormous walk-in closet, its glass-fronted cabinets filled with gowns, was the only place where some trace of her still lingered. At least, I assumed the wardrobe had belonged to Signora Brunelli.

I asked Teresina about the gowns as she chopped onions, tomatoes, and something that smelled like licorice. Yes, she said, all the *vestiti* had belonged to La Signora Brunelli. La Signora went to Paris every year and bought gowns from the top designers.

"Is there a photo of her anywhere?" I asked.

"Of Signora Brunelli?" Teresina clamped her lips tight. "Il Principe had them all removed."

"There isn't one photo?"

Teresina looked at me. No, studied me. Then she wiped her hands on a towel and said, "*Aspett'*. Wait." She went to her room and returned with a framed photograph.

I was expecting a glamour portrait, something shot in a studio. But this was just a snapshot, and not a very good one. A frail-looking woman with gray, slightly disheveled hair, stood in a garden. Maybe it was Giovanna's garden. The woman wore a plain white sleeveless dress. She had a faded regal quality, like a forgotten queen. At one time, you could just tell, she'd been statuesque and haughtily commanding. But by the time this photo had been snapped, no amount of makeup could hide the truth of her decline. Her lips, sadly smiling, were painted with way too much lipstick and her eyelids drooped as if from the weight of too much mascara and medication. She reminded me of someone, but I couldn't think who. Certainly not her daughter, Giovanna.

La Signora was holding on to the back of a wrought-iron garden chair. Maybe steadying herself. Teresina was standing beside her, smiling broadly, surprisingly photogenic.

"Who took the picture?" I asked.

Teresina didn't answer. She took the photo back and polished it with a corner of her apron. "This was soon before La Signora . . ." She brushed a tear from her eye.

It was difficult to believe that the woman in the photograph had been married to Marcello. I just couldn't see them as a couple. She looked several years older than him. In fact, she looked like an old lady. Marcello was mature, of course, but he did not look like an old man.

"Did they—" I stopped, trying to frame the question as delicately as possible. "Did they get along?"

"Get along?" Teresina repeated the words but obviously didn't know what they meant.

"Were they happy?"

"Ah, Il Principe and La Signora?" She thought for a moment, then shook her head. "No."

And that was that. No further information was offered.

"Did he cheat on her?" I asked.

"Cheat?"

"Other women."

"Ah!" She knew immediately what I meant. "Si." She looked into my eyes. "Many."

And I wondered for a moment if Teresina had been one of them.

Teresina, like all Romans, had a siesta between one and three. This didn't mean that she, or any other Roman, slept for the two hottest hours of the afternoon. All it meant was that she took those hours as personal time, to do as she pleased.

When Teresina disappeared, I headed for the walk-in closet.

As I opened the doors, the closet let out its faint, sweet exhalation. I smelled powder and a delicate perfume.

The only place I'd encountered period haute couture before was at Rethreads, a thrift shop in Portland. But Rethreads was mostly junk. La Signora's closet was a gold mine.

Old clothes had always fascinated me. Slipping into a fancy dress from another era, a garment that some other woman had once eyed, admired, paid for, and worn, always gave me a weird thrill. As a girl I loved to play "dress up" with my mom's clothes, and since Carolee was a garage-sale junkie, I'd been introduced to a lot of different dress styles.

Each of La Signora's dresses was carefully hung on an upholstered hanger. Balls of netting were stuffed into their empty bodices, to retain their shape. Tissue paper protected beaded necklines, sequined jackets, appliqued skirts. As I carefully made my way down the rack, I saw the names Dior, Balmain, Lanvin, Yves Saint Laurent, Chanel, Balenciaga, Courrèges, Givenchy.

There was a whole section in the closet just for accessories. Scarves and gloves were neatly folded and put away in boxes and drawers. There were maybe twenty purses. Shoes were arranged in separate cubicles. Everything was perfect. It was like a shrine.

I pulled out a long pink box and opened it. Inside, nestled in tissue paper, lay a pair of long purple gloves. When I say long, I mean they went up past my elbows. They were soft as sin, and drawing them on was like drawing on a second skin. You couldn't have fat arms and wear gloves like these.

La Signora's hat collection was pretty amazing. Some rested in big hatboxes with corded handles, others sat atop small pedestals. I took down a small purple hat with a bit of black veil and clamped it on my head.

It was so strange to think that women used to wear hats all the time.

On the dress rack I spotted something white and shiny. I couldn't believe my eyes. It was a mini-dress made out of what appeared to be white vinyl. *Extremely* cool.

I held it up in front of me. Looked in the mirror. Imagined.

By six that evening, I was pacing like a tiger in a cage. Teresina looked aghast when she came in and saw that I'd pulled up the windows and pushed open the shutters.

But I didn't care. I needed light and life. A hum of voices, clicking footsteps, and traffic sounds floated through the windows. A

muggy August breeze stirred the long draperies. I desperately wanted
to be outside.

"Is there a secret way to sneak in and out of this palazzo?" I asked
Teresina.

"Signorina?"

"This place is so huge. It takes up a whole block. You'd think
there'd be some secret door to get in or out."

Teresina shook her head. "I do not know, signorina."

"How does your friend get in?"

"My friend?"

"Your lover."

She looked at me.

"The person who was with you in your room," I said.

She didn't answer.

"I can't believe he—or she—came through the front door." Still
no response. "Teresina, I promise I won't tell."

"Later," she said after an endlessly long pause. "I show you when
it is dark."

It was molto weird having a pretty maid about my own age. Being
American, I instinctively felt that I should consider Teresina as a
friend. I didn't realize that I was trespassing on a very old and pretty
strict social apartheid that kept servants and their masters separate,
no matter how close they were.

So Teresina never seemed to warm up to me, no matter how
friendly I tried to be. She kept her distance. She answered questions
but did not confide. She kept her emotions, her secret feelings,
under wraps.

At eight-thirty she served me dinner. A place for one had been set
in the dining room. When I asked Teresina if she'd like to join me,
she stared at me in surprise.

"No, signorina. I eat in the kitchen."

And that was that.

At about eleven o'clock, however, she knocked and came into my
bedroom. "Signorina," she said, "I cannot do this thing. I cannot
show you the secret door."

"Why not?" I was all prepped up for my secret little adventure. "You said you would."

She nervously clasped her hands. "No one is to know of this door."

"I won't tell anyone." I raised a hand. "I swear."

She bit her lower lip and looked at me. "Even I am not to know of this door. If Signorina Giovanna found out—"

"She *won't* find out," I insisted. "How could she? I promise you I won't tell. I *promise*."

"Why do you want to know about this door?" she asked, her voice a whisper, as if we were conspirators.

"Because I want to get in and out without the paparazzi seeing me. I can't stand being cooped up here all the time."

"Ah. You want to go outside," she said. "*Fuori*."

I nodded.

"You want to meet Signor Giovanni," she suggested. "In secret."

"No."

"He is your *amore*," she said. "Your lover."

"No! Swear to God."

She sighed. Frowned. Turned away. Whispered, "This door, signorina. It is very deep and dark. The way is very old. It is not easy or pretty."

"I don't care. Look." I pulled out the bank note that I'd been saving as my trump card. "I'll give you a hundred euros. Just to show me."

She bit her lips again, then snatched the money from my hand. "Come. But place on a coat. It is very cold."

I didn't say a word. Just observed. Memorized.

"Take off your *scarpe*," Teresina whispered, slipping off her shoes. "They make too much clicks."

I did as I was told.

Like thieves, holding our shoes, we left my wing and sneaked through the shadows of Palazzo Brunelli. The marble floors were cool and slippery. Down the inner stairway, then through a nondescript door and into a service passageway. "That goes to the street," Teresina whispered, pointing to a door. "Come this way."

We entered a huge, dark, vaulted room. "The old kitchens," Teresina said. She paused so we could slip our shoes back on, then snatched up a flashlight hidden behind a cupboard door. I followed the beam of light as she hurried through the cavernous room. In the darkness I could just make out a giant fireplace and huge wooden tables.

"Watch your—" Teresina patted the top of a low arch and slipped down into an inky pool of blackness.

Five steps. A rising smell of damp. A left turn. More steps.

Teresina was moving fast. She pushed open another door. Now we were in a low, narrow, tunnel-like passage with a curved ceiling. It was cold and dank and had a peculiar smell. Stale air and damp brick and something else, something faint but foul. The putrid smell grew stronger as we scuffed our way along. I had to breathe through my mouth so I wouldn't gag.

"What's that smell?" I asked.

"*La fogna,*" she gasped, clamping her nose.

"La what-a?"

"How do you say—shit pipes."

"You mean sewers?"

"Si. La Cloaca Maxima. The big shit pipe of Rome." She stopped and pointed the beam of the flashlight up to the ceiling so that we could see one another in its reflected light. We were standing in front of a small door. "This part is very terrible," she warned, pinching her nose and covering her mouth. "Do you desire to go ahead?"

I nodded.

Teresina opened the door.

"Oh my god!" I coughed. The smell was so pervasive, so horrible, that it made my eyes water. I knew I would gag instantly if I let the odor fully into my nose.

"Hurry," Teresina said. "Now it is not so far."

We were in what appeared to be a cavern, on a ledge high above a wide, dark river. The sound of rushing and dripping water echoed in the space. The cold air was saturated with a stink so profound that it was beyond comprehension.

I didn't know how much longer I'd last. I blindly followed the beam of Teresina's flashlight. She turned from the ledge and darted up another flight of stairs, through another door, and then raced up what must have been a hundred or more stone steps. At the top, she snatched down a big iron key from a hook and inserted it into the lock of a small square door.

Pushed.

The door was heavy. It opened slowly, with a faint groan.

I saw light from a streetlamp. Smelled fresh, warm Roman air.

Teresina held me back. "Never go out quick," she said. "Make sure no one is on the street."

She peeked around the door. Nodded. "Come."

We were in what looked like a sunken doorway several feet beneath street level. As we climbed the last steps, both of us panting and gulping in fresh air, I saw that we were nowhere near Palazzo Brunelli.

Chapter
14

Two days later, Palazzo Brunelli suddenly erupted into a state of high alert. I didn't know what was going on, but something was definitely up.

A whole battalion of cleaning ladies arrived. In the giant salone I saw squads of them down on their hands and knees, scrubbing, waxing, polishing the marble floors. Others washed windows and dusted. Chandeliers were taken down and cleaned. Rugs were hauled down to the courtyard, draped over wooden posts, and severely beaten.

New smells from cleaning unguents, waxes, and polishes drifted through the giant rooms where the women chattered, laughed, and panted with the exertion of their labors. Some of the women looked as old as my grandmother.

I wandered through the main rooms of the palazzo with a pleasant smile on my lips, trying to remain as invisible as possible while sussing out the situation. Two of the Little Doves had flown over from Giovanna's quarters to supervise the cleaning staff. The starched wings of their wimples flapped as they raced around, beads clacking, pointing up, pointing down, leaning close to inspect, nodding. They looked almost happy, like they enjoyed being part of the work crew. Especially since they didn't have to lift a finger themselves.

"What's going on?" I asked Teresina.

She, too, had been possessed and was in a state of cleaning

frenzy. No one had come over to our wing to help her, so she was doing all the work herself.

"La Principessa," she panted, racing back and forth with a dust mop. "She arrives tonight."

Marcello's mother, whom everyone referred to as La Principessa, had decided to leave her villa on Capri and come to Rome for a few days.

"La Principessa is *very* strict," Teresina told me as she hauled out a mop and bucket and started to swab the floors. "Everything must be *perfetto*." She suddenly looked haggard, like she was running a marathon with flagging energy.

"I can help you," I said.

She made a face. "What? No, signorina!"

I rolled up my sleeves. "Just tell me what to do."

It took some persuading. I was breaking all known codes of behavior by offering to help. Finally, treating me like a little girl, Teresina gave me a cloth and said, "You can—" and made a motion of dusting.

An hour later, during what should have been Teresina's siesta, we were cleaning windows together. On the Via Giulia side of the salone there was a whole rigamarole that had to be gone through so that the paparazzi wouldn't be able to see in. But as I knew, this was the hour when no one hung out on the street below. Everyone in Palazzo Brunelli was so terrified of the paparazzi that they'd never taken the time to figure out that the paparazzi took a siesta break like everyone else in Rome.

"What's La Principessa like?" I asked Teresina. "Is she nice?"

"Nice?" Teresina's rag squeaked on the glass. "What is nice?"

"You know, pleasant. Easy to get along with."

Teresina let out a strange noise and said, "When you meet her, signorina, you will know."

It didn't sound promising.

No matter what I did, I couldn't get Teresina to confide in me.

"Did the Principessa get along with La Signora?" I asked.

"No."

"Why not?"

Teresina shrugged and wrung out her rag. "People with money," she said. "They are all a little crazy, eh?"

"Maybe La Principessa was jealous of La Signora," I hazarded. "Sometimes mothers don't like the women their sons marry."

Teresina shrugged. She stopped, sighed, gave her sweating brow a dramatic swipe, and climbed down from the ladder. Then she sort of withdrew into herself, like I used to do when my mother came over to clean my apartment. I felt a pang of sympathy for Teresina. I could tell she resented having to work all the time as a servant. Who wouldn't? I didn't blame her for snatching a little fun in her room— but I was still curious as to who her playmate was.

Teresina yawned and pulled a pack of cigarettes from her apron pocket. She offered the pack to me. Temptress. I shook my head.

"OK when I—?" She blew out an imaginary puff of smoke.

"Sure."

We stood there by the ladder, taking a break. The cigarette she smoked smelled vilely delicious.

"So—eh." Teresina cleared her throat. "Soon comes your mama."

"And my dads."

"And they all comes here, to Palazzo Brunelli, eh?"

I nodded.

"OK," Teresina sighed. "I make ready their rooms. *Domani.* Tomorrow."

I heard a familiar sound and peered out into the courtyard below. Johnny was sitting on his Vespa and revving the motor. He backed the motorbike out of its spot, swung around, and puttered across the courtyard to punch in the gate code.

Teresina joined me at the window. She looked down at Johnny and then looked at me, a knowing little smile on her lips. I knew what she was thinking.

We were standing there by the window when the door to my wing suddenly flew open and Giovanna, trailed by Sister Angelica, rushed in. Teresina gasped and flipped her cigarette out the window.

Giovanna stopped and stared at us like we were thieves caught in the act. Sister Angelica hung back behind her, hands folded within her robe.

"What are you doing?" Giovanna said.

Was she addressing me or Teresina? Her brusque, dismissive tone could have been for either one of us. She looked from Teresina to me, down at the wet cloth in my hand, and back to Teresina.

When neither one of us responded, Giovanna barked something in Italian to Teresina. Teresina shot her a sullen glance and left the room.

I wasn't prepared for this meeting with Giovanna. I was wearing shorts and a sleeveless T-shirt with my other shirt tied around my waist; my feet were bare and my hair was a mess. Giovanna, on the other hand, was wearing one of her long rustly gowns, this one mousy gray and without decoration of any kind. It looked like a version of the robes worn by the Little Doves.

"I came to tell you that my grandmother is arriving," Giovanna began.

"I wish you'd knock before you come in," I said.

The comment clearly threw her off guard. "Yes, but I am in a hurry, you see."

"Everyone seems to be in a hurry."

"Yes. There is so much to be done." She took a couple of halting steps into the salone. "Grandmother rarely comes to Rome now. And in August, *never*."

"Must be an important occasion," I said.

Giovanna sniffed. "She is coming to see you, of course."

For a moment I felt like I was drowning. I'd jumped in too deep and the current was sucking me in and rushing me along too fast to catch my breath. Marcello's determination to woo me was both wonderful and terrible at the same time. Wonderful because I now had a glimpse of what my life could be like as the new Signora Brunelli. I would never have to worry about money again. *For the rest of my life.* But terrible because I didn't love my husband and his daughter obviously hated my guts. What La Principessa would think of me was anyone's guess.

"I'm looking forward to meeting her," I lied. In truth, my knees got a little shaky just thinking about it.

"Papa desires that we all dine," Giovanna said. "Together. Here. Our family and yours. A *festa*, a party."

"Sounds great."

"And nonna—my grandmother—desires that you take tea with her tomorrow afternoon."

"Fine." My mind raced through my meager wardrobe.

Giovanna turned to go, then turned back and said in a puzzled voice, "You are not helping Teresina with her duties?"

"I offered," I said. "She has way too much to do here by herself."

Giovanna turned bright red. "Signorina Gilroy," she stammered, "guests in Palazzo Brunelli do *not* help the servants." She clasped her hands and nervously twisted them. "If my father found out, he would be furious."

"Then you'd better not tell him," I said.

At that, she and the Little Dove swept out of the room.

The scent of fresh flowers permeated the air. By late afternoon it was so strong that I left my wing and wandered out into the main part of the palazzo.

I'd never seen so many blossoms in my life. Vases brimming with enormous bouquets adorned every table, chest, and shelf. There were orchids and roses and dozens of other flowers that I couldn't name. Long-stemmed exotics I'd never seen before were arranged in enormous urns.

The smell, combined with the waxes and polishes, was so strong it almost made me swoon.

Two guys were taking care of the flower arrangements. On a movable dolly, they had what looked like an entire florist shop, the blossoms jammed into white plastic water buckets. One of the Little Doves was supervising. She had a sour look on her face, as if she disapproved of the flower boys, both dressed in tight jeans, skimpy T-shirts that showed their belly buttons, and Doc Maartens. The older one had dyed blonde hair and four rings in his left ear. The younger one looked like a decadent cherub.

They eyed me and smiled. I smiled back. I had this sense of instant rapport, the way I usually do with gay guys.

"The flowers are beautiful," I said.

"Si," said the one with earrings. "Beautiful. Like you."

I giggled to let him know I was on to his game. "No, like you."

"You are most very kind," he said. "Americana?"

"Si," I said.

"I love the Mistah Sistah," he said, snapping his fingers and dancing to imaginary music. "Wow-a." He did a quick twirl on the polished floor and plopped a flower into an arrangement he was working on.

The world was too small. Here in Rome, these guys had heard of Mistah Sistah, the man my former lover was about to marry, or maybe already had married. But of course it made perfect sense that they'd know about Mistah Sistah because gays always know what's going on months before the rest of the world.

"Janeefer Lopez," said the cherub. "Jel-Lo."

I nodded. "Leonardo DiCaprio."

"No." Blondie shook his head and tsked. "In Italy, Leonardo da *Vinci.*"

The Little Dove pursed her lips, made a clucking sound, and pointed to another vase. Cherub filled it with water and consulted with Blondie about which flowers to put in.

Blondie held up a long-stemmed flower with a feathery yellow blossom. "Do you like?"

"*Bella,*" I said.

"*Bello,*" he corrected me. "From Capri. All." He made a sweeping gesture that took in all the flowers in the salone. "From La Principessa's garden."

The Little Dove couldn't take it anymore. She said something in a sharp, scolding tone. Blondie smiled and made a rude farting sound. The angry nun reprimanded him, but Blondie ignored her and looked at me.

"You are a guest at Palazzo Brunelli?" he asked coyly.

I nodded.

"You are the guest of Il Principe?"

I nodded. "But he's never here."

"Ah." He nodded. "You like to dance?"

"I love to dance."

"Ah. We too." He pointed at his partner. "Baby." Then pointed at himself. "Carlo."

"I'm Venus."

"Venus." He pronounced it *Vein*-oos. "You like to go dancing with Baby and me?"

"Sure. When?"

Carlo shrugged. "*Stasera?* This night?"

"I don't think I can."

"Very big party at Asclepio," he whispered. "Very cheek. Everyone famous will be there."

"I don't know. Maybe." I thought of what fun it would be to go to a big party in a Roman club with Johnny.

"*Ecco.*" Carlo scribbled out an address and tore it off his pad. "See here?" He came close. "Asclepio. On Isola Tiberna. Here is address. You come, you say, 'Carlo and Baby.'"

"Carlo and Baby," I repeated.

"You must come," he said. "We look for you."

Baby smiled, showing his bright golden front tooth.

A couple of hours later, trunks, suitcases, and crates of food began to arrive. A balding overseer wearing a black suit directed a sweating, grunting cadre of workmen. The men hauled their loads up from the courtyard on their backs, like pack animals. Once they were inside, the overseer checked what they'd brought and pointed them toward La Principessa's suite of rooms or toward the kitchens.

The palazzo was jammed with people hurrying back and forth, getting things ready. There was noise and laughter. I wished I could be a part of it, at ease and somehow connected. Instead, feeling shy and a little furtive, I hung back and tried to be unobtrusive, watching the proceedings from doorways and behind pillars.

In the midst of all the hubbub I saw Johnny, wearing a dark blazer and a tie, hurrying through the salone. My heart gave a lurch and I almost called out to him. I watched as he conferred for a moment with the overseer and then darted out the front entry door.

I took that as a signal to return to my wing, and had just left my shadowy observation spot when Johnny raced back into the salone. This time he saw me.

At first he smiled. So did I. I could feel my face lighting up. But then, as if remembering how I'd shaken him off the day before, he frowned and turned away.

I didn't cry until I was safely back in my palazetto.

No one had invited me to meet La Principessa when she finally arrived. And since I wasn't part of the Brunelli family, I figured I'd better stay in my own wing for the rest of the evening. I felt like Palazzo Brunelli was being divided up into three distinct territories: La Principessa's, Giovanna's, and mine.

With all the comings and goings that day, the paparazzi must have guessed that something was up, or maybe they had some advance intelligence, because more and more of them appeared on Via Giulia. By eight o'clock I counted twelve men and three women. All of them had camera equpment. They smoked and gabbed and gestured and talked on their cell phones. There was a kind of anticipatory excitement in the warm Roman air, that anticipatory buildup you feel before a celebrity arrives.

Then, suddenly, someone shouted, "*Eccola!*" and they all rushed like a pack of wolves down the side street toward the front gate of Palazzo Brunelli.

I couldn't see what was going on but heard the echoing jabber of their voices. It occurred to me that the window in Teresina's kitchen looked out on that dark, narrow street, so I hurried there, opened the window, and leaned out to see what was happening.

A very long and very black and very shiny limousine was slowly nosing its way through the paparazzi. The photographers looked crazy. Like a cluster of wasps, they buzzed alongside the limo, pressing their cameras to the windows. Bulbs flashed. Voices pleaded. They rapped their knuckles on the car door and pressed closer and closer until finally two policemen on motorcycles roared around the side of the limo, shouting something and forcing the paparazzi back.

I was totally caught up in the drama of it.

Teresina's door opened and she raced out, panting and straightening what looked like a new black dress. She let out a startled gasp when she saw me. "Ah! Signorina!"

"What's going on?" I asked.

Teresina poked her head out the window. "Ah! La Principessa is arrived!" She fumbled with her hair, trying to pull it back and hold it with barrettes. "I must hurry!"

"Where are you going?"

"Ah, signorina! You do not understand! When La Principessa arrives, everyone must be there to meet her!"

"The whole staff?"

"Si. *Tutti*. Everyone!"

More than anything, I wanted to get a glimpse of La Principessa and see the woman I'd be dealing with at teatime tomorrow.

I put my hands on Teresina's shoulders to calm her down, then carefully inserted the barrettes. "Do you have another black dress?"

"*Cosa?*" Teresina's eyes widened when I told her what I wanted to do.

OK, it was crazy. I admit that. But I just got carried away in the excitement of the moment.

Teresina was terrified. She was afraid I'd be seen and she'd be blamed. For what? Wearing one of her maid's dresses? She lived with this constant fear that she was going to be fired.

"No one's going to recognize me," I reassured her, squeezing into one of her black uniforms. "I'll hang back in the shadows. She won't even see me." I ran to the dressing room and grabbed one of La Signora's blond pageboy wigs.

Teresina let out a horrified wail when she saw me. "Signorina! You cannot do this thing!"

I followed her out of our wing and down the corridors that led to the main salone. She walked stiffly, as if she were my prisoner. I could hear an excited murmur of voices. At the doorway that opened onto a far corner of the salone, Teresina left me and went to join the rest of the staff, all of them attired in black uniforms and standing very straight, like an army at attention, staring expectantly at the front doorway. I stayed behind, at the very back, ready to bolt.

Car doors slammed in the courtyard. Everyone in the salone seemed to take a deep breath and stand even straighter. It was so quiet that I could hear voices outside. They were slowly walking up the stone stairway toward the front door of the palazzo.

When La Principessa entered, it was like she had an invisible force field around her. The crowd of servants moved back. She stood there, framed in the ancient doorway, the limpid evening light behind her, and slowly looked from left to right, like a captain reviewing her troops.

Her dress was bright red. A long white scarf was affixed around her shoulders and a wide-brimmed white hat was pulled down on her forehead. She wore large tinted glasses, the kind movie stars wear to hide their crow's-feet. The whole ensemble was like camouflage so you couldn't tell how old she was.

From where I was standing, she looked remarkably young. Her skirt, I noticed, ended a couple of inches above the knees. She had very shapely legs.

"*Buona sera,*" she said in a soft, husky voice.

The entire room echoed in unison, like schoolchildren, "*Buona sera,* Principessa."

She stood for a moment longer, surveying her staff. Then she gave a special nod and smile to several in the front row. "*Dov'é Giovanna?*" she asked.

Which I knew meant, "Where's Giovanna?"

A Little Dove came forward and whispered something in La Principessa's ear. Whatever it was, it didn't seem to please her. "Giovanni!" she called.

Johnny appeared from outside. La Principessa smiled at him and took his arm. The crowd parted as the two of them moved deeper into the salone.

But suddenly La Principessa looked toward a wall near me and lifted her chin as if she were scrutinizing something. All eyes, including my own, followed hers to a large painting.

"My Correggio is back," she said.

"Yes," Johnny said. "The museum returned it yesterday."

"No more tours for my Correggio, eh?" La Principessa headed toward the painting.

I flattened myself against the wall, behind some of the other staff, and tried to sink down so my face wouldn't be seen. To my horror, the Principessa was examining everyone, smiling graciously if they passed muster or frowning if she spotted something out of kilter—a missing button or an apron or shirtfront less than gleaming white.

Johnny saw me before she did. His face registered shock, then bewilderment, then a kind of unspoken "What the hell are you doing?"

I remained totally passive, a servant among servants. My heart pounded as they moved closer.

Then, as in a nightmare, La Principessa's all-seeing eyes darted back to me. Her eyes locked onto mine.

She turned to Johnny. "Is that girl new?" she asked, and before he could answer, turned back to me. "*Com'e ti chiama?*" she said.

I froze. I stared at her like an idiot. I didn't know what she'd asked, so I just nodded.

La Principessa turned back to Johnny.

"I think she's deaf," Johnny whispered.

"Ah. Poor thing." La Principessa continued toward her Correggio. When she was out of sight, I managed to slip away.

Why shouldn't I go to the party? Why shouldn't I go and meet Baby and Carlo at a club and dance the night away? What was keeping me in Palazzo Brunelli?

Nothing but my own fear.

Fear of what? I asked myself.

I was under no obligation to remain locked up. I was free to do whatever I wanted whenever I wanted. I had no intention of sitting around like a stupid mistress waiting for Marcello to get back from Torino. His continued absence was starting to piss me off.

And something else, too. In two days my mom and dads would arrive in Rome and I'd be locked into family things.

"Your last night of freedom," I said to my reflection. The white vinyl minidress from La Signora's closet fit me amazingly well. I pulled on the long purple gloves. "Make the most of it."

* * *

I didn't want to be seen, so I had to leave by the secret passageway. I dreaded it. The thought of having to pass through that horrible stench down in the sewers made my stomach queasy. But I had no choice. If I was going out, that's the way I'd have to go.

It would not be cool to leave Palazzo Brunelli by the front gate. A couple of hopeful paparazzi were still hanging around out there, even though it was almost midnight. And I didn't want Giovanna to spot me on her surveillance cameras. Especially since I was wearing her mother's minidress.

I waited until the palazzo was completely silent before I ventured out on the first leg of my escape route. Stilettos in hand, I tiptoed through the corridors to the main salone, then skittered through that dark, cavernous room toward the interior stairway beyond it. The floors were as slippery as a skating rink.

I was about to start down the wide stone steps when I caught a glimpse of movement in a corner of the salone. Someone was entering the room.

I ducked behind a column, my heart pounding.

The footsteps were soft, measured.

I peeked around the column.

It was La Principessa, in a long white nightgown and diaphanous robe. She reminded me of someone in a museum, walking slowly, taking her own sweet time, examining all the rare and beautiful treasures on display.

She stopped for a moment in front of one of the giant glass doors that led out to a balcony. I could see her silhouetted against the faint golden light filtering through the shutters from Piazza Farnese below. She stood very erect, hands clasped, and stared out into the shadows of the flower-scented room.

I heard her mutter something in a low, conversational tone. Then she made her way over to a pedestal with the bust of a man on it. She murmured something, heaved a sigh, and kissed the bust, caressing the marble hair and stroking the cold stone cheeks.

I was out of there.

I tiptoed to the staircase and practically flew down. I remembered all the props and procedures of the secret passageway. The flashlight was waiting in the ancient kitchens. I ran up stairs, down stairs, through doors, down corridors.

The smell was waiting. I couldn't escape it.

When it came time to enter the sewer, I wrapped my long silk scarf around my nose and mouth. Like a deep-sea diver, I took a couple of test breaths to get my rhythm going. Then I opened the door.

My eyes were watering as I darted through the tunnel as fast as I could. By the time I unlocked the door to the street, I was gasping and fighting dry heaves.

Then, blissfully, I was outside, prepped and ready to meet the mysteries encountered on a muggy summer midnight in Rome.

The cab driver was a fat, sweating man of about fifty with a drooping lower lip and a bald head that shone like a hubcap. He looked at my boobs, then at me, then took the sheet of paper I held out.

"Ah, Asclepio, si."

It was pronounced Ass-*sclep*-ee-ohs.

We were there in about five minutes. The cabdriver pointed. Isola Tiberna was an island in the middle of the Tiber River, closed to traffic. I had to cross over via a pedestrian bridge.

It wasn't hard to find the club. The one little square in front of Asclepio was packed. There was an awning out front, but all the noise and music was emanating up from a cellar. The club's only identification was a blue neon sign of two winged snakes wound around a stick.

It was one of those club scenes where you have to wait in line for hours to get in unless someone comes out and chooses you, like Cinderella. Scores of young Italians, Americans, and Japanese were thronged around the doorman, waving their hands and begging for admittance. The doorman, like some snotty guardian to the underworld, would hardly look at them.

He spotted me as I hobbled across the square. It was paved with cobbles and was treacherous for stilettos. I smiled from afar. He wouldn't smile back, but he certainly was interested in my legs.

By the time I reached him standing behind his podium, I was a little breathless. "Carlo and Baby," I said.

"Si." It was smooth as silk. He escorted me to the top of the stairs and said something I couldn't understand. I nodded. He pointed down. I entered.

God, what a scene.

First of all, you had to walk down about a hundred stairs. The walls were brick. The air was steaming hot and smoky. There weren't many lights. And this boom of techno-rave music came pulsating up the stairs like a pounding heart. There was a loud roar of voices beneath it.

I entered an enormous underground cavern. It was packed. There were bars and dance floors. Lasers sliced through the darkness. One huge space led to another, then to another. I had no idea how I'd ever find Carlo and Baby.

I put on my party smile and waded into the room. Some guy flashed his black lashes at me and said something as I passed. Then another guy squeezed by a little closer than was necessary, trying to cop a feel. Finally, I found a free corner and squeezed in, wishing I had the courage to go order a bottle of water.

As my eyes adjusted to the dark, I got a better idea of the layout. There were tables around the sides of two of the dance floors. You could sit there and order drinks that glowed in the dark from barefoot waiters who wore white bikini shorts and headbands that were supposed to look like golden snakes. The dance floors were arrayed around a huge round shaft with the club's snakes-around-a-stick hanging in the center. Real snakes make me faint, but these snakes were spectacular. Colored lights coursed up their glass bodies so that they seemed to be writhing. There was a stainless-steel DJ booth below them.

The sound was spectacular. It came from everywhere.

The people on the dance floor were moving in a trance of lights and music and drugs.

A woman stepped down hard on my toe as she brushed past. I let out a cry, jerked my foot away, and turned to look at her.

"Ah, *scusatemi, scusatemi,*" she apologized.

Our eyes met.

We recognized one another.

It was Flavinia. Johnny's Communist pal. Or girlfriend.

She was as shocked to see me as I was to see her. Neither one of us knew what to say. Her initial look of sympathy for having stepped on my toe gave way to one of guarded hostility. She took a drag of her cigarette and seemed to swallow the smoke.

"*Come vai?*" she said in her deep, dusky voice.

I knew this meant, "How are you?" So I answered, "*Bene. Grazie.*" Which meant, Fine, thanks.

Her dark eyes glimmered. She gave her thick loose hair a flick. She looked me up and down, taking in my white vinyl mini and my purple gloves. She was wearing a skintight lycra top with a loose cotton skirt. She had a voluptuous figure, all tits and hips.

"Ciao." She flipped her head back in a kind of dismissive way and disappeared into the crowd.

I wondered if she was here with Johnny. For a second, I was tempted to follow her.

An instant later I was blinded by a really bright flash. It took me a moment to realize what was happening. Carlo was standing on one side of me, Baby on the other. They were both smiling so hard that they looked like weird animals about to lunch on something.

Me, maybe.

The flash went off again. Carlo said something. They switched their positions, tugged me out into an open area, and the flash went off again, then again, and once more.

Somewhere in the back of my head a warning voice said, *Paparazzi.*

"Hey," I said, "I don't want my picture taken."

"But you are beautiful," Carlo said. "You like to dance?" He and Baby led me out to the dance floor and immediately began dancing around me. The photographer melted into the crowd.

Carlo and Baby were high on something. I could tell because I wasn't. The pupils in their eyes were contracted, they were sweating profusely, and they had ecstatic looks on their faces.

The photographs had me worried. "Who took the photos?" I said—yelled, rather, since that was the only way to be heard above the music.

"A friend of us," Carlo said, holding me around the waist and spinning me back and forth. "You look *bellissima!* Don't worry."

Now I *was* worried.

Could I trust him?

Probably not.

When the show started, I stumbled off the dance floor as fast as I could.

Snakes. Real snakes. Huge pythons or boa constrictors or cobras or something. Two guys and two girls came out on the little round spotlighted stage in front of the DJ booth and began playing with them. The guys had on bikini shorts, the girls wore tiny bikini tops and bottoms and high heels. The enormous snakes slithered up and around them as the music changed to something low and kind of scary and smoke rose from holes in the floor.

I thought I'd pass out.

I was the only one moving. Everyone else seemed to be hypnotized by the writhing snakes. Carlo and Baby looked like they'd entered a trance.

I wanted air. Air and water. I felt panicky. It was a reaction to the snakes. What if one of them got loose and came sliding through the crowd and latched onto my bare leg?

I gulped down deep Buddha breaths as I squeezed through the crowd as fast as I could. I ran smack-dab into Johnny and didn't even see him, I was trying to get away so fast.

"Venus?"

The sound of his voice triggered some primitive impulse in me. I whirled around, saw him, and practically hurled myself into the safety of his arms.

It all happened so fast, neither one of us knew what was going on.

I lifted my face to his. He pulled me tight. My gloved arms encircled him. We kissed.

We kissed again.

We kissed harder.

A camera flashed.

I broke away, started to cry, and ran out of the club.

Chapter
15

I had a lot to think about as I dressed for my afternoon tea with La Principessa.

Marcello's mom had come to Rome to size me up. Instinctively, of course, I wanted her to like me. And, just as instinctively, I knew that she wouldn't.

She'd no doubt be like Giovanna. No matter what I did or said, no matter how nice or polite I was, she would find some reason to hate me. I imagined the queenlike Principessa staring disdainfully at me across a chasm of class and education and breeding.

So to hell with it, I thought. I'm just going to be myself, because she'll hate me no matter what I do.

I didn't need to impress this woman. It wasn't as if I were some gold-digging interloper scheming to marry her wealthy widowed son. Her son was the one begging to marry me.

I made no attempt to look sedate or virginal. I'd listened to Whitman and Daddy's fashion advice and come loaded down with black in many variations. Besides my black leather mini, I had a beautiful sheathy sort of strapless black cocktail dress. And black heels so gorgeously sexy they could have been a pinup on a foot fetishist's calendar. The dress and shoes cost a frigging fortune at Saks, but Whitman had gallantly paid for everything.

"In Rome, you're allowed to be beautiful and sexy," he said. "Men *and* women. It's called *la bella figura*."

"What's that mean?"

"Cutting a beautiful figure. You know, poise. Style. Chic." He mimicked some fashion poses.

"Looking fabulous all the time."

"Yes. Rome's not like Portland, thank God, where everyone lives in baggy blue jeans and dumpy sweatshirts. The Italians revere the body. They treat it like a piece of art."

He was right, of course. I'd been paying attention to what the Romans wore. Italian women did *not* wear blue jeans. Or if they did, they wore them skintight with high heels.

"*Che bella*," Teresina said approvingly when she saw me in my black strapless cocktail dress. The big dark rose tattoo over my breast might freak out the princess, but that was her problem, not mine.

"How should I wear my hair?" I asked, fiddling with it in front of the mirror. "Up?"

Teresina studied me. "No," she finally said. She pulled my hands away from my head and fluffed out my hair so that it hung naturally around my shoulders. "*Cosí*. Like that."

I felt like I was on my way to a job interview. Butterflies fluttered in my tummy.

Which led me, of course, smack-dab face-to-face with the one huge issue that I still could not face. Was I or wasn't I? I'd missed one period, which wasn't uncommon. If I missed the next one, I had some serious issues to deal with.

Tips on poise and posture came back to me from my one week in modeling school years earlier. I straightened my spine. I slowed my step. I resisted a frantic urge to pull out my mirror and study my image for the flaws that I knew were there.

You're just you, I said to myself, walking past the gauntlet of staring Brunelli portraits. Venus Gilroy from Portland, Oregon, U.S.A.

A maid I'd never seen before came up to me as I entered the giant salone. "*Prego, signorina*." She led me to a sofa. "*La Principessa venga subito*."

I nodded as if I knew what she was saying.

The maid left me alone. But the minute she left, I once again had that feeling that I was not alone. That I was being watched.

I cast my eyes up to the frescoed ceiling, searching for hidden surveillance cameras. But all I saw up there was a lifelike gallery of Brunellis, saints and nobles, full of secrets, all of them floating above the ordinary world. Some of them peered down over a painted railing into the salone below. I could almost hear them whispering, *Look at her. Look at that one. She comes here as a potential bride of Prince Marcello, one of us, and she falls for his chauffeur instead! There's definitely something wrong with that girl.*

It occurred to me that important social encounters had taken place in that room for hundreds of years. Maybe the Brunelli mothers always interviewed prospective daughters-in-law there.

It was like waiting for an audience with a queen.

When La Principessa entered, it was with that same regal air I'd noticed the day before, as if she were surrounded by invisible bodyguards.

She was cordial but not exactly welcoming.

"Signorina Gilroy," she said, extending her hand.

I stood. Suddenly I realized that I didn't know how to address her. So I took her hand and said, "Hi, very nice to meet you."

We shook. I shook, rather. Her own hand remained inert.

"Please," she said, indicating that I should sit.

"Thank you."

Then we just sat there. I sat there, I should say, while La Principessa stared at me. I kept my knees together and my ankles crossed in this totally weird and unnatural position I'd learned in modeling school.

La Principessa had been a terribly beautiful woman. She was still beautiful, but now she had to work at it. Her skin was flawless. Her auburn hair was stiffly perfect. I saw nothing saggy under her chin. She had enormous almond-colored eyes with a catlike upturn that suggested a sexy mischievousness out of keeping with the power she wielded. Her eyes had been lifted at least once, and she carefully used a whiter makeup around them. Her lips were full and sensual, colored a creamy coppery shade. Her long aquiline nose was nowhere near the size of Giovanna's beak.

I had to admit, Marcello's mother looked like a million bucks. Her clothes had the kind of timeless elegance and unwrinkled style that would forever elude my own mom. La Principessa wore a white knee-length belted silk dress with a dark patterned silk scarf artfully draped around her shoulders and held in place by an enormous gold pin. Sheer black silk stockings showed off her remarkably shapely legs. Her large breasts were so expertly cupped that they showed no sign of age or gravity.

Yes, she must have been quite a beauty. And she kept herself in fabulous shape. That clinging silk dress showed everything.

She sat there with the imperturbable calm of someone who needed nothing and was accustomed to getting whatever she wanted. She wore her status as matriarch of the Brunelli family as if she were wearing a crown. It was both awesome and unsettling.

"Is there a picture of you somewhere?" I asked.

"A picture?" Her voice was very deep.

"A painting. These are all Brunellis, aren't they?"

"Ah. Yes." She nodded. "There is a painting of me. But it is not on display."

"Did you grow up here?" I asked, trying to keep the conversational ball bouncing.

"Eh?" She frowned. "You mean, did I grow up here in Roma?"

"Yeah—yes—si. In this house."

She let out an amused laugh. "I came to live here when I was a young woman. Younger than you are, I think." She leaned back, staring at me with those cat eyes. "If I may ask, how old are you, Miss Gilroy?"

"Twenty-five."

"Ah." She nodded. "I was already a mother at your age."

"Mm."

"Now—" She made a dismissive gesture with her hands. "Now women do not want to have babies. Once there were too many, now there are too few. We have a zero population growth here in Italy."

I blanked. I had no idea how to respond. Luckily, the maid came in just then carrying a tea tray with a china pot and cups and a small, round cake sprinkled with powdered sugar. La Principessa pointed to the table beside her. The maid put the tray down, curtsied, and left.

I'd never seen anyone curtsy in real life before.

La Principessa ignored the tea and narrowed her focus on me. I noticed that she couldn't keep her eyes off my rose tattoo. "You look strangely familiar, Miss Gilroy. Have I seen you somewhere before?"

I shook my head and smiled sweetly, hoping she wouldn't identify me as the deaf maid she'd noticed yesterday.

"Tell me about your family," she said.

I cleared my throat. "Well, I've got a mom and two dads."

"Two?"

"Yeah. They're gay. They've been together for twenty years."

"Twenty?" Her perfectly penciled eyebrows rose.

"Yeah. That's like a hundred and twenty straight years."

"And these two men raised you?"

"With my mom."

"All together?"

"My dads were mostly in New York," I explained, "and my mom was in Portland. So I went back and forth."

"It must have been terribly confusing."

I shrugged. "Not really. Just different."

She studied me a moment longer, then turned to pour the tea. "I hope you like a good English tea. Earl Grey."

"It smells good."

"I knew nothing of afternoon tea until we moved to England," La Principessa said in her accented English. "Tea was the only thing that made life in England bearable. Tea and gardening."

"You have a pretty garden here," I said.

"Ah! Giovanna showed you?"

"She said it was one of the oldest gardens in Rome."

"Yes, and always tended by the Brunelli women. For five centuries." She handed me a cup of fragrant tea. "Are you a gardener, Miss Gilroy?"

I thought about it for a moment. "I could be," I said.

"Do you like children?"

I knew what she was getting at. "I love kids."

"Tell me, Miss Gilroy, do you have a career?"

"Not really."

"No? But I'm certain Marcello told me that you were a model."

"Oh, that." I felt the heat rise in my cheeks. "That didn't last very long."

"What did you model?" La Principessa asked.

And suddenly I had it all figured out. She knew the answers already. She'd run a security check on me. She could gauge my truthfulness from every answer I gave.

"I modeled lingerie," I said.

"Ah," she said. "For a department store? Or was it photographs for *Vogue?*"

I shook my head. "It was just a job," I said. "I needed the money."

"Si, si," she said quietly, "I understand." She took a sip of her tea. "My son Marcello is quite infatuated with you, Miss Gilroy."

"I know."

"His wife—well, she was not an easy woman to live with. She was not healthy. For many years. It was very difficult for Marcello. Because he is a passionate man."

"Yes, I know." And I thought of all those times when Marcello had said and done things that shocked me because they *were* so passionate, so completely unlike anything an American guy would ever say or do.

"Passionate," she repeated. "Like his father." She looked across the salone toward the bronze bust I'd seen her kissing the night before.

The word, or a memory associated with it, momentarily tripped up her poise and brought a sheen to her eyes. "Passion makes people do very odd things, Miss Gilroy," she said finally.

I nodded.

"Very odd things. Things they would not otherwise do."

I sensed what was coming.

"Passion disorders the mind, you see. It disorders reason."

"I'd rather have passion in my life than reason," I said.

"You say that," she said, "because you are very young."

"Maybe I say it because I'm passionate."

"Yes, my dear," she said, in a tone of voice that was suddenly and shockingly confidential, "but you can afford to be passionate, can't you, because you have absolutely nothing to lose."

"What do you mean, I have nothing to lose?"

"My dear, Marcello doesn't love you," she said pityingly. "He loves your youth. Your freshness. Your lovely body. But—"

"But not me?" I was suddenly really hot and really defensive.

"Miss Gilroy," La Principessa said calmly, "my son is a man who runs eight businesses with a net worth of over seven hundred million euros. He has saved the Brunellis from financial extinction. It has been his life's work. And work is all he knows. He had no happiness with his wife. So periodically he"—she made a subtle hand gesture—"dallies."

"I'm not his mistress," I interrupted her. "I've never slept with him."

"Yes," she said. "That was very smart of you."

I felt like I'd been slapped. The implication was that I was deliberately scheming to marry Marcello—for his money, of course. When the truth was, I'd put him off and put him off because my heart was teased but not tugged.

"Look, I didn't plan any of this," I said. "I didn't try to make Marcello fall in love with me. I tried to talk him out of it."

"Miss Gilroy, I am not here to judge you."

"Yes, you are," I said.

"No." She held up her hand as if giving a pledge. "I myself have been judged. Very severely. I would not do that to you. To anyone. But there are standards, Miss Gilroy. Social considerations. Family considerations. I must think of these things. I must put the reputation of my family ahead of everything else. I must try to be practical instead of passionate."

"You're saying that I won't fit in and you don't want me to fit in."

"Miss Gilroy, the Brunellis are one of the oldest papal families in Rome. We have our own coat of arms. We have founded a religious order. Brunellis have lived in this palazzo for over five hundred years."

"And have any of you ever been happy?"

"I beg your pardon?"

"*Happy*. I mean, pardon me for saying so, but no one in this place, dead or alive, looks even remotely *happy*."

La Principessa stared at me with very wide eyes.

"And that's all that Marcello really wants," I said. "He just wants to be happy."

La Principessa pursed her lips and stiffened her spine. "Happiness is an accident, Miss Gilroy. It is not the primary focus of life."

I licked my dried-out lips. "Happiness is part of human nature," I said. "Just like passion."

"Exactly. So happiness is as brief as passion."

"Just because it's brief doesn't mean you shouldn't go after it."

We were both getting kind of agitated. La Principessa was losing a bit of her cool. I noticed that she was rubbing one of her beautifully manicured hands along her silk-covered thigh. She wore a gorgeous ring, thick gold with a huge malignant-looking stone.

"Miss Gilroy," she said, "I offer you one hundred thousand American dollars to leave Rome."

I was shocked. Speechless.

La Principessa moved in for the kill. "I will give you a check drawn on our American bank. I give you my word of honor that you will be able to cash it."

I stared at her. She stared back. Brunellis stared down from the ceiling above. They stared out from portraits. Even the blind bronze eyes in the busts seemed to be staring.

At me. To see how I'd react.

A hundred thousand dollars.

"If you accept," said La Principessa, "you must leave Rome today. I will arrange it."

I stared down at my teacup, sitting on the table.

"You will sign a contract," said La Principessa.

Sunlight pierced through the slatted shutters, throwing ladders of shadow across the marble floor. La Principessa seemed to be talking from a great distance.

"You will of course never see Marcello again," she said.

My eyes darted up toward that gallery of Brunellis staring down from the ceiling, watching *The Principessa and Venus Show* below. I wondered what kind of deals they'd made in their time. How they'd gained their power, and how they'd exerted it.

I'd never been in a situation like this before. Someone offering me money to disappear.

Offering me money to disappear because I wasn't "appropriate."

La Principessa might be a good fighter, but she'd made a major tactical error. She'd told me what the Brunellis were worth. When you've got that kind of money, a hundred grand ain't even a sneeze. Even I, who'd never had anything but a negative balance in my checking account, knew that.

A hundred grand was an insult.

I was worth a lot more than that.

Thanks to La Principessa, I had reached a turning point in my life.

I finally stumbled onto my own knowledge of power.

And I saw clearly, for just a moment, how power worked. The mechanics of it. The moves. The countermoves. The bribes and payoffs.

"Shall I fetch my checkbook?" La Principessa asked.

"No," I said. And smiled at her.

"Perhaps you want cash."

I shook my head.

"What *do* you want, Miss Gilroy?"

I pointed to the tea tray beside her. "Just a piece of that cake, please."

Carolee's plane was about an hour late. I watched the big Alitalia jet taxi up to the gate and wondered what to expect.

My mom never flew. She was afraid of flying and hadn't traveled anywhere in years. When I offered to fly her over to Rome and she accepted, no one was more surprised than I was.

I admired my mom's bravery, her willingness to actually try to conquer some of her endless fears. But I was expecting the worst. Maybe she'd had a panic attack, or started screaming. It was a long haul from Portland to Rome, and it involved a change of planes.

Hat in hand, Fabio stood a little behind me as we waited at the security gate. Fabio was one of those guys who love to ogle women. Discreetly. He didn't have a clue that I knew this about him. But all you had to do was follow his eyes as he walked through a public place, like the airport, to know what was on his mind. He feasted on tits and ass.

Some women get all uptight with oglers like Fabio. But I've always considered sex and the sexual urge a basic part of being human. I ogle as much as any guy. Fabio's ogling was kind of tender and appreciative and full of yearning for the unattainable.

On the way out to Fiumicino, we'd communicated enough so that I knew he was a recent widower. He'd been married for thirty-five years when his wife died. He seemed to be both bereaved and horny.

I kind of felt that way myself. Because I'd decided I had to give up Johnny. I didn't want to. But it was the only way to give Marcello a chance to make me fall in love with him.

In the midst of all my turmoil about Johnny, I'd finally figured something out. I had this propensity to get totally stuck on a guy, almost to the point of obsession. I wove all kinds of impossible stories so that the guy would fit my fairy-tale scenario. And of course he always disappointed me because I'd concocted a fantasy personality for him.

That's what I'd done with all three of my husbands. That's what I had done most recently with Tremaynne. I had ignored all his warnings. I hadn't listened to him, not really, when he tried to tell me who he really was.

And here in Rome, I was fantasizing about Johnny, not Marcello. But now that Marcello was due back from Torino, it was time for me to give him my full and undivided attention and see what came of it. I *wanted* to fall in love with Marcello. The urge was even stronger after my meeting with La Principessa. Something in me wanted to prove to her that it wasn't just money I wanted, it was her son.

I caught a glimpse of Carolee's distinctive hair, a kind of orangey red soufflé, rising up behind the line of dark-haired Italians making their way through the security gate.

Something strange was going on.

As the line moved forward, I saw that a small Italian man was walking beside my mother, clasping her hands and staring up into her eyes with what looked like passionate adoration.

For a moment, I wondered if she'd been arrested. Maybe she was having a seizure, or was really sick. She looked down at the Italian with half-closed eyes, her lips quivering.

"Mom!" I called.

She looked at me, waved, nodded, and turned back to the man beside her. He stroked her hands and looked as though he was pleading with her. She gestured in my direction and shook her head. The man fumbled in his pockets. Withdrew a piece of paper and a pen. Scribbled something and handed it to her. Carolee looked at it, said something, and carefully folded the paper. The man leapt up like a little dog and kissed her on the neck. My mom burst into tears. They looked at one another. The man tugged her down and stood on his toes to kiss her, barely able to encircle her enormous cleavage with his arms.

Then my mom backed away, put up a hand as if to say *stay away now*, and lurched toward me like a silent-film star.

We embraced. She was very hot, almost soggy. Seemed to have scarves everywhere. Smelled of wine. "Oh, sweetheart," she said, "oh, sweetheart. I can't believe I'm here in Rome!"

"Mom, who was that?"

"Cesare!" The very mention of his name made her whirl around to look for him.

He was standing off to one side, hands in pockets, forlorn as a dog left in a kennel. Carolee raised a scarf and gave him a doleful wave.

"Mom?"

She turned to me. "Oh, Venus. I have so much to tell you."

Fabio parked his cap on his head and stepped forward. "Signora?"

Carolee straightened up. "Yes?"

"May I assist?"

"Assist?" Mom looked at me, confused.

"This is Fabio, Mom."

"Fabio? Oh, not . . . ?"

"No. Fabio's the chauffeur, Mom."

"Oh, the chauffeur. Of course."

"Signora?"

"He's offering to take your carry-on, Mom."

"Oh. My carry-on." She put out her hand before giving him the bag. "Hello, Fabio. I'm Carolee. Venus's mother. From Portland, Oregon."

I couldn't believe what I was seeing. Mom and Fabio looked at one another. A spark jumped from his eyes to hers. They both smiled shyly.

This is going to be one hell of a week, I thought.

Mom had never had good luck with men. Or with women, either, for that matter; her one sapphic adventure had been disastrous. But suddenly passion had blossomed for her, and his name was Cesare.

"That's Italian for Caesar," she informed me as we drove back toward Rome from the airport.

"As in salad," I said.

"Yes, but it's pronounced *Chay*-sa-ray." She sighed. "Oh God, what a sweet, sweet man." But as she said this, I saw her eyes steal a glance at Fabio up in the front seat.

Mom had met Cesare on the flight from Portland to Chicago. They were seated side by side. At first, Mom hadn't paid any attention to him because she was in her own world of terror. She was beyond anxiety. It was all she could do to keep herself from running out of the plane. She was experiencing the classic symptons of panic: increased heart rate, breathlessness, an overall clammy feeling of incipient disaster. She had a relaxation tape especially developed for people who have a fear of flying, but she hadn't been able to concentrate on the soothing words.

"It was the weirdest thing, sweetheart," she said, patting my hands. She'd perked up considerably once we got into the limo. "I just had the strongest feeling that it was *do or die*. Everything in me was screaming, Get off this plane, it's going to crash! But I knew if I did, if I gave in to my fears, it was all over for me."

"What do you mean?"

She shrugged. "It was like I was being given one last chance. And if I didn't take it, then there was nothing left but to sit at home the rest of my life and watch reruns on TV."

So there she'd sat in her economy class seat, with the fan blowing and her seat belt fastened, confronting one of the greatest fears of her life. Evidently Cesare had sensed what she was going through because he leaned close and said, "Signora?" When Mom opened her clenched eyes, she was looking into his. He smiled tenderly and held up a rosary. "You wish?"

"Oh, no, thank you," Mom whispered. "I'm not Catholic."

Cesare sort of nudged her. He pressed the rosary into her sweating palm. "Take. Hold. It will help."

So Carolee, who hadn't a clue as to how to use a rosary, nodded and clenched the beads.

She managed to hold herself together until the plane began to taxi. That got her heart racing again. She felt breathless, lightheaded, sick to her stomach. She was sweating through her antiperspirant. As the engines revved and the plane started down the runway, she let out a soft agonized moan, pressed herself back against her seat, and prepared to die. It had been the scariest moment of her life.

That's when Cesare had taken her hand.

At first she hadn't registered what was happening, what he was doing, so she didn't resist or take offense. And when she did realize what was going on, she simply gave herself over to the moment. She felt his firm, warm, comforting hand covering her own. No words were spoken. When she managed to glance over through her half-closed eyes, she saw that he wasn't trying to put the make on her. In fact, he was staring straight ahead, his lips pinched, as if he needed a little reassurance himself.

For Carolee, it was like some bad spell had finally been broken. It wasn't like she was suddenly free of her fear of flying or her agoraphobia, but they no longer had the kind of crippling power over her they once had.

She'd felt, she said, like a newborn. "A newborn just takes the world as it comes," she said. "It trusts that it will be taken care of."

And that had been the beginning of her sixteen-hour romance with Cesare Scarpetti, all of it played out on the plane in economy class and, briefly, in a concourse at Chicago's O'Hare Airport.

Even though his English was limited and her Italian nonexistent, Mom had managed to extract all the essential information she needed from Cesare. He was not married. He never had been married. He lived with two sisters on a chicken farm east of Naples.

"A chicken farm?" I said.

"Yes. I mean I'm *almost* positive."

"What did he say?"

"Well, honey, his English is not what you'd call fluent. When I asked him to explain, he sort of clucked."

I leaned forward. "Fabio, what's the word for chicken?"

"For chicken? *Pollo.*"

"Yes," Mom said, "that's the word. *Pollo.* He has a pollo farm."

Cesare had been visiting his nephew, Vincenzo, in Portland. This nephew was the son of a brother who had emigrated to America decades earlier and recently died. Vincenzo was a computer programmer.

As the Alitalia jet approached Rome, the sixteen-hour affair had grown more passionate. But how could it continue? Carolee had only her week in Rome, with me, and Cesare had to return immediately to his chicken farm.

"He begged me to call him," Mom said, looking down through tear-glazed eyes at the piece of paper on which Cesare had scrawled his phone number. "*Begged* me, sweetheart."

"So call him," I said.

"Oh, honey, sometimes these things are just sort of . . . of the moment."

"And sometimes they're not."

She looked at me. Then her eyes wandered up toward Fabio again. And he picked up her radar. He craned his head around and flashed her—not me—a smile.

Carolee, pleased and embarrassed, smiled and looked out the window. "This is supposed to be the land of love," she said.

"Yeah." I tried to replace Johnny's daydream image with Marcello's.

"Italian men don't seem to be afraid of a plus figure," Mom said.

Maybe she was right. Fabio was certainly doing his best to appreciate her in his rearview mirror.

I didn't ask her to go, but the next morning Carolee insisted on accompanying me back to Fiumicino to pick up the dads.

"You don't have to, Mom. Just stay in bed. We can all go out sightseeing later on."

Sitting in the huge bed, against the plumped-up pillows, she looked like a happy little girl. "Oh no, honey. I want to go with you."

Everything in Palazzo Brunelli overwhelmed her. She followed me around like a nervous puppy, gasping "I can't believe I'm here" at every turn.

The electricity in the car between her and Fabio practically made my hair stand on end. And I never realized how sneaky she was until we arrived at Fiumicino and she said, "Honey, why don't you go in and surprise the dads. I'll wait out here in the car with Fabio."

Perfect, I thought, making my way into the terminal. Like daughter, like mom. They both fall in love with chauffeurs.

The dads had spent a couple of days in New York and flown from JFK to Rome. I expected to see them relaxed and happy, glad to be back in their favorite city, but one look told me something was wrong. Whitman had that quick, tense walk of the wounded and the furious. Daddy, a couple of steps behind, was engrossed in an animated conversation with a tall, dark-haired woman wearing dark glasses.

Whitman caught my eye first and clicked on a smile. He said something to Daddy, who looked away from the woman and saw me. He pointed me out to the woman, who took off her dark glasses, smiled, and waved.

Who the hell was she?

"Hello, sweetheart," Whitman gave me his usual chaste pucker.

"Venus!" Daddy drew me into an embrace and rocked me back and forth. "Sweetheart, I want you to meet Gabriella Mangione."

"Hello." The dark-haired woman took my hand and smiled. Then she looked at Daddy. "She's beautiful. She looks just like you, John."

"Except, of course, that she has breasts," Whitman said, his tone acid.

"Well, John . . ." The woman looked up at him, smiled, and took his hand. "It was quite a surprise, eh?"

Daddy nodded.

Whitman stared at them. "John, let's go."

The woman did not acknowledge Whitman. She kept her eyes on Daddy. "I live in Rome now," she said.

"So you decided to come back home," said Daddy.

"Si. Rome was harder to stay away from than I thought."

They looked at one another, some unfinished business obviously holding them.

"John?" Whitman said.

The woman appeared to be crying. No, she *was* crying. She opened her purse and pulled out a handkerchief to dab her eyes and nose. Then she pulled out a business card and tucked it into Daddy's jacket pocket. "Call me?" With that, she was gone.

We all looked at her retreating figure.

"Who was that?" I asked.

"That," said Whitman, "was your father's first wife."

Chapter
16

I'd been pretty much on my own since coming to Rome but now I was surrounded by family. Mom and the dads settled into "my" wing of Palazzo Brunelli.

All three of them seemed to be in a weird state. In the case of the dads, it had something to do with running into Daddy's first wife, Gabriella Mangione. It was one of those small world stories. Daddy and Whitman had been sitting in business class, and after the plane left JFK and reached cruising altitude, "this woman" (as Whitman referred to her) had come up from behind and tapped John on the shoulder.

Gabriella was the woman my dad had met in Rome almost thirty years earlier. He'd married her and they'd moved to Boston, where Daddy worked as a young architect. Then something had happened—I never knew what, exactly, because Daddy never talked about it and I never pried. All I knew was that when Gabriella got her American citizenship, she divorced Daddy and disappeared.

She had always been a mystery woman in my mind. Kind of sly and conniving.

Carolee was fascinated. "Oh. My. God. Are you going to call her?" she asked from the front seat of the limo.

There was a moment of awkward silence before Whitman said, "Yes, John, are you going to call her?"

Daddy laughed and shook his head with the wonder of it all. "I might," he said. "Just out of curiosity."

"Oh, sure!" Carolee said. "I would!" She leaned across the console and tried to explain the situation to Fabio. "John and I were *married*," she said, indicating Daddy in the backseat.

"Eh? You are married?" Fabio didn't sound very pleased.

"No," Carolee said. "We *were*."

"Ah." Fabio nodded. "No more."

"No. No more. John is *gay* now. Whitman is his *domestic partner*."

Fabio looked at the dads in the rearview mirror.

"But before he met me, or Whitman," Carolee went on, "John was married to an *Italian* woman. But she ran away and he never saw her again."

"Carolee," Daddy said, "for Christ's sake."

"Well, it's interesting," Carolee said. She leaned closer and touched Fabio's knees. "Don't you find it interesting, Fabio?"

"Si."

"See? It *is* interesting. The way our lives work out. The people we meet. The people we leave. The people we find. So anyway," she said to Fabio, "after thirty years or so, John *saw* this Italian woman again. His *first* wife. She was on the same *plane*!"

Fabio shook his head and murmured, "Mama mia."

Daddy and Whitman were too engrossed in their own thing to notice what was going on in the front seat. But I could see. It was plain as daylight. Mom had turned into this chatty, flirtatious creature who was attempting to seduce the man behind the wheel.

And from the looks of it, she was succeeding.

The plan was for everyone to relax for a few hours before the big dinner party with the Brunellis. After my encounter with La Principessa, I thought that she would cancel this meeting of the clans. But everything appeared to be going ahead as planned. As we entered Palazzo Brunelli, a squadron of uniformed maids was bustling about in the salone and the cavernous dining room.

"Look at all those gorgeous flowers!" Carolee exclaimed. "I hope they don't set off my allergies."

"This is rather pleasant," Whitman said as I led them through the palazzo to my wing. "Is that a Correggio on the wall over there?"

"Yeah," I said, "they just got it back from a traveling museum show."

"Nice trompe l'oeil ceiling," Daddy observed.

"What's trompe l'oeil?" I asked.

"It means 'deceive the eye'." Daddy pointed up at the gallery of Brunellis standing behind that railing overhead and looking down into the room. "Things painted so realistically that they fool you." He explained how the painter had manipulated perspective so that the Brunellis appeared to be standing at full height, when, in fact, they were squashed down and painted on a curved ceiling.

They weren't so intimidating after all.

When Marcello returned from Torino, he came straight to me. When I saw him, my heart gave a stutter, like a cold engine trying to turn over. I could sense his longing. I could see his hunger. His eyes never left mine. He pulled me into a tight embrace and kissed me, his hands sliding down my back. He sucked in a deep breath when his hands reached my behind. I let them feel me. His tongue went into overdrive.

I pulled away, flustered, not quite ready to give myself up to him.

"Darling," he whispered, smoothing my hair. "My darling Venus."

He was dressed beautifully, as usual, but he looked haggard.

"I missed you every moment," he said. "Did you miss me?"

I nodded.

"Oh, Venus." He pulled me into his arms again. Pressed me close. "It was only the thought of you that kept me going."

His passion was overwhelming. I felt myself being pulled in, like into the undertow of a huge wave.

I followed his lead and sort of sidestepped toward the bed. He pulled me down beside him, then gently pushed me back so that we were lying side by side.

I looked deep into his eyes. I saw that he loved me. I felt for some weird reason like I wanted to cry.

Cry and give myself up to him. Because just looking into his eyes,

I knew that none of my three husbands had ever loved me as intensely as he did. Tremaynne had come closest in the passion department, but Tremaynne had never truly given of himself. He gave his body, but not his soul, and it was Marcello's soul that I could see in his dark, glistening eyes.

"Darling," he whispered, gazing at me, his hand running down to cup my breast.

I was right on the verge of giving in, right on the cusp of making this really crucial decision, when I heard Carolee's voice and her scuffling feet.

"Venus? Where are you, sweetheart?"

We both sat up, like teenagers caught necking.

Mom was as embarrassed as we were. "Oh," she gasped when she saw us. "Oh. Oh, I'm sorry. I didn't—"

"Mom, this is Marcello."

Marcello, ever gallant, brushed at his mussed hair and leapt to his feet. "Signora Gilroy. What a pleasure." He put out his hand.

My mother was like someone hypnotized. She stared at Marcello with dazed eyes. "Oh, I . . ." She looked at his hand, then slowly took it. And then—I could have died—she *curtsied*.

Fucking curtsied! In her bathrobe and scuffs. Her face green with the seaweed mask that she'd slathered on. "How do you do, Prince Brunelli?"

Marcello smiled and looked at me. "I do just fine, thank you."

"I'm looking forward to meeting your family," Mom said. "It was so nice of you to invite all of us to dinner."

"Mom," I said, "did you want something?"

"What? Oh, oh yes, sweetheart. I just wanted to know—when you're calling someplace in Italy—I mean, from Rome to another place in Italy—how do you do it?"

Marcello asked what number she was calling. When Mom told him, he said, "Ah, that is close to Napoli."

Mom and I exchanged looks. She gave me a nervous smile.

Marcello told her what to do, even offered to make the call then and there on his mobile phone, but Mom shook her head and said, "No, I don't want to disturb you. I'll just go and call from my room. I'll charge it to my home phone number, of course."

"Please," Marcello said, "dial direct."

"Oh, OK, thank you, I will." Mom turned and scuffed away in her slippers.

I sighed and looked at Marcello. "Well, that's my mother," I said.

"She's charming," he said. "And you met my mother as well, eh?"

"Did she tell you?"

"Of course."

"What did she say?"

"She said you were charming." He sat down beside me.

"Don't lie," I said.

"But she did! She said you were charming."

Charming? Obviously she was lying. "And what else?"

"She said you were very direct. Mama likes that."

"She's pretty direct herself."

"Yes, I know. Many people find her overwhelming. But she had to take care of many things when my father died, you see. She had to learn how to run his business. To take charge of things."

"She doesn't think you love me," I blurted out.

"What?"

"She thinks I'm all wrong for you."

"Eh?"

"And maybe I am."

"No!" He pushed me down again and held me tight. "If you love me, that's all that matters." He planted little kisses on my neck, on my chin, on my ears. "Do you love me, Venus? Say that you do. I will be so happy."

I didn't have time to say anything, because just then his mobile phone started playing a tune. "Ah!" he exclaimed, annoyed, sitting up and answering. "Si. Ciao, Giovanna."

I had no idea what they were talking about, but Giovanna's loud, nasal voice sounded irritated, and as the conversation progressed, Marcello started to sound angry. Finally he let go with a gush of Italian that seemed to go on forever, and hung up.

He looked at me. "That was Giovanna."

"Is there a problem?"

"Only those she creates," he said to my surprise. "No, it was nothing. Your fathers. They wanted to go out for a cappuccino and couldn't get out. Because of the security." He stood up. "The endless goddamned security."

He pronounced it god-*damn*-ed.

"Why do I live this way?" he asked. "I despise it. I feel like a prisoner."

He looked at me as if I had an answer. But I didn't. I felt the same way myself.

Marcello the multimillionaire prince felt like a prisoner. But so did Venus Gilroy, the pauperess. Never having mastered the art of money, a bankrupt at twenty-five, always, always, always in debt, constantly worried about the bare essentials, like having my junky old Toyota die on me and paying my rent on time and scrounging up enough for a Double Whammy espresso now and then, my prison was very different from the one Marcello inhabited.

But, in a queer way, that sense of imprisonment did, in fact, make us alike. The prince and the pauperess had something in common after all.

"Sometimes," Marcello said, "I would like nothing more than to go and live in my cabin at Pine Mountain Lodge. Away from everything. Away from labor strikes. Away from mobile phones. Away from everyone but you."

"You could do that," I said. "If you really wanted it."

He smiled. "And would you come and live with me at Pine Mountain Lodge in Idaho?"

"I might."

He put his hand out and stroked my cheek. Stared, tenderly.

Someone should write a book about what goes on in a woman's mind before she makes love to a guy for the first time. The endless internal debates. The way she weighs the pros and cons, from an emotional, sexual, and financial perspective.

This kind of thinking, holding back, was new to me. Up until then, I hadn't really paid too much attention to the deeper meanings of sex. I'd never put a cork on my libido. I was so afraid that I'd never be loved, that I loved—or talked myself into loving—anyone who showed an interest in me.

All of them inappropriate. All of them disappointing. Because I'd somehow learned from my mother never to judge anyone. It was a good lesson, as far as it went, but it left me at a definite disadvantage sexually and emotionally. It robbed me of any ability to judge character. When you can't judge character, you end up with losers and heartbreakers.

Marcello was definitely not a loser. And his wealth, I had to admit, was something of an aphrodisiac. But it was not because of his money that I was there, an inch away, looking into his eyes and feeling his warm breath on my cheek.

I did feel a connection to Marcello. I found him incredibly handsome and sexy. But I had never been able to respond to him sexually, or emotionally, which amounts to the same thing. And I wondered then if it had something to do with Daddy. I'd never studied psychology so I didn't have any theories. I knew vaguely that Freud had said men wanted to marry their mothers and women wanted to marry their fathers. But there was this built-in incest taboo that kept it from happening in real life. So was I attracted to Marcello because he reminded me of my dad, and afraid to fuck him because it would be like fucking my father?

It didn't seem fair. Or even plausible.

Maybe I was just afraid of him because he was an older man and I didn't want to acknowledge wrinkles and sags, the love bites of age.

How shallow of me.

I have to admit, too, that for the first time in my life, I was aware of the mechanics of desire. I knew from our shared past at Club Peek-a-Boo that Marcello fantasized about women who were pouty and impatient. Women who were sexually alluring but who had little or no interest in him. He had to conquer them. He had to win. He always looked for the challenge.

My holding back increased his ardor. But I wasn't holding back because I hoped to get something by letting him screw me. For once in my life, I was actually trying to listen to whatever wisdom there was in my poor overworked heart. I didn't want need or fear of loneliness to color my decision.

But I did want desire to be part of the equation. Desire can't really be faked, even though millions of women try to fake it every day. Without desire, I couldn't imagine making love to anyone. Desire was the flame that got the kettle boiling.

And that got me to thinking about Johnny.

No matter how hard I tried not to think about him, I thought about him. I even saw some ghostly vestige of Johnny in Marcello. Something about the line of Marcello's jaw, and the square bevel of his chin, and the flashing depths of his eyes, and even the shape of his ears reminded me of Johnny.

Get a grip, girl, I said to myself.

"Venus," Marcello murmured, "come closer to me, darling. I want to feel your heart beating next to mine."

I snuggled closer.

"You are so beautiful," he whispered, stroking my breast. "So natural. So sweet. So rare."

I tentatively put my hand out and touched his silvery hair. He closed his eyes as if this little gesture was ecstasy, then he caught my wrist and brought it to his lips.

A shiver ran through me. I moved a little closer.

He stroked my waist and then my hips and he cupped his hand around my behind and pulled me so close that I could feel his hard dick through the fabric of his trousers.

"Venus," he whispered. "*Ti amo.* I love you."

I believed him.

That in itself was a kind of miracle.

"I want to make love to you," he whispered.

"Now?"

He nodded, then moved his head down to my breasts, nuzzling them, eyes closed, smiling like a sleepy, contented baby. "Mmm. So soft and warm."

With most guys it's, like, dive in and hook your lips around that soft titty sandwich as fast as possible. Most of them don't have a clue about e-zones or e-behavior. So Marcello's slow-moving sensuality was working wonders. A woman doesn't want to feel trapped or scared by a guy's lust, she wants to participate in it. Even guide it, up to a point . . .

So I slowly unbuttoned my blouse for him. As I did so, he stared into my eyes with this look of incredible gratitude and longing. Then he exhaled a very warm breath and turned his attention to my breasts.

"*Deliziosa*," he whispered, planting voluptuously soft kisses and laying his stubbly cheek against them. "*Carina*."

I stroked the back of his head as he nuzzled closer, his nose burrowing into the cleft between my breasts, his fingertips playing with the lacy silk fabric of my hundred-dollar bra from Saks.

My head was above his. His thick silver hair gave off a smell of cigarette smoke and lavender-scented shampoo. I looked down at him. Felt a scary, melting kind of tenderness. The tension in his body had relaxed and he was curled up like a baby, eyes closed, his breath hot on my breasts.

How would I know unless I tried it?

I'd set up all these roadblocks to keep him at a distance. He'd respected them. He hadn't forced or coerced me. He'd been patient, caring, kind, and generous.

Maybe I'd really be surprised. I had a feeling that he'd be a good lover. Better than good. *Great*. If I just gave him a chance . . .

And gave myself the chance to find out.

I was finally ready.

The light turned green.

Marcello let out a snore.

I looked down and saw that he was fast asleep.

In a group, we made our way from my wing, down the corridors, to the giant salone.

The dads looked like a million bucks. They were both wearing Armani suits, Daddy's charcoal gray, Whitman's black. Whitman had on some elegant thin black leather shoes with pointy toes that he'd bought in Rome on a previous trip.

Their confident, determined stride reminded me of the way

they'd walked in New York. The way I'd always had to move a little faster in order to keep up.

I walked between the dads, almost like a bride, holding their arms. My gown rustled. My jewel-encrusted watch glittered. I took deep Buddha breaths. "Do I look OK?" I asked for the tenth time.

"Sweetheart, you're beautiful," Daddy said, giving my hand a re-assuring pat.

"You actually look chic," Whitman said from my other side.

Trailing a few feet behind us was Carolee.

My mom just wasn't accustomed to dress-up special events, the way my dads were. I didn't know where she picked up her fashion ideas, but not from any magazines I knew. Her dress was white, fairly simple, but it had all these gauzy M&M-colored veils that floated around her like wisps of polka-dot smoke. Her legs were still pretty but the hard sheen on her white hose made them look surgi-cal somehow.

"Oh darn!" she exclaimed. "Wait a sec, will you?"

We unlinked arms and turned. "What's the matter?" I asked.

"I can't walk as fast as you. I'm not used to wearing heels any-more, and these damn floors are as slippery as cat shit."

Whitman left my side and offered Carolee his arm.

"Why, thank you, Whitman," Mom said appreciatively. "When you're not being a bitch, you're a real gentleman."

Even Whitman laughed.

We started off again. I could hear Whitman and Carolee talking behind us.

"I'm so nervous," Mom whispered.

"Why?"

"They're so *important*. The Brunellis."

"They sit on the toilet, Carolee, just like you and me and the Queen of England."

"Well, I know, but look at how they *live!* I mean, this place is a friggin' *palace*."

"Yes," Whitman said, "I do have to admit that I never thought I'd see our daughter in a palace."

Our daughter. A proud little thrill of family love coursed through me.

Carolee let out a loud, emotional exhalation. "Oh. And doesn't she look bee-you-ti-full?"

I pressed Daddy's biceps and he flexed. It was an old joke we had.

"Did you call her?" I whispered.

"Not yet," Daddy whispered back. "My head's still swimming."

"It was weird to see someone you were married to before Mom or Whitman."

"What did you think of her?"

"Gorgeous," I said. "Drop-dead gorgeous."

Daddy nodded. "Still. After all these years."

I looked at him. Wondered what kind of hold this woman, Gabriella Mangione, still had on his heart.

The first people I saw as we entered the giant salone were La Principessa and Giovanna. They were sitting on the enormous sofa and staring at us. La Principessa was all in black. Giovanna had on one of her weird floor-to-ceiling dresses, this one a blood-colored velvet with big puffy sleeves and a high bodice that flattened whatever tits she had. Her hair was so elaborately coiffed it was impossible to follow its serpentine twists and turns and knots. In an odd way, she looked like a little girl dressed up for a party.

"Ah, *eccoci.* Here they are." Marcello approached and greeted us, shaking everyone's hand but kissing me on the cheek.

I was hyperaware that everyone was watching us, watching Marcello and me, to see how we acted as a couple.

You are beautiful, I told myself. *Remember that.*

Introductions. The dads graceful and at their ease, or at least able to act as if they were. Mom smiling a lot and nervously looking around.

"What an extraordinary dress," La Principessa said to Mom. "Wherever did you find such a creation?"

"I made it," Mom said. "From a Butterick pattern."

"Made it?" Giovanna sounded incredulous. "You mean, on a sewing machine?"

"Mm-hm. My old Singer. Who made your dress?" Mom politely asked Giovanna.

"The Little Doves," she said. "They make all my clothes."

"The Little Doves are nuns, Mom."

"A religious order," La Principessa explained. "Founded by the Brunelli family five hundred years ago."

"Oh, I just love nuns!" Mom exclaimed.

La Principessa looked at her. "Do you?"

"Oh, yes. Audrey Hepburn in *The Nun's Story?* I cry every time I see it. And *Nunsense.* Have you seen that? It's a riot!"

I saw La Principessa turn her head ever so slightly and glance at Marcello. I knew what was in that glance. My cheeks were burning. Then La Principessa turned her regal attention to me. "Miss Gilroy, how are you this evening?"

"*Bene, grazie. E Lei?*"

"Ah! She speaks Italian." La Principessa smiled. She looked at me and started talking. In Italian, of course. I didn't have a clue what she was saying and looked over at Marcello.

"Ah. My mother, she says she is feeling well, thank you, and she is delighted to welcome you and your family to Palazzo Brunelli. As I am."

A white-jacketed waiter appeared with a tray of champagne.

"Allora," Marcello said, "may I have the honor of proposing a toast?"

"But shall we not wait for Giovanni?" La Principessa asked.

"He's probably with his Communist comrades," Giovanna said.

Who, I wondered, was Giovanni? Not Johnny. Why would they want to wait until their chauffeur joined us?

Just then the sound of racing footsteps came echoing up the internal staircase. We all looked in that direction.

Johnny hurried into the salone, his hair wet, a sheepish look on his face. He ran toward us, getting up his momentum, then expertly slid all the way across the huge, slippery floor, right up to La Principessa, seated on the sofa.

"*Scusatemi, nonna,*" he said, bending down to kiss her cheek. "I'm sorry to be late."

"Liar." La Principessa pursed her lips in a grudging, coquettish smile and let him kiss her. Then she pinched his cheek.

Johnny straightened and looked at all of us. Looked at the dads. Looked at my mom. Looked at me.

Marcello stepped forward. "Finally, he is here," he said. He put a hand on Johnny's shoulder. "May I introduce my son, Giovanni?"

Chapter
17

I was an emotional wreck, but I didn't show it because seven people sitting around an enormous oak table in a palazzo in the heart
of Rome were scrutinizing me.

La Principessa didn't want me to marry Marcello, her son, so I
knew she would be the most critical. She was looking for wealth, intelligence, and beauty in a daughter-in-law. She was looking for
pedigree. And she was determined not to find any in me. But La
Principessa was too much of a lady, or too good a poker player, to let
personal emotions register on her face. She was smooth as syrup,
graciously presided at the head of the table, inclining her head to listen to Whitman on one side and Giovanna on the other, a pleasant,
noncommittal smile lifting the corners of her lips. Occasionally her
large cat eyes glanced in my direction, paused for a moment, then slid
away again. Who could tell what she was plotting? Certainly not me.

Marcello wanted me to shine, because of course he wanted his
mother to be impressed. He had that weird male fantasy that
women all like one another just because they're women. He loved
me, Marcello did, and I knew it. There was a kind of safety in that
love. Every time he looked at me, I could feel the warmth of his
emotion. And I wanted to return it. More than anything in the
world, I wished I could look at him with a clear, clean heart full of
pure, pulse-racing excitement.

But Johnny, sitting almost opposite me, made that impossible. I could feel his eyes willing me to look at him. Demanding that I turn my attention to *him*. I refused. Or, rather, I couldn't, because I felt like a total moron. I mean *total*. How could I not have guessed he was Marcello's son? There were clues all over the place. It was just that nobody had ever formally introduced him to me as Giovanni Brunelli, and he had never identified himself as Giovanni Brunelli. He'd probably enjoyed playing with me, pretending to be a chauffeur. Dumb, gullible girls probably fell in love with him all the time. I wanted to melt under the table, just disappear, so I wouldn't have to think about him.

Giovanna, Johnny's sister, Marcello's hawk-nosed daughter, La Principessa's ugly granddaughter, Keeper of the Security Codes, Mistress of the Gates, wanted me dead. Or at least out of Palazzo Brunelli. I was an enormous threat to Giovanna. Of course she didn't want me to marry her dad. That would upset her own empire. And my presence probably tarnished the sacred memory of her dead mother. But Giovanna also had grounds to hate me because I'd exposed her as a thief in her own home. What card could she play now? I wondered. How could she get rid of me without exposing herself? She'd seen those photographs of Giovanni and me on his Vespa and she was probably hoping that there was something between us, between Giovanni and me. If she could catch me out, she could report my treachery to her father. And of course she'd want to sour the opinion of La Principessa against me, too. She was a scary one, Giovanna.

Unlike my mom, Carolee, who didn't believe any one—and especially her daughter—was guilty of anything. It was because of me that Mom was having this Roman adventure, and in her eyes I was forever beautiful and talented in some mysterious way that has always escaped me. I could do no wrong. She would always love me, always believe in me, always believe me. It's comforting to have that kind of unconditional love. It's like always having a big favorite pillow to rest your head on. But I could tell by the bright, unnatural smile she kept glued on her lips that Mom was extremely nervous, afraid she'd breach some code of Old World etiquette and be forever damned, and me with her. She was worried that she might ruin what she saw as my fairy tale come true, do something to upset the fragile balance of events that had led us there, to a palazzo in Rome. Mom was seated next to Giovanni and kept nodding emphatically at everything he said. She was drinking wine and her cheeks were getting flushed. I sensed disaster.

Whitman, my faux pa, was keeping a watchful eye on me while simultaneously working overtime to charm La Principessa. Every table manner I had, I'd learned from Whitman. He'd grown up in a family that ate every meal on bone-china plates using silver utensils and cloth napkins. From Whitman I had learned how to approach soup, twirl spaghetti on a fork ("No more than ten strands at a time so they fit easily into your mouth"), and distinguish between a salad fork and a dinner fork. In his world, people actually said things like, "Shall we have some sorbet to cleanse the palate?" This was my big test, of course, dining with an ancient papal family in a Roman palazzo, and I wasn't going to let Whitman down. I blessed him, actually, for giving me the basics of dining etiquette. And at one point, Whitman seemed to bless me. His sharp eyes noted that I picked up the right utensil and he gave a barely perceptible nod of approval before turning back to dazzle La Principessa with his mouthful of bleached and perfectly capped teeth.

And then there was my Dad. He was seated beside me, next to Marcello, and the two of them were engrossed in a conversation about Italian architecture: who was greater, Borromini or Bernini? My dear old dad was actually younger than Marcello. And with his easygoing, affable air, and his abstraction from the painful side of reality, he didn't have a clue what his daughter was really going through as she sipped acqua minerale from a heavy goblet, ate her grilled fish, and tried as hard as she could not to run crying or screaming from the dinner table.

I poured too much olive oil and balsamic vinegar on my salad and quickly glanced around to see if anyone had noticed. I wasn't used to the Italian habit of pouring out your own portions of oil and vinegar from dainty crystal decanters; I was accustomed to premixed, refrigerated dressings squeezed out of a big easy-grip bottle.

I pretended everything was fine and ate a couple of oil-soaked leaves. The wine was so tempting. I'd let the server pour me a glass because I was too shy to say no. There it sat, untouched, glowing in the diffused late-summer twilight.

Thank God for Whitman and Daddy. Whitman was having a serious opera talk with La Principessa.

"Tebaldi in her prime," La Principessa reminisced. "There was no one like her."

"What about Callas?" Whitman asked.

"A great artist," opined La Principessa, "but a miserable woman."

"You mean she was personally unhappy."

"You cannot take an audience home with you," said La Principessa. "Your home must be separate from the stage. A home must be where you experience real emotions, real love, not the exaggerated emotions of grand opera."

"You were on the stage once, weren't you." Whitman didn't pose it as a question, he stated it as a fact.

"I?" It was hard to tell whether La Principessa was flattered or annoyed by his suggestion. She dismissed the question with a deft hand gesture and a secretive smile.

On my other side, Daddy was saying, "I can appreciate the Baroque, of course, but it always looks so theatrical to me."

"Si si," agreed Marcello. "But you do agree that Bernini and Borromini were great architects, great innovators, great manipulators of space."

"Yeah, but they were only rediscovering what the Romans knew fifteen hundred years before them."

And across from me, I heard Johnny say to my mom, "So you went back into your past lives?"

"Mm-hm," Mom said, sipping her wine. "It's not so hard. You have to be receptive, of course."

"And you actually saw yourself here in Rome, in a temple?"

"I was one of the Vestal Virgins," Mom informed him.

"But that's fantastic," Johnny said. "What was it like?"

"Well, it was fine for some of the girls, I'm sure. But I got walled up alive." She leaned toward him and whispered, "I broke my vows."

At this point, La Principessa rose from her chair and invited everyone to join her in the giant salone for coffee. Whitman offered her his arm and La Principessa, after just a moment's hesitation, took it. The rest of us followed.

I was longing to escape back to my room, but Mom was a little unsteady in her heels. I took her by the arm so she wouldn't slip on the waxed marble floors, and steered her to the nearest comfortable chair. "Thank you, sweetheart," she said, stroking my arm and sort of pulling me down beside her. "That Giovanni is the nicest young man," she whispered. "He talked to me all through dinner."

"Yeah, I noticed."

"His English is perfect. Of course, he did go to Princeton."

So that was one of the East Coast schools Johnny had attended but wouldn't name when I'd asked him. "Did he tell you he's a Communist?" I asked.

"A Communist? Here in Italy? Giovanni?"

To my horror, Johnny heard his name and thought Carolee was summoning him. He turned and came toward us, a smile on his face, his dark eyes on me. "Yes?"

Carolee was flustered. "Oh, nothing. It was just something Venus said. A joke, I think."

"A joke?" Giovanni grinned in anticipation. "Tell me."

"Well, she said you were"—and here my mom, under the influence of two glasses of wine, began to laugh—"she said you were—a Communist!" Tears were running down her cheeks by the time she got it out. "You! The son of one of the richest men in Europe!"

I managed to stand up and turn away from Johnny's gaze and my mother's red-faced fit of laughter.

"But I *am* a Communist," Johnny said.

"Oh, right," howled Carolee, "and I'm the Queen of England!"

"What is so funny?" Marcello asked, coming to join us.

"Your son," Carolee said, dabbing at her eyes with one of the veils floating from her dress, "is pulling my leg. He says he's a Communist."

"Yes, let us hope it is only a phase," Marcello said.

"It's not a *phase*," Johnny said, annoyed. "It's a political party that takes into account something other than the greed and selfishness of capitalism."

"Ah, Giovanni." La Principessa shook her head reprovingly. "You know nothing about communism."

"I beg your pardon," Johnny said politely, "but I know a great deal about political theory."

"You may know about political theory, my boy, but you are too young to know much about human nature. Communists," pronounced La Principessa, "are exactly like everyone else. Greedy. Self-serving. Lazy. Looking for a free handout so they don't have to work."

"And all of them are atheists," Giovanna added. "What kind of a society can you hope to achieve when the people have no moral backbone?"

"You're calling the church a backbone?" Johnny said. "I would have called it a crutch. A *broken* crutch."

Giovanna turned to Marcello. "Papa, why do you always let him torment me about my beliefs?"

"Torment?" Johnny let out a whistle. "Is having a rational discussion a form of torment to you, Giovanna?"

"Faith is not rational," his sister cried.

"That's for sure." Johnny turned to his father. "You somehow think that because of my privileged upbringing—and yes, I will admit that it was privileged—I can't feel the same things that an ordinary man feels."

"Now you sound like Berlusconi," huffed La Principessa. "The billionaire Prime Minister who writes Neapolitan love songs to make the people think that he is one of them. You are not one of them, Giovanni," La Principessa informed her grandson, "so why do you wish to pretend you are?"

"I don't wish to pretend anything, Nonna," Johnny said.

La Principessa looked up at Whitman, standing beside her chair, holding a cup of espresso. "My grandson rides a Vespa," she informed him. "Here, on the streets of Roma. With paparazzi, kidnappers, and terrorists on every corner. Can you imagine how I worry?"

Marcello let out an exasperated sigh. "Giovanni, I have asked you—"

"*Warned* you," Giovanna piped up, speaking to Johnny but looking at me.

"I am not going to live like the rest of you!" Johnny said. "I am not going to live like a prisoner. If I can't live like a free man, what's the point of living at all?" With that, he turned and stormed out of the room.

La Principessa let out a sigh. "Marcello," she said, "I think you should all come to Capri. Eh? Giovanni always loves it there."

"I like it there, too, Nonna," Giovanna said in a childlike voice.

"Si si. Everyone likes it there." La Principessa patted Giovanna's long bony hand. "That's when we are a happy family, eh? When you all come to Capri, and play in Nonna's beautiful garden, and swim in the sea." She turned her attention to Carolee, Daddy, and Whitman. "I invite all of you. Come to my villa in Capri."

The only one she didn't look at was me.

Chapter
18

Finally, finally, finally the evening came to an end. We all said good night or *buona notte*, and went off to our respective bedrooms.

At last, alone, I was free to indulge the chaos of emotions that I'd managed to keep hidden from everyone.

Torn between two lovers, a father and a son . . .

Yes, torn. I wasn't being what Whitman called a "drama queen." My heart really felt like it was going through a shredder.

I wanted to cry, out of habit I suppose, but an oddly rational voice in me asked what good that would do. It said, *Crying is not appropriate for this situation.*

What was appropriate?

Running away.

Yes, running away. That way, I wouldn't have to face any of it. I could simply refuse to participate in an impossible situation.

But run away to where? I had no place to run to. The past was three failed marriages, a dinky apartment, a dead-end job, and never having enough money. The future was a big fat question mark.

The one thing I did know, the one thing that I was now absolutely certain of, was that Marcello loved me. It was a great mystery, almost like a weird sort of miracle. I'd been totally skeptical, certain that all he wanted was my body. As usual, I'd sold myself short. That old beggarly, abandoned, poor-little-me voice lodged deep in my emotional soundtrack chided me for entertaining thoughts above my station. *That kind of man can't love you,* the voice scoffed. *You're not worthy of his love or his money. You have nothing to offer. The only charms you have are physical.*

And because I felt that way, I had viewed Marcello's ongoing pursuit as little more than horniness. Which would have been fine if I'd been horny in return. If I'd desired Marcello as much as he desired me. My attitude, I realized now, was horribly cynical. It cheapened the potential of our relationship by assuming it could only exist on one level, the physical.

But something had happened earlier that day to change the way I viewed Marcello Brunelli. It was nothing spectacular. Exhausted, he'd fallen asleep in my arms. I studied him as he slept. His face softened, the tense lines of worry and agitation disappeared, as though he'd had an injection of botox. He looked...not young, but younger. And serene.

It was kind of amazing, really. This guy, one of the richest men in Europe, trusted me so much that he could fall asleep nestled against my breasts. It made me feel oddly maternal. A sense of sweetness and strength flowed through me. My own power for loving, that ancient instinct that gives a special meaning to life, stirred and stretched.

Marcello had awakened. His eyelids slowly rose. There was no sign of confusion, panic, or embarrassment. He had looked into my eyes and smiled.

And that's what had changed me. That's when I knew he really did love me. It was all in his eyes and his smile and his confidence.

Marcello was offering me a future that I could barely imagine. Marriage. Riches beyond measure! But the package also included a handsome son, a wicked daughter, and a mother who had already offered me a hundred grand to disappear.

If I loved Marcello enough, truly loved him with all my heart and soul, we could overcome the obstacles of his family.

But did I love him that much?

How could I, when Johnny had taken a big bite out of my heart.

It was like a vile joke. A reminder that no fairy tale can come true without the main character overcoming *major* obstacles. You had to lose something to gain something. You had to be tested. (That, at least, was what I had been taught in my junior-college psych-lit class called "Happily Ever After: The Wisdom of Fairy Tales.")

I truly wanted to believe that Johnny had somehow tricked me into falling for him by withholding crucial information. If I'd known he was Marcello's son, my pathetic reasoning went, I would never have entertained those first flirty feelings of attraction. If I'd known who he was, I would have steered my relationship with Johnny in a different direction from the get-go.

Right?

✓ *I would have looked into his large, lustrous eyes without a thought of how irresistible they were, or that I wanted to dive into their dark, midnight depths.*

✓ *I would have viewed his head of black curly hair without imagining how silky-thick it would feel if I ran my fingers through it.*

✓ *I would never have grasped his waist the way I had, tightening my hands on either side of those hard, trim muscles as we raced through the streets of Rome on his Vespa.*

✓ *I would have kept my flesh numb to the heat of his flesh.*

✓ *And if I'd had a clue as to who he really was, there was no way that I would ever have sat with Johnny Brunelli in a romantic Roman piazza overlooking the Pantheon and sipping a double espresso to increase the buzz of being with him.*

Looking back, I could see how it all happened. I could chart out the growth of my attraction to Johnny almost to the minute.

✓ *Admiration for his daring dexterity in traffic.*

✓ *Reverence for his knowledge, and gratitude for the way he shared it.*

✓ *The mindless pleasure of being with someone young, smart, fun, hip, gorgeous.*

✓ *Plus, of course, he'd saved my life. He'd arrived just in the nick of time and prevented those gypsy kids from killing me. When a guy saves your life, you're indebted to him for forever, whether he's cute or not.*

And then there was The Kiss. I'd replayed that moment of panic and passion a few thousand times since it happened. The way he grabbed me, the sudden surprise as we recognized each another, the strange realization, as it was happening, that we were going to express our secret feelings for each other with a kiss, and that we didn't want to stop ourselves.

My feelings for Johnny had become particularly intense after The Kiss. But it was The Kiss that finally brought me back to my senses, to my belief in fair play, to my determination to give Marcello a chance to recapture my faltering attentions.

The funny thing was, all my original feelings for Johnny had been predicated on the assumption that he was someone other than who he really was. As a chauffeur, he was closer to my ingrained social standing, therefore more accessible, than he was as the Princeton-educated son of a multimillionaire.

Father or son?

It was a real dilemma.

Because what made me think that either Marcello or Johnny would want anything to do with me once they discovered that I was pregnant with Tremaynne's baby?

"Venus? Sweetheart, are you awake?"

I was and I wasn't. I'd been in a state of catatonia for hours. My stomach felt weird and I didn't know if it was the oily food, the start of an overdue period, or my first bout of morning sickness.

"Sweetheart?" I turned toward the whispered voice. Heard the scuffle of Mom's slippers on the marble floor. Suddenly she was in my bed, pulling me into a squeeze, all hot and riled up about something. "I hope I didn't wake you. I just couldn't sleep any more."

"Jet lag," I said.

"I tossed and turned. Then I heard something being slid under my door." She fluttered an envelope in my face. "You won't believe it." Before I could respond, she'd pulled a letter from the envelope.

"'My beautiful Signora Gilroy,'" she read, then looked up as a thought suddenly occurred to her. "That *is* me, right? I'm *Signora* Gilroy—Mrs. Gilroy—and you're *Signorina* Gilroy—Miss Gilroy."

"Yes, Mom, you're Signora and I'm Signorina."

"Thank God!" Mom said. "Otherwise this letter would be for you instead of me."

"Just read it, OK?"

"'My beautiful Signora Gilroy,' with 'beautiful' misspelled and underlined twice, 'on behalf of all the mens of Roma, I wish to tell you how very gratitude I am'—"

" 'Gratitude I am'?"

"That's what it says. '... how very gratitude I am for your beauty,' only he spells it 'booty.' "

"Who's this from anyway?"

"Just listen." She breathlessly read on. "'I congratulate,' misspelled, 'you on the size of your beauty.' "

"Booty," I laughed.

Mom ignored me. "'I wish to partake'—well, I really shouldn't read this part," she said, sitting back on her haunches and fanning herself.

"Read!"

" 'I wish to partake of your charming magnitude and offer the—the'—something—"

I grabbed the letter. " '... and offer the pleasure'?—something with a *p*—'the pleasant? the pleasure? of—of—' "

Mom grabbed the letter back. " '... the pleasant or pleasure of dinning—' "

"Dining, obviously."

" '... of dinning on my money.' "

"He thinks you're beautiful and he wants to take you out to dinner," I paraphrased. "So who is it? Fabio?"

Mom leaned close, eyes narrowed. "How did you know?"

"He's had his eyes on you ever since you arrived."

"Has he? Yes, I guess he has." She fiddled with her hair and tried not to smile. "But what about my sweet little Cesare?"

"What about him?"

"Well, he adores me too," Mom said. "*Ti adoro.* That's what he said to me. *Ti adoro.* It means 'I adore you.'"

"Fine, he adores you, but he lives down in Naples."

"Yes, but we talked on the phone and Cesare wants me to come down there."

"Are you going?"

"I don't know," Mom said. "What do you think I should do?"

I was suddenly a little alarmed. Felt like a mother who's asked to help her daughter make some major life-changing decision.

"He wants you to visit him?"

Mom nodded. "On his chicken farm."

"You mean, like, stay with him? Go down and stay with him in his house?"

"Well . . . yes . . ."

"And sleep with him, obviously."

Mom blushed and gave her freshly tinted red hair a major fluff. "He didn't say that."

"Well, Mom, sometimes it's just understood."

I watched her. My mom, anxious as a sixteen-year-old before a date. She'd long ago given up believing another guy would ever enter her life. After Daddy left, she'd never found another romantic outlet for the huge amount of love she had to give. All she had was me.

"For heaven's sake," she said, "I haven't had sex in about two thousand years."

"Nothing's changed, Mom."

"I suppose it's like riding a bicycle." She brushed the hair away from my face. "I'll tell you a secret, honey. I have absolutely no idea how to act with a man."

"You don't act, Mom. You stay you. Who you are."

"But who am I?" she asked. "I don't know anymore. I mean, here I am in Rome. Thousands of miles away from Portland, right? From home, right? From all the things that made me *me*. Do you understand what I'm saying?"

I nodded.

"My life started to change the minute I dared myself to get on that plane. Once I did that, once I faced that horrible fear, it was like I was free of something. Free of the old Carolee."

"There was nothing wrong with the old Carolee, Mom."

"Except that she never went anywhere. Or did anything. And no one ever saw her. No one ever looked at the old Carolee. Men, I mean. And suddenly here I am in Rome, and one guy is telling me how beautiful I am, and another guy's begging me to come down to his farm. So I don't really know who I am or what I should do and I need some advice because it's all so completely frigging crazy."

My mom coming to *me* for advice about what to do when two men are vying for your attention. I kept the irony of it to myself. "Which one do you like better," I asked. "Fabio or Cesare?"

"That's the problem. I like them both."

"So why can't you see both?"

"Well, sweetheart, I've only got a week. How can I spend any time with you if I'm running around with Fabio here in Rome and visiting Cesare down in Naples?"

"And what about Capri? La Principessa invited you."

"Maybe I'd better call work," Mom said. "Tell them I need a few extra days."

It was before seven, and Mom had gone back to bed, and I'd fallen back into my catatonic state, when Marcello tiptoed in. "Darling, are you awake?" he whispered.

He was wearing a linen suit and a dazzling white shirt with starched cuffs and collar and a patterned tie. I could smell a lemony tang of aftershave or cologne.

"Where are you off to this time?" I said.

He winced. "Darling, I've been summoned to Parma."

"Why?"

"The plant there is—ah, what does it matter. My entire life is spent dealing with emergencies."

"You're failing slacker class." I said. "I'm giving you an F."

He sat on the edge of my bed and ran his hand along the curve of my body, then leaned close and planted a kiss on my cheek. "I promise I will be back tonight."

"If you can't ever be with me," I said, turning away, "I may as well go home."

"Venus—"

"How can I ever get to know you, really know you, if you're gone all the time?"

"I was planning to be with you today. But the plant in Parma—"

"I mean, you say you want to marry me. But I don't even know you. I *can't* get to know you. Because you're working all the time."

"I will try to change that," he said. "I will arrange it so we can go to Capri. Mama has already left."

It was right on the tip of my tongue. I was ready to blurt it all out. I wanted to tell him everything: about his mother's attempted bribe, his daughter's thievery, his son's kiss, even about my maybe-baby. I wanted to clear the air, put us on an honest footing.

And test him. Really test him. See how he'd react, what he'd do.

"Marcello," I said, "we really need to talk."

"Yes. We'll talk in Capri. I'll take you to the Blue Grotto."

"No, we need to talk now."

"Allora." He glanced at his watch. Then his phone rang. His body tensed and his voice changed. He rose from the bed and began yelling into the tiny phone, chopping and jabbing the air. A vein rose on the side of his skull. He paced around the room as he spoke and kept glancing at his watch. Finally, after a final shout into the phone, he hurried over to plant another kiss, this one fast and forceful, on my lips.

"Darling, I am absolutely late for my plane. I'll call you later in the day and see you tonight for dinner. Have fun with your family, eh?"

With that he turned and hurried from the room.

After breakfast, Daddy, Whitman, Mom, and I set out for some sightseeing. Whitman, who'd written a travel guide to Rome years earlier, had planned out an exacting, exhausting itinerary. I didn't care where we went or what we saw. My mind was elsewhere, my stomach queasy, and I just wanted to follow along without thinking.

Being with my three parents on a limousine tour of Rome wasn't like zipping around the streets on the back of Johnny's Vespa, though.

It felt kind of weird, all of us being together like a family on vacation. Mom and the dads got together on "big" social occasions (my birthdays and weddings) but otherwise led pretty separate lives. Seeing Mom and Dad together was always kind of weird. That John and Carolee were a once-viable marital unit amazed me because they were so completely unalike.

For one thing, Mom had never quite figured out the clothes thing.

I did a fast double take when she appeared in my room and said, "OK, I'm ready for Rome!" I didn't scream, roll my eyes, or say something cutting. I decided that I was just going to let Mom be Mom, or Carolee be Carolee. Being in Rome with two Italian men begging for the pleasure of her plus-size company, she was on a once-in-a-lifetime high.

I felt like *her* mother in a weird way. Like a mom who knew it was time for her daughter to fly the coop but was worried that she'd crash into a wall.

She'd been nervously humming a tune off and on since she arrived, and finally put some words to the melody as we made our way through the hallways of Palazzo Brunelli. "'Three coins in the fountain . . .'" She hummed away at the song until she suddenly turned to Daddy and said, "Have you called your first ex-wife yet?"

There was a pause before Whitman said, "Yes, John, have you called her yet?"

"Such a beautiful woman," Mom said. "Did she ever tell you exactly *why* she ran off? Why she just disappeared like that?"

Daddy ignored the question.

"I'd be sooo curious," Mom went on. "Wouldn't you, Whitman? I'd want to know *why*. You know, John, this is really a perfect opportunity for you to find out. It might help to heal the wound and bring some closure."

"On the other hand," Whitman said, "it might just open things up and make everything really nasty."

Daddy doesn't like to deal with emotional issues. I could sense that he was tensing up, so I put my arm through his and gave his biceps a surreptitious squeeze. He flexed, to let me know he was OK.

There was no sign of Johnny or Giovanna or La Principessa as the four of us made our way through the vast, shuttered, flower-filled public rooms of Palazzo Brunelli and out to the courtyard.

Stepping outside was like stepping into a furnace. The sun, even at 10:30 A.M., was like a fiery fist. We'd heard at dinner the night before that all of Europe was broiling in an unprecedented heat wave.

"My God, it's so sultry," Mom said, slinking carefully down the stone stairs in her inappropriate footwear. She was wearing high-heeled sandals, black Lycra shorts, and a long, loose, red blouse that looked like a man's shirt, with the collar left casually open all the way down to her black boob tube. How she'd transported that wide-brimmed straw hat, I don't know, but there it was, with a red gossamer streamer floating off behind. She gripped the stone balustrade with one hand and waved at Fabio, waiting by the limo, with the other.

"Mama mia," he said appreciatively, giving himself a quick fan.

Carolee giggled. "Si si," she said. "But Mama's going to be very hot!"

"Carolee, you might want to rethink the shoes," Whitman said, watching her tortuous descent. "They're very sexy, but I don't think they'll take kindly to cobblestones."

"Cobblestones?" Mom shot him a nervous glance. "I thought we were just going to stay in the car. You know, look out the window at things. With the air-conditioning on."

"No, dear. We'll be walking. Outside. To get to places."

Mom looked hopefully at me. "There's a pair of black flats in my room."

"I'll get them." I dutifully ran back inside, down the hallways, into my palazetto, marveling that even the grandest of palaces became familiar over time. Part of me was already at home in Palazzo Brunelli. Knew its general layout. Knew what I'd find in each giant room.

I tapped in the code, darted into our suite, found Mom's flat-heeled shoes, and headed out again.

You know that feeling you get when you see a long wooden banister? The devilish kid in you wants to jump on and slide down. I was having a similar moment now. As I sped down the waxed marble hallways of Palazzo Brunelli, I wanted to slide across the entire giant salone the way I'd seen Johnny do the night before. Sort of a cross between flying and skating. I was wearing shoes with thin leather soles—perfect for this sort of Wonder Woman technique.

I was going pretty fast as I came out of the hallway and into the salone. My runway was about eighty feet of slippery, slideable marble from the end of the hallway to the first step of the internal staircase.

The trick was to gain momentum without slipping on the waxed tiles. It was like running on ice. I sprinted another twenty feet and then let go.

It was a ridiculously wonderful sensation. I whizzed effortlessly across the massive room, watched by all the Brunellis gathered overhead in the frescoed domed ceiling and lining the walls. For just a moment, a feeling of freedom, a kid again, almost Wonder Woman.

I'd gauged how far I could slide before my momentum failed, and I was only about halfway there when Johnny came running up the internal staircase and into the salone. He saw me and put on his brakes, but he started to slide, too. I screamed something like, "Ooohhhhh!" and Johnny shouted something like, "Aaahhh!" We fixed horrified expressions on each other as our bodies slid like approaching cars on an icy street.

We crashed.

Sort of fumbled to grab hold of each other and keep our balance, but I shot out to one side and rammed into a big overstuffed chair. Johnny spun like a skater and desperately grabbed a huge floor lamp for support. It came down with him.

"Oh my God," I moaned.

"You all right?"

I turned to look at him and started to laugh. "Yeah. I'm OK. Are you OK?"

"I'm OK," he said. "But the lamp's not OK."

OK, so we got a little hysterical. It was funny. Maybe not as funny as my gasping shrieks of laughter warranted, but funny all the same.

Johnny stood up, righted the lamp, and started toward me. But when he put his left foot down, he winced and let out a sharp gasp. "Ow! Jesus Christ in China!"

I was instantly sober, afraid he'd broken his ankle or leg. And I, of course, was responsible.

I helped him over to a sofa. "Do you think something's broken?"

He examined his ankle. "No, but definitely sprained."

"I'm so sorry."

He looked up at me as I stupidly hovered over him, not knowing what to do, not knowing whether I should touch the ankle or call an ambulance or what. "It's OK," he said calmly.

"I feel like such an idiot!" I blurted out. "Sliding across the room like a stupid kid!"

"Venus, it's OK. Really." He touched my arm.

My face was hot and I was sweating. The pulsing sensation in my gut grew stronger. I knew what was happening, and it had nothing to do with last night's dinner.

I needed to get back to my room double-quick.

But Johnny wanted to talk. "You looked beautiful last night," he said.

"Thanks. But look, right now I need to—"

"I knew what you were trying to do," he said.

That stopped me. "Do what?"

"You know what." He sat back, spread his legs, and smiled.

No man should have a smile like that. There should be a tax on it. Or maybe a ban. "I don't know what you're talking about."

"Yes, you do," Johnny said. "And you succeeded."

"Succeeded in what?" I clenched my thighs and thought of St. Agnes in agony.

"Why don't you—why don't we—"

Oh. My. God. It was coming. In a moment, it would be staining my beautiful new white silk panties from Saks.

"Johnny, I've got to go. I've really got to go."

"Will I see you later?" he called.

I was already halfway across the salone and pretended not to hear.

Chapter
19

I could have gotten out of the sightseeing. I could have stayed in my room and lain on the bed in variations of a fetal position. I didn't have cramps, but I could have said that I did, and that would have been a very handy excuse.

But I decided staying alone in Palazzo Brunelli was not wise. I didn't want to be there by myself.

So I took care of matters. Tucked a few extra tampons into my cute little microweave purse. Stood in front of the full-length mirrors in La Signora's closet and sucked in a round of deep Buddha breaths, the way Whitman had taught me to do when times were tense. Then, slowly this time, with a firm, deliberate tread, I left my suite, walked through the hallways of Palazzo Brunelli, and straight out to the courtyard.

Johnny wasn't in the salone, or if he was, I didn't see him. I was keeping my eyes straight ahead. Avoiding all temptations.

The limo was waiting at the gate. Mom was sitting in front. I slipped in the back with the dads.

"Sweetheart, we were about to send in a search party," Mom said.

"Sorry."

"Did you bring my shoes?"

"Oh, shit. I'm sorry. I'll go back."

"No!" Mom said. "I'll be fine."

"We shouldn't waste any more time," Whitman said. "If we don't get to the Capella Sistina in about ten minutes, the lines will be so long we'll never get in."

"Right," Mom said. "Let's go!"

"Avanti?" Fabio said. "We go now?" He punched in the code. The security gate opened and the limo nosed out into the street.

Daddy stroked my arm, took my hand. "What's wrong?"

I laid my head on his shoulder. "Just my period."

Just my period.

No big deal.

My body, like that of every woman since the dawn of time, was cycling through its eternal internal preparations for motherhood, sloughing off the old in preparation for the new. Because the working womb never gives up its reproductive readiness, its hope that it will catch a sperm at just the right moment and create life, no matter what the consequences.

This period meant a lot more to me than Mom and the dads would ever know.

It signaled the end of my connection to Tremaynne.

It meant that I wasn't pregnant with his baby.

I was free.

That's what I kept telling myself as we drove north along the Tiber, crossed a bridge, and headed down a wide avenue called Via della Conciliazione.

Whitman had everything planned out to the nanosecond. He never traveled anywhere without first getting a travel-writing assignment. On this trip, he was writing a story called "Three Romantic Days in Rome" for an airline magazine.

First we marched into the Vatican Museums, so that Carolee and I could see the Sistine Chapel (which Whitman insisted on calling "the *Cappella Sistina*").

I kept close to Daddy, holding on to his arm like a little girl. It was a blessing not to have to think, or make decisions. I just followed along, through the security check, up a circular staircase, down miles of corridors. The rooms hummed with the muffled din of thousands

of tourists from every country in the world. Tour guides held up umbrellas or little flags for the groups nervously following behind them.
Ahead of us, Mom was valiantly clicking along at the brisk pace dic-
tated by Whitman.

A series of dull, declarative sentences tolled in my head. *You're
not pregnant. You're not having his baby. You don't have to worry about
that anymore. Tremaynne is no longer part of your life.*

Part of me was relieved and even happy in a shocked sort of way.
The lifelong responsibility of having a child, of being a single parent, had been lifted from my shoulders. But of course it brought
back a flood of Tremaynne-memories, memories of my passion for
him, my love, memories of our crazy honeymoon, of how we'd escaped death together only to part at the end of what should have
been our beginning.

I followed my parents, Whitman in the lead, through a complicated series of galleries, hallways, and small chambers into a long,
narrow room crammed with people staring up at the barrel-vaulted
ceiling.

Mom cried, "Oh my God!" and burst into tears.

It was the Sistine Chapel.

Like everyone else, I looked up. I saw the ceiling Michelangelo
had painted. The colors stormed my eyes with their throbbing radi-
ance. Rich magentas, glowing blues, vibrating yellows, vibrant greens—
a palette of such amazing intensity and luminosity that even my
poor ignorant heart instinctively shared its splendor and soared in
wonder to see it.

There, in the center of the ceiling, was the famous image of the
outstretched hand of God, finger extended, about to jolt Adam to
life.

I knew the story of Adam and Eve, sort of, but the rest of the
Bible was a complete and utter mystery to me. "What does it all
mean?" I asked Daddy.

He tried to explain. He was the son of missionaries and the Bible
had been belted into him. He went through the pictorial narrative
on the ceiling scene by scene, pointing out the prophets and the
sibyls and explaining in shorthand the various stories. I heard about

half of it. My head was buzzing with the strangeness of it all. Disobeyed laws, expulsion from paradise, God being born on earth to a virgin . . .

From the Vatican Museums, Whitman insisted we walk to St. Peter's. Fabio had parked the limo somewhere and joined us outside. Carolee, starting to feel the effects of her high heels, took his arm for support.

Tremaynne never loved you. It slipped like a dark shadow into my thoughts as we crept along the sun-drenched streets. *You are a terrible judge of character. You are afraid to love "above your station" so you always look for the lowest common denominator. That's how you keep yourself down and poor and miserable.*

Daddy patted my hand as we walked. "We all really like Marcello," he said.

I smiled dumbly.

"How is it going with him?" Daddy asked.

I shrugged. "I don't know. He's never there. He's always working."

"Well, sweetheart, that's what men do when they run their own businesses."

"I know that. I understand that. But when do they live their lives?"

"Work becomes their life," Daddy said. Then, after a pause, "You'll have to get used to that, sweetheart."

"If I stay in Rome, you mean. If I marry Marcello."

"He loves you very much," Daddy said, stroking my hand. "Last night he asked me if I had any objections."

"To what?"

"Your marriage. He wants to marry you."

"I know." I looked into Daddy's calm blue eyes, seeking a moment of rest. "What do you think I should do?"

"Do you love him?"

"Sort of. I don't know. I keep waiting for, like, some revelation. Something to make me sure."

"Maybe the revelation is that there isn't a revelation."

That hadn't occurred to me. When it came to love, I was always waiting for the oracle of my heart to whisper yes or no. But after three failed marriages, it was obviously time to fire the oracle.

We followed Whitman through a gigantic colonnade and entered a giant square with a colossal church at one end.

"Oh my God!" Carolee whipped out her disposable camera and had us all pose in front of St. Peter's. Then she asked me to take one of her with Fabio. Then we made our way into the cool cavernous interior of St. Peter's.

But Carolee was stopped at the door by a black-robed priest acting like a bouncer at a club. "Signora." He pointed at her legs. "*Non permesso.*"

"What?" Carolee's face clouded with confusion. "Did I do something wrong?"

First Fabio stepped forward to speak to the priest. Then Fabio conferred with Whitman. Then Whitman conferred with the priest, the two of them pointing and examining Carolee as if they were judges and she were a prize heifer at the state fair. Finally Whitman said, "It's your Lycra. He's being an asshole and saying your shorts or whatever they are are inappropriate."

"Inappropriate?" Mom was flabbergasted. "But I got them at Nordstrom!"

"He says they're too tight," Whitman reported. "And Venus has to have a scarf or something on her head."

"A scarf? I don't wear headscarves!"

The sour-faced priest wouldn't budge. Mom and I were banned from entering St. Peter's. I thought of that scene in the Sistine Chapel, the *Expulsion from Paradise*. But it was really weird to imagine that God would give a shit about my not wearing a scarf, or that Mom was wearing Lycra.

Whitman didn't accept defeat lightly. "Thank God you're in layers," he said to Carolee, explaining his scheme. A minute later, we were ordered to stand around her, outside the doors to St. Peter's, as Mom unpeeled her Lycra shorts. That left only the long red shirt, which Whitman thought might pass for a dress. "They may say it's too short," he warned her as we made our way toward a different door.

"What about my scarf?"

Whitman said, "Carolee, may I?" and whipped the red gossamer thingie off her straw hat and gave it to me.

I gingerly tied it around my head, knowing how absolutely ridiculous I looked.

We were all trying not to laugh as we entered St. Peter's. This time, no one stopped us.

OK, I'd been in New York. I'd been in big buildings and tall buildings. I'd even been in St. Patrick's and a church Whitman called St. John-*too*-Divine. But this was like nothing I'd ever seen or been in before. It was gigantic.

The funny thing about St. Peter's, though, was that there wasn't really that much in it to see. It felt kind of huge and empty.

The most famous piece of art in it was Michaelangelo's *Pieta*, which stood behind a thick wall of glass. Whitman said a few years back a madman had taken a hammer to it. The glass wall was there to protect it from further assaults.

I studied the marble figures, trying to understand the meaning behind them. Mary, the virgin who'd given birth to Jesus, the son of God, was tenderly holding her dead son after he'd been taken down from the cross, where he'd died to save humankind.

Save us from what?

I just didn't get it. The story was like an intricate jigsaw puzzle that I couldn't piece together.

It got hotter and hotter as the day wore on.

After St. Peter's (Whitman called it *San Pietro*), we got back into the blessedly air-conditioned limo and Fabio drove us to Trastevere. We had lunch at a restaurant on a square that I recognized from my sightseeing days with Johnny. There was a fountain in the middle and a church at one end. We'd gone through that square on Johnny's Vespa to get to the café where Johnny's friend Flavinia had insulted America. Not far from there, I'd been attacked by the gypsy kids.

I had a history with that square.

The gypsy beggar kids would have made a good story, but I didn't want to worry Mom and the dads. Or tell them about Johnny.

They were all in the midst of their own secret dramas. Not so secret in Mom's case, since she spent much of her sightseeing time gazing into Fabio's eyes. At lunch, she chugged down two glasses of red wine and began to laugh uproariously at everything Fabio said—which wasn't much, because his English was limited and he was shy about using it.

Daddy and Whitman seemed estranged somehow. It made me uncomfortable because usually they were totally fixated on each other. But now, and ever since they had arrived, there was a funny disconnect between them.

Whitman and Daddy each had a "past" in Rome. They'd both spent a lot of time here in their younger days. I didn't know much about those days, except that Whitman had studied singing and had some kind of affair with a rich Italian. Daddy had briefly worked in a Roman architectural firm and met the mysterious Gabriella Mangione here.

Daddy's distracted air made me wonder what was going on. Was he reliving his past with Gabriella? Was he reliving those bygone days when he was still a practicing heterosexual? Days before Carolee, before Whitman, before me?

After lunch, Fabio drove us to the Forum (or *Forum Romanum*, as Whitman called it).

It was hard to believe this jumble of ruins had once been what Whitman called "the epicenter of Rome." As we walked down the Via Sacra ("the Sacred Way," Whitman informed us, "used as the official path by all ancient processions"), he reconstructed mighty temples, halls, markets, and basilicas from a few broken columns, brick walls, and slabs of pitted marble.

Carolee, wobbling on her high heels, clutching Fabio's arm, asked where the Vestal Virgins had lived.

Whitman pointed. "Right there. Via Hymen 23."

Carolee disengaged herself from Fabio's arm, teetered toward the ruins, and stood in front of them with a look of reverence. "This used to be my home office," she informed Fabio, who looked to Whitman for a translation. "Oh, look, it's circular," Carolee marveled, stepping across the threshold.

"It looks kind of small," I said, joining her.

"Well, we were all much smaller back then," Mom informed me. She sighed.

"What did the Vestal Virgins do?" I asked. "I mean, besides being virgins."

"We kept the sacred flame burning. Day and night."

"That's it?"

"I'm sure there was more," Mom said. "But that's the part I remembered in my past-life soul retrieval. That and being walled up alive." Her voice rose. She was still a little high from the wine at lunch. "For having sex! Big deal!"

"Where do you think they walled you up?"

"Over there!" Mom pointed. "I can feel it! Oh my God!"

If I hadn't caught her, she would have passed out in the foyer of her former home office.

"It was the heat," Whitman said. "Wine and hot sun do not mix well."

We'd left the Forum and were sitting at the edge of the Trevi fountain, the last tourist attraction of the day.

"It wasn't the heat," Mom murmured. "Or the wine."

"Then what was it?" Whitman asked.

"A memory," Carolee said.

"Of?"

"Of how unfair it was. How scared I was. How young I was."

"Mom," I said, "that was, like, two thousand years ago."

"These things become part of your psychic karma," Mom assured me. "You're doomed to repeat and repeat certain things until you actually confront them head-on. Only then can you change your destiny. Move on. Boogie to a new tune."

Daddy had left for a few minutes, saying there was a store nearby that he wanted to check out. Fabio had gone to get some bottled water for Mom. The rest of us—Mom, Whitman, and I— stared silently into the crazy drama of the Trevi fountain. Horses reared up, sea gods blew on conch shells, water poured off rocky ledges and splashed noisily into the basin below. The water sent a cool breath up into the small piazza that surrounded the fountain.

Whitman asked my mom what she needed to confront.

"My life," she said. "Sex."

"What about it?" Whitman said.

"Everything. All my inhibitions. All my fears. They all come from being walled up alive. Just because I wanted to have a little fun."

"But you knew celibacy was part of the job description," Whitman said.

"Oh, well,"—Mom shook her head—"all it takes is one . . . burning glance . . . and I'm ready to boogie. That's how I've always been. But something always goes wrong. So I'm afraid to let myself go. I want to. I try to. But something inside always holds me back."

"A fear of looking ridiculous," Whitman said. "That's why I hold back."

"You?" I thought he was kidding and let out a snort of laughter.

"Yes, me. Expressing love," Whitman said. "Saying 'I love you.' It's the most difficult thing in the world."

"No," Carolee said, "the most difficult thing is when you don't have anyone to say 'I love you' to."

We were all silent, staring at the fountain, but then Mom started to hum that tune again.

"Carolee," Whitman said, "did you know this *is* the fountain?"

Mom stopped humming. "The 'Three Coins in the Fountain' fountain?"

"This is it. 1954. Technicolor and CinemaScope." He laughed and sang the corny lyrics as Mom dug through her purse. She came up with three coins.

The American quarter she gave to Whitman. The euro coin she gave to me. And for herself she had a silver dollar. But not just any silver dollar. Her *lucky* silver dollar. It was from 1883, and she'd won it in a contest when she was in grade school.

"Mom," I squawked, "you're not throwing in your lucky dollar!"

"Why not?"

I shook my head, suddenly superstitious. "Let me give you a dime or a euro or something."

But my insistence only made her more stubbornly determined. "I'm going to throw it. You have to give up things to get things."

"But it's worth, like, a thousand dollars!"

"Venus." Whitman put a hand to silence me. "Let your mother throw the coin."

"What exactly do we do, Whitman?" Mom asked.

"We stand and throw the coins over our left shoulder."

"And make a wish?"

"Yes, make a wish."

"Out loud?"

"No. Silently. It's between you and your heart."

Suddenly we were all kind of solemn, the way you are before superstitious moments. We stood up and turned away from the fountain, staring out into the noisy throng of tourists seated and moving around its perimeter.

I watched Mom close her eyes. She was breathing really hard, concentrating. Whitman glanced at me, nodded, and did the same.

"Ready, sweetheart?" Mom asked.

I made my wish. Closed my eyes.

"On the count of three," Whitman said. "One, two, three . . ."

We flipped our coins into the fountain. Opened our eyes. Smiled.

But suddenly Mom's face was stricken with what looked like paralyzing fear. "Whitman," she gasped. "Oh my God. Which shoulder did you say?"

"The left."

Carolee let out a strangled cry. "Oh God! I threw it over my right!"

Before we could stop her, she'd plunged into the fountain.

With Fabio's help, Mom got her silver dollar back. Then, dripping wet, she threw in another coin, this time over her left shoulder. And then she turned to Fabio and gave him a clumsy kiss.

It all created quite an uproar in the hot little square.

When Daddy returned, we all headed back to the limo and Fabio drove us back to Palazzo Brunelli.

I saw the envelope as soon as I entered my bedroom. Mom was with me, soaked and chattering. I didn't open it until she was gone.

Inside, there was a photograph of me kissing Johnny Brunelli. Taken with a flash in Asclepio, the nightclub.

There was no message. No blackmail note. Niente.

Which made it creepier. Who had sent it? Giovanna? Carlo and Baby? Maybe Johnny himself?

My name was not written on the envelope.

I asked Teresina about it. "Where did this envelope come from?"

She shrugged. "I do not know, signorina." She said she hadn't been there between noon and four o'clock.

"It seems funny that with all the security around here, people still manage to get in and out."

"Signorina?"

"Never mind."

I didn't want her to think that I was freaked out. I sat down on the huge bed and stared at the photo.

Was it a warning? An indictment? A prelude to blackmail? Or just a beautiful memory captured on film?

Chapter
20

I'd never had a day alone with Whitman. I'd had maybe an hour alone, or, when I was a kid and went to visit him and Daddy in New York, maybe a half a day. But never a full day alone as adults.

So I was a little surprised when my faux pa asked me to accompany him on his second day of research for the "Three Romantic Days in Rome" article. He said he wanted to see if an out-of-shape American could keep up with the fast-paced itinerary he'd created.

Daddy said he couldn't come because there was "something else" he had to do. Mom bowed out, too, saying she couldn't deal with the heat and that Fabio had promised to take her to a beach somewhere. Marcello hadn't returned from Parma, La Principessa had fled back to Capri the day before without so much as an addio, and I didn't have a clue what Johnny and Giovanna were up to. So rather than twiddle my thumbs in Palazzo Brunelli, I agreed to go with Whitman.

We sneaked out like thieves, expecting the street to be full of paparazzi, but it was so hot that even the photographers had disappeared.

I was impressed at how well Whitman knew Rome. "Let's take this shortcut," he'd say, turning into a tiny alleyway before I even had time to find the street name on my foldout map.

Whitman could get around mapless and knew all the bus routes.

"Not that you'll ever have to take the bus, sweetheart, if you marry into the Brunelli clan. But to really see Rome, you need to see it like Romans do."

I loved getting into the orange Roman buses and lurching around the city and watching the dark-eyed, dark-haired people and even getting my ass pinched. ("Rome is a *hands-on* city," Whitman said.) It was way more fun than sitting in the limo behind tinted bullet-proof glass.

Around one o'clock we left Hadrian's Tomb (*Mausolea d'Adriano*, Whitman insisted on calling it) and strolled across the Tiber on a bridge called Ponte Sant'Angelo. The bridge was lined with statues of sweetly smiling angels carrying what looked like torture equipment. When I asked Whitman about them, he said, "Those are the instruments of the Passion."

"Whose passion?"

"Christ's. On his way to the cross."

It was weird and unsettling and I just didn't get it. All over the city, there was a creepy undertow of violence and pain and death. Whitman showed me weird sights, pointing out sculptures and paintings that were gruesome reminders of mortality—leering skulls with hungry smiles and tortured martyrs having their heads chopped off or their eyes gouged out or their skin flayed or being dipped in vats of boiling oil.

It wasn't all blood and gore, though. The city Whitman showed me was also filled with a kind of joyous, giggly beauty. I saw slender marble boys (never girls) or mischievous little boys with fat butts and jowly faces, perched on high, dim ledges in church chapels; statues of saints in wild-eyed ecstasy ("Look," Whitman said, "she's having a spiritual orgasm"); and fluffy, weightless angels that were nothing more than heads in a pair of wings.

The sheer theatrical drama of Rome was unending. It was so totally unlike America, and so totally *totally* unlike Portland, Oregon. Everywhere you looked in Rome there were statues. They stood high up, on the parapets of buildings and colonnades, silhouetted against the sky, and greeted you in street-level piazzas, always giving what looked like a blessing or a salute. A lot of the deities or saints or apostles, or whatever they were, had been sculpted in the seventeenth and eighteenth centuries ("the exalted Renaissance," according to Whitman, "which gave way to the exuberant Baroque, which evolved into the ridiculous Rococo"). But the city was also studded with fragments of really ancient statues, like the giant sandaled foot Whitman showed me on a narrow side street in an area called the Ghetto, and the colossal head of an emperor fiercely glaring from a courtyard of the Capitoline Museums.

I got this sense—it's hard to describe—that the city was churning with mysterious presences, mysterious powers, mysterious fates. Whitman kept pointing out little shrines set into the sides of buildings, where the time-smudged face of a saint or Madonna peered out from behind votive candleholders and withered bouquets.

"Carpe diem," Whitman said as we walked across the Ponte Sant'Angelo from Hadrian's Tomb. "It's Latin. Know what it means?"

"Consumer beware?"

"No. Seize the day. Live for now."

"Are you telling me or you?"

He shrugged and stopped to look down into the sluggish brown waters of the Tiber. "That's the lesson of Rome," he said with a melodramatic sigh. "Everything ends. *Tutto è finito.*"

I couldn't stand it anymore. I had to know. "Whitman, is something wrong between you and Daddy?"

Whitman sniffed. For a moment I thought he was going to cry. But he didn't. He flicked his hair back—the new cut required constant flicking—and started walking again, leading me from the bridge into a warren of dark, narrow streets.

"Whitman? Do you want to talk about it?"

"It's nothing," he said. "Your father's sick of me, that's all."

"What?"

"He's tired of me. Bored with me."

"Since when?"

"Since he met that first ex-wife of his on the plane."

"Gabriella?"

"Why do you think he's not with us today? Hm?"

"He said he had something else he had to—"

"He had to meet *Gabriella*. A nostalgic rendezvous at her charming little antiques store. Which happens to be somewhere along this street."

Whitman stopped to peer into the windows of the small and very exclusive shops that lined Via dei Coronari.

"If we happen to run into them," he said, "pretend that we're doing the shopping research for my travel story."

"Whitman, this is ridic—"

"You take that side of the street and I'll take this one. Cough if you see them."

"Try some of the squid," Whitman said. "It's cooked in its own ink."

I shook my head, unable to look at the little purply things swimming in a sauce the color of licorice.

"So tell me how it's going," Whitman said, chewing on a squid.

"I don't know what to tell you."

"Can you imagine yourself living with that family?"

"I don't know." I hazarded my own question. "What did you think of them?"

Whitman chewed some more. "Well, Marcello's charming. And handsome. And refreshingly unsnobbish for a multimillionaire. Overall, I like him."

"What did you think of Giovanna?"

"Signorina Schnozzola? She gave me the creepolas."

"Really?"

"It wasn't just the nose, although God knows a beak like that is hard to ignore. She could spear fish with it. And the clothes, what are those all about? Half nun and half Renaissance princess."

I longed to tell him about the watch, about Giovanna's drug-fueled past, about the accident that had crippled her. But I resisted because I didn't want Whitman to ask me where my information came from. I was trying hard not to think about Johnny.

"You'll have to watch out for that one," Whitman cautioned. "She's extremely angry about something. Obviously you're a huge threat to her."

"I don't want to be," I said. "I haven't done anything to her."
Whitman patted my hand. "Sweetheart, there are certain things
you just do not understand. Like money." He took a sip of his
Pellegrino and flipped back his hair. "Look, you've entered into a
different class here. You understand that, don't you?"

I nodded, wanting every bit of information he could give me.

"A different social level," Whitman continued. "Part of it is the
family's history. They have a pope in their background."

"Why is that so important?"

"It isn't. Not for an American, anyway, because we're all immigrants and we have so little history. But for an Italian family to have
a pope in their lineage, well, it connects them to what was once the
most powerful force in Italy."

"Who was this pope anyway?"

"Calixtus the Sixth. He was incredibly corrupt, but that doesn't
matter. He was a pope. And that confers a special status on the
Brunellis. They're part of a whole papal network, members of cer-
tain societies and all that. It's dying out, but it still carries weight.
And the papal connection is what gives Marcello his title, you see.
The title goes back to Calixtus the Sixth, who was actually the bas-
tard of a prince but conferred titles on his family once he was pope.
Are you following?"

I nodded. Leaned closer, like a conspirator.

"So with the Brunellis you've got the status that comes from nobility," Whitman said. "But you also have the status that comes from
big money."

"Marcello's businesses are worth seven hundred million euros," I
whispered.

"Did Marcello tell you that?"

"No. La Principessa."

"She's lying," Whitman said. "They're worth a lot, the Brunellis,
but not that much. Not anymore. The whole Brunelli empire has
been really hard hit in the past five years. That's why Marcello's diversifying like crazy. Building Pine Mountain Lodge in Idaho, and
investing in real estate in Shanghai, and looking for opportunities in
Asia and Mexico."

"Because he's lost so much money?"

"It's called spreading around your assets."

"How do you know all this?" I asked.

Whitman flicked his hair back and fixed me with those laser blue eyes. "Sweetheart, I'm from a rich, horrible family, too, remember? I'm not part of it anymore, but I know how it works. And I still have old friends I can call. And I know a bit about Rome and what goes on because I used to live here."

"You said 'rich and horrible.' Why are the Brunellis horrible?"

"I didn't mean they're personally horrible," Whitman said, "except maybe that daughter, Signorina Schnozzola. But, you know, like any old rich family, they've got secrets to hide and lots of skeletons in their closets."

"Like what?"

"Well, if you ever read the paper, sweetheart, especially the business section of the *New York Times*, you'd know that the Brunellis have been getting some very bad press lately." Whitman studied me for a moment, then leaned close and spoke in a low voice. "Some of their businesses have been linked to the fascist era."

"That's World War Two?"

Whitman nodded. "Correct. It's a political thing. The charges may never be proved, but the PR damage to the Brunelli name is huge." He sat back and folded his arms. "That's why it's such a joke that his son goes around pretending to be a Communist."

"He's not pretending," I said. "Johnny *is* a Communist."

"Johnny?"

I blushed and looked away from Whitman's eyes. "That's what he told me to call him."

"Johnny the Commie," Whitman said, keeping his eyes on me. "He's awfully cute, isn't he?"

I evaded that question and asked another. "But isn't the whole Communist thing over? Like in Russia and Eastern Europe, they got rid of Communism, didn't they?"

"Yes, but it's still a political party here in Italy. Not as powerful as it once was, but still a force to be reckoned with. Of course a lot of rich young people dabble in left-wing politics. Like Johnny. I mean, obviously he's just doing it to spite his father."

"Maybe he really believes in it," I said. Whatever *it* was. My knowledge of communism was as vague and ill-formed as my knowledge of the Catholic Church. I wondered what the principles and beliefs behind Johnny's political affiliations really were.

"Tell me," Whitman said, pushing away his plate of squid, "did you have a secret pow-wow with La Principessa?"

"She hates me," I said. "She doesn't want me to marry him. Marcello." I didn't mention the hundred grand bribe she'd offered; it was too humiliating.

"No surprise there," Whitman said. "The empire's crumbling and she's protecting her assets. That's what they're all doing. That's why you're such a big threat to them."

"But I don't *feel* like a threat," I said. "I don't *want* to be a threat. I'm not *trying* to be a threat."

Whitman suddenly leaned across the table and tucked my hair behind my ears. "Sweetheart, I've known you since you were five years old. You're my daughter, and even if your father leaves me for that woman, I hope you'll continue to think of me as your faux pa."

"Whitman, he's not—"

"Just listen to me without being defensive, OK?"

I nodded.

"I tried to tell you this before you left. It's just that—well, sweetheart, for all your experience, you're just incredibly naive about some things. You've entered a very different world here. This is not about marrying some poor American jerk who doesn't have a pot to piss in. Like your other husbands. If you go through with this, you have to be prepared for a lot of resistance. From a lot of different people. Despite all the glamour, and all the money, and the limousines, and the fabulous palazzo, and the beautiful clothes and exquisite jewels—"

"I'll be miserable," I finished.

Whitman raised a hand. "No. I did not say miserable. Not all rich people are miserable. But great wealth does change people. People who have a lot of money want to keep it, and make more, and the last thing they want is to give it up."

"I'm not asking anyone to give up anything!"

Whitman nodded. "What I'm trying to say is, this may all look

like a fairy tale to you, but it's not. In this world you're in now, people are not always what they seem. So you've got to be prepared for
resistance. You've got to be prepared for enemies. And sometimes
enemies can fool you. Sometimes enemies have the sweetest smiles."
Whitman smiled. "If you want Marcello, Venus, you have to be prepared to fight."

I knew something was wrong the second we entered Palazzo
Brunelli. All sorts of people were scurrying about, grim-faced, tight-
lipped, intent on some important matter. From somewhere deep in
the palazzo came the sound of sobbing.

As Whitman and I made our way toward my suite of rooms, we
saw a cleaning lady shaking her head and tapping a rosary against
her chest.

Whitman asked her if something was wrong.

"Ah, signore, signore," the old woman wept, clutching her hands,
"Il Principe. *Lei è morto!*"

"Oh my God." The color drained from Whitman's face.

"Whitman, what is it?" I braced myself for catastrophe.

Whitman put his arm around me. "Let's go into your suite."

My hand was shaking as I punched in the code.

Carolee was waiting for us in the salone. The moment she saw us,
she leapt up and shouted, "Something terrible's happened!"

Whitman eased me down into a chair. "Honey, Marcello's dead."

"What?"

"Take some deep Buddha breaths," Whitman said.

Carolee shot over to my side. "Dead?" She looked at Whitman as
she hugged me. "That's not what they told me."

"The cleaning lady just told me he was dead."

"No," Carolee said, "not dead. But he collapsed."

"Collapsed?" I numbly repeated. "Marcello?"

"We were having such a nice day," Mom said. "Fabio took me to
a beach. But then he got a call from Giovanna. You know, Marcello's
daughter. She was hysterical. I could hear her screaming and crying.
She told Fabio he had to come back to Rome immediately because
she needed him."

So Mom and Fabio had packed up their wine and bread and cheese and returned to Rome. At this very moment, Fabio was driving Giovanna and Giovanni to Parma, where Marcello had been rushed to a hospital.

"But why did he collapse?" Whitman asked. "Was it a heart attack?"

"Don't know." Carolee shrugged and rocked me against her bosom and kissed my forehead, as if I were a little girl. "Didn't anyone call you, sweetheart? It seems like they should have told you."

I'd turned my cell phone off in the first church Whitman and I visited that day and had forgotten to turn it back on. I felt like a zombie, in a kind of waking dream, as I reached into my purse and retrieved it.

No messages.

Chapter
21

It wasn't until the following day that I found out what was going on. Teresina scurried into my bedroom and said, "Signorina, signorina! *Telefono!*"

It was Johnny. He said he was calling from the hospital in Parma. "We've been up all night," he said.

"What happened? Is he OK?"

Johnny let out a long, low sigh. "Yeah, we think he's OK. They're doing a lot of tests."

"What happened?"

"He was in a meeting. He collapsed."

I could barely say the words. "Heart attack?"

"No. Apparently not. They thought it was. At first. A heart attack. Or a stroke. But it wasn't."

"So what was it?"

"They think it might have been exhaustion. A viral infection brought on by exhaustion."

Now I sighed. "He never stops working."

"Well," Johnny said, "now he'll have to. At least for a while."

The plan was to bring Marcello back to Rome, where his own doctors could examine him and administer another battery of tests. Then the family would all go to Capri.

I felt like I was being shoved out of the picture. And why not?

What claim did I have on Marcello Brunelli? I was nothing more than a girlfriend—and not even a very good one. I had no status within the family, no right to ask questions. I wondered if I was going to be included in their plans or sent packing.

"Hey," Johnny said, "I should tell you—he's been asking for you."

"He has?"

"Yeah. I think he wants to see you—I mean, be with you—more than with us."

I didn't know what to say, except, "So, he's conscious? He's talking?"

"Oh yeah, he's talking," Johnny said.

"What did he say . . . about me?"

"Listen, I've gotta go," Johnny said.

"Can I talk to him? Just for a minute?"

"We'll be back tomorrow. Ciao, Venus."

I had no idea what protocol I should follow, but I was determined to greet Marcello when he arrived back in Rome.

Teresina called me into the kitchen when she saw the ambulance pull into the street below. I joined her at the window and we watched the frenzy of the paparazzi as they literally crawled over the ambulance.

"*Animali*," Teresina muttered under her breath.

No translation necessary.

I'd been waiting all day for Marcello's return. I'd told Daddy, Mom, and Whitman to go sightseeing without me. There was nothing they could do, and I wanted to handle this by myself.

I stepped outside just as the ambulance was parking in the courtyard, the limo slowly nosing in beside it. A police car outside the gate kept the paparazzi at bay.

As the metal security gate rolled into place, and before a single car door opened, I made my way down the stone stairway and positioned myself by the rear doors of the ambulance. Two attendants got out and glanced at me as they headed toward the back of the vehicle.

"Signorina Gilroy!" Giovanna hurried out of the limo and limped toward me. "Wait!"

"Giovanna!"

The voice stopped Giovanna in her tracks. I looked over and saw Fabio opening the back door of the limo. Seated inside was La Principessa.

Giovanna peered over her shoulder at her grandmother.

"Giovanna," said La Principessa, "*venga*." She beckoned with her hand.

Giovanna returned to the limo, where she stood with lips clenched and hands clasped in front of her bony chest, glaring at me. Johnny got out and stood next to the front passenger seat, his face anxious and tired.

With Fabio's help, La Principessa made a graceful exit from the limo. She was wearing large dark glasses and dressed all in black. Versace, maybe. Or Armani. Incredibly chic. *More like a widow*, I thought, *than a mother*.

We looked at each other as she slowly crossed the courtyard. I did not smile and neither did she. When she reached my side, she motioned for the attendants to open the ambulance doors.

They slid out a stretcher.

Marcello was strapped to it, all but his neck and face covered by a white sheet and blanket.

He looked so vulnerable. My heart gave a lurch and I stumbled toward him. I wanted to touch him but was afraid of hurting him.

But then he opened his eyes and squinted in the hot glare of the sun and saw me, and the smile he gave me was Marcello's. I burst into tears and bent down beside the stretcher. "Marcello." I stroked his matted hair.

"Darling." His voice was a whisper. He pursed his lips and made a kissing sound.

I thought he wanted me to kiss him, so I did. Gently. With his mother looking on. And after I'd kissed him, after our lips had met and I had drawn back an inch, he murmured something in my ear.

"We mustn't tire him, Signorina Gilroy." La Principessa gave another signal and the attendants hoisted up the stretcher and carried Marcello into Palazzo Brunelli.

No one told me, so I had to ask Teresina. "Where is Marcello?"

"Il Principe?" She twitched her mouth and gave her downy mustache a quick stroke. "In his room, signorina."

She cocked her head and frowned when I asked if she would take me there. "You don't know where to go?"

And I had to confess that no, I didn't.

There were a whole lot of things in Palazzo Brunelli I didn't know and would have to find out on my own.

Teresina led me down one floor and into a section of the ancient palazzo that I hadn't seen before. From what I could tell, this area was directly beneath my own. It looked older somehow, and far less showy than the rooms above.

"La Principessa is there," Teresina whispered, pointing to a massive oak door. She turned and pointed to another door directly across from it. "Il Principe there."

Neither of the doors had an electronic security lock. I didn't see any security cameras mounted up near the ceiling, either. But Marcello's door opened just as I raised my hand to knock.

Giovanna was as startled to see me as I was to see her. We both gasped in surprise. It looked as though Giovanna was about to leave, but now, seeing me, she drew herself back inside the room and closed the door to a crack. And through that crack she stared at me as if I were a door-to-door salesman or a Jehovah's Witness. "Yes? What do you want?"

Her hostility threw me. Once again I lost my emotional footing. Felt like an intruder. "I was hoping I could see him."

"Who?" Giovanna asked.

I kept my temper in check. "Marcello, of course."

"Oh." Giovanna glanced over her shoulder. "He's resting."

"I'll come back, then. When would be a good time?"

A look of disdain rippled across her face like a sour breeze. "It would be better if you leave, Signorina Gilroy."

Did she mean leave now, and come back later, or did she mean leave Palazzo Brunelli permanently and never come back?

"He wants to see me," I said, remembering the words Marcello had whispered in my ear as he lay on the stretcher.

"He's to see no one." Giovanna smiled. "The doctors insist."

"Are the doctors with him now?" I asked.

She looked affronted, as if it were beneath her to answer my questions. "No, not at this moment."

"Who's with him?" I persisted.

"His *family*, Signorina Gilroy." With that, she closed the door in my face.

What was supposed to have been a fun time with Mom and the dads turned into something more like a shared vigil. As the shadows gathered in Palazzo Brunelli and darkness fell over Rome, we all sat together in my salone, not knowing what to do.

"Maybe we should leave, sweetheart," Carolee said.

"All of us?" Whitman leaned forward from the depths of the sofa to examine what Teresina had laid out for us on the marble-topped coffee table.

"I don't know," Mom said. She looked up, startled and grateful, when Teresina came over to refill her empty wineglass. "Oh, grazie, sweetheart. Just half a glass is fine."

"I don't think we should leave," Daddy said.

Whitman gave him a sidelong glance. "No," he said quietly, "I'm sure *you* don't want to leave Rome just yet."

"The question is," Mom said, "what can we do?" She looked down at the tray of sweets Teresina was offering. "Oh, thank you, sweetheart. What are they?"

"Nipples of Venus," Whitman said.

Mom smiled nervously. "I beg your pardon, Whitman?"

"Nipples of Venus," Daddy repeated. "That's what they're called, Carolee. The pastries."

"Oh! Good heavens!" Mom looked at her pastry. "Well, I guess I can see why they'd be called that."

"I think we stay right here," Daddy reiterated. He'd been rearranging everything on the table so that it all lined up according to an exact pattern in his head. "At least until we know exactly what the story is."

"You mean, how this affects Venus," Whitman said. He looked at me. "So let's replay the details. You haven't seen Marcello since he returned in the ambulance, right?"

"Right," I said.

"And when you tried to see him, you were stopped by Signorina Schnozzola."

"Who's that?" Mom asked.

"The daughter," Whitman said. "She wouldn't let you in. Is that right?"

I nodded.

"And she didn't say when you could come back to see him?"

I shook my head.

"And the mother, La Principessa, hasn't given you any information either," Whitman said.

I shook my head.

"But you know Marcello wants to see you?"

"Of course he wants to see her," Daddy said. "He's in love with her."

"How do you know Marcello wants to see you?" Whitman repeated.

"You sound like a lawyer," Daddy said. "Don't cross-examine her."

"John," Whitman said. "You have absolutely no understanding of how families like this one work. For the Brunellis, this is a crisis. Marcello is the head of the family. If he should die—"

"He's not going to die," I cut in. "It's exhaustion. Because he works too much."

"You obviously didn't hear my hypothetical *if*," Whitman said. "I said, *if* he should die, there would be major changes in the family fortunes. They all know this. Marcello runs a business empire. If he croaks, who takes over? What happens to the moola? That's the big question for them. Inheritance."

"Whit," Daddy said, squinting with exasperation, "what the hell does inheritance have to do with the situation at hand?"

"Wake up and smell the latte, John! This is all about money!"

Now it was Whitman's turn to look exasperated, as if we were all morons failing his class in economics. He rose from the sofa and paced around us. "Look, they don't *want* Venus to see Marcello because it could upset their balance of power. *Capisce?*" He drew his fingers together and tapped the side of his head. "They don't *want* Marcello and Venus to meet alone because they're terrified she'll exert some kind of power over him."

I let out a snort. "Power over him?" It sounded ridiculous . . . and a little scary. "What power?"

Whitman looked at me. "The power of love," he said. "We are talking *love* here, aren't we, Venus?"

I looked away.

"This is a perfect opportunity for them to drive a wedge into your relationship," Whitman went on. "If Marcello collapsed because of exhaustion, he's probably weak as a baby right now. Full of drugs. Maybe a little confused, maybe even a little frightened."

Hearing Marcello described this way, I started to sniff back tears. I remembered how he had looked on the stretcher.

"When people are in a weakened state," Whitman continued, "they just can't operate the way they usually do. So yes, Marcello may be asking for Venus, begging to see her, *pleading*, but the family and the doctors are not going to let him."

"I think I saw a TV movie like that once," Carolee said. "What was it called? *No Tears for Tomorrow* or something. This older man—"

Whitman cut her off. "It happens in the gay world all the time," he said. "Someone gets really sick or dies and the family takes over, and the lover or the partner is put out on the street. And there's nothing they can do about it. Because they don't have one essential legal document. A marriage license."

"I think maybe we're jumping to conclusions here," Daddy said.

"Of course I'm jumping to conclusions," Whitman snapped. "I've been through all this before. Right here in Rome. I've seen it happen."

And suddenly, without his saying so, I knew it had happened to him.

In the silence, we heard the muffled ringing of a phone and Teresina's voice as she answered it. A moment later she hurried into the room, her eyes wide. "Signorina, La Principessa, she wishes to speak with you."

"Good evening, Miss Gilroy." La Principessa's voice sounded flat, businesslike.

"Good evening."

"I'm calling to ask what your plans are."

I was going to say, "I don't know," but caught myself. I didn't want La Principessa to think that my plans were dependent upon *her.* "I want to see Marcello," I said.

She was silent.

"Nobody's really told me what happened," I said.

"Marcello was in a business meeting. In Parma. In the board room at one of our factories there. He said he felt a little light-headed, but he pushed on with the meeting. Labor negotiations," spat La Principessa, her voice suddenly harsh as acid. "The same thing that drove my husband to an early grave."

"So it was exhaustion?"

"Who told you that?" she demanded.

"Johnny. *Giovanni.*"

"One moment." She covered the receiver and spoke to someone else in a low, chastising voice. "It could be exhaustion," she resumed with me. "That certainly played a part in Marcello's collapse. But it may be something far more serious."

My heart was thumping. "Oh? Like what?"

"It is better we do not speak of that now, Miss Gilroy."

"I wish you'd tell me," I said. "I want to know."

"These are family matters, Miss Gilroy. I would not want to burden you."

"It's not a burden. I want to know."

She let out a perturbed sigh. "We are all under a great deal of stress right now, Miss Gilroy. I'm sure you can understand that."

"Of course."

"I am in the car. Giovanni is with me. Fabio is driving us back to Naples."

"Naples?"

"To our boat. We are going to Capri." She paused. "I am very sorry, but under the circumstances I must withdraw my invitation to you and your family. You will please convey my regrets to your mother and fathers."

"Yes, I'll do that."

"Giovanni is going to help me get Villa Brunelli ready. As soon as he is able, Marcello will come to us on Capri. Giovanna will make certain that her father is comfortable."

Yes, I thought, *and what about me?*

"We are always together in Capri, at Villa Brunelli. Every August. For many, many years we have done this. This is the first time my family did not come to me in August, Miss Gilroy. And you see what happened as a result." It was the only time her voice sounded a little wavery, as if a speck of sentiment momentarily got the better of her.

I assumed she wanted me to feel guilty. As if it were all my fault. Well, maybe it was. But there was nothing I could do about it.

"As I said, I'm calling to ask about *your* plans, Miss Gilroy."

My plans? The truth was, I still didn't know what my plans were. Except that I was not going to leave Rome without seeing Marcello first. The more they tried to keep me away, the more determined I was to see him.

"Giovanna is skilled at making travel arrangements," said La Principessa. "She would like to be of assistance."

"I'm sure she would," I said.

"Simply tell her when you wish to leave and Giovanna will take care of all the details."

"Let me ask *you* something," I said. "Did Marcello ever tell you that he wanted me to leave?"

There was a moment of silence. "Well," she said, "it is, shall we say, *understood*."

"Understood by who? I mean, whom?"

"By me, Miss Gilroy. Marcello's mother. I am his only mother and he is my only son. We are very close. We share a special bond."

"I guess so, if you can read his mind."

"I have much experience in this sort of thing, my dear."

Her dismissive tone pissed me off. "What sort of thing, *my dear?*"

She sighed again, as if I were a tiresome child. "Marcello and his girls. Usually they're a bit more tactful. They understand when it's time to depart."

"I'll leave—" I said.

She was silent, listening intently.

"—when Marcello asks me to."

I waited for a response. Heard a sudden sizzle of static. Either she'd lost reception or hung up on me.

I lay in that huge canopied bed and thought, *This bed was not made for one person.*

I thought of Marcello on his stretcher. The tight white sheet and blanket. The straps that held him secure.

It was not the Marcello I knew, full of life, full of energy, full of daring.

I remembered him in Portland, climbing up my fire escape. Remembered our trip to Cannon Beach, and getting clobbered by a big wave. Remembered his kisses. Real grown-up kisses.

The dark glow in his eyes every time he looked at me.

The way he'd fallen asleep like a baby at my breast.

I should have known then. I should have seen how exhausted he was.

Now that it had happened, I could look back and see how his collapse was inevitable. He was a man who drove himself to the brink. Who kept going, no matter what. Who did not give up. A man who had everything money could buy except the time to enjoy it and the right person to enjoy it with.

And I knew—or some part of me now sensed—that what I had always been for Marcello was just that: a person who embodied the fun and freedom he never had. He was reaching out to me for exactly that reason. Maybe that was even why he said he loved me.

It didn't matter that I didn't see *myself* that way. The flip side of "fun and freedom" is "poverty and loneliness." It didn't matter that my personal self-perception was not in synch with the way Marcello saw me.

He idealized me.

What I saw as a flaw, he saw as perfection.

And the *chivalry*, or whatever you call it. That old-fashioned way of treating a woman, as if I were a princess. I'd never experienced that before. It was a quality that didn't seem to exist in my generation. The guys I'd known and married didn't have a clue.

And the sense of *romance*. Of the big gesture. Not one rose, but fifty.

What was wrong with me that I couldn't accept that? Didn't I believe I was worthy of it?

There was something in Marcello that wanted to *give*. And I'd mistrusted that. I'd seen it all as middle-aged lust. Lust was there, no doubt about it, but the only problem for me was that I didn't feel it in return.

I wouldn't let myself.

I'd never tried. Not really. I'd put up mental barriers.

I kept hearing those words he'd whispered to me from his stretcher: *Darling, come to me. Please come to me.*

There was always the fear in Palazzo Brunelli that I was going to trip some unseen alarm and set off a piercing security alert. The fear of the thief and trespasser.

As I slowly made my way through the giant rooms and hallways and down the internal stairway, I wondered about the past of Palazzo Brunelli. I wondered about all the lives, great and small, that had been lived there. Generation after generation, for half a millennium. What secrets were locked in the tombs of those proud, rich, aristocratic Brunellis staring out into the darkness from their portraits? How many of them had hidden hard-ons beneath their religious robes?

Were there ghosts? At one point, I was certain that I saw a thin, dark shadow slip past an arched doorway at the end of a corridor. The hair on my arms and the back of my neck stood on end.

I turned away and hurried on until I reached the door to Marcello's room. Pressed the latch. Expected to be blasted to kingdom come by a siren.

Silence.

The heavy door swung open.

I was barefoot. Didn't make a sound as I crossed the enormous room to where he lay.

I crouched next to the bed. It was a huge old thing, like mine, with a towering carved headboard and four thick, carved posts.

Marcello was sleeping. He was on his back. His hands were outside the bedcovers. He was wearing a white, collarless pajama top that was starched like a dress shirt. His face was turned toward me.

I leaned closer, to get a better look. To smell him. He was breathing softly through his nose, but then took a deep breath and blew it out through his lips. His eyelids twitched and his long black lashes fluttered. He was dreaming. What was the dream? Was I in it?

And then, suddenly, his eyes opened.

He stared at me, trying to get his bearings.

"Venus?" he whispered.

"It's me," I whispered back.

We looked at one another.

"I just wanted to see you," I whispered. "Make sure you were all right."

He closed his eyes when I stroked his hair. Then he took my wrist and brought it to his lips. "I'm so glad you are here."

"They don't want me to see you," I whispered.

He nuzzled my lower arm against his face. I could feel the rough stubble of his whiskers. "Who, darling?"

"Your family. They want me to leave Rome. Leave you."

"Do they?"

"Yes."

"I shall have to do something about that," he whispered.

"Are you going to be all right?" I asked.

"Oh yes."

"I've been so worried. I didn't know—"

"This has made me realize many things." He pulled me closer. I was half on and half off the bed.

"What things? That you have to slow down and not work so much?"

"Yes," he said. "Yes. And do things now. Now, Venus. Not later. Now."

"You never came to my slacker classes," I said.

He let out a low sleepy laugh. And then closed his eyes and said, "Will you marry me?"

"Your family'd be very upset."

He opened his eyes. Stroked my face. "Will you marry me, Venus? No, don't draw away." He tugged me up onto the bed, to his side, and held me close and stroked me. "I know it scares you. I know all the objections. And do you know what?"

"What?"

"I don't care. For once in my life, I don't give a damn."

I let him stroke me.

"You don't have to be afraid," he whispered, kissing my forehead, my cheeks, my ear, my neck. "I will take care of you. I will protect you. I will cherish you."

I let out a weird sound, sort of like a whimper. I didn't know where it came from. All I knew is that no man had ever said he would take care of me, or protect me, or cherish me.

Cherish me.

"If you do not love me now," he said, "you can learn to love me."

I nodded. "But I have nothing to offer you."

He let out a short soft moan and pressed his face to mine. "Ah! No one has ever said that to me before."

"But it's true."

"I love you," he said. "What you bring me is something that has no price tag on it."

"OK," I burbled.

"Will you? I promise to make you happy."

I nodded. My tears dripped onto the starched cotton sheets.

Chapter
22

I fell in love with him in that huge, dark room in Palazzo Brunelli. Marcello told me he'd moved into the room after his father died, because his mother wanted him closer to her. His father had used it as an office. But when Marcello's father died, the estate was in a shambles. The war and postwar changes had wreaked havoc with manufacturing and the economy. It had been La Principessa, to everyone's surprise, who stepped up and took over the running of the various businesses. Marcello, meanwhile, was groomed to take over the faltering empire as soon as he turned twenty-one. That had been his life's work: to restore the ailing fortunes of the family and to inoculate them against future economic shocks.

A remarkable woman, La Principessa. I learned a lot more about her. It didn't make me like her any more, but it did help me to understand her position.

According to Marcello, his mother had been a great beauty in her day.

"In Roman society, like your father?" I pictured La Principessa as a gorgeously gowned princess swanning around in old Roman palaces.

Marcello smiled. "No. Mama actually comes from a rather humble background. That's why there were so many objections when my father married her."

Somehow I found that comforting. Beauty really is a wild card that can change a person's fortunes.

In that enormous room, lying beside Marcello in the dark, I said things that needed to be said. Things that I had been afraid to say earlier, but that had to be said if we were going to share a life together. Things like, "Marcello, you know your mother doesn't want you to marry me."

"Yes, I know that," he said.

"She offered me a lot of money if I'd leave."

"A hundred thousand, wasn't it?"

I nodded, surprised that he knew.

"And you did not take it." He sighed into my hair.

"She's not going to be happy about this."

"Probably not," he said. "But it is my happiness—our happiness, yours and mine—that must come first now. Mama will come around, you will see. She fears change, like everyone else."

"And your daughter—"

"Giovanna?"

"She hates me." I simply stated it. I did not color it. I did not ask him to take sides. But I wanted him to know.

"Giovanna has had a troubled life," Marcello said. "The problems with her mother, and I was always away."

Which led me to another topic that had always been taboo. The ghost I knew only as "La Signora."

"Tell me about your wife," I said.

"Can't it wait?" he whispered, drawing me tight. "It does not seem right to talk of her just now."

But I was determined to find out what I could. "Did she have a lot of money?" I asked.

"Hmm?" Marcello seemed lost in thought. "Yes. A lot."

"Did you marry her because of her money?"

"Yes," he said, his voice low. "And I have never forgiven myself. Because it meant nothing, my marriage. It was hollow at the core. From the beginning. It was like one of those false building fronts you see in Hollywood. That's how too much of my life has been, Venus. That's what I want to change now, before it's too late."

Beauty was one wild card that could change a person's life. Money was another. Women married for money all the time. But when a man did, it seemed degrading and predatory.

I asked how long he'd been married.

"Thirty years," he said. "I was a boy when I married her. I let Mama talk me into it. For the good of the family, she said. But of course it was really because we needed capital. Our factories needed to be modernized."

"You never loved her?"

"I tried. But I was acting out a charade. And by giving up any hope for a real life, for a life that was my life, or in any way emotionally fulfilling, I got—well, something else."

"Modernized factories," I said.

Marcello was silent.

Thirty years. They'd been married longer than I'd been alive. I remembered the photo Teresina had shown me of La Signora standing in a garden, how old and vacant-eyed she looked. It was difficult to imagine her as light and lively and young, buying and wearing all those designer dresses that still hung in the giant wardrobe, going out to parties and balls and galas with Marcello at her side.

"It was not her fault," Marcello said. "It was my fault. And when she got sick, I—I don't know, I was not much help."

"Was she sick for a long time?"

He nodded. "Many years. It was quite ugly. I shouldn't have kept her here. She should have been in a hospital, or a nursing home. But she wouldn't go. She refused. So I locked my door. I had to. There were times when she tried to kill me."

I propped myself up on an elbow and looked at him.

"It was her illness," Marcello explained. "It made her violent. She heard voices. Sometimes she had to be restrained." He combed his fingers through my hair. "Now it is time for me to unlock my door."

I thought he was being poetic, but Marcello pointed to a door on the far side of the room. "Why don't you open it for me?"

"Now?"

"Yes. Unlock it, and then you can come to me at any time."

"Or you to me," I said.

He pressed my hand to his lips. "Unlock it for me."

By then my eyes had adjusted to the dark. I crossed the room and eyed the mysterious door. Beside it stood an inlaid wooden cabinet. Inside the cabinet, right where Marcello said it would be, lay a large, heavy key.

I took the key back to show him, but he'd fallen asleep. I didn't want to wake him, so I gave him the softest, lightest kiss I could, and returned to the mysterious door. Fit the key into the lock. Turned it. Heard a click as the ancient tumbler mechanism engaged. Pressed down the thick iron handle.

The door gave a soft groan as it swung open.

My heart was pounding. I'd seen too many horror movies and half-expected La Signora to spring out with a knife in her hand and a crazed look on her face.

Nothing.

Silence.

I looked up and into what I assumed to be a hidden stairway. It was pitch black and emitted a breath of dry, stale air from its dark throat.

Marcello had called it *"la scalinata dell'amore"*—the stairway of love. He said it connected his room with my room above.

I took a couple of short, tentative steps into the tunnel of blackness. Stubbed my toe on a stone riser. Felt around for a light switch. Nothing. Of course there wouldn't be lights in something built hundreds of years ago. They would have used candles.

I had a sudden vision of all the tunnels and staircases threading through this ancient building, hidden from view but used for short-cuts, escapes, and assignations, pulsing like arteries with the secret life of Palazzo Brunelli.

I looked up into the dark void, daring myself, rooting myself on. *Come on, Wonder Woman!*

But no. It was just too dark and too unknown.

I'll do it tomorrow, I thought, *during the day.*

I closed the heavy door but did not relock it.

* * *

Love.

No wonder people are always writing songs about it.

Once you let it into your heart, it's like a high colonic to your spirit. It makes you feel lighter, stronger, cleaner.

It was quietly dazzling, this newfound love I had for a man named Marcello Brunelli. Maybe it's what a miracle feels like, because a miracle is something that isn't supposed to happen, but does.

I loved him. He had finally succeeded in coaxing me to open up my heart and let him in.

I'd agreed to marry him—*before* I slept with him. If that wasn't a miracle, I didn't know what was.

There would be endless problems. I didn't care.

His family would hate me. I didn't care.

He was going to change his life for me.

I felt pregnant with happiness. I carried around a kind of sweet, excited glow in the pit of my tummy.

But I wasn't going to see my new fiancé for the next three days. Marcello's doctors were going to administer a whole battery of tests to try to ascertain what had caused his collapse, and he would be at the hospital or in clinics all day, every day.

He put on a brave front, but like anyone else, he was terrified that the tests would reveal some horrible disease that was going to cut short his life.

"I have so much to think about now," he'd said. "So many new plans. A whole new life to figure out."

He wasn't the only one.

Since Fabio was going to be busy driving Marcello around, Mom decided that she was going down to Naples the next day to visit Cesare.

"We need to go shopping," she said. "Cesare lives with his two elderly sisters, and I want to make a good impression on the family."

Whitman, working on Day Three of his "Three Romantic Days

in Rome" article, said he would accompany us. His face went stony
when Daddy said he had some shopping of his own to take care of.

"Hunting for antiques on Via dei Coronari?" Whitman said, his
tone dangerously peevish.

"Yes, as a matter of fact."

Whitman sucked in a deep Buddha breath and turned to Mom
and me. "Come along, girls. *Venga, venga, venga.*" He snapped his fingers and literally pulled Mom and me from our chairs. "Don't daw-
dle. Let's go. We've got some serious shopping to do."

"Let's meet for lunch," Daddy called after us. "I'll make a reservation at La Tavola Antica. Two o'clock?"

"Maybe," Whitman said. "Venus and Carolee can meet you, but I
might be busy."

We stood at the bottom of the Spanish Steps, panting like dogs
in the fearsome heat, tourists crawling around us, two giant palm
trees waving their glittering fronds in the piazza next door. The
little stone fountain at the base of the steps was shaped like a
boat.

"Let's see," Whitman said, looking at Mom, "for you, something
summery but modest. And for you"—he turned his critical attention
my way—"another wedding dress. Black this time, I think. Or gray.
A tailored suit perhaps. Something simple and chic."

"I've got my pink leather minidress," I said.

Whitman sighed. "Darling, you are not going to marry a Roman
prince wearing a pink leather minidress."

We were, as usual when it came to questions of taste, locked into
immediate battle.

"Why not?" I challenged. "I'm the one marrying him."

"It's a wedding ceremony," Whitman said, "not a rock concert.
It's meant to be dignified. Think of yourself as walking down an
aisle instead of dancing on a table."

"Why don't you let Mom and I—"

"Mom and me," he corrected.

"Why don't you let Mom and me do this alone," I said.

"Because you'd never find the right shops," he said, "or the right dresses. Not to mention accessories. Come along now. This way."

He led us down Via Condotti, where we shopped for three hours straight. It was exhausting, and of course Mom and I didn't know what we wanted, but Whitman knew just exactly what we should or shouldn't try on.

"Look at this one, Carolee," he said in one shop, holding up a dress for Mom to examine. "It's perfect."

"Do you think so?" Mom obviously didn't.

"Of course. It's great with your hair color, as long as you keep it that shade. It's matronly for the elderly sisters, but look here—" He unbuttoned a top piece. "For Cesare, after his sisters have gone to bed, you can undo this part and show him you mean business."

"It looks a little daring, that way," Mom said.

"Carolee, forgive me for being frank, dear, but if my tits were as big as yours are, I'd show them off."

"You would?" Mom sounded dubious.

"Did Anita Ekberg hide hers? Did Sophia Loren hide hers? Straight men *love* big tits."

"Not when they hang down to your knees," Mom said.

And so it went on as we trudged up and down Via Condotti and into all the little side streets around it. The two salesgirls in the Armani store were so snotty that I almost started to cry. As Whitman led me through the racks, the girls rolled their eyes, tittered, whispered, and were generally rude. Finally, Whitman took matters into his own hands.

"Who is the manager here?" he demanded. (This all went on in Italian, but he gave us an English blow-by-blow afterward.)

"She is busy," said one of the snotty salesgirls.

"I suggest you call her at once," he said.

"I told you, she is busy."

"Call her," he shouted, "or you'll be out of here on your asses. Do you know whom you're dealing with?"

The girls suddenly went silent, not knowing if he was referring to himself or to me.

A smart-looking young woman of about thirty came over. "I am the manager, may I ask what the problem is?"

Whitman pointed to the two salesgirls. "They are the problem. I have never experienced such rude behavior in my life. We came in here hoping to find some clothes for my daughter," he pointed at me, "who is to be married to Prince Marcello Brunelli."

The store went completely silent. Everyone froze.

"Perhaps I should tell Prince Brunelli how your salesclerks treated his bride-to-be," Whitman said. "I'm sure he'd be interested to know, and so would all of his friends."

The manager licked her lips and turned to the salesgirls. She said something in Italian and the girls disappeared. She turned back to us with a smile. "Please accept my apologies. Those girls are temporary. My regular staff has left for the August holidays. Would you care to come downstairs to our private fitting room?"

"Gilroy," Whitman said to the hostess at La Tavola Antica, "*una tavola per quattro.*"

"Si." The hostess checked her list. "*Ma il reservazione è per cinque, non è vero?*"

"No," Whitman shook his head, "*quattro.*"

"*Va bene. Prego.*" The hostess motioned for us to follow her.

"What was that all about?" Mom asked.

"I said it would be a table for four; she thought the reservation was for five."

"Oh, look," Mom said, eyeing a long table covered with crushed ice and artfully inlaid with fresh fish and crustaceans. "You never see anything like that back home."

"Have you and Daddy eaten here before?" I asked Whitman as the hostess pulled out our chairs and got us comfortable.

Whitman nodded. "We ate here on our honeymoon."

"Honeymoon?" Carolee unfolded her thick linen napkin, her eyes darting around the restaurant, taking it all in. "I didn't know you'd been married, Whitman."

"Yes, dear, to your ex-husband." He turned away and motioned for the waiter.

Mom wasn't sure how to take his comment. "Oh, that," she said.

"Yes," Whitman said. "That." He asked the waiter to bring us a big bottle of Pellegrino and turned back to Mom. "It's not marriage with a license, of course. The higher authorities don't believe we deserve such credentials."

Mom said, "That will change, Whitman."

Whitman stared at her for a moment. "You know, Carolee, you are pretty damned remarkable."

"I am?" Mom blushed, unaccustomed to compliments.

"How many women would sit at lunch with their ex-husband's lover?"

"In Rome," I said.

"In Rome," Whitman repeated. He looked around the restaurant and his eyes grew moist. "Where it all began. And probably where it's all going to end."

Suddenly his face crumpled and his eyes filled. I actually thought I was going to see Whitman Whittlesley the Fourth burst into tears. I'd never seen him cry before and it was a startling sight. But of course he recovered himself immediately. He took a deep Buddha breath and said, "There's the bastard now."

He meant Daddy, who followed the hostess over to our table. He was carrying a cardboard envelope and grinning. When the hostess queried him about the fifth chair, should she leave it or remove it, Daddy told her to leave it. "Gabriella's joining us," he said.

Sometimes life is really weird. A moment later, Gabriella Mangione entered the restaurant and made her way toward our table. Toward Daddy, I should say. She removed her dark glasses, smiled, and kept her beautiful dark eyes trained on him. Daddy smiled back. He stood up and helped her into her chair. A whiff of soft, seductive perfume hit my nose as she sat down.

So there I was, sitting with my Dad, his two ex-wives, and his male partner.

"Well," Whitman said, "isn't this a surprise."

Gabriella was all in white. A beautifully tailored white linen suit and white silk blouse glowed against her burnished skin and thick black hair. She had a permanent tan, but her skin looked soft, lustrous even. She was wearing a gold bracelet, gold earrings, and a gold necklace.

"I suppose you two have been catching up on old times," Mom said to Gabriella.

"Yes," Gabriella said, "old times. Eh, John?" Her smile was dazzling. She extracted a gold cigarette case and lighter from her purse and turned to us. "Do you mind if I smoke?"

"Yes," Whitman said. "I mind." He gave his hair a dangerous flick.

Gabriella cast him a cool glance as she put her cigarettes away.

"You live here in Rome, Gabriella?" Mom asked.

Gabriella nodded. "Yes, I was born here."

"But then you left, didn't you?" Whitman flicked his hair and gave her an innocent, quizzical look.

Gabriella looked at Daddy. "Yes. When I married John."

"And then where was it you went after that?" Whitman asked. "I mean, after you got married, and after you got your American citizenship, and after you left John? Disappeared, I should say. Where did you go then?"

Gabriella smiled at him but did not show her teeth. She crossed her long, shapely legs and shifted sideways in her chair.

"I'd just be curious to know, that's all." Whitman turned his attention back to the wine list. "John never really knew where you went. Didn't you have to have her declared dead, John? Or something?"

Gabriella closed the fingers of her left hand and examined her manicured nails.

"Gabriella had her reasons for leaving," Daddy said.

"I'm sure she did," Whitman said, flicking his hair. "She had an American passport. The most valuable passport in the world—back then, anyway. Are you still an American citizen, Gabriella?"

Gabriella fiddled with her bracelet. "I have dual citizenship," she said.

"I'm sure that makes it easier for business," Whitman said. "You're an antiques dealer, aren't you?"

Gabriella smiled and nodded. "My shop is on Via dei Coronari. You must come and look."

"We already have," I said, but then shut up because Whitman kicked me under the table.

"Gabriella knows all the dealers in Rome," Daddy said. "Look at what she found for us." He opened the cardboard envelope and extracted a photograph. "Guess who?"

"They will never guess," Gabriella said.

We all leaned forward to examine the photo.

It was a studio portrait of a big-breasted woman wearing a low-cut peasant blouse, a clingy dark skirt, and dangly earrings. She was barefoot, standing beside a basket of grapes and holding up a small accordion, her mouth open, as though she was playing and singing a bawdy song.

"It would appear to be from the late 1940s or early 1950s," Whitman said. "Either a stage act or a posed scene from a film."

"A stage act," Gabriella verified.

"Gypsy or contadina?" Whitman asked.

"Contadina," Gabriella said. "From the south. From Napoli."

We all shook our heads, unable to guess who it was.

"That," said Daddy, "is none other than La Principessa Brunelli."

"I knew it!" Whitman snatched the photo and stared at it. "I knew she'd been on the stage."

The facts were few and far between, and most of the photographic evidence had been destroyed. But according to Gabriella, everyone in Italy knew that La Principessa Brunelli had once been a singer called, simply, Lita. The story was that Prince Brunelli, Marcello's father, discovered Lita singing in a Naples dive and fell head over heels in love with her. Lita married him and immediately retired from the stage. Her career hadn't lasted long enough for her to become famous, but her marriage to Prince Brunelli guaranteed that she would never be forgotten.

"So she wasn't born into the Roman aristocracy," Whitman crowed. "I knew it." He leaned over and stroked my arm. "She was a *commoner*, darling, just like you."

The Lita photograph got us all excited and even I had a glass of wine. I hadn't had any form of alcohol for weeks and one sip went straight to my head.

"I'd like to propose a toast," Daddy said. We all lifted our glasses. "To the past and what it's taught us, to the present and what we have now, and to the future, which no man can outguess."

We clicked glasses.

"And to my partner, Whitman," Daddy said, rising and going to put his arm around Whitman's shoulder. "Today is our twenty-first anniversary."

Whitman looked up at him but said nothing.

I thought, *Just like them not to mention it.*

Daddy fished a small ring box from his pocket and handed it to Whitman.

"If anyone's going to cry," Whitman warned, "they can leave the table at once." He opened the box. "Oh." He pulled out a ring.

Daddy took it from him. "This ring is two thousand years old. It dates back to a time when men could actually draw up contracts that made their unions legal in the eyes of the law."

"I gave that book to you for Christmas fifteen years ago," Whitman said. *"Same-Sex Contracts in Hellenistic and Pre-Christian Rome."*

Daddy took Whitman's hand and slid the ring onto the fourth finger of his left hand. "Whitman, you're as annoying today as the day I met you, and just as lovable. I hope you'll consider spending the next twenty years of your life with me."

Whitman, looking up at Daddy, flicked his head and said, "Yes, I will," in a barely audible voice. He turned beet red when Daddy leaned down and kissed him.

"Bravo," said Gabriella.

"Gabriella helped me find it," Daddy said.

"Thank you, Gabriella." Whitman nodded at her. "You may smoke now."

Mom reached over and patted Gabriella's hand. "Is there a man in your life, Gabriella?"

Gabriella laughed, a deep husky laugh. "No. No man. A woman. Daniela. Fifteen years now."

"Holy daughters of Sappho," Whitman said.

"That's why Gabriella left me," Daddy said. "Neither one of us knew we were gay."

"I think perhaps we knew, John, but we did not want to know."

"I'll be darned," Mom said.

"Let's eat," I said. "I'm starving."

Chapter
23

I looked everywhere but could not find the door that opened onto the secret stairway leading down to Marcello's room. I surreptitiously went through every room in my suite, including the rooms Mom and the dads were in, opening doors and peering inside.

I was about to ask Teresina if she knew where it was but then thought better of it. It was, after all, supposed to be a secret.

Since I couldn't visit Marcello via the secret stairway, I made my way down to his room just as I had the night before. But this time his door was locked.

I stood there in the darkness wondering what to do. Maybe they'd kept him in the hospital overnight. He hadn't phoned, so I didn't know. I knocked and softly called his name. There was no response. I knocked again and put my ear to the heavy door, listening for his footsteps. Nothing. I put my lips to the keyhole and whispered, "Marcello!" Nothing stirred. Everything was absolutely silent. But then, back in the shadows at the far end of the corridor, I suddenly sensed a pulse of movement and turned to see what looked like a vanishing fragment of darkness. The hairs on the back of my neck rose. I hurried back to my bed, afraid to look behind me, not knowing if what I'd sensed was from this world or the next.

* * *

The next morning, the dads announced that they were going down to Naples with Mom. "You don't need us here," Daddy said, "and frankly, your mother's in dire need of a guide."

"Two guides," Whitman said. He smiled at Daddy, then at me, then down at his new 2,000-year-old gold ring. Obviously the dads had made up and were back to being an inseparable twosome. It turned out that their motives for going to Naples with Mom weren't entirely altruistic: Whitman had snagged another lucrative freelance travel-writing assignment. "For the travel section in that horrible glossy magazine called *Money Today*," he told me. "They've taken that old five-dollar-a-day idea and updated it to five hundred."

"We're going to Pompeii and Herculaneum, too," Daddy said. He and Whitman loved touring ancient sites.

Outside, in the courtyard, next to the security gate, I hugged them all good-bye.

"You'll be all right?" Daddy asked.

"I'll be fine."

"You know how to reach us," Whitman said.

"Yes, Whitman."

"Show me the paper."

Like a dutiful little girl, I opened the paper he'd given me.

"Can you read everything?"

"Yes, Whitman." I admired his beautiful, clear handwriting. "Here's the hotel name, here's the address, here's the phone number, here's the fax, here's the e-mail."

"Call us if you have any problems," Whitman said. "We're only two hours away by fast train."

Mom, looking a little stiff in one of her glamorous new outfits, held me tight. "Give our love to Marcello," she said. "And if you see Fabio, tell him I decided to go to Naples with your fathers."

"He doesn't know about Cesare?"

"Well, I just *mentioned* Cesare. You know, how we met and that he wanted me to visit him in Naples. And Fabio"—she put a hand to her breast—"Fabio just went crazy!"

"Crazy how?" I asked.

"Jealous, sweetheart."

"*Gelosia*," Whitman said. "Thank God I don't suffer from that."

Mom let out an excited laugh. "Oh, sweetheart, am I crazy to be doing this? Going to Naples?" She kissed me. "Yes, I am totally frigging crazy!"

Their taxi pulled up and I punched in the code for the smaller door set within the sliding security gate. They filed out, piled into the taxi, waved, and were gone.

Parents, I thought. *You can never be an adult when your parents are around.*

I went through all the rooms again, searching for the door to the secret stairway, and again I couldn't find it. The only place I hadn't looked was in Teresina's room off the kitchen. And that was off-limits. At least when Teresina was there.

When I knew she'd gone out, I poked my head in. I saw a small room with one window and a tiny bathroom. A single bed with an iron frame and a white chenille coverlet was shoved into the corner. The poster of the pissed-off chick in the leather bikini aiming a machine gun was still on the wall. Knickknacks and photographs, including the one of La Signora, were carefully arranged across the top of a wooden dresser. She had a whole collection of weird little porcelain animals dressed like Victorian people. A very fancy and expensive camera sat on the windowsill. I slipped into the room and opened the one other door in the room. It was a narrow closet with two of her maid's uniforms, a couple of white aprons, and several dresses—gowns, I should say. I knew without checking that they had to be from La Signora's collection of designer couture.

Was Teresina stealing them to sell? Or to dress up in? Again, I wondered how much I could trust my maid. It was kind of creepy to think that someone who was supposedly working for me might have a very different agenda from the one she was supposed to have. But there was nothing I could do about it. If I confronted Teresina about the dresses, I'd be admitting that I'd been in her room. And maybe La Signora had given her those clothes, the way Princess Diana always gave away hers. And the dresses didn't belong to me anyway.

I resumed my hunt for the door. Where on earth could it be?

Obviously it was well hidden. I tried to visualize the layout of my rooms above Marcello's. But given the size and age of Palazzo Brunelli, there was no telling if the walls on my floor matched up with the walls beneath them.

The only way to find it was to climb the stairs up from Marcello's room and see where I came out.

I made my way down to his room. This time, I didn't knock first. I pressed down on the handle and the door opened and I walked in.

Five startled faces greeted me. Giovanna, two nuns, and a short, sad-looking man with a carefully trimmed gray goatee were seated around Marcello, who was sitting up in a bed covered with papers and two laptop computers.

Giovanna quickly rose from her chair and advanced on me. "He's working," she said accusingly.

"Venus." Marcello beckoned me over to the bed. "Ah, my darling. I'm glad you are here."

I could feel Giovanna's eyes boring into me as I leaned down to kiss him. "I didn't know when you were going to the hospital."

"He should be getting ready now," Giovanna said. "He should not be doing any of this. He has been *forbidden* to work."

"I am simply making a few necessary alterations," Marcello said. "Some legal rearrangements."

Giovanna drew in a tense, aggrieved breath and turned her ashen face toward mine, as if I were the one responsible for this outrage. She blurted out, "He's putting Giovanni in charge!"

Marcello either did not hear or chose not to hear the anguish in his daughter's voice. "Venus," he said, ignoring Giovanna and indicating the sad-looking man with the goatee, "this is our family lawyer, Salvatore Degli Atti."

Signor Degli Atti was also working on a laptop. He held it against his short thighs with his left hand as he half stood, bowed his head, and shook my hand with his right. "Pleasure," he said.

"It's time for your medicine, Papa." Giovanna gestured to the nuns, who bustled over to fetch pills and a glass of water. The pills were shaken into white paper cups, set upon a silver dish covered with a white cloth, and offered to Marcello. "A pharmaceutical candy store," he said, eyeing the contents. "I don't think any of these pills help me."

"Take them, Papa."

"Giovanna," he said sharply, "stop treating me like an invalid!" He swallowed the pills and impatiently shooshed away the nuns. "Now go. You make me nervous. Go. *Va, va.*"

The nuns, heads bowed, left the room just as Giovanna was bringing a wheelchair to the side of Marcello's bed. "Clear away your papers, Papa, and I'll help to you to get dressed."

"No," Marcello said. "Venus will help me."

I smiled and sat down on Giovanna's vacated chair.

"And put that goddamn-ed wheelchair away. I'm quite capable of walking out to the car."

"Papa, I—"

"I said take it away!" he bellowed.

Giovanna stood frozen, her hands gripping the handles of the wheelchair. "But—you heard the doctors—"

"Go!" he shouted. "I will meet you at the car in fifteen minutes."

She turned, close to tears, and quickly left the room.

"She makes me feel like an old man," Marcello grumbled. He leaned toward me and whispered, "I am not an old man." Then he said, louder, "In fact, I've never felt better in my life! I don't look ill, do I?"

He did, a little, kind of drawn, but nothing like the way he'd looked on the ambulance gurney. "You look a lot better," I said.

"I am fully operational," he said.

I caught the spark in his eye.

"Salvatore," Marcello said to the lawyer as he shut down and closed his computers, "you have my instructions. Is everything clear?"

"Yes, Excellenza. Perfectly clear."

"Good. Then I can expect to have the documents in a few days, and you will act as witness and notary when I sign them."

Signor Degli Atti nodded, shut down his laptop, gathered all the papers on Marcello's bed, and stuffed everything into his capacious briefcase.

"There's one more thing I want you to look into," Marcello said.

"I didn't want to mention it when Giovanna was here. But I'm thinking of reducing or eliminating the endowment to the Little Doves."

Signor Degli Atti stared at him, open mouthed. "But—"

"If I cannot get married in my own church," Marcello said, "by a priest on my own payroll, then I think the Little Doves should start looking elsewhere for their bird food."

Signor Degli Atti cleared his throat. "You must discuss this with the Principessa, Excellenza."

"As head of the Brunelli family, I am in charge of their endowment, and I am free to revoke it at any time."

"But—the endowment dates back centuries, Excellenza."

"If they wish to discriminate—which I don't need to remind you, Salvatore, they have done for centuries—they must accept the consequences. Don't you think so, Venus?"

"Why can't you—we—get married in their church?" I asked.

"For the simple reason, my darling, that you are divorced."

"What if I converted to Catholicism?"

"You couldn't. The Church is forever closed to you."

"No, Excellenza," said Signor Degli Atti, "that is not strictly true. Signorina Gilroy could become a Catholic, but as a divorcée she could never remarry."

"I don't think that's a religion that speaks to me," I said.

Marcello laughed. "Nor to me. But for hundreds of years Brunellis have been married in that church, our church, paid for with our money. So it will be up to us, Venus, to break all those centuries of tradition."

"That makes me feel horrible," I said.

"It makes me feel free," Marcello said. "Wonderfully free."

"Alone at last," Marcello said, pulling me onto the bed the moment Signor Degli Atti took his leave.

I gave myself up to the moment. We kissed. He pulled back the covers and invited me in, beside him.

"I'm supposed to help you dress," I whispered.

"First you must help me to undress," he whispered back.

So I did. I wasn't shy. I unbuttoned his cotton pajama top and opened it wide, exposing his chest with its stiff mat of salt-and-pepper hairs. After helping him out of the top, I unbuttoned his pajama bottoms and started to tug them down. The jammies got snagged on his hard dick, which suddenly poked out of the fly and fell back on his stomach with a little thud.

"Sorry, nurse," he said.

I laughed. "Just don't let the Little Doves see that."

"I ask you, isn't that an indication that I am well?"

It turned into a game. When he was naked, I tried gently to get him out of his bed, and he tried to get me into it.

"Not now," I said.

"Why not? I thought you were supposed to help me be a slacker."

"Giovanna might come in."

There it was. I'd come full circle. I heard myself voicing the same objection Whitman used to voice to Daddy when I was a little girl visiting the two of them in New York. I remembered hearing Whitman whisper from their bedroom, "No, not when she's in the next room."

Eventually I got my patient out of bed and helped him to dress for the doctor's appointment. He was a little slower than usual, and I could sense his impatience with himself for moving at something less than his usual breakneck speed. His closet was lined with suits, starched dress shirts, and ties folded in drawers, but there were few casual clothes. I didn't see a single pair of jeans. Marcello settled on a pair of linen trousers and a short-sleeved silk shirt. That was as informal as he could get.

"Venus," he said, "before I go, there is something I want you to have." He went into an adjacent room and returned with a ring. "This, more than anything, makes it real for me."

I was speechless. The ring was a thick band of gold with a huge blue stone protruding like an eye and encircled by diamonds. Seeing it, understanding its significance, I turned into a complete chicken. Drew away as if it were poison. Said, "I can't accept that."

The comment seemed to take some of the wind out of his sails. He gave me a pained look. "Have you changed your mind?"

I shook my head. No, I hadn't changed my mind. But the ring, if

I accepted it, made our commitment real. Sealed my future with Prince Marcello Brunelli. Changed my life forever.

"I want you to have it," he said. "Give me your hand."

Still I hesitated.

"I want to slide it on your finger."

I looked into his eyes. I searched them. There had to be a trick. This kind of thing didn't happen to girls like me.

You know how, in those old novels, women always faint when they confront strong emotions they're not equipped to deal with? That's how I felt. As if life, with all its crazy twists and turns and tragedies, was throwing me a destiny unlike any I'd ever dreamed of, and I couldn't assimilate all the possible ramifications fast enough. It was like being at the edge of a diving board, blindfolded. I stood there, frozen.

"Venus?"

"I'm afraid," I said.

"Afraid of me?"

"No. Not of you. Not of you." I couldn't tell him who I was really afraid of. It was me. I was afraid of myself, of what I might become.

"Please," he said, holding out his hand.

I put my palm in his. He stroked it. Gently lifted the fourth finger of my left hand. Slipped on the ring. Kissed my hand. Looked into my eyes.

My heart was racing. I felt the heavy weight of the ring. It completely covered the phantom ring I'd had tattooed on my finger for Tremaynne. That part of my life was over.

"Darling . . . ?"

I looked at him. I thought, *Those are the eyes you're going to be looking into for the rest of your life.* They were beautiful eyes, soft with love, tender with patience, steady with resolve.

I think it was the first time I actually said it out loud. "I love you."

That night we became lovers.

I'd found out where the entrance to the "staircase of love" was hidden in my room.

Earlier in the day, I had been as confused as Alice in Wonderland when, candle in hand, I climbed up a very steep flight of stone stairs from Marcello's bedroom, found the almost invisible handle of a door at the top, and entered a room full of dresses. At first I couldn't register what they were. They hung suspended like an army of bodiless phantoms guarding a rich woman's tomb.

When I got my bearings, I realized I was in La Signora's dressing room.

Pretty weird, but, I had to admit, kind of cool. The back wall of her built-in wardrobe, where all her expensive designer clothes were stored, was actually a door.

Finding this door, knowing that it served as a direct connection from Marcello's room to my own, gave me a strange sense of power. It was like being inducted into a secret society. Who else knew about it? How many generations of lovers, candle in hand, had tiptoed up and down this hidden shaft? It saddened me to think that Marcello had had to lock it, to safeguard himself against his own wife.

I was in possession of a very special key. By having it, I knew I had become part of the history of Palazzo Brunelli. Part of me now belonged there. And I realized that it was up to me to make Palazzo Brunelli my home. I had to take possession of it, imprint my reality on its ancient rooms. I had to do this despite hostility and resistance.

"Signorina, signorina!" Teresina found me as I was soaking in a hot tub of lavender-scented bathwater, pondering what to wear for my secret nocturnal visit to Marcello. That night I wanted to be really special. I wanted it to be a night neither one of us would ever forget.

Teresina breathlessly waved a paper that already looked as if it had been read to shreds. "Signorina, look! Look!"

It was a Roman tabloid. She showed me the front page with its headline: *Non è un segreto! Marcello sposarsi a Venus!*

"What does it say?"

"'Not a secret. Marcello to'—uh—" She snapped her fingers trying to think of the word. "*Matrimonio.*"

"Marry?"

"Yes. 'Marcello to marry Venus.'"

There it was, in print. A thrill of horror and amazement ran through me. How could they know? Who had told them? I squinted through the steam at the accompanying photo. It was a blurry shot of Whitman, Mom, and me taken through what appeared to be a shop window. When and where? None of us had had a clue that we were being tailed and photographed. I thought back to the scene in the Armani shop. How Whitman had identified me as the future wife of Prince Marcello Brunelli.

There was my answer.

Someone in the shop, maybe one of the snotty salesgirls or maybe the manager, had spilled the beans to the press.

What could I do about it? Nothing. I just hoped Marcello wasn't upset.

Later that night, when the palace was quiet, I opened the secret door in La Signora's wardrobe and held up the small aromatherapy travel candle Mom had given me. The tiny flame barely touched the darkness. I started down the long steep tube of black.

The air was dry and cool on my naked body. All I was wearing was the ring he'd given me.

At the bottom, I opened the door into Marcello's room.

He was sitting up in bed, working on his laptop. He looked up and saw me. He took a deep breath but didn't say a word. He closed his computer and put it on the bedside table. Turned off the lamp.

I stood there, naked, holding my little candle. I could see his eyes shining in the silvery darkness. He pulled aside the bedclothes and sat on the side of the bed.

I took a step toward him.

"No," he said. "Stand there for just a moment. Let me look at you."

An old vicious voice, the voice all insecure women carry around like a monkey on their shoulder, hissed in my ear, *What could he possibly see in you? Your body isn't perfect. Far from it. One of your tits hangs lower than the other. Your thighs are too—*"

Marcello stood and held out his hands. "My Venus has come to me at last."

* * *

Sex is what millions or billions of women have every day, sometimes because they want to, often when they don't. Sex is the mechanics of physical union, the hydraulics of desire.

When sex takes on an extra dimension, it becomes lovemaking.

Lovemaking is not a duty, it's a privilege.

I discovered this in Marcello's arms.

And I think he discovered the same in mine.

It was like nothing I'd ever experienced before. Even Tremaynne, who'd brought me to such crescendos of pleasure, was a novice when compared to Marcello. It wasn't just that Marcello was so much bigger. It was that his attitude—his "thereness"—was so powerful. It was me, Venus, that he was making love to. It was my essence that enraptured him. And when I returned his hot pleasure, he was seized by such joy that I felt almost dangerous.

Chapter
24

Life is crazy; no one knows that better than me (I?). One minute you're a sad, bored, thrice-divorced loser with a minimum-wage job you hate, wondering how you're going to stay dry when you finally become a bag lady in rainy Portland, and the next you're wed to a rich Roman prince.

It was the fourth time I wasn't married in a church. That didn't bother *me* so much because I hadn't been raised with any kind of affiliation to the multitude of churches God supposedly calls home. But for *Marcello*, not to be married in Santa Madre di Dio, the church attached to Palazzo Brunelli and funded by the Brunelli family, was a big deal. He was bucking centuries of tradition.

For me.

He made light of it. In fact, he seemed elated. "The more I cast off," he said, "the lighter I feel."

For an American with hardly any traditions at all, except being forced to watch *Auntie Mame* every holiday season with the dads, it was hard to understand the burden Marcello carried as head of an old and very prominent Roman family. Everyone thought of him as a supersuccessful man who had everything he wanted. "The only thing that is missing," he confided to me, "is my life." He felt like a pack mule who'd been forced from an early age to bear the full weight of his family's obligations and expectations. Everyone depended upon him, took him for granted, assumed he'd never stop. He never cut himself any slack.

And he'd never been happy. He'd never enjoyed himself, or so he said.

"There's so much in me that I want to discover," he said during one of our long postcoital conversations. "I have achieved for my family, but not for myself. Never for myself."

"What do you want to achieve for yourself?"

"I want to feel that my life is my own. For once. I want to find out who I really am."

"Aren't you Prince Marcello Brunelli?"

"That's who the world sees. The outer man. But what about my inner man? Who am I really, in my heart? Someone who has never been allowed to express himself except through money and power."

"And sex," I added. "You express yourself pretty well through sex."

He cradled me in his arms. "Do I make you happy?"

I nodded.

"You don't feel like you're in bed with an old man?"

I shook my head, ridiculously close to tears and I didn't know why. "You're the best lover I've ever had. The others were boys—"

"Ah! My darling!"

He pulled my body to his. Looked deep into my eyes. Kissed me. We went at it again.

Three nights. Countless kisses. The awakening thrill of feeling him inside me. The slow, delicious pulse that brought me to a kind of panting delirium. There in the warmth of his carved oak bed I found out what it was like to make love to a man who wasn't afraid to be romantic and tender, who called me "darling" and "*carissima*." I don't know how many times we made love. His passion and sheer physical joy claimed my body and my heart.

"Your breasts are so beautiful," he whispered, gazing at them, stroking them, sucking them.

If I let myself believe him, everything about me was beautiful. Everything that I'd hated and found fault with in the mirror was transformed by the reflection of Marcello Brunelli's love.

Amore, they call it in Italy. A-*more*-ay, with a soft trill of the *r*. Love.

He was giving me more and more amore. I was like a sponge, expanding with the hot, sweet juices oozing from his heart.

It was like being in our own secret world, a world known only to us, a world that began when the moon rose and ended with the first light of dawn. During the day, he was officially an invalid, someone who'd suffered a mysterious collapse and was still considered unwell and undiagnosed. Giovanna accompanied him to private clinics and specialists all over Rome. At night, he was anything but an invalid.

"I think I shall name a clinic after you," he said. "You are better than any doctor at restoring my health."

He said I made him feel young. He said he'd never felt young. He said he'd been robbed of his youth.

Take mine, I thought. *Take all the misguided, boneheaded, ill-judged mistakes that made up my "youth" and help me to transform them into a life and a relationship that's mature and lasting and wonderful.*

I was surprised when he pressed to be married as quickly as possible. He shrugged off his annoyance with the tabloid that had prematurely announced our wedding by saying "For once the *cretini* have something right." Given his prominence, it seemed like there'd be endlessly complicated details to take care of before we could proceed. But Marcello, like a general on a fast-moving campaign, took care of everything. Since I was a divorced non-Catholic, the wedding couldn't be held in Santa Madre di Dio and wouldn't be sanctified by the Church. So our union would be a civil ceremony held in Palazzo Brunelli. Various legal documents were required because I wasn't a citizen of Italy or the European Union. So Marcello pulled every string he could. He knew those in power, the ones who could shake an apple from an empty tree. "There are times when being a prince comes in handy," he said.

We waited until Mom and the dads returned to Rome after their Naples adventure. I told them over dinner.

"Marcello and I are getting married tomorrow."

Mom dropped her fork and burst into tears.

"It's not going to be anything fancy, OK? It's not in a church. It's going to be out in the big salon—"

"Sa-*lone*-ay," Whitman corrected.

"Salone. No priest, no minister, just an official Marcello knows who can officiate at civil ceremonies."

Daddy came over to kiss me. "Is this what you want?"

And I was able to say calmly, with the certainty of a grown-up, "Yes, it is."

Whitman said, "You didn't sign any prenuptial agreements, did you?"

"I haven't signed anything."

"I want to see every document," he said. "We'll fax them to my lawyers for legal commentary before you sign anything."

"I'm sure Marcello will take care of everything," Mom snuffled, wiping her eyes. "He's such a gentleman." She beckoned me over and pulled me close to her hot and heavy bosom. "Oh, Venus. Oh, my little girl. You're going to be a friggin' princess."

Marcello's mother, La Principessa, did not come to the ceremony, and his daughter, Giovanna, absented herself by saying she was ill, and his son, Giovanni, was unavailable because he had to fly to London to deal with some urgent Brunelli business.

I knew perfectly well that if Marcello had married the "right" woman, a nondivorced Catholic, his family would have been there at his side. Their disapproval of me couldn't have been any plainer.

It didn't seem to bother Marcello in the least. He was jovial and excited. A bit slower than usual, but a perfect host.

Me? Don't ask. Part of me was cowering with fear, still unable to accept the truth of his love and the reality of his wealth. By going through with this, my life would be changed forever. I knew that. And maybe that's why I felt so oddly superstitious, as if all those invisible gods and saints and devils and angels that flew through Rome, touching the lives of mortals, were suddenly crowding into the vast salone of Palazzo Brunelli and working out the jigsaw puzzle of my fate.

I concentrated on the fact that I loved him. A miracle had oc-

curred. For once in my life I had fallen in love with a stable, generous man instead of a debt-ridden, insecure boy.

And he'd fallen in love with me.

I couldn't question the whys and wherefores, because it was a
miracle. And you don't analyze miracles. You accept them. Humbly.

Everything was ready. We'd talked about the ceremony and how
we would manage it. The giant salone with its domed, frescoed ceiling and huge windows was as beautiful as any church and almost as
large. The room was filled with fresh flowers—not, this time, from
La Principessa's garden in Capri. A string quartet played soft, unobtrusive music.

At four o'clock, Marcello took his place in front of a tall marble
table with gilded legs that ended in claws. He was wearing a soft,
dark suit with a starched white shirt and a patterned wine-colored
tie. Mom stood beside him in one of her new outfits, a purple crepe
suit that set off the carrot color of her hair. The dark-suited official
who would pronounce us man and wife stood stiffly behind the table,
which almost looked like an altar. Teresina, wearing a simple black
dress, was there, and so was Fabio, who looked uncomfortable in his
gray suit. Signor Degli Atti hovered in the background.

The string quartet stopped playing. The giant room grew quiet.

"Ready?" Whitman whispered. We were standing behind a set of
doors that led into the room from a corridor.

I nodded.

"You look beautiful," Daddy said.

I squeezed his hand.

"Beautiful," Whitman nodded. "I'm so glad I made you buy that
dress."

"You didn't make me buy this dress," I whispered. "You said it
made me look—"

"I was wrong," Whitman said. "OK, everyone, Buddha breath."

We all sucked in a deep breath.

The string quartet began playing again. It was a beautiful melody
I'd heard somewhere, someplace, sometime long ago, maybe at some
high-toned event the dads had dragged me to. My throat tickled,
felt dry, as if my voice were evaporating. I kept myself from licking

my lips. Looked down at myself. Thought, for one brief, disjointed moment, of Mistah Sistah in his white wedding gown performing his hip-hop "Wedding Bliss Diss."

A cynical rap. One that appealed to people who didn't believe in love songs. Or love.

"Here we go," Whitman said. He opened the door and Daddy and I stepped out into the salone. I took Daddy's arm and Whitman's arm and as the music played we slowly walked to where Marcello was waiting for me with glistening eyes. When we were a few feet away from him, the dads stopped and I took the final steps on my own.

I looked up into Marcello's eyes. He didn't smile and neither did I. The moment was solemn. I took his arm. We faced the official.

He was about to begin when we heard the sound of footsteps behind us. Arms linked, we both turned.

I tightened my grasp on Marcello's arm.

"Sorry," Johnny said. He limped into the room. "I made it after all."

Afterward, there were the usual hugs and kisses and handshakes. Johnny shook my hand. "Congratulations," he said.

"Thank you." I racked my brain trying to think of something to say. "How's your ankle?"

"It's OK. I just have to wear an elastic bandage around it."

"I thought—we thought you were in London."

"I'm leaving in a few minutes," Johnny said. "There are a few things I must discuss with my father before this meeting."

We looked at each other for a moment longer and then I turned to my new husband, who was making sure that everyone had a glass of champagne.

Toasts, sips, laughter, more toasts.

"Excuse me one moment, will you?" Marcello walked to the far side of the room with his son. I tried not to look but couldn't help myself. They were having an animated discussion about something. It almost looked like an argument. Marcello shook his head, chopped the air, shrugged his shoulders. Johnny, who'd come with a leather briefcase, retrieved some papers and showed them to his father. Marcello intently studied the papers and then pointed to something on one of the pages. More discussion. Johnny looked tense and nervous and unhappy. He ran his hands through his hair and rubbed his neck as if it were stiff or cramped. He was wearing a dark suit instead of his usual jeans and T-shirt.

As they stood together, caught up in their conversation, I could see more of Marcello's features in Johnny than I ever had before. I must have been blind not to make the connection earlier.

Saint Agnes, I prayed, *I don't really know you, but if you're out there, and you can hear me, please help me to be a good wife to Marcello.*

I knew that Johnny's life, like my own, had changed dramatically in the past few days. Marcello was drawing back from his micromanaging business approach and handing over the day-to-day operations of the Brunelli empire to Johnny. Johnny, like his father before him, had been groomed for this. And maybe he was just as unwilling as Marcello had been. I had the sense that Johnny was going along with the plan but inwardly resisting it. How would he reconcile his Communist ideals with running an international business?

I felt sorry for him, suddenly saddled with a new and incessantly demanding life.

While watching the exchange between Marcello and Johnny, I was simultaneously making inane small talk with Mom, the dads, Teresina, Fabio, Signor Degli Atti, and the official who'd officiated. I wasn't used to drinking and the glass of champagne I'd nervously downed went instantly to my head.

I sat down, a dumb smile on my face, and looked up at all those Brunellis staring down from the ceiling. Were they disapproving? Or welcoming me into the family?

Marcello joined me on the sofa. "Sorry, darling, but Giovanni needed my advice. This is his first important business meeting in London."

I looked over my shoulder and saw Johnny standing by himself, tucking papers back into his briefcase. I could imagine Marcello at that age, doing the same thing, looking just as miserable. "Will he be all right?"

Marcello sighed. "Eventually, yes. He will make mistakes, just as I did. He must learn how to harden himself."

"Maybe that's not his nature," I said.

"No, but that is the nature of business."

Johnny fastened his briefcase, ran his fingers through his hair, and straightened his shoulders. He was preparing to leave. He looked my way, a forlorn expression on his face.

"I'm going to go say good-bye." I rose and crossed the room. Johnny kept his eyes on me. I forced myself to look at him and prayed that I could dissolve all the emotions he summoned up. "Are you leaving now?" I asked.

He nodded. "Plane to catch."

"Well—I don't know when I'll see you again."

He looked down at his feet, then over toward the door; then his eyes moved back to mine. "I hope you'll be happy, Venus."

I nodded. "You too."

He lowered his voice. "I hope this is what you really want."

I smiled, but it was more of a defense mechanism than anything else.

"Because I thought—" He stopped and looked away.

I put my hand on his arm and whispered, "I hope we can be friends."

Johnny nodded.

I stood there and watched him go.

erable, though. He'd known she was going to visit another suitor, and when she returned from Naples, Fabio did everything he could to spend time with her. But potential romantic trysts were foiled because Fabio, as Marcello's driver, was basically on duty day and night. He had to be ready to go anywhere and at any time. He and Mom had been able to snatch only a few stray minutes here and there.

"So which one are you more interested in?" I asked. "Fabio or Cesare?"

She reddened and went into the bathroom to fluff her hair for the ten millionth time. "I like both of them," she said. I heard the faint hiss of an atomizer.

"You're not choosing?"

She poked her head out of the bathroom and looked at me. "Sweetheart, I hardly know either one of them."

"But you slept with Cesare," I reminded her.

Mom let out a low, funny laugh and turned back to the mirror. "Sleeping with a man doesn't tell you anything about him."

"Wrong! It tells you everything."

Again, her head appeared around the corner of the bathroom door. Our eyes met. "Is it . . . that *good* with Marcello?" Mom asked. "Or that *bad?*"

"That good."

"I have a feeling that Fabio would be better than Cesare in that department, but now I'll never know." Mom checked her purse for plane tickets and passport. "OK," she said, "I'm starting to hyperventilate a little. I'm starting to feel nervous about the flight. All those hours on the plane."

Teresina rapped on the door. "Signora, Fabio is here. He drives you to *aeroporto*."

"Hallo." The next moment, Fabio walked in. He and Mom looked at each other. "Please," he said to me.

It took me a second to realize that he wanted me to leave. He wanted a moment alone with my mother. He had her in his arms before I was even out of the room.

* * *

Next, it was the dads. They didn't want me to go to the airport either.

"Gabriella's going to drive us," Daddy said.

"Such a wonderful person," Whitman gushed, pulling on a pair of thin cotton gloves.

"You're wearing gloves now?" I laughed. "In the summer?"

"To protect my ring," he explained. "It's a piece of ancient art and deserves respect. And I can't wear just one glove—that would look too pretentious—so I have to wear both." He suddenly came over, took my fingers and raised my hand, rocking it back and forth in the light. My ring and jeweled watch flashed and glittered and shot out hard, brilliant sparks. "Do you have any idea how much these are worth, Venus?"

I shook my head. I was afraid to ask. I didn't want to place a monetary value on them.

He released my fingers. "Don't wear them out on the street, honey, unless you have armed security with you."

I'd always been amazed at the dads' methodical orderliness. Their matching leather suitcases sat side by side on the bed, contents neatly folded and arranged. Whitman scanned his, then closed and locked it. Daddy scanned his, then closed and locked it.

"OK," Whitman said, "before we go, your fathers want you to promise them that you'll be careful."

"Careful?"

"Careful. Especially with those paparazzi. They're worse than terrorists. They'll do anything. Remember Princess Di."

"Keep your eyes open," Daddy cautioned.

"Wide open," Whitman nodded. "*Stai attento*. Put that one in your phrase book. Pay attention. Because for all your worldly experience, honey, you're still very innocent in the ways of the world."

"The Old World, anyway," Daddy said.

"Right," Whitman said. "And we don't want you to get into any trouble."

"Marcello's a good man," Daddy said. "He'll take care of you."

"He's obviously trying to recapture something of his lost youth," Whitman said. "It's not uncommon at that age."

"Whit," Daddy said, "he's only a couple of years older than we are."

"Not if we're measuring in gay years," Whitman said. "Gay men age at two-thirds the rate of straight men."

Daddy looked at me and rolled his eyes.

"John!" Whitman snapped his fingers. "The photo!"

"Oh, right, the photo." Daddy pulled a cardboard envelope from his carry-on and handed it to me. Inside was the photo of La Principessa taken when she was the cabaret singer Lita.

"If your mother-in-law gets too high and mighty with you," Daddy said, "just wave this in front of her."

"Yes," Whitman said with a dangerous smile, "you can remind La Principessa of her *theatrical* origins. The secret she doesn't want anyone to know."

And then, following the departures of my mom and the dads, my husband picked up and left, too.

"Darling," he said, after an agitated phone call, "I have to go to London. Immediately."

And when Marcello said *immediately*, he meant immediately. He dialed Fabio with one hand and called up some information on his laptop with the other. Plane schedules appeared. Rome–London.

The emergency had something to do with the big meeting that Johnny was supposed to be managing. Things weren't going well. The company officials, accustomed to dealing with Marcello, not his son, were displeased and unhappy. Johnny apparently didn't have all the facts and figures that were needed, and he didn't know how to finesse a board.

"Marcello," I said, watching with amazement as the Brunelli machinery leapt into action, "what about your health?"

"There's nothing wrong with me. The doctors haven't been able to find a thing, not a single goddamn-ed thing."

"You collapsed," I reminded him. "Just a few days ago."

"I was tired. Run down. Maybe it was the flu. I'm fine now."

"We haven't even had our honeymoon yet."

"This will be for only one day," Marcello said. "Tomorrow, when

I am back, we'll drive down to Naples. And then we'll sail. First to Capri—a short visit to Mama. And then—wherever we want."

"Can't I go with you to London?"

"Darling, this is not a good idea. I will be in meetings with Giovanni the entire time. I must help him. Much is at stake. What fun would it be for you, sitting in a hotel by yourself?"

"I'd find something to do. I've never been to London."

"Darling, listen to me. I am going to be irritable and distracted. You do not want to be with me at this time. But I promise you, the minute I return—" He pulled me close and kissed me.

Chapter
26

So once again I was alone in Palazzo Brunelli. Only this time I was married.

It was time to think about our living arrangements. I'd been sleeping with Marcello, down in his suite, and returning to my rooms in the morning. But how and where would we live now that we were married?

The whole concept of day-to-day domestic space as I had come to know it in America was different in this ancient palazzo. I thought of my dinky studio apartment and laughed. I thought of American houses, all so predictable in what they had and where they had it.

Here, I was still at odds with the scale of things around me, dwarfed by the size and grandeur of the rooms. It was a strange sensation, one that made me feel weirdly vulnerable. There were too many unknowns, too much space and too many shadows. I was forever looking over my shoulder; some inner reflex was keeping me on my guard. If I was going to live there with Marcello, I'd have to make myself at home. Literally. I couldn't just be a spectator to life as it was lived around me in Palazzo Brunelli. I had to know the inner workings of the place.

Soon after Marcello's hasty departure, I received one of Giovanna's elaborate embossed notecards. It was an invitation to join her for lunch. The weird formality of the invitation amused and irritated me. But if I was going to share the same palace, it was time to establish some sort of working relationship with Giovanna.

She was, after all, my stepdaughter.

A tiny, bespectacled nun answered the door and peered up at me, her face so wrinkled it looked like a dried apple. Where was Sister Angelica, the nun who'd been in Giovanna's rooms the last time I was there? This Little Dove opened the huge door and pointed to Giovanna's salone. *This time I'll wait no more than five minutes*, I thought, taking a seat.

Giovanna appeared a moment later. She was wearing a long, pleated black robe—it looked like a cross between a choir robe and an old lady's dress—with a wide collar of lace laid like an intricate spiderweb around her neck and across her shoulders. The garment completely hid her body; there was no indication of waist or hips or breasts. She nodded and flashed me a brief, anxious look. "Papa has gone to London," she said.

"He said he had to go. To help Johnny."

"Johnny?"

"Giovanni."

"Ah, yes, you call him Johnny, don't you."

I said nothing, merely stretched out my left hand and rested it on my crossed knee. Giovanna's eyes flew immediately to the ring sparkling on my finger. She stared, breath whistling in her cavernous nostrils.

"Sit down, Giovanna," I said. "Let's talk."

She hesitated, then limped over to sit across from me. The tiny nun entered with a tray, poured two thimble-size glasses of a thick, greenish liquid from a crystal carafe, and left. Giovanna gestured toward a glass but I ignored it.

"Are you worried about your father?" I asked.

"Yes, of course. He's not well. He should not go to London." She sucked in a sudden, wheezing breath, as if trying to hold back a sob. "I worry about his soul. I pray for him day and night."

There didn't seem much I could say on that subject.

"Is it true?" Giovanna said, nervously clenching her long white fingers. "Is he going to starve my Little Doves?"

"Starve them?"

"Stop their endowment."

"I don't know."

"He can't! He mustn't do that!"

"Giovanna, I have nothing to do with your father's business decisions."

"But of course you do." Her tone indicated the depths of my stupidity. "It's because of *you* that he's going to cut off their endowment."

I sat up straight and took a deep breath. "Giovanna, that's not true."

"He can't marry you in the Church, so it's the Church he blames."

"Blames for what?"

"For having moral standards! Because *he* obviously has none."

I kept my mouth shut. I thought, *Let her spew it all out. Listen.*

"I pray for his soul," Giovanna went on, a catch in her voice. She looked at me, her eyes blazing. "Because in the eyes of the Church, you must understand, he is not married."

"But in the eyes of the law," I said, "he is. We are."

"Yes." I thought I heard a sad note of resignation in her voice.

"Giovanna, I want to talk to you about some things."

"What things?" She stiffened, instantly suspicious.

"Living arrangements. The security system. The people who work here."

She leaned forward and coughed, quite rudely, in my direction. "Excuse me, I must have a breath of air."

I watched her limp toward the ancient garden that separated her living quarters from her security office. She closed the glass door behind her and stood with her back pressed against it, staring up at a sky that was turning dark and tumultuous after days and days of broiling heat.

Watching her, I came to the sudden, startling realization that she literally could not bear to be with me. My very presence acted on her like a suffocating poison. Well, too bad. I wasn't going to skulk away. She had to deal with me sooner or later.

I understood, of course, that my stepdaughter's animosity was entirely defensive. She felt toward me what I once had felt toward Whitman, back when Daddy first left and I suddenly had to deal with his strange and demanding lover, the person he'd chosen over Carolee and me. I hated Whitman's guts back then, just as Giovanna now hated mine. He'd usurped my mom's throne, and that made him dangerous and despicable. Giovanna probably felt the same way about me. Like it or not, I was now her stepmother.

I tried to be charitable toward Giovanna. After all, her world, like mine, had just been turned completely upside down. If we could just acknowledge that, admit to our mutual confusion, maybe we could find some way to live together.

It must have been difficult for her, coping with a deranged mother and a father who wasn't around much. And, unfortunately, there was nothing she or anyone else could do to disguise the unavoidable fact of her ugliness. You couldn't say, "Giovanna has a great personality," because she didn't, or "She has beautiful eyes," because Giovanna's eyes had no warmth in them.

No wonder she was so emotionally dependent upon the Little Doves. The Little Doves were the ones who'd raised her, and who'd always taken care of her. Not warm and loving mother figures—more like cold and resentful nannies who didn't dare complain if she treated them like servants, because that, essentially, is what they were. It was her family's fortune, after all, that kept the Little Doves in birdseed.

Poor Giovanna. As I watched her thin black shape wheezing for breath out in her ancient garden, I felt a vague glimmer of sympathy for the bleakness of her life, the pain and tortured emptiness of it. It was impossible to imagine her in a relationship.

Maybe in time I could break through to some bright, sparkling personality trapped beneath the pinched, arrogant monster she'd become. Fish out the fun-loving little girl who had turned into an emotionally constipated zealot.

I eyed the tiny glass of liqueur. Picked it up. Sniffed. Rosemary?

Took a sip. Shuddered. Vile. Put the glass back down and tried to soothe my outraged taste buds.

There was a rustling sound and I looked over to see the tiny nun making her way across the salone. She rapped once on the glass door to the garden. "*Pranzo*, signorina."

It was time for lunch.

The nun put a plate of salad before me.

"You're not having any?" I asked Giovanna.

She shook her head. "No. I am allergic."

There were several different leaves in the salad, different shapes, different colors. It was the kind of fresh mixed-leaf salad the dads would serve. I loved their salads. My mouth watered, remembering the medley of tastes. I drizzled olive oil and balsamic vinegar on the bed of leaves and dug in.

Giovanna watched me intently.

"I'm sorry you couldn't come to our wedding," I said, knowing full well that she could have but chose not to.

"I was very ill," she said.

"With what?"

"Severe vomiting and diarrhea."

I almost believed her. She did look kind of peaked, maybe even a little feverish. There was a glittery look in her big dark eyes. She reminded me of someone I'd seen in the Brunelli portrait gallery, a black-robed woman clutching a crucifix and staring fervently toward heaven, her head tossed back as if she were in the throes of a major crisis.

"Do you enjoy the salad?" Giovanna asked, taking a sip of water.

I nodded. "Do the Little Doves do all your cooking?"

"For me, personally, yes. Because I have so many allergies."

"And Teresina will be cooking for Marcello and me?"

Giovanna suddenly looked uncomfortable. "Teresina is gone," she said."

"Gone?"

"I dismissed her early this morning."

"Dismissed her?" I put the napkin to my mouth and fished a weird-tasting bit of salad leaf from between my teeth. "Why?"

"She was a—" Giovanna would not or could not look at me. "Teresina did some terrible things."

"Such as?" I wasn't going to just let this pass. I liked Teresina. I had every intention of keeping her on.

"She was a traitor!" Giovanna hissed, her face turning red. "She was having an affair with a paparazzo! One of the scum on the street! Yes, it's true! She even managed to get him into Palazzo Brunelli. God only knows what they were planning to do."

"How do you know this?"

"Her lover was arrested this morning. I caught him on camera and called the police. He was disgusting. He said Teresina put him up to it. He said she'd arranged it so that he could photograph you—*nude*."

"What?" I couldn't believe it—and yet I believed it, and cursed myself for being so gullible.

"The police found a whole cache of his photographs in Teresina's room."

My breath seemed to be evaporating and my mouth was growing very hot. "Photographs?"

"Of you," Giovanna said. "They were confiscated by the police. And I hope to God, for your sake, they are never seen."

I wondered if Carlos and Baby were in on the scheme. And I wondered if Teresina's boyfriend had taken that photo of me kissing Johnny at Asclepio. And I wondered if Teresina was the one who'd left that photo on my bed, to frighten and prepare me for the blackmail that was to come. To think that all this while, the secret lover she'd entertained in her room, letting him in through the secret door, was none other than one of the photographers she professed to hate. It made me sick to think of her duplicity, and heartsick, too, because I had come to trust her.

"Was Teresina arrested?"

"No." Giovanna fiddled nervously with her napkin and continued to avoid my eyes. "She denied everything, of course. Pleaded. Cried. Begged. I told her she had fifteen minutes to pack up her filthy things and leave."

My heart was racing. My eyes had started to water—why, I didn't know. I let out a dazed Buddha breath and dabbed at the sweat that had broken out on my forehead.

Giovanna regarded me over the rim of her water glass. "Anyway, now you will be moving down to my father's rooms."

"No," I said. "I like the rooms where I am. They're a lot more comfortable. Sunnier."

"Papa will never move up there."

I said nothing, just looked at her.

"Too many memories," she said.

"Well, I'll talk to him about it and we'll decide."

She inclined her head in what I took to be a nod of acquiescence.

"I want to know more about the security—" I began.

"That is my job!" she snapped, instantly tensing up. "I am in charge of that. Papa put me in charge."

"I understand that. But I want to know more about it. How the system works. It's important, if I'm going to be living here."

"I have designed all the security," she said. "It is too complicated for you to understand."

"I'll be the judge of that."

"Do you have a degree?" she asked. "I have several. One in security analysis and delivery systems."

I smiled and said, "I'll talk to your father about it."

"Talk to him about what? There is nothing to talk about. He is as stupid as the rest when it comes to understanding the need for security gates and security codes."

"And security cameras."

"At strategic points, yes."

"Are there any in my rooms?"

She hesitated and looked down at her hands, clenching the long bony fingers in her lap. "We needed them for my mother. That is why they were installed."

Had she been monitoring me all along? I wondered how much she'd seen and heard. "I want them taken out," I said. "Immediately. I'll talk to Marcello about it."

The Little Dove appeared to take my salad plate. Her hands

were old and misshapen. She used only the thumb and forefinger, like lobster claws. Was she in pain? If so, she gave no sign of it. She wore a plain gold band on her ring finger. A bride of Christ. Wed to a supernatural deity. No personal life of her own. Weird.

"Will you take an espresso?" Giovanna asked.

I couldn't quite get my hostess into focus. My heart was pounding and I was sweating. "No, thank you. I'm feeling a little strange. I think I'll go lie down."

It hit about an hour later. And when I say hit, I mean *hit*. My stomach felt like it had been slammed by a giant fist. Sharp, shooting pains radiated out from my gut. I moaned and shivered and curled up in a fetal position under the covers, trying to get some relief.

What was it? Flu? Something I'd eaten? Salmonella? E. coli? I hadn't had any shellfish, or any eggs, or any meat that could have been bad. Some cereal for breakfast and then a light lunch with Giovanna.

"Teresina," I called weakly. Then remembered that she was gone.

I fell into a sweaty, stuporous doze and woke some time later with the realization that I had to get to the bathroom, fast. I lurched out of bed and made it to the toilet just in time. My guts clenched and roiled as I spewed out a noxious green porridge. The pain in my stomach was hot and relentless. I retched until I was spent and panting on the cool marble floor beside the toilet. Then I felt it from the other end and managed to sit down on the toilet just a second before it came gushing and squirting out in an evil tide of stink.

The water pressure was low—all over Rome, I'd been told, because of the heat wave. I had to wait for what seemed like hours for the toilet to fill so I could flush it again. And then again. And then again.

I thought a hot bath would feel good but couldn't bring myself to turn on the taps and wait for the tub to fill, so I wobbled back to bed. I felt slightly better, the way you do after vomiting, but my anus stung as though I'd been shitting scorpions and my lips burned like a flamethrower's. I fell into bed and must have passed out. I didn't wake up until another hot fist grabbed and twisted my gut.

Moaning, I made my way back to the toilet.

That toilet, with its peculiar shape and the low, murmuring sound it made while filling, became very important to me over the next few hours, as I expelled every atom of food from my body. I braved a look each time, trying to read the intestinal sludge that came out. What could have caused this?

Had Giovanna passed her mysterious illness on to me, the "severe vomiting and diarrhea" she said had forced her to miss our wedding? Or was it some form of food poisoning?

I went through everything I'd drunk or eaten that day. Boxed cereal for breakfast, a German brand of muesli that Marcello liked. Milk with the cereal. A cappuccino made by Teresina. A glass of fresh-squeezed orange juice. Then . . . ? Nothing until lunch. A tiny tiny sip, it hardly counted, of that green liqueur. Some bread. Cold cuts: a couple of pieces of salami and cheese. Mineral water. And then the salad.

The salad.

I saw it again, in full color, heaped on the plate before me.

I remembered seeing Giovanna eating a salad during the meal our two families had shared. But earlier today she'd said she didn't eat salad because she was allergic.

I mentally picked through the leaves of the salad. I couldn't name them, but most I'd seen before. The Italians ate dandelion leaves, which were new to me but hadn't caused any upset when I'd had them at other meals. There were some bitter, crunchy greens. Some kind of reddish leaf snipped up and scattered throughout for color. Extremely bitter, almost metallic tasting. I remembered because I'd gotten a piece stuck between my teeth. I could feel it there, wedged in, and after easing it out with my tongue, and into my napkin, I had sneaked a surreptitious look.

A coarse, thick, red-and-gray-veined leaf.

Hadn't I seen that leaf somewhere before?

Where? Where would I see a leaf in Palazzo Brunelli?

In Giovanna's ancient herb garden.

"Jesus Christ," I whispered, staring up at the ceiling, soaked in sweat, my entire intestinal tract ablaze.

It wasn't possible.

Yes, a voice echoed in my ear, *it is possible.*

My wicked stepdaughter had poisoned me.

Day was turning to night. How long had I slept? I crawled out of bed, so lightheaded I nearly fell, and lurched through the giant rooms, steadying myself by holding on to pieces of furniture, until I came to the kitchen.

I tried Teresina's door. Locked.

I craved water. Cool water. Put my parched lips to the spigot in the kitchen. But choked as I tried to swallow it. The water, as it went down, seemed to intensify the burning sensation in my gut.

By now it was clear to me that I had to get help. I had to go outside my palazetto and find someone to help me. I didn't even know how to call a doctor.

I wobbled out to the vestibule and stood in front of the security keypad, head hammering, vision blurred, trying to remember the exit code. My hand was shaking and I could barely lift it and extend my finger. I tapped in the code. Waited for the sound of the lock being released. Didn't hear it. Tried the door. It wouldn't open.

That pitiful groaning sob I heard was my own. The sweat was drying on my feverish body. I was so cold that my teeth chattered. And I was so hot. My guts were sizzling.

I managed to reset the keypad and again tapped in the code. Nothing.

I stood there, hunched over, clutching my stomach, trying to slap down a mounting wave of panic.

All the past residents of Palazzo Brunelli were ganging up on me, I thought crazily. All those haughty hawk-nosed aristocrats peering out from oil paintings and frescoes had conferred and decided my portrait would never hang with theirs.

"Help!" But I knew no one would hear me. I could barely hear myself. My strength was ebbing away fast.

I made it back into the kitchen in time to heave into the sink.

There wasn't anything left in me, but my stomach was determined to wring out every last drop.

The telephone.

First I tried the one on the table in the vestibule. There was no dial tone. I held the dead receiver in my hand, trying to understand the extent of Giovanna's hatred, the planning that had gone into this. I wondered if she had made up the story about Teresina—maybe Teresina was innocent, and Giovanna had fired her just to get her out of the way, so no one would be there to help me.

It then occurred to me that Giovanna might be watching me at this very moment on her bank of monitors. Staring impassively at her screens, watching her loathed stepmother die. Or maybe smiling, discussing with a flock of Little Doves the effects a certain toxic leaf had on the body when ingested.

Where were the cameras? I didn't see any.

I fumbled my way back to my bed. To La Signora's bed. The intricately carved pattern of vines twisting up the bedposts and across the headboard hid a malevolent harvest of poisonous fruits.

"Giovanna," I panted, looking out into the room, unable to stand straight, "if you can see me, call a doctor. Please."

How ridiculous. Why would she call a doctor? She wanted me dead.

The thought of her observing me, as she'd no doubt observed her mad mother, filled me with a kind of impotent fury. I wanted to block her vision so she couldn't see my torment.

How quick and clever are the devils of the world. This one sat at her computer control boards like some kind of malignant deity. A few strokes on her keyboard and I was her prisoner in hell.

Where was my cell phone? I could call Marcello. I had the number that got through to him anywhere in the world. But where was the damned phone?

Gone. I was so exhausted that I stopped searching. Gave myself up to the certainty that my mobile phone had been stolen. Perhaps by Teresina. Perhaps by Giovanna. Perhaps by a Little Dove.

My God, but they were cunning.

"Oh! Oh!" I doubled over as the pain squeezed my gut.

Then it was time for another round on the toilet. By the end of it, I was sobbing. Or would have been if I'd had any fluid left in my body. I was dried up and dried out, like a squeezed sponge on a hot brick. I made the sounds of crying, but my eyes were dry and scratchy.

I was going to die here, alone. God only knew how many assassinations had taken place in Palazzo Brunelli over the centuries. And Giovanna would fix it somehow so that she wouldn't be caught or even suspected. Marcello would never know that his daughter had killed his young bride. He would grieve but he would never know the truth.

The world was in slow motion now. Every move had to be carefully considered. There was no energy left to waste.

I crawled back to the bed—the huge bed where Brunelli women had given birth and made love and died, generation after generation. I hoisted myself up and onto it. Lay there panting with the effort. Twisted my body into various contortions, hoping that one of them would ease the relentless burning pain.

"Help me."

I didn't know who I was asking for help. There was no one there. It was just a general-alarm SOS to the universe.

The light in the room was disappearing, sucked out on the rising tide of night. Shadows pooled in the far corners. It was unbearably quiet. Usually at this hour I could hear the rising clamor of the evening passeggiata, when Romans took to the streets. But it had started to rain, so people were staying indoors. I could hear the sound of raindrops as they pitted against the windows. Water. Moisture. I craved it but knew I couldn't reach it. I listened for the sound of bells tolling the hours, that beautiful sound that was so magical and poignant to my American ears.

I heard nothing. Maybe death was stopping my ears.

I recognized the smell.

In my confused state, I thought it was the smell that had awakened me.

It was the faint smell that hid in the mattress, in the bedclothes, that was embedded deep in the wood. It was oddly comforting, like some remembered smell of my mother when I was a frightened kid and she took me in her arms.

Had I slept?

I must have. The room was dark.

The pain had dropped a notch and I felt empty and otherworldly, as if I'd stepped across some physical boundary.

A shadow moved near my bedside. I didn't see it so much as feel it. Something that had been sitting on the bed beside me rose and moved a few steps away. I strained to see who it was. I thought it must be a friend. It was associated with the smell.

Was it beckoning me? I couldn't be sure. It flitted away from the bed. It seemed to be waiting for me to follow.

But I couldn't move, could I? I was immobilized. Weak as a moth on a cottonball soaked in chloroform.

The shadow made what looked like an impatient gesture.

I moved my foot. First one, then the other. Then each limb. Then I turned my head back and forth. I did all this very gently, testing for pain and my own limits. I must have looked like a doll coming to life.

"*Venga, venga,*" a strange voice whispered. The shadow was urging me to hurry. "Presto, presto."

I felt light as a wraith, as if I'd shed every last milligram of bodily weight. I rose up—almost floated—and moved toward the shadow.

"*Venga,*" it urged, motioning for me. "*Presto.*"

I was light, lightheaded. I felt my way through the room, trying to discern the shadow moving within the blanket of darkness. I had no idea where I was going. I was not making decisions. I was following.

The shadow slid into the small anteroom that led to La Signora's dressing room. When I got to the anteroom, the shadow was gone. I knew where it was.

I opened the door and entered the wardrobe and dressing room of my predecessor. The vague smell that had awakened me in bed was stronger and sharper in there, the stubborn, lingering scent of a woman who refused to vacate her old haunts.

Something was different, some outrage had been committed, but

I couldn't immediately recognize what it was. My eyes needed several seconds to adjust to the deeper level of darkness.

Then I saw it.

A massacre.

La Signora's dresses had been ripped from the hangers where they'd been so carefully preserved and lay heaped and hurled and torn and kicked across the floor. Shelves had been ransacked of hats and shoes, drawers yanked open and disemboweled, their delicate contents pulled out and strewn like entrails.

Teresina, in a final fit of rage? Or La Signora herself . . .

I looked up and saw the shadow moving back and forth, a piece of agitated darkness, a black candleflame, at the very back of the closet.

"*Prego. Mi può liberare!*"

I didn't know what she meant.

"*Il porto,*" she said, her voice a pleading whisper, "*il porto!*"

Porto meant "*door.*"

Once I made that connection, I realized why I was there, in that wardrobe. La Signora was helping me to escape. I'd been too weak and addled to remember the hidden stairway of love.

I waded through the carnage of cold, tangled fabrics to the secret door at the back of the wardrobe. Realized as I tried to pull it open how weak I was. I felt light as a flame and just as insubstantial. Like I could be blown out and become part of the world of darkness and shadows at any moment.

Would, if I didn't get out.

The door sprang open.

Freedom.

I moved slowly down the stairs, toward the door at the bottom, the door into Marcello's room. From there I could get out, find help.

Giovanna had not won.

There was only one key, and I had it.

At the bottom, beside the door, the shadow was waiting for me. I knew it with a kind of unquestioned clarity. I could feel her ravaged, anguished spirit forever pushing against the boundaries of her confinement, longing to be released.

"La Signora," I whispered. Silence. "La Signora, I know it's you." Silence. "I'm not afraid of you. But it's time for you to go." Silence. "I know you loved Marcello." A faint sound, like someone crying in the dark. "I love him, too. I'll take care of him. That's what you want, isn't it?"

"*Mi liberai*," the voice begged. "*La porta! Aperto!*"

When I opened the door, I felt something brush past me like a gust of hot, dry wind. And by that time, I was no more than a leaf swept along in its wake. I stumbled out into Marcello's bedroom and that's where they found me, sprawled on the cold marble floor.

Chapter
27

When I came to and saw Marcello's anxious face, and saw the love in his eyes and felt the warmth of his hands pressing mine, I thought, *Don't ever forget how unbelievably lucky you are, girl.*

I believed him when he told me that it was Giovanna who'd found me and called the doctor. "She saved your life, darling. That terrible flu might have killed you." He was proud of her, his daughter; she'd finally done something he approved of.

I said nothing about Giovanna or her special salad. Giovanna's time would come. I pulled my husband as close as I could without disengaging my feeding and hydration tubes. I ran my hands up his arms, across his chest, and managed to draw him down to my breasts, where he lay warm and pliant, like a love-sated child.

"I'll never leave you again," he whispered.

And he kept his word. From that point on, we weren't separated for more than a few hours at a time.

It's easier to write about greed, hatred, jealousy, treachery, and betrayal than it is to write about love.

But ask anyone what it is they most want in life, and they'll say *love*.

It's the most important and valuable emotion of all. Without it, all you're left with is greed, hatred, jealousy, treachery, and betrayal.

Maybe love isn't an emotion. Maybe it's more of an instinct. An ancient inner skill we're supposed to develop to keep us from destroying one another.

Here's what I know about it: Love gives meaning to life. It makes life worthwhile. It makes pain bearable.

And it makes revenge oh so much sweeter.

For I have to admit, fantasies about getting even with Giovanna would periodically swim up from the murk beneath my enchantment. I pictured myself taking her by the hair and slamming her big ugly nose into a vise and turning the handle as she screamed and flailed. And other not-so-nice things.

But I was ultimately more interested in my love for Marcello than I was in getting back at his daughter. This love was something I'd never experienced before. I'd always thought of myself as a loving person. Every time I got involved, I eagerly handed over my stash of love. But here's what I learned: When you offer free candy, people snatch it away and don't give you anything in return. It's free, so they assume it has no value and they don't have to share.

Sharing is something I never did with my three previous husbands. I mean, *I* did, I shared, but they didn't. Either they didn't know how or they didn't want to learn. I'm not blaming them. I was half of the equation.

I'm saying all this about love because it was such a discovery to me when I finally found it. It was like I'd been driving all my life on an unknown highway and finally was able to pull into a rest stop.

Not that I rested much.

The sex with Marcello was so orgasmic that I discovered a weird new vocal repertoire. I don't know where the sounds came from. They were loud and uninhibited, not words so much as various tones of moaning, gasping, crying, panting.

And laughing. Afterward, we'd lie back and laugh. I don't know why. Maybe laughter expressed the sheer dizzying exhilaration of being in love and making love.

Oh my God, how he loved me. What a lover he was.

* * *

Once I was well, and he was well, we embarked on our crazy honeymoon.

Who was the leader? We both were. We led one another.

I wanted to see Italy, my new homeland. But I didn't want to sail, and I didn't want to go to Capri. I just didn't want to deal with La Principessa's disapproval. So Marcello got his Lamborghini out of storage and we took off.

On my honeymoon I learned that my husband, Marcello Brunelli, was a bigamist. He was wed to me and to his silver Lamborghini Miura, an unforgivably expensive sports car with a broad, low-slung hood and a motor directly behind the passenger seats. The car was named after a Spanish bull, but it reminded me of a powerful shark with staring, upturned eyes. There was no music system because in a Lamborghini, Marcello said, the engine noise was part of the overall pleasure. You were supposed to enjoy the high muffled whine, which became ingrained in the back of your brain the way the sound of a jet engine does when you fly. With the windows down, you could hear the mufflers' throaty, powerful roar. It was not a car made for tall Americans. Marcello, at five foot ten, came close to the roof. But the leather seats were wide and surprisingly comfortable. There was hardly any room for luggage, so we traveled light.

Marcello's other wife was a demanding creature, I must say, requiring endless tune-ups, parts, and washings. And oh my God, the excited conversations she inspired at gas stations and body shops. Because the Miura was a sacred icon for car lovers, a fantasy of perfection that people had heard of but rarely got to see in the flesh. Men would touch her, pat her, stroke her.

And I discovered that there's driving and then there's *driving* . . .

We'd be flying down an autostrada at a hundred miles per hour and I'd think of my taped-up and exhausted old Toyota back in Portland, barely able to wheeze up hills and always threatening to drop dead. Where was she now, my ancient, rusted-out Corolla? She'd probably been towed and stowed in some Portland lockup for battered, abandoned vehicles.

The life she represented, my life as a perennially broke minimum-wage earner counting out pennies for a gallon of regular unleaded, was over.

Nevermore, quoth the Raven.

I was like a snake that had slithered out of my old, battered skin and felt the sun, all warm and delicious, on my new one.

We drove all over Italy, moving on or staying put as the mood struck or as parts and servicing were needed for Marcello's second wife.

We drove through Tuscany and Umbria, passing vineyards and olive groves and stopping in ancient stone-built villages perched on hilltops. It was the beginning of harvesttime and a dusty golden light floated in the air. For several days we holed up in a little medieval castle outside of Florence, making love all morning and wandering into town every afternoon to explore and find a good restaurant for dinner. We visited churches and art galleries and palaces and archaeological sites. Sometimes we got a private tour from the director or the owner or the person in charge, but most of the time we were tourists like everyone else, paying our admission fees and gawking with the others. Marcello enjoyed this. I think, for him, it was a way of being ordinary. He'd never been ordinary in his life.

We strolled, holding hands, wearing dark glasses, unrecognized. Or I'd take his arm and rest my head against his shoulder. Or we'd just stop, overcome by a view of Florence, and kiss. We seemed to be melting into one another.

I began to understand why Daddy and Whitman loved Italy so much. For me, it was a landscape of revelation. I felt like I was learning things just by being in it. The cadence and pronunciation of the language was sinking in. I tried out words and phrases, blushing with the effort but incredibly proud of myself when I got them right.

I wanted to see more, so we went to Venice. When we got into a water taxi and started down the Grand Canal, I burst into tears. Marcello thought something was wrong with me. He took me in his arms and asked what was the matter. And all I could say was, "It's so beautiful."

Because it was.

I was an American girl, after all. I was used to freeways and malls, not canals lined with palaces and baroque churches.

In Venice, I felt like I was hypnotized. I didn't smell the garbage as we glided down the canals in a private gondola Marcello had hired at two in the morning. It was still warm as summer, with a soft muggy breeze. All the tourists had gone to bed and Venice was ours. Hardly any lights were on. A slice of silver moon hung in the black-velvet folds of the sky. The gondolier, being paid a small fortune, guided us through the watery tunnels of the sleeping city. It was so quiet you could almost hear it sinking.

At the time, I wondered if this extended honeymoon of ours was the only way Marcello could keep himself from working, and that was why it went on and on. It was like a dream he didn't want to end.

His life, unlike mine, had been totally defined by work. Work was all he'd ever known. He was a man who was accustomed to being constantly busy, his ass on the line 24/7. He wasn't a wage earner like most of us. His working life wasn't about putting in eight hours and collecting a paycheck that was never big enough. He owned businesses all over the globe. He negotiated deals. He moved millions of monetary units—euros and dollars and yen—every day.

And now Giovanni had taken over those duties. Like his father before him, he was constantly on the move, forever away on business trips. Marcello spent about two hours a night talking to his son, trying to guide him through the perils and pitfalls of high-end capitalism.

"It must be done," he said. "He must learn."

I never spoke to Johnny, but every now and then Marcello would say, "Venus wants to say hello," and shove the phone into my hand. So we'd have to talk. Molto awkward. But we did it, hanging on to some shred of relationship—what it was, I doubt either one of us knew.

When Marcello was talking to Giovanna and tried that same "Venus wants to talk to you" trick, I said in a voice loud enough for her to hear, "No, Venus doesn't want to talk to her" and refused to take the phone. Later, when he asked me why, I just didn't have the heart to tell him that it was because his daughter had tried to poison me.

Plus, like him, I didn't want to wake up from the dream of our honeymoon. I wanted to wallow in the enchantment of a new love. I didn't want to acknowledge that other world, the ugly one Giovanna lived in. What I had with Marcello was ours alone, a world unto itself, something we created ourselves, outside of Palazzo Brunelli.

It was inevitable. I'd actually been hoping. Not planning, just quietly hoping.

We were in Sicily when I told him, standing in a meadow overlooking the seaside Temple of Demeter.

"I'm pregnant," I said.

I'll remember his expression until the day I die. A kind of stunned incredulity, as if a pie had just been thrown in his face, followed by a dazed grin, as if he'd gotten a sudden rush of oxygen to the brain.

"You're having my baby?" he said.

I nodded.

Suddenly he was delirious with joy. He laughed and raised his arms to the blue sky. Scooped me into his arms. Held me close, hummed a tune, danced with me on the hillside.

"I must call Mama," he said.

"Not yet." I squeezed him as tight as I could, pressing my face to his chest. "I want it to be our secret—just *ours*—for a little while longer."

But, sooner or later, I knew I'd have to face La Principessa again, this time as her son's wife.

His *pregnant* wife.

Chapter
28

Capri is a small island in the Tyrrhenian Sea just off the tip of the Sorrento Peninsula. It was the one place in Italy where I'd been before, but I was only twelve when the dads took me there on that superfast trip tied up with one of Whitman's travel assignments. All I remembered of it was eating pistachio ice cream in a square and falling in love with a chocolate-eyed, dark-haired boy who was eating strawberry gelato next to me. And Daddy's buying me the little porcelain box that I'd brought with me to Rome as a good luck charm.

Now, fourteen years later, I was returning to Capri to visit my mother-in-law. This time around, I wasn't Venus Gilroy, I was Princess Brunelli. I was on a boat owned by my husband, who was a prince, and I was almost six months pregnant.

Marcello, looking nautical in white trousers and a blue blazer, was standing up in the helm, guiding the boat. I sat below, on the rear deck, hands clasped over my belly.

I had a lot on my mind as my skipper-husband revved the boat's powerful engines and blasted its horn, and we slowly glided out of the harbor at Naples.

It was a brilliantly clear day. Mt. Vesuvius rose in the distance, peaceful and benign in the warm spring sunshine. But we'd visited Pompeii and Herculaneum the day before, and images of the plaster casts archaeologists had made of people killed and buried in the eruption of 79 A.D. still haunted my thoughts. When I saw them, the ancient past came alive in a creepily vivid and poignant way. The casts captured the agonized forms of real people caught completely unawares. One day they were going about their business, probably wondering how to make ends meet, and the next day the mountain where they grew grapes blew its top, toppled buildings, whooshed its poisonous breath down the slopes into their lungs, and then buried them with ash and pumice. One cast was of a mother trying to protect her child.

It reminded me that Mount St. Helens had erupted in 1980, the year I was born. Mom had told me about the big flakes of ash that came raining down on Portland, coating the streets. It was scary and unsettling to realize that something I wanted to think of as stable and pretty, like Mount St. Helens, was, in fact, completely unpredictable and could suddenly turn as dangerous as Vesuvius.

As we headed out into the calm waters of the Bay of Naples, my thoughts turned apprehensive. It was like a dark, cold current sucking at my legs, trying to tug me down.

Get a grip, girl.

But, in truth, I knew that something was wrong. Way wrong. Molto wrong. The Brunelli empire was in big trouble. Some kind of scandal, or the threat of one, was looming on the horizon, and whatever it was, it was gnawing away at Marcello like a cancer.

I felt terrible for him and wanted to help, but I didn't know what I could do. It didn't seem like I could do anything because this was about *them*, about the Brunellis and their businesses, about a world they'd created for themselves long before I'd entered the scene.

Marcello wouldn't talk about it with me. I think he was too proud, or too embarrassed. And he wanted to protect me.

"It will blow over," he said when I first asked him about it.

But it hadn't blown over, and whatever it was, it fueled a feeding frenzy among the paparazzi that started toward the end of our honeymoon, when someone snapped our photograph poolside at Villa d'Este on Lake Como, and never stopped. When we finally returned to

Rome, not because we wanted to but because Marcello said he had to, it became almost impossible to leave Palazzo Brunelli.

"Darling, I think it might be wise if you went somewhere else until this blows over," Marcello said.

I stared at him in disbelief. "I'm not leaving. I'm staying here with you."

He looked both relieved and anxious.

Someone should write a book about the paparazzi.

I used to have the same lame fantasies as everyone else, like, oh, wouldn't it be fun to be so glamorous or famous that you couldn't go anywhere without people taking your picture? I never believed those stars who complained about never having any privacy. Yeah, right. They *loved* never having any privacy. That's all they lived for, to get their photos taken.

But the truth is, the paparazzi are scary. They're violent. Dangerous, because they'll literally do anything to get a photograph. And it wasn't fashion photography they were after. They didn't want snaps of Marcello and me all glammed up and smiling as we arrived at charity galas and cultural events. They wanted hard-core tabloid trash, tears, grimaces, anger, surprise, bad hair. Their aggression reminded me of those gypsy kids who'd attacked me months earlier. The hassling got so bad that finally I just stopped going out. I was worried about the baby. There was no telling what one of those camera-crazy assholes would do. I wasn't going to risk it. So mostly, except for trips to my ob-gyn, I stayed inside Palazzo Brunelli.

But on a hunch that it might come in useful one day, and that I should get it now, before my swelling belly made it difficult to walk, I did make a secret foray down into the foul-smelling, sewerside passageway beneath the palazzo and filched the old iron key from its hook beside the door. I didn't tell anyone, because I wasn't supposed to know about this ancient escape route that Teresina had shown me.

Teresina had been replaced by Maddalena, an older woman who dressed in black, smelled of garlic, had a big wart on her chin, and hardly said a word to me. I didn't know if she was resentful or just shy, and when I tried to speak to her using my limited Italian, she stared at me as if I were crazy. Maddalena kept a little red cell phone in her apron pocket and would talk and talk and talk on that. She spoke so rapidly and in such a low voice that I never knew who she was talking to or what she was saying. I suspected one of her callers was Giovanna, who'd sequestered herself in her part of the palazzo and had absolutely nothing to do with me.

Whatever story was breaking regarding the Brunellis, I didn't mention it to my mom or the dads. Silly, I suppose, but I wanted them to think everything was just dandy. I couldn't tell them, anyway, because I didn't know what, exactly, was going on.

What did I know, really, about the inner workings of this rich old Roman family? I saw the external trappings of their lives, the treasures they'd accumulated over the centuries, but that was all. For all I knew, they were part of the Mafia.

And that scared me. It seemed implausible, ridiculous, but how did I know what kind of unholy alliances the Brunellis might have formed to build and maintain their power? All kinds of crimes might be hidden in the pages of their ancient family ledger.

And yet . . . I *knew* Marcello. I knew the essential goodness of his heart. I knew that he loved me. And it was impossible to reconcile what I knew of him with these other fears and imaginings that had begun to haunt me.

I also knew that life could change in the blink of an eye. I knew that, but I didn't want to know that.

One day I saw Maddalena reading a tabloid with the headline: *Impero Brunelli può darsi investigare.* When she saw me, she quickly folded up the paper, grabbed her broom, and hurried away.

I hurried, too, right to my Italian–English dictionary.

The headline meant something like *Brunelli empire may be investigated . . .*

"Investigated for what?" I asked Marcello.

"I don't want to discuss it!" he said angrily.

"Why not? It's important!"

"It's a vendetta," he shouted. "Directed against this family. Based on lies. Old lies."

"Marcello, I'm your wife. I should know."

"No," he said, softening, stroking my face, "you shouldn't. Because it's false and ugly and I don't want it to taint you."

I started to cry. "I'm not a delicate little flower, you know. I can handle it. Maybe I can help you."

"You've already helped me more than you could ever imagine," he said quietly. "But in this case, darling—no. There is nothing you can do. I do not want you to involve yourself."

Easier said than done. Day by day, week by week, the crisis pushed me out of Marcello's line of vision. I'd been smack-dab in the center of his attention for months. Now I was relegated to the sidelines. He spent hours in meetings with the family lawyer, Signor Degli Atti. Then, one day, three more lawyers appeared. A team—I was certain—working on some sort of defense strategy. Then two more men—auditors, I was told—came on the scene. Then accountants. Palazzo Brunelli was buzzing. My former rooms were appropriated as a temporary office. Men in dark suits, women carrying file folders and papers and computer disks, scurried up and down the secret stairway of love. One day I went up there just as a workman was hauling away three clear blue garbage bags stuffed with shredded paper.

"Are they shredding documents?" I asked Marcello.

"Every business must do that," he said. Then, sensing my concern, he added, with an amused smile, "Don't worry, darling, it's not illegal."

I believed him because I wanted to believe him. I had no reason not to believe him, even though his talks with Giovanni now stretched on long into the night. I could hear him arguing—at least it sounded like arguing. He spoke so rapidly that I could make out only a few words. Now he never said "Venus wants to talk to you" or thrust the phone into my hand.

Something was taking an awful toll on him. He started to look drawn, wan, haunted. He was unable to sleep; if he did fall into a doze, his moans and twitches would wake me up. Sometimes, early in the morning, I'd wake to find him standing in his bathrobe, staring out the window.

He was always distracted, even when he was with me, and I had to work hard to get him back. I didn't want him to lose the reality of me, of us, of our baby.

Because despite all the agitation, despite all my fears and worries and wild imaginings, our child was growing, filling me up. Nothing could stop that. There were times when the baby would turn or twist or kick or punch and the soft tender glow of new life would overwhelm me.

Then one day Marcello kissed my belly and said, "We are going to Capri."

He needed to get away. He needed a break from the stress. In order to give him that, I was willing to face La Principessa.

I hadn't spoken to her since my family's visit the previous August. She hadn't attended our wedding. When Marcello told her I was pregnant, she hadn't asked to speak to me and did not offer congratulations. Though he never said so, I knew Marcello had been hurt and puzzled by her behavior. Her silence made perfect sense to me, though. I knew it was because she couldn't bear the thought of me as her daughter-in-law. Someone who'd soon present her with a second-generation grandchild.

I didn't expect our visit to Capri to be pleasant—at least not for me. I hoped for Marcello's sake it would be a relaxing distraction from his daily grind of anxiety.

Now, as I sat on the deck, fretting in the sunshine, my husband turned to look down at me from the helm. Our eyes met and I was suddenly flooded with love for him, overwhelmed by it, as if a wave had crashed over my head and left me spluttering for breath. He smiled and pointed.

We had reached Capri. Marcello was guiding the Brunelli yacht into Marina Grande, the harbor on the north side of the island.

Surrounded by high walls and set back from a footpath, Villa Brunelli was hidden amid a magnificent garden on the south side of the island. The path, Via Krupp, named for the German industrialist who had paid for its construction back in 1900, wound along high limestone cliffs overlooking the sea and a trio of offshore rocks called the Faraglioni. It was a magnificent setting, and the views from the terraces of Villa Brunelli were breathtaking. I could understand why La Principessa would never want to leave her island paradise.

She was not there to welcome us when we arrived, and Marcello's face turned stony when a maid told him that his mother was busy and would join us later in the afternoon. He turned to me and asked what I'd like to do.

"Explore," I said. "What would you like to do?"

"I would like to show you the Blue Grotto. If you are up to it."

I took his hand. "Let's go."

"Do you want to see the house first?"

I shook my head. I just wanted to be with him. It had been so long since we'd been alone together, having adventures.

Marcello had mentioned the Blue Grotto so often that I was curious to see it for myself. He'd first encountered it as a boy, when his parents spent summers on Capri, and revisiting the Blue Grotto had become a yearly ritual. He was extremely superstitious about it and believed that if he didn't see the Blue Grotto once a year, something terrible would happen, to him or to someone in his family.

It seemed like an odd belief for a man who was otherwise so firmly grounded in the hard-core business of business, but I'm not one to question or mess with other people's superstitions. We all have them, no matter how rational we pretend to be.

Marcello wanted to show me the entire island by boat, so we returned to Marina Grande and set off in a small launch. Capri is only about four square miles, so you can make a slow, leisurely circuit in less than two hours.

Suddenly we were happy. Maybe it was just being alone, on the sea, in the sunshine, with a soft warm breeze in our faces. The water shimmered, a rich, shifting palette of blues and greens and everything in between, very different from the eternal steel gray of the Pacific off the coast of Oregon. I nestled beside my husband, who steered the boat with one hand and kept his other arm around me.

The ancient Romans, he told me, called the island Capreae and used it as a summer resort. "Look up there," He pointed to some grass-covered terraces at the top of a giant limestone cliff. "Those are the ruins of a villa where the emperor Tiberius lived. And that"— he pointed to a high, sheer-sided crag near the ruins—"is the Salto di Tiberio."

"What is it?"

Marcello pulled me a little closer. "From the top of that rock, he would have his victims thrown into the sea."

"Cute." I imagined the terrified screams of the emperor's victims as they plunged to their deaths.

We continued down the eastern side of the island, where the sights were less gruesome, passing natural rock formations and a grotto dedicated to the nymphs, and then skirted past the Faraglioni rocks and along the south coast. There was a smaller harbor on this side of the island, and the ruins of a monastery. I scanned the cliffs high above, trying to get a glimpse of Villa Brunelli, but it was too well hidden.

The wind suddenly picked up as we rounded Punta Carena, the southwestern tip, and headed up the rocky western side of the island. Marcello swore under his breath.

"What's the matter?"

"We cannot get into the Blue Grotto unless the sea is very calm."

It got choppier as we headed north. The silvery tips of the waves flashed and sparkled in the sun. By the time we reached the small beach next to the Blue Grotto, the launch was bobbing like a cork on the incoming waves.

The Blue Grotto had been carved out of the rock in prehistoric times by the relentless hammering of the sea. Back then, you could walk inside because it was a cavern with a rocky floor. But gradually, the sea level rose and filled it up. So in order to get into the grotto today, you have to rent a small, specially designed boat and row in. There's so little space between the sea and the entrance that you have to lie down until the boat is inside the cavern.

The fat, elderly man who ran the boat concession saw Marcello, waved, and hurried out to meet us at the little pier. He and Marcello got into an animated conversation. The man—Beppo was his name—

bowed and scraped and called Marcello "Excellenza," but he wouldn't rent us a boat. The sea wasn't calm enough. It would be better tomorrow.

Marcello insisted. He cajoled and charmed and threw in just enough princely authority and more than enough money to make Beppo change his mind. But the only way he'd agree, Beppo said, was if his top rower, Franco, took us out.

No, Marcello said, he would take the boat out himself. He knew how to row. He'd been boating in the waters around Capri since he was a boy. He knew the Blue Grotto better than anyone.

"*Prego*, signora." Beppo appealed to me. "Go with Franco. Is best."

I looked up at Marcello. He shook his head and started arguing with Beppo. My guess was that it was some kind of macho test. Marcello needed to prove that he was still in control, still in shape, still the master.

Finally Beppo threw up his hands in defeat and said, "*Va bene!*"

Marcello had won. "It will be fine, darling," he assured me, helping me into the rowboat. "This may be our only chance and I don't want you to leave Capri without seeing the Blue Grotto."

"You're sure you can do this?"

The hurt look he gave me made me sorry I'd asked. "Venus, do you really think I would do this if I thought there was any danger? You're carrying my child!"

I kissed him. "I trust you."

"Unless you think—unless you don't want—"

I settled myself on the prow seat. "No, I'm ready. Let's go." I did not want to be a spoilsport. I did not want him to think that I was questioning his abilities or that I was frightened. I knew that this was an important thing for him to do, to show me the Blue Grotto, a place that had special significance in his life.

Marcello took up the oars and began to row.

Except for the little inlet where the rowboats were rented, there was no beach. We stayed close to the giant limestone cliffs that plunged down into the sea, just far enough out so that the waves wouldn't propel us into the offshore rocks or the cliff face.

"Beautiful, no?" Marcello smiled at me.

It was. The color of the sea was mesmerizing. And Marcello actually looked happy, more relaxed than I'd seen him in months.

"*Ecco.* There is the entrance." He nodded toward a low arch in the cliff face.

"The ancient Romans called it Gradola," he said, puffing as he rowed. "They said there were witches and monsters inside."

"I hope we don't run into any."

"No, darling. The only monsters or witches inside the Blue Grotto are the tourists. So many in the summer that each boat is only allowed inside for three minutes."

"Three minutes? What can you see in three minutes?"

"The light," he said. "It's extraordinary. Once you see it, you will never forgot it."

"I can't wait."

"It will bring good luck to all of us," Marcello said. "You'll see."

I leaned forward in the little boat and kissed him.

It was to be the last kiss I ever gave him.

When we reached the entrance, Marcello instructed me to lie down on the floor of the boat so I wouldn't bang my head as we entered. The boats were constructed with this in mind, and had foam padding in them. There was a special technique for the rower, he said. Whoever was guiding the boat had to lift the oars and lean back, almost parallel to the water, at just the right moment as the boat glided in.

I slowly got onto the floor of the boat, my belly making the procedure more cumbersome than it was supposed to be, and lay on my side with my head turned so that I could look into the darkness of the cavern. I couldn't see anything inside, just a yawning black emptiness. It was like peering into a dark, dripping mouth.

"Are you ready, darling?" Marcello asked.

"I'm ready."

I heard the splash of the oars as they dipped into the water. The boat glided forward. The prow entered the mouth of the cavern. It was suddenly very dark, and after the sunny dazzle of the sea outside, I couldn't make out a thing. I stared ahead, into the dripping blackness.

Then I heard a muffled groan and a sharp intake of breath. The boat rocked. I looked back and saw Marcello, still outside the entrance. He'd dropped one of the oars and was frantically clutching his left shoulder. Before I could register what had happened, before I could even say anything, he dropped the other oar, let out an agonized choking sound, and tried to stand up. But just then, the boat gave a sudden little leap as it was propelled forward by an incoming wave. I saw Marcello throw out his arms for balance. Heard a loud thunk. Saw him fall backward into the water.

"Marcello! Oh my God!"

And then it was like one of those witches or monsters that the ancient Romans believed inhabited the cave had suddenly come to life and was determined to separate us. The backward momentum of Marcello's fall propelled the boat further into the grotto. When I screamed his name, it richocheted back and forth, like a trapped spirit.

"Marcello!" My first thought was to jump in after him. But I was almost six months pregnant, and a rotten swimmer. "Marcello!" My only hope was to row back to the entrance and drag him into the boat. But the oars were gone. He'd dropped them into the sea.

And I couldn't see him anywhere. All I could see was the low, rounded arch of the grotto entrance with a blinding scrim of white light pressing against it. I didn't hear any splashing or cries.

"Help!" I screamed. "Someone help!"

I nearly upset the boat as I scrambled breathlessly to get up and onto one of the seats. A long pole with a hook on the end was affixed to the boat. I grabbed it and tried to propel myself along the dripping rock walls, toward the entrance, toward Marcello.

"Marcello! Marcello! Sweetheart!"

At first I was so blinded by my panic that I couldn't take in my surroundings, but as I frantically worked to maneuver the boat, using the long pole, I became aware of the light inside the grotto.

An extraordinary blue glowed all around me. It emanated upward, from the water, calm and serene and utterly indifferent to my terror.

I still dream of that color. I dream that I am in that color, in that place, in that Blue Grotto, and that when I reach out from the boat, Marcello's hand clasps mine, and all is well.

Chapter
29

They found Marcello's body in the Blue Grotto. The waves had carried him into the cavern, where he'd been snagged in the embrace of an underwater rock formation.

I answered questions. I told and retold the story. I realized at one point that they didn't want to believe me. They had their own version.

Oh my God. The madness that surrounded the news of his death. It gave everything such a grotesque, surreal air.

I don't know how I got through it all. I felt crushed beneath the weight of my misery, buried alive in the rubble of my happiness.

That wasn't a baby I was carrying: it was a hot, heavy ball of grief. All I did, all I could do, was sniffle, snivel, cry, and moan. It was more than just *my* loss that I was dealing with. I was crying for our baby, too. He would grow up without a father. He would never know the man who had worked so hard to win me, to make me finally accept his love.

La Principessa took care of everything. I was dazed, useless in a foreign country. Marcello's mother knew all the proper protocols and legal formalities. She took care of everything, but she offered absolutely no comfort. In the shock of my misery I longed for just one sympathetic embrace, one shoulder to cry on. But La Principessa kept her distance. I was distraught and disheveled, but there was never a hair out of place on her perfectly coiffed head. Her eyes remained dry. Her voice didn't shake. When she spoke to me, her tone was sharp, almost scolding, as if I were a simpleminded servant.

Well, I know now that death can make you furious. It wasn't *my husband* who'd been killed, it was *her son*. And no doubt, in her eyes, I was to blame.

She didn't consult with me on anything; she simply told me what she was going to do or what needed to be done. I saw no reason to object. Marcello's body, zipped in a black plastic bag, was helicoptered to Rome. An autopsy had to be performed. The funeral, La Principessa informed me, would be held in the chapel attached to Palazzo Brunelli. "It will be a requiem mass," she said. "Our bishop will preside. Marcello will be buried in the family crypt."

I spoke up for the first time, my voice hoarse and whispery from crying. "I think he wanted to be cremated."

"Brunellis are not cremated," La Principessa informed me.

"But he told me that's what he wanted," I managed to squeak.

"Marcello did?" Her eyes blazed. "When?"

"On our—on our honeymoon."

"My son told you on your honeymoon that he wanted to be cremated?" She sounded incredulous. "Why would he do that?"

"I don't know. But he did. One morning. Right after—"

"Yes?"

"Right after we'd made love." I hardly dared look at her, but I didn't want to be intimidated, so I looked right in her eyes. "He said now he could die happy. And when he died, he said, he wanted to be cremated and his ashes scattered in—in—" I sucked in a shuddering breath. "—in the Blue Grotto."

La Principessa waited a moment before responding. She swallowed and straightened her shoulders. "Marcello's body will go in the family crypt."

And that was that.

In life she couldn't have him, but in death he was all hers.

La Principessa and I traveled to Rome together, in the same helicopter that carried the body of my husband, her son. Fabio met us and drove us to Palazzo Brunelli, where we were attacked by the paparazzi. It was horrible. They swarmed around the car, screaming questions, banging on the windows, a flock of crows fighting for a piece of news-carrion. All the while, La Principessa sat as far away from me as she could and stared straight ahead, a seated figure carved in stone, her eyes hidden by dark glasses.

She'd had years to develop her armor against the media, but I was freaked out and afraid. I cradled my belly and tried to breathe deeply as the barrage continued. When something smacked hard against the window beside me, I gasped and looked to see what it was. But it wasn't a what, it was a who. Teresina. She'd somehow gotten close enough to slap her hands against the window. Her face was crazed with anger, her mouth open, spewing out what sounded like invective. It was like glimpsing a creature in hell. I didn't dare open my window and hoped that Teresina couldn't see me through the polarized glass. I hoped that whatever she was screaming wasn't directed specifically at me.

The police finally forced back the crowd, and the limo slowly maneuvered through the gate and into the courtyard.

Like a shadow, I followed La Principessa up the stairs and into the palace, unable to separate myself because I wasn't sure what I was supposed to do next. I needed the guidance of a wise and experienced mentor to help me deal with the sudden shock of losing my husband.

The entire staff had gathered in the vestibule. Everyone wore black. The women had little black scarves pinned in their hair. The men had black handkerchiefs in their breast pockets. I heard muffled sobs.

It was a receiving line. They were there to offer La Principessa their condolences. I got the distinct impression that they weren't there to acknowledge *my* grief. I was an outsider, barred from their sympathy.

I followed La Principessa as she walked down the receiving line, slow and stately as a grieving queen. Rosaries clacked, fists beat against hearts, faces were contorted into masks of misery. As she passed, some of the women gave a cry and reached out to touch her, to fumble for her hand, rewarded when their mistress pressed their fingers before moving on.

They didn't do that for me. When I passed by, right behind La Principessa, they seemed to draw back and eye me with suspicion, as if they suspected me of murder.

If they didn't like me, I realized, it was my own damn fault. I'd never established any rapport with them. Except for Maddelena, I hardly knew their names. Instead of making Palazzo Brunelli my home, I'd lived in it as if I were living in a hotel. I'd felt I had no authority, no right to trespass in their domain. I wasn't in charge— Marcello was, or La Principessa was, or Giovanna was. Anyone but me.

But a thought now occurred to me, for the first time: was Palazzo Brunelli mine? As Marcello's wife, did I have a right to it? Had he made a stipulation in his will to that effect?

"*Ma dov'è Giovanna?*" La Principessa asked when she reached the end of the line. She looked around for her granddaughter.

"Nonna!" There was a renewed spurt of sobbing from the women in the crowd as Giovanna appeared, arms outstretched, hair loose and streaming, wearing a long, black velvet gown. Her nose, horribly red and swollen, looked like a raptor's beak that had been rummaging around in a bloody gut. "Ah, Nonna!" She flew to her grandmother's arms.

La Principessa held and consoled her, stroking her wild black hair, whispering soft little endearments. When I took a step toward them, meaning to acknowledge Giovanna's daughterly grief by touching her arm, Giovanna drew back as if I carried the plague. She stared down at my pregnant belly and let out a wail. La Principessa caught and held her granddaughter, trying to soothe away her hysteria. I stood there with my arm half-extended, aware of all the eyes that were upon me.

Our rooms were now directly across from each other, making for an awkward procession through Palazzo Brunelli.

I silently followed behind La Principessa as she took the sobbing Giovanna down to her suite. I thought I might be invited in.

I wasn't.

I stood there in the ancient corridor that separated La Principessa's rooms from Marcello's and mine and watched her door close. Not quite in my face, but almost.

I fought back a spurt of anger. For a moment, I was tempted to barge into La Principessa's rooms and . . . what? Demand that she acknowledge me? Demand that she give me, her son's wife, whom she hated, some sympathy?

I cupped my hands around my belly. Who was I, standing there in that ancient Roman palazzo? I was Marcello's wife. I was carrying his son and heir. I lived there. It was my palace, too.

I wanted my mommy and daddies.

When I called them and choked out the news, they made arrangements to come immediately, in a group. But one of their flights was delayed in Frankfurt because of a security alert, so it took them two days to reach Rome.

Meanwhile, I was stuck, alone, in Palazzo Brunelli. With Marcello gone, I couldn't take anything for granted anymore. It was like living in a perpetual earthquake, the ground shifting constantly beneath my feet. I wanted to hole up in Marcello's rooms and cry— sobbing had become like a full-time career—but I was afraid that if I did that, they'd just leave me there. I had to make an effort to be around La Principessa in order to know what was going on. And until I knew what was mine, I felt that I had to have La Principessa's permission to do anything.

But my mother-in-law wasn't in her rooms when I went there to ask if Fabio could go and pick up my parents. Instead, an elegant young woman who was apparently serving as La Principessa's personal secretary opened the door, a cell phone glued to her ear. She held up a hand indicating for me to wait a moment while she finished the call, then snapped the phone shut. "You are Signora Brunelli? I am Raffaela. How do you do?" We awkwardly shook hands. "I am very terribly sorry," Raffaela said.

I nodded, sniffing back a fresh onslaught of tears.

"What may I do for you, Signora?"

"I have to talk to La Principessa. About picking up my parents. At the airport."

"Ah, yes. I am sorry, but you see, La Principessa is not to be found. I don't know where she goes, perhaps upstairs in the grand salone." Her cell phone played a fast, irritating tune. "Ah, Dio!" She rolled her eyes and shook her head. "I am to deal with the media. It is—what is the word? Outrageous! What they are saying."

"What are they saying?"

Raffaela checked the numbers being displayed on her cell phone and then switched off its tune. "That there is a connection."

"A connection?" Whatever it was, my brain wasn't making it.

"Between the investigation and Il Principe's death! That someone kill him, or he kill himself, or you—" She was going to say more, but stopped herself.

"Or me what?"

She gave me a fake little smile and shrugged her shoulders. "They want to make a good story, so they say these things."

"There is no story!" I blurted out. "It was an accident. I think he had a heart attack." And the horrible scene in the Blue Grotto, all rewound and ready to go, played itself out yet again.

Raffaela lowered her voice. "You were with him, eh?"

I nodded.

"They want to know these details. All I can say from La Principessa is 'no comment.' It is not enough for them." She looked at me, her dark eyes frank and appraising. "Do you wish to tell them?"

"Tell them what?"

She shrugged. "I don't know. Details. What happened." She poked her head out and quickly looked up and down the corridor. Her voice was a low, urgent whisper. "You know you could sell this, eh?" I must have looked bewildered because she suddenly hissed, "This story! Your life! How he died!"

I took a step backward. I didn't know which way to turn. I felt like I was trying to orient myself within the distortions of a funhouse. Or maybe it was a madhouse.

"I know an agent," Raffaela whispered. "She will love it. You're even pregnant. *Perfetto!* Shall I ring her?"

I clasped my belly and turned dazedly in the corridor.

"We could make a book out of it. Fifty-fifty. You are an American, no? They could love it in Hollywood. Antonio Banderas and Drew Barrymore."

I left her there and made my way back upstairs, toward the sa-lone, where I found La Principessa. She was sitting with a corpulent man who had sagging, age-speckled jowls, thin black hair, and was wearing a red robe. They both looked up in surprise when I entered the room. I thought La Principessa was going to ignore me, but after a moment she said, "This is Cardinal Buonaventura."

The man in red inclined his head and put out his hand. I didn't know if I was supposed to shake it or kiss his ring. His fingers were cold and soft. He had thick, pouty lips that made him look like a prissy old queen in an antiques store.

"Signorina Gilroy," he said.

It took me a moment to register what he'd said. "No," I said, "I'm Signora Brunelli."

La Principessa and the cardinal exchanged glances.

"Well," said the cardinal, "that is what we must establish."

"Sit down," La Principessa said to me.

There was an awkward silence. I took note of all the flowers. The salone was stuffed with them, huge wreaths and complicated arrange-ments that choked the room with their sad, heavy scents. Finally the cardinal cleared his throat and said, "Signorina—"

"No," I said, "*Signora.* We were married. I was Marcello's *wife.*"

There was a rapid exchange in Italian between La Principessa and the cardinal. Then La Principessa looked at me. "I am trying to make the funeral arrangements," she said. "But there are difficul-ties."

"What difficulties?" I asked.

"The Church does not recognize your marriage."

I stared at her, my mouth open in disbelief.

"There can only be a high requiem mass if my son, Prince Brunelli, died in a state of grace."

"What does that mean?" I remembered Marcello's last smile. Our last kiss. Didn't those final moments of happiness register as grace?

"It means," said La Principessa, "that he accepted the Church and its teachings."

"And all her laws," Cardinal Buonaventure added sternly, lifting a porky finger.

"Yes," La Principessa said quietly, "her eternal and inflexible laws." The glance she gave him was brimming with barely concealed anger. "Tell me, Pietro, why is it that the laws of the Church are so inflexible, except when the Church itself is in trouble?"

"Principessa?" he said.

Her voice turned steely. "You know what I mean, Pietro. When there is something the Church wants to hide, some problems with morality, shall we say, it seems there is always a way to get around those inflexible laws."

"You are asking me to do something I cannot do."

"Of course you can."

"Marcello was married to a divorced woman," the cardinal said.

That was me. I sat there like a total wonk, a piece in some complicated chess game the two of them were playing.

"Pietro, how long have we known one another?" La Principessa asked. "Fifty years, eh? Sixty, if we are honest about it. You remember what Napoli was like during the war. And afterwards. What we did to stay alive. Eh?"

The cardinal grunted.

"You were there with me. I remember all kinds of things that we used to do. To stay alive. Do you remember any of those things, Pietro? Eh?"

The cardinal scratched his cheek.

"You are always urging me to write my memoirs. Perhaps there are some things I could ... leave out." La Principessa leaned forward and touched his knee. "Or—put in?"

The cardinal smoothed back the strands of his thin black hair.

"All I am asking for, Pietro, is a high mass sung in Latin with Bishop Sangiovanni presiding."

"But Principessa—"

She cut him off. "Marcello deserves that. The Brunellis deserve that. For all we have done to help you and the Church. And for our past history, Pietro, yours and mine."

Cardinal Buonaventura stood and made a little bow. "I shall send word to the bishop," he said.

I didn't feel that I could invite my parents to stay at Palazzo Brunelli, so Whitman booked rooms for them at a nearby hotel and said they'd take a taxi in from the airport.

Now I had to figure out how to get outside and to their hotel. Two armed policemen had been posted outside the gate, and a plastic barrier erected to keep back the paparazzi, but it was still impossible to get in or out on foot without being noticed and pursued.

It looked like the secret passageway beneath the palace was the best solution. Thank goodness I'd had the foresight to snitch the key.

I slowly opened the door and stepped out into the sunshine of the quiet little piazza. It was such a relief to get out of Palazzo Brunelli, where the air felt heavy, thick, saturated with so much misery that it was difficult to move, to breathe.

I locked the door behind me and then stood there, blinking up at the blue sky, like a prisoner released after years in the pen. It was only a momentary release. A second later I was engulfed by a black wave of misery.

My life, which had been full of such unexpected joy and happiness and love, was suddenly bleak and barren and uncertain. A Marcelloless future as a single mom stretched out ahead of me.

I yearned for him, craved him, ached for him.

I still couldn't believe that he was gone.

His absence was unacceptable. It *hurt*.

We'd had so little time together.

Each one of those days, I realized, was precious and unrepeatable.

I tried to control myself, fighting for deep whole breaths, Buddha breaths, but couldn't, and gave myself up to a fit of sobbing. I hadn't slept or eaten much and I felt exhausted, totally wrung out.

I stumbled over to the little fountain gurgling in the middle of the square and sat down at its base. I was hunched over, my face buried in my hands, keening with an onslaught of grief, when a soft voice said, "Signora? *Che cosa fa?*"

I couldn't speak, just shook my head.

"*Perchè piangerai?*" the voice asked.

I looked out from between my soaked fingers. A young woman, hugely pregnant, maybe due any day, was staring at me with soft, worried eyes. I sniffed and wiped at my face. "I'm OK," I whispered.

She handed me her handkerchief, pressing it into my hand when I refused. "*Americana?*" she asked.

"Si." It was such a sweet little handkerchief, linen, with flowers embroidered along the edge. I hesitated to use it.

She took it from me and gently wiped my face. "You are lost?" she asked, carefully forming each word.

I thought about that for a moment, then shook my head.

"Do you wants help? *Dottore?*"

"No, grazie." I didn't need a doctor.

She dipped her handkerchief in the fountain, squeezed it out, and ran it lightly around my eyes and along my forehead and cheeks. It was cool and comforting. "Your bambino," she said, pointing to my belly. "Boy or girl?"

"Boy," I said.

"Ah." She nodded and smiled. "Me too."

And then, as if in acknowledgment, my son-to-be gave a swift little kick. I made a sound as if I'd been goosed and, without thinking, took the young woman's hand and placed it on my belly. Another kick. We looked at each other.

"*Che robusto!*" she laughed.

I slowly got to my feet. She helped me up, then indicated that she would walk with me. Her presence was so sweet, so comforting, that I couldn't refuse. I showed her my street map, pointing to my destination. She took me by the arm, her touch as soft and warm as a kitten's, and led me through the streets. And when we reached the hotel, she said, simply, "*Buona fortuna*, signora," and waddled away.

Buona fortuna. That meant "good luck."

* * *

They were standing in the lobby when I came in. Oh my God. *Dio mio*, as the Italians say. I was so glad to see their familiar faces. We all looked at one another and burst into a collective sob.

"Mommy." I went to her first.

They took turns holding me, kissing me, crying with me, then we all huddled together in a grief scrimmage. It was exactly what I needed.

Whitman had to tear himself away in order to continue an argument he was having with the hotel manager over the price of their rooms. Mom stayed close, one arm around my waist, the other stroking my belly, murmuring and clucking and weeping. Daddy led us over to an ornate sitting area. "You'll never guess who's staying here," he said.

"In this very hotel," Mom added.

They didn't have to say more because I suddenly caught sight of JD in the gilded mirror of the lobby. She screamed when she saw me, threw up her arms, and, after some quick instructions to the porter who was carrying all her luggage, ran over to me. "Venus! Oh! My! God!" We embraced. "Oh, babe," she said, suddenly pulling back and trying to look grief-stricken. "I heard. Marcello. Your prince. Fucking *dead!*"

I couldn't speak. I was too shocked to see her.

"Oh honey—or should I call you princess?—I am so fucking sorry. You must be, like, *totally* bummed out."

"What are you doing here?" I asked.

"We're on tour!" JD said.

"On tour? You mean, touring Europe?"

"Yes, touring Europe on tour. Mistah Sistah!" she exclaimed, obviously seeing the blank look on my face. "The Wedded Bliss Diss Tour!"

"Oh."

"It's been, like, totally fabulous. They fucking *love* us."

"Are you in the act?"

"Sort of. Anyway, oh my God, Venus, we just played Frankfurt. The fucking opera house! We've been, like, everywhere. Even fucking Finland!"

"That's wonderful, JD." Some horrible gremlin in me hated her for being so happy. "How's Mistah Sistah?"

"He's cool. Totally cool."

"How's marriage?"

JD shrugged. "He does his thing and I do mine. I met the *coolest* countess in Berlin," she whispered in my ear.

I just couldn't hold it together anymore. I turned away and started to sob.

"Oh, Venus. Oh God, here I am just thinking of myself, as usual. When here you are, a fucking *widow*. And way pregnant, I see." She sighed on my behalf but was hardly able to contain her manic energy. "So he, like, drowned? Oh my God, that must have been so fucking horrible. When's the funeral, babe?"

"Day after tomorrow."

"Shit! Wouldn't you just know it? We'll be in Greece. We're leaving in like two hours." She gave me a featherweight hug and pressed a card into my hand. "Call me if there's ever *anything* I can do for you."

"Death brings out the worst in people," Whitman said. "Especially rich people. That's just how it is, sweetheart."

I'd been pretty circumspect, but I did drop a few hints to my parents that my mother-in-law and stepdaughter weren't being very nice to me in my hour of need.

"Everyone's a little crazy," Mom said. "It was so sudden. Everyone's probably in a state of shock." She drained her glass of Chianti and started picking at me. It was something she always did when we were both in a highly emotional state. Maybe it was some kind of prehistoric mother–child grooming/comfort ritual. She picked little bits of crust from around my eyes and stray hairs from my clothes and flakes of dandruff or skin wherever they'd fallen. It was driving me crazy, but I didn't say anything because it obviously made her feel better.

We were all gathered in Daddy and Whitman's room, sitting out on the little terrace that Whitman said cost one hundred euros extra a night. I was parched from so much crying and drank bottle after bottle of Evian. I couldn't handle fizzy Pellegrino anymore; it gave me heartburn. I was peeing for two, so I had to get up and go to the bathroom about every five minutes.

"I know it's difficult," Daddy said, "but you've got to make a plan and stick to it."

"She can't make a plan," Whitman said, "until she knows what her husband left her. Did he have a will, darling?"

"I don't know. We never talked about it. There was so much else going on."

"Poor Marcello," Mom said, "I just can't believe he was as corrupt as they say."

"As who says?" I snapped.

Mom looked over at Whitman.

"That's what the papers are saying," my faux pa explained. "Suggesting, anyway. And the Italian magazines. And Gabriella's been e-mailing your dad."

"Marcello didn't tell you what was going on?" Daddy asked.

I shook my head and grabbed for a Kleenex. "He wanted to protect me."

"Of course he did," Mom cooed, picking at something near my right ear as I sobbed.

"Well, if he wanted to protect you," Whitman said, "let's hope he set up a secret account in the Cayman Islands."

"He said it would all b-b-b-blow over," I blubbered.

"Yeah," Whitman said, "like a hurricane."

"Gabriella says that the government's going after the Brunellis because of the Parmalat scandal," Daddy said.

"What's that?" I asked.

"Oh, nothing," Whitman said. "Just the Enron of Italy, that's all."

Daddy explained. "Parmalat was a family-owned company that lied about its assets. It went on for years, getting bigger and bigger, without anyone bothering to check into it. And then it all collapsed like a house of cards and the government was left looking like an idiot with a thumb up its ass."

"So now the government has to pretend like it's on top of things," Whitman said, "and investigate the Brunellis."

"It could drag on for years," Daddy said. "What's she supposed to do in the meantime?"

"I think she should come back home," Mom said. "I'll fix up my little den. We'll make it nice and cozy. I don't think there's room for a crib, but we can buy a cute little bassinet. I see them at garage sales all the time."

My son's a prince, I thought. *He's not going to sleep in a used bassinet in my mother's den.*

"I don't think she should leave," Whitman said.

"Why not?" Mom said. "She doesn't have a friend in the world *here*. And we all want to be with her when she has the baby."

"It's just not a good idea for her to leave," Whitman said, "until she gets some kind of a settlement from the Brunellis."

"How can she get a settlement if there's nothing left to settle?" Mom asked.

"Oh, they won't be wiped out, even if they're guilty. Not the Brunellis. They may have to sell off some of their assets, but they are not going to starve."

"Gabriella's girlfriend is a high-powered attorney," Daddy said. "I think we'd better talk to her."

And so it went, on and on, throughout the afternoon and into the evening. They discussed the complexities and legal ramifications of my fate until I was too exhausted to listen anymore. I fell asleep on Mom's bed and dreamed of Marcello. He was in a boat, rowing out to sea, and I jumped into the waves, frantically signaling to him to stop, to take me with him. But he sternly shook his head and shouted for me to go back to the shore.

Chapter
30

The night before Marcello's funeral, I tapped on La Principessa's door.

Raffaela answered. "Yes, Signora?" Her voice was cool.

"I need to see La Principessa."

"No, I am afraid you cannot."

"Do you know where she is?"

"Mm, yes, but she do not wish to be disturbed."

"It's very important," I whispered.

Raffaela looked at me, arms crossed, lips pursed, cell phone in hand.

"I need to see Marcello. To say good-bye." My eyes filled and my throat contracted. "I know he's in the chapel. I know there's a way to get there, from inside Palazzo Brunelli, but I don't know what it is."

Raffaela considered what I said, then stepped out into the corridor. "You do not tell her I showed you, eh?"

I couldn't have found it by myself. It was on Giovanna's side of the palace, and we had to go through an old connecting tunnel and then outside, through a narrow cloister. Raffaela pointed to the door, touched a finger to her lips, and slipped back into the darkness.

My heart was pounding as I entered. There were no lights on, but I saw the casket immediately. It was in front of the altar, raised up on a cloth-covered platform, surrounded by banks of flickering candles and enormous bouquets of flowers. A heavy scent of incense—a smell I'd encountered in other Italian churches—mingled with the sickly-sweet odor of the flowers.

I heard a low, monotonous chanting, one lead voice intoning and others repeating, hypnotically, over and over. A flock of Little Doves was kneeling in wooden pews on the right side of the chapel, reciting rosaries in unison. On the left side sat one lone figure, all in black, her bowed head covered with a long, gauzy black veil that fell past her shoulders.

I started up the aisle.

The aisle of the chapel where we couldn't be wed. Because of me. Because of my history. Because of who I was.

I stopped, suddenly aware, acutely aware, of all the religious laws that Marcello had broken in order to marry me. In this environment, I was completely unwelcome. Didn't, in fact, exist. I was not even recognized as Marcello's spouse.

My plan was simple: to walk up to the front of the chapel and stand by my husband's casket and say good-bye to him. But a terrible weight seemed to be bearing down on me, pushing me back. I knew I had to fight it, had to move forward. I looked around the chapel for something to focus on, something that would help me. Statues held out their arms, but they weren't beckoning to me.

I felt a sob heaving its way up from the black lagoon of my sorrow. I tried to muffle it, but out it came, along with his name. "Marcello." I clung to the side of a pew and wept.

The figure wearing the black veil turned to see what was going on.

Move, I commanded myself. *Stop crying and walk!*

My legs felt like lead. I seemed to weigh a thousand pounds. It was like one of those horrible dreams when your body won't behave the way you want it to. I mopped my eyes and sort of slid up to the next pew, grasping it, and then to the one after that, until I made it to the front and stood before my husband's closed casket. I stood there gasping for breath, knowing he was inside and that I'd never see him again; then I went up and embraced the hard black surface, laying my cheek on it, covering it with snot and tears, stroking it the way men used to stroke his Lamborghini when we were on our honeymoon.

A heart attack. The muscle that pumped the blood of life from his brain to his toes had seized up like an angry fist, throttling him from inside. The loving heart that had beat next to mine beat no more, but the loving went on. The loving was real.

I don't know how long I was there. But at one point I was aware that the terrible black weight had lifted, flown off, left me.

I watched as La Principessa slowly rose from her pew and approached me, her eyes gleaming behind the gauze of her veil. She stood there, next to me, for what seemed like an eternity. Then she put a hand on my back and gently tugged me away from the casket.

The organ thundered.

The high, pure, virginal voices of the Little Doves rose to the highest corners of the packed chapel.

"Is that Latin they're singing?" I whispered to Whitman. He knew about masses because he'd been sent to a Catholic boys' school in Boston.

He nodded. "They're going to sing the entire mass," he whispered back. "It's hardly ever done anymore."

A procession of robed men and boys walked up the aisle. One of the men waved a big golden incense burner billowing thick, spicy smoke. It was so thick, in fact, that I started to cough. Then some guy wearing a strange-looking hat and complicated robes appeared.

"That's the bishop," Whitman whispered. "He'll say the mass, and those priests will help him."

Thank God Whitman was there to tell me what was going on. I didn't have a clue. I'd never witnessed a ceremony like that before. It was solemn and awesome and completely incomprehensible. Mom and Daddy and I followed Whitman's lead, rising and kneeling and sitting on cue.

Inside, everything was precise and choreographed, but outside, in the street, it was a total zoo. Mom had given me a breathless rundown when she first arrived. The funeral was by invitation only and lots of people were turned away. Barred from the service, news crews and paparazzi scavenged for juicy tidbits among the crowd. Protesters held up signs demanding justice for the Brunellis. Famous men and beautiful women arrived in limousines. "It took us almost half an hour to get through security," Mom reported. "We were right behind Gina Lollabrigida!"

Whoever she was.

The chapel was packed. It was a celebrity event, only I didn't know any of the celebrities and I didn't give a damn if they were famous or not. I wondered how many of the beautiful women staring so hard at me had been in love with Marcello and hoped that he'd marry them.

We sat in the front pew on the right side: Fabio, Mom, Daddy, me, Whitman, in that order. I sneaked a glance at the pew across from us on the left. La Principessa, Giovanna, and Giovanni.

I hadn't seen Johnny for months, but a couple of hours earlier he'd tapped on my door and offered to escort me to the chapel. I was shocked to see him and unprepared for the ricochet of my emotions. Because when I first opened the door, not knowing who it was, and looked into his eyes—it was Marcello I saw, not Giovanni. I almost cried out. Instead, I just cried. And Giovanni was nice enough to hold me in his arms and let me bawl.

I was grateful for his offer to escort me. His silent companionship as we walked through the mazelike corridors of Palazzo Brunelli gave me strength for the ordeal ahead. At one point I even took his hand. I squeezed it. And he squeezed back. He was not my enemy, he was my friend. He grieved too, as a son.

I tried not to look at him now, in the chapel, but couldn't stop myself. He'd changed so much in the months since I'd last seen him. He looked older. He looked tired.

Well, we all looked tired. Grief is exhausting. I hadn't slept for days, and Mom and the dads were dealing with jet lag on top of everything else.

Giovanni had his father's profile. It would become more pronounced as he got older and grew into his role as the new Prince Brunelli. I wondered how he was dealing with the stress that had been heaped onto his shoulders. What did he think about communism now that he was a megacapitalist having to fight the government for the sake of his family?

Everything and everyone changes, I thought. *That's what life is, trying to deal with sudden changes, unexpected detours, mystifying roadblocks.* I had had some experience of that already, but Marcello's death had given me a new understanding of life.

Life is precarious, and so is love. Both are precious gifts not meant to be squandered.

I was miserable, but I was lucky. I was loved. Daddy held one of my hands and Whitman the other. Daddy's other hand held Mom's hand, and she held Fabio's. I could feel the current of life running through us, warming us, holding us together.

The reception afterward was held in Palazzo Brunelli. Gorgeous food. Immense bouquets brought up from Villa Brunelli on Capri. White-jacketed waiters offering drinks and collecting plates. All that was missing was Marcello. Someone had propped an oil painting of him up on a tall easel, but the pose was stiff and formal and I didn't think it looked anything like him.

I didn't know what I was supposed to do and hung back with Mom and the dads.

"Sweetheart," Whitman said, "your place is over there, in the receiving line."

I looked over to where La Principessa, Giovanna, and Giovanni were standing side by side, shaking the hands of guests as they arrived. "Nobody said anything to me," I whispered.

"You've got to stand your ground." Whitman took me by the elbow and steered me over to the Brunellis.

Giovanna, when she saw me, pressed closer to La Principessa, making it impossible for me to wedge myself between them. If I stood on the other side of La Principessa, I would be first in line; if I stood next to Giovanni, I'd be last.

"Wife comes before mother," Whitman said, giving me a little shove.

La Principessa showed no reaction when I took my place at the head of the line. She continued to receive the guests, accepting subdued condolences, air kisses, handshakes. But my presence seemed to galvanize Giovanna.

"What do you think you are doing?" she hissed behind her grandmother's back.

"Giovanna," La Principessa said softly, *"calmati."*

But Giovanna wouldn't be calmed. As I stood there shaking hands, Giovanna reached behind La Principessa and plucked at my dress, trying to pull me out of the receiving line. I slapped her hand away. She did it again. This time, I grabbed her wrist and violently thrust her arm away. Giovanna let out a weird little moan and took a step backward. She grabbed me by the shoulder, spun me around.

"How dare you!" she gasped. And spat in my face.

I just stood there, in shock.

She was lame and wearing a long, heavy dress, so when she aimed a feeble kick at me I had plenty of time to sidestep her. I didn't know what to do, only that I had to do something, so I grabbed that huge nose and give it a good squeeze.

Giovanna let out an ear-piercing shriek.

"That's for trying to poison me," I hissed, shoving her away. I wiped the spittle from my face, so hot and furious that I was way beyond any kind of social protocol or nicety. I'd had it with her. With all of them. "She tried to poison me," I said to La Principessa. "She tried to kill me with a poisoned salad."

"Giovanna." La Principessa's voice was a shocked whisper.

"No," Giovanna wailed. "She's crazy, Nonna! Vulgar and immoral and crazy. Papa didn't want to marry her. She trapped him!" Her wild eyes flew from face to face in the crowd that was growing around us. "Yes! He told me so!"

That was the last straw. "You lying—"

"First she seduced my father; then she seduced my brother!"

"Giovanna!" Johnny took an angry step toward her but she backed away.

"Do you deny it?" she taunted. "Do you deny that she kissed you? Shall I get the photograph?"

Johnny's face turned bright scarlet. He turned to look at me, his eyes wild.

I couldn't let her get away with this. If she was determined to make a public scene, then I'd give her one. I stepped forward, like a defense attorney at my own trial, but it was Giovanna I addressed. "Your father loved me. And I loved him. It's as simple as that. You can believe it or not, Giovanna, but I know it's true."

Mom quietly extricated herself from the immobilized crowd and came to my side. Daddy and Whitman followed.

I was fuming. I could feel the anger pulsing out of me in waves. The sensation was so intense that I thought it might harm the baby. I stood there clutching my belly, looking at the sea of faces, taking deep Buddha breaths to calm down.

"Giovanna." La Principessa's voice was quiet. "Go to your room."

Giovanna shook her head and lifted her jaw in defiance of her grandmother. "No." She sounded like an angry, spiteful little girl.

"Giovanna." La Principessa's voice was a notch tighter. "Did you hear what I said?"

It was obviously a test of wills. In this family, what wasn't? With the Brunellis, it was all about authority, chains of command.

Giovanna sneered in my direction. "You get nothing from us. Nothing! Except my father's bastard."

The crowd seemed to draw in one shocked breath. Their eyes now turned again to me.

"Come." La Principessa extended her hand. At first, I thought it was for Giovanna. But it wasn't. She was beckoning to me.

"Giovanni," she said, "take care of your sister, please."

Mouth open, face blotched, Giovanna stared down at her grandmother's hand holding mine. She looked like she was in the grip of some completely unknown emotion. Her eyes were huge, glazed with fury or madness. She gasped and wheezed and quivered. And then, as everyone watched, a thick red drop of blood gathered at the tip of her nose, ballooned into a globule, and dripped to the floor. Giovanna didn't seem to be aware of what was happening. People drew back as another bright red drop splashed down on the white marble tile.

"Ah!" Giovanna touched her fingertips to her nose. "My stigmata!" She craned her face forward, showing off the spigot of dripping blood. Her upper lip was stained red. She smeared the blood over her face as she made a circuit of the horrified onlookers, smiling at them, saying, "You see? My stigmata!"

"Giovanna. Come." Her brother took her gently by the arm and steered her away. As they passed Marcello's portrait, Giovanna plucked it off its easel and clutched it to her thin bosom. She shot me one last malevolent glance before Johnny led her off.

Nobody knew what to say. We just looked at one another.

Finally La Principessa gestured to a waiter and pointed to the blood-stained floor. Then, still holding my hand, she turned us around so we faced the line of guests.

"This is my daughter-in-law," she informed the crowd. "Marcello's wife."

Getting Mom and the dads off was a big deal. They didn't want to go but had to. Jobs were waiting. Money had to be earned. All the ordinary stuff that makes up life had to be resumed.

Mom begged me to return with her. But I steeled myself and said no. I was no longer Venus Gilroy, the girl who lived in a messy studio apartment and worked for minimum wage and worried that her wheezing old car would collapse. I was the widow of Prince Marcello Brunelli, one of the wealthiest men in Europe. I was carrying his child. And I intended to get for my child everything that Marcello would have wanted him to have.

"I could stay here," Mom suggested. "That's what Fabio wants me to do."

"Mom, you can't just move into Palazzo Brunelli with me."

She nodded, trying not to cry. "I miss my little house," she admitted. "Isn't that ridiculous? You dream about getting away, going somewhere, falling in love . . . it all happens . . . and then, one day, you realize that you miss your African violets and your gas stove and your eiderdown comforter and all the friends who kept you going." She did some final picking at me and tried to cheer herself up. "It's pretty here in Rome, but it would be hard to ever feel at home. Don't you feel that way, sweetheart?"

"I haven't figured out where home is yet." But the deeper truth was, I couldn't let go of the eternal city. I didn't want to. Not until I was certain that it didn't want me.

"I tried to explain all this to Fabio," Mom said. "And to Cesare. You can have great sex, I said, without speaking one another's language. But at some point you stop having sex, and then you have to talk. Well, at least I have to talk. In English."

I rode with them in a taxi out to the airport. Since Marcello's death, I'd become hyperaware of all the good-byes in life. How many times do you say good-bye and not even think about it? You just assume it's temporary. But sometimes it's not.

I couldn't go through security without a ticket, so we had to say our good-byes outside the first gate.

"John, the phone!" Whitman said.

"Oh yeah, the phone." Daddy pulled a black cell phone from his shoulder bag and handed it to me. "This is for you, sweetheart. It's all set up and we'll pay for the service, so you don't have to worry about it."

"You're to call us at any time," Whitman informed me.

"Night or day," said Daddy.

He showed me how they'd programmed in their home number, their cell phone numbers, Mom's home and cell phone numbers, their lawyer's number, my ob-gyn's number, the maternity hospital's number, and Gabriella and her girlfriend's number.

"I think we've thought of everything," Daddy said.

"Every possible catastrophe," Whitman said.

"And if you decide you don't want to come back to us," Mom said, "we'll come back to you. We'll all be right there at your side during labor and delivery, wherever you are."

"I can't believe we're going to be grandparents," Whitman said. "It's not fair. My hair isn't even gray yet."

One final embrace.

I waved as they disappeared into the first round of security and waited until they reappeared on the other side of the barrier. Then

I pressed a number and watched as Daddy answered his cell phone.

"It's your daughter," I said.

"Hello, sweetheart."

"I just wanted to say I love you."

"I love you, too."

I said the same thing to Whitman and to Mom. Because I believe in love. When you love someone, tell them. You never know if you'll ever see them again.

We opened our doors at exactly the same moment and then stood in our respective doorways, surprised, looking at each other.

"I was about to come and knock on your door," La Principessa said.

"I was about to come and knock on yours."

"How strange." She stepped back and opened the door wider. "Will you please come in?"

Raffaela was stuffing a pile of folders and loose papers into a briefcase as I entered. She gave me a smile. "*Buon giorno*, Signora."

La Principessa spoke to her in Italian as they made a quick inspection tour of La Principessa's suite. I noticed three leather suitcases stacked next to the bed. A final consultation and then Raffaela left us alone.

"I am leaving," La Principessa said, smoothing down the silk of her dress. "Returning to Capri."

I didn't say anything.

"I hate Roma. The dirt. The paparazzi. It's no longer for me. I want my garden. I want some peace."

So did I. But I didn't say that. I didn't say anything.

We stood there, deadlocked. Futures had not been discussed.

"Would you care to sit down?" La Principessa gestured toward a small seating area in front of her marble-clad fireplace.

I sat down.

Her rooms, or at least this room, were smaller than I'd expected, but far more luxurious. Every detail was perfect. Not a thing was out of place. Every fabric was exquisite. The cozy, pampered femininity on display was completely at odds with the rest of Palazzo Brunelli, which tended toward the huge, the cold, the forbidding. The one oddity was the covered painting above the fireplace. At least I assumed it was a painting. Or it could have been a shrine of some sort. Whatever it was, it was hidden behind folds of fabric that could be drawn apart like a curtain.

La Principessa stood behind the chair opposite me, clutching its upholstered back. "I spoke with Giovanna's doctors today," she said. "They told me she must not leave the clinic."

After her violent outburst at the funeral reception, Giovanna had tried to kill herself with an overdose of OxyContin. Apparently the drug had first been prescribed for leg and back pain and she'd become addicted to it. One of the Little Doves found Giovanna face down in a pool of vomit and managed to resuscitate her. She'd then been taken away to a private clinic in Switzerland.

"I hope you can find room in your heart to forgive her," said La Principessa.

I nodded. In time I would. Life's too short. I wasn't one to bear grudges forever.

"She seems to be showing some of the same behavior patterns as her mother." La Principessa nervously patted the top of the chair. "Her mother, you know, once tried to poison Marcello."

"Yes, he told me."

"Such a strange thing, the mind."

I nodded.

"We know so much, and yet we know so little."

I nodded.

"And the past—well—" She turned and walked over to a sun-filled window, standing with her back to me and looking out toward the Tiber. It took me a moment to figure out what was happening. I saw her shoulders twitch, and then her whole body tremble, and then there was a faint, mewlike sound and she dropped her head into her hands.

I got up and went to her. Laid a hand on her silken shoulder. But I didn't cry with her.

She turned to me, the mascara dripping down her tear-stained face. "I have wronged you," she whispered.

I led her to a chair. Got her box of tissue from the bathroom. Poured her a glass of water.

"I wanted so much not to like you," she said. "I wanted to punish Marcello—for choosing you."

I said nothing.

"And now, you see, it is I who have been punished. My son died thinking I had turned away from him."

I said nothing.

"It is so strange," she whimpered. "I dream of him every night."

"So do I."

"He is my little boy again. Full of energy. He runs to my arms."

In my dreams, Marcello was usually in a boat, rowing away. But sometimes he was in my bed, making love to me, and the sensation was so intense that I sobbed myself awake and then had to deal with his absence.

"I carried him," La Principessa said, "just as you are carrying your child."

"His child," I reminded her. "Your grandchild."

She turned her face away. Sniffed. Dabbed at her nostrils. Was unaware, or didn't care, that her face was a tear-smeared wreck. "A boy loves his mother before he loves anyone else. She is everything to him. You will find that out for yourself."

"In three months."

She studied me, turning to regard me from different angles. "You remind me a bit of myself, you know. The way I was when I first came here from Napoli. A young bride. Beautiful. Ambitious—"

"I'm not—"

She put up a finger. "There is nothing wrong with ambition, *cara mia*. But in my day, you see, the only ambition a woman could have was to marry well."

"Didn't you hope that your career would—"

"I had no career," she broke in. "Not until my husband died and I was forced to take over the Brunelli businesses."

"But didn't you sing—or something?"

"Sing?"

"Yes," I said. "Sing. Your name was—"

"Lita." She stood and took a couple of rapid steps as if she meant to walk away, but then, just as abruptly, she stopped and turned back to me. "Did Marcello tell you?"

"No. My dad found an old picture."

"An old picture." She sat again. "Madonna."

"It's pretty. You look happy in it."

"Ah, yes, but you see, Lita was always happy. She sang, she danced. She was a young girl with nothing—except a pretty face and a wonderful body and lots of ambition."

"Did he make you give it up?" I asked.

"Who?"

"Your husband."

"He wanted me only for himself." She pointed to the covered painting above the mantelpiece. "Pull the cord there."

I did. The curtains parted. Behind them, a young, sultry, raven-haired woman with her head thrown back but her long-lashed eyes gazing provocatively at the viewer smiled through half-open lips as she caressed one of her large, creamy breasts.

"My portrait," said La Principessa. "It's not on display, you see, like the other Brunelli portraits."

I stared in wonder.

"Are you shocked?" she asked.

"No," I said. "Just surprised."

She laughed softly. "Marcello used to beg me to open the curtains so he could look at it."

Hmm. Interesting. How old was he? I wondered.

"The secret Lita." La Principessa stood and regarded the painting. "The woman hidden behind the curtain. The poor girl who got her wish. She married a prince and became so rich"—she pulled the cord and the curtains once again covered Lita—"that she forgot who she was, who she'd been, where she came from." She looked at me. "Forgot that once she, too, had been young, and happy, and in love. And then lost her husband. And felt lost herself."

"I feel lost now," I said, "because no one's told me what I can expect for the baby. You act as though you don't want me here. Like you don't even want to see Marcello's baby."

"Yes, I know. I have been terrible." She bowed her head.

"I don't care what you think of me anymore, but I do care about what happens to my baby. Marcello's baby. He's a Brunelli, whether you like it or not. And that means that he—"

"Will be well taken care of," said La Principessa. "Sent to good schools."

"Loved," I said. "By his family."

"Yes, of course."

"And as Marcello's wife—"

"As Marcello's wife, you will also be well taken care of." She lifted a finger and let out a sardonic little laugh. "If there is anything left once those vultures finish with us."

"If I stay here, in Palazzo Brunelli—"

"You would be much more comfortable on Capri."

I stared at her, trying to gauge her sincerity.

"There's a charming little villa right in my garden," she said. "You'd have your privacy. And I wouldn't have to worry about you here, alone, in Roma, with all the paparazzi and the newspapers. It would be quiet, but while all this terrible nonsense is going on—"

Hmm.

"I'm being selfish, of course," said La Principessa. She touched my hand, tentatively, then took it in her own. "I want my family around me as much as possible."

Chapter
31

It really is an enchanted isle, Capri, but it took me a long time to accept the enchantment. I couldn't focus on the beauty, only the pain.

Grief, I discovered, has a natural life of its own. Every day it would slip in like a cold black tide to suck and slap at the shoreline of my emotions. Eventually I learned to navigate its deep, dark waters. Learned not to fear them, anyway. Because after a while, the tide would go out again, and I'd be back on dry land.

Gradually, I stopped reciting my daily litany of "if onlys": If only we'd had more time. If only he hadn't been so stressed out and exhausted. If only we hadn't gone to the Blue Grotto. If only he'd been wearing a life jacket. If only I'd jumped in and saved him. If only he could see his child. If only, if only, if only . . .

But life isn't in the "if onlys." Life is here and now, the present moment, with its smorgasbord of pains and pleasures. "If only" leads nowhere. It strands you on the outskirts of life, leaves you clinging to the past and trying to rewrite the future.

In the days and weeks following Marcello's death, I learned so much. The knowledge changed me, changed my life. Nudged me into maturity. I'd look back at that girl I used to be, that all-American Venus Gilroy, and I'd think, *Poor thing*. Because she *was* poor, and that old Venus Gilroy was stuck in a kind of permanent adolescence and didn't know it. She had a big shiny all-American heart to go along with her all-American naiveté. She had a kind of perennial all-American hope that everything would turn out fine and the ending would be happy. The new Venus—Princess Venus Brunelli—was much wiser.

Well, being pregnant does that. It's like you've been given this great secret, handed down through the ages. A kind of mysterious understanding, and a funny kind of bravery.

And hope.

It's pretty amazing.

It's beautiful, Capri, and, like Rome, it weaves you into its captivating spell. For one thing, it's warm. Africa isn't all that far away. And even though the sun doesn't *always* shine, Capri is always flooded with light. The wind-dimpled sea spreads out around it, absorbing and reflecting and infusing the air with a soft bright intensity that makes colors throb and glow. Little breezes, so regular they've been given nicknames, like pets, wander up and down, around the cliffs and over the island. And it smells divine because there are so many flowers.

At first, I pretty much stayed in the garden. La Principessa was a vigorous and passionate gardener and, much to my surprise, did most of the work by herself. Over the years, she had created a series of interconnected gardens around Villa Brunelli. Each garden, she explained, had its own personality.

I would slowly wander along the paths, inhaling the scents and feasting my eyes on the brilliant colors. I'd stand at the viewpoints and look out over the sea with its shifting patterns and hidden mysteries. I would swim in the long pool. Float on my back, my belly growing big as a beach ball.

Always dreams of water. With or without Marcello. Lakes, rivers, oceans. Moving along in a current.

Gradually, I could feel myself coming back to life. That's what it felt like. I walked further. I went outside the gates. There were no paparazzi to bother me and the locals seemed to take me under their wing. Maybe that was because La Principessa was regarded as a kind of goddess on Capri, and nobody wanted to piss her off. I was called La Principessa Pregnante and accorded a lot of respect. And I worked hard to make friends. I insisted on helping with the shopping and would accompany Maria, the cook, or La Principessa herself, as they made the rounds of the shops. It was a great way to practice my Italian: *pomodori* (tomatoes), *pesce* (fish), *pane* (bread), *frutta* (fruit), and, *naturalmente* (of course), *bambino* (baby).

Having a baby in bambinoland is a great conversation starter. As I waddled into my third trimester and really started to show, women would come up to me on the little streets and lanes of Capri and touch or rub my stomach as if it were a magic amulet.

Life away from the idyllic isle was "frankly insane," as Johnny put it, and to escape, he came to Capri as often as he could. Sometimes it was for a weekend, sometimes it was for a day, sometimes just for an afternoon.

Maria always told me when he was due to arrive. His grandmother always made his favorite dishes, and we shopped for the ingredients together. That's how I learned what he liked to eat. *Risotto con frutti di mare*—risotto with seafood—was his all-time favorite. Mine, too, once I tasted it.

If everyone on Capri was a little in love with La Principessa, they were definitely infatuated with Giovanni. He was now Il Principe. Prince Giovanni Brunelli. But to me, he was Johnny, as he'd always been, the smart, sexy guy on the Vespa, my first tour guide in Italy.

Maybe it was because we were so close in age, but we fell into an easy familiarity. He would always meet in private with his grandmother, but afterward, he'd wander around the gardens, restless, trying to defuse the pressures of his life, and we'd bump into each other. Sit and talk.

The investigation into the Brunellis' business holdings continued. Johnny called it "a farce of the first order" but was determined to see it through and clear the family's name.

One afternoon I was sitting in the little vine-covered pergola near the pool, studying my Italian, when I heard a splash and looked over to see him gliding beneath the water, sleek and swift as a dolphin. He surfaced with a gasp, shook the water from his thick black hair, and waved.

"What are you doing?" he called.

"*Studio italiano.*"

"Ah!" He climbed out of the pool and stood in the sunshine. He was wearing one of those little bikini swimsuits European men are so fond of. There was something touching about his body, the leanness of it, the paleness of it, the triangular patch of black hair on his chest. "How about we go for a ride?" he said.

I looked down at my belly.

"You'll fit," he said.

And I did, but just barely. Johnny had an old motorbike that he used to get around the island. It was smaller than the Vespa he kept in Rome. "I'll go very slowly," he said, handing me a helmet.

"*Si, è meglio quando varemmo lento.*" Which I hoped meant, "Yes, it's better if we go slow."

"I'm impressed," he said, smiling.

"*Grazie,*" I said. "*Allora, avanti.*"

I like that word *avanti*. It means "let's go," or "forward."

It felt strange to have my arms around him again, this time with his father's baby between us. But it also felt perfectly right, perfectly fine, perfectly friendly.

He knew all the roads. He'd been coming here ever since he was a boy. We putt-putted over to the town of Anacapri and then followed a hairpin road down to the beach near the Blue Grotto.

Johnny stared out at the calm sea. Then he looked over his shoulder and said, "Would you do something with me?"

This time the water was perfectly calm. I lay down in the boat right at the dock so I wouldn't have to maneuver my body from a sitting position to a prostrate one later on. I lay there like I was in a cradle, watching as Johnny pushed us off and began to row.

The boat slipped easily through the water. I was scared as hell but I knew I had to go through with this, just as Johnny did, and for some of the same reasons.

The sky was clear. The sun was warm and bright. Birds sang and sailed high overhead, roosting in the giant limestone cliffs.

We were at the entrance now.

"Are you OK?" Johnny asked.

"Yes."

"I can turn back, if you want."

"I don't want us to turn back."

"OK. Here we go."

He leaned backward, holding up the oars, and the boat slid quietly into the Blue Grotto.

Neither of us spoke.

Johnny rowed further into the cavern. Then stopped. We floated.

This time I saw the Blue Grotto without the billowing sheen of terror and panic that had colored my last visit.

Look at it, I said to myself.

I pulled myself up so I could see over the sides of the boat.

The color was unearthly. It was like being inside a liquid jewel. The sun poured down into the sea outside the entrance and then shot back into the grotto, refracting the pure blue of the sky upward, through the water and into the soft, warm air. The color was alive, shimmering, shifting, like a strange kind of music. It seemed indifferent to human sorrow, and yet it embraced and held you as long as you were in it. A soothing blue womb of life.

For Marcello, it had all ended here, in this magic blue grotto that he said would bring good luck.

"Papa," Giovanni whispered, "*addio. Ti amo.*"

Good-bye. I love you.

The baby kicked.

We hardly said a word afterward. But it felt as though we'd passed through something, gone through a trial together. That's how it felt to me, anyway.

We climbed back on the motorbike and slowly made our way up to Anacapri and then east to the little town of Capri, where Johnny parked in the main square.

"How about a gelato," he said.

"You're reading my mind."

We crossed over to the gelato stand. The owner knew me because I often went there with Maria. I loved the ice cream. It had become a craving.

There was one question I'd been dying to ask Luigi, the owner of the gelato stand, but my Italian wasn't good enough and the question itself seemed kind of crazy. But when the dads had brought me to Capri fourteen years earlier, we'd stopped in that square so I could have a gelato. I couldn't remember details exactly, but it had to be that square because that was where all the tourists congregated and where all the main shops were located. What I did remember very clearly was the color of my pistachio ice cream, a green I'd never seen before. And that as I was eating it, I spied a dark-haired boy staring at me as he ate a dish of strawberry. We acknowledged each other with shy, secret looks and I, of course, fell in love with him.

That happens when you're a twelve-year-old American girl on your first trip to Europe and having an ice cream in the main square of Capri. The world opens up and you let it in.

What I wanted to ask Luigi, but never did, was whether or not he'd had his gelato stand there fourteen years ago. And whether or not he could remember me and my dads. But of course it was ridiculous. Tens of thousands of tourists had passed this way since then.

"Ah! Principessa Brunelli! Il Principe Giovanni!" Luigi smiled and nodded. "*Che cosa vuole?*"

I told him I'd have my usual: pistachio.

Johnny ordered *fragole*. Strawberry.

"*Per sempre*," said Luigi as he artfully scraped up our orders and mounded them on cardboard dishes. "Always the same." He winked at me and nodded toward Giovanni. "Since he was a little boy."

"Really?" I turned to Johnny. "Always strawberry?"

He nodded.

"How long have you been coming here?" I asked him.

"To Luigi's? Ever since I was kid. He's been here as long as I can remember." He smiled at some secret memory. "In fact, this is where I first fell in love."

"Really?"

"Mm." He dug into his gelato with the tiny plastic spade.

"How old were you?" Oh, how I loved that creamy green pistachio. And my baby did, too. I just knew it.

"I must have been—thirteen? Fourteen maybe?"

"What happened?"

"Nothing."

"But you fell in love?"

"Well, that's what it felt like."

"But what happened? I mean, how did you fall in love? Who was it?"

He shrugged and ate. "Don't know."

"Well, did she have a name?" I persisted.

"Yes, I suppose she did. But I don't know what it was."

"I give up," I said.

"Well, nothing happened, you see? We stayed on Capri, with Nonna, every summer. And every day I'd bike down here just as the ferry arrived. So I could watch all the crazy tourists. And one day, I got my gelato and I was wandering around looking at people and I saw this girl. There was something about her, I don't know what it was. She just intrigued me for some reason. So I sort of hung around the edges of the crowd and watched her."

"You never said anything?"

"No, of course not. She was a tourist, with her parents I suppose. She ordered a dish of"—he pointed to my rapidly disappearing gelato—"pistachio gelato, and she was eating it and then she saw me."

I looked into his eyes.

"And we looked at one another. And there was something—" He shook his head. "Something in the way we looked at one another. Something that passed between us. Just for one moment only. And that's when it occurred to me for the first time."

"What did?"

He shook his head, puzzled. "That you could look at someone—just look at them—and—"

"Fall in love?"

"Yes. It's a strange feeling when it happens. That first time. You never forget it."

I nodded. Looked away. My head was reeling.

"Has that ever happened to you?" Johnny asked.